"LORD OF THE OAK. LORD OF THE HOLLY. WE STAND BEFORE YOU. Lords of the First Forest, we come to witness."

The air trembled. A shiver ran down Struath's spine as the energy flowed around him and through him, through all of the watchers—a circle of living power surrounding the Tree. A shudder rippled through the massive trunk. The sweeping boughs of the Holly shook as the Lord of the Waning Year offered the challenge. The Oak rattled its spindly branches, accepting.

Then the Holly attacked. The finger-length spikes of its leaves carved long gouges in the Oak's trunk. Struath sang with the others. Each day since Midsummer, the Oak-Lord's strength had dwindled, and with it the strength of the sun. Tonight, his power was at its lowest ebb, yet somehow, the Lord of the Waxing Year must prevail.

A great bulge ran up the trunk of the Tree. Twigs burst out of the Oak's naked limbs. They grew thick and strong, swelling with power. The Oak lashed the Holly, the sharp retort of cracking branches punctuating the singing. Green boughs sagged. Red berries, large as fists, rained down.

The Holly's limbs shriveled, retreating before the burgeoning power of the Oak. Even as relief surged through him, Struath heard a high-pitched whine. The chanting faltered.

The Oak split with a horrifying shriek of rending wood. Shards of wood, longer than any spear, catapulted through the air. Men and women fled screaming, trampling those in their path. Struath stood frozen as one of the flying spears shattered a man's head. Another impaled a woman on a birch where her body hung, twitching.

The Tree shrieked again. Struath raised his head as the Oak shuddered and ripped away from the trunk of the Tree. Blackness filled the jagged scar. In the blackness stars red as blood gleame~~~ ~~~ swirled, slowly coalescing ~~~ ~~~ realized. An outstretched ~~~ uncurling as if reaching f~~~

HEARTWOOD

Trickster's Game # 1

BARBARA CAMPBELL

DAW BOOKS, INC.
DONALD A. WOLLHEIM, FOUNDER
375 Hudson Street, New York, NY 10014

ELIZABETH R. WOLLHEIM
SHEILA E. GILBERT
PUBLISHERS
http://www.dawbooks.com

First Printing, May 2005
1 2 3 4 5 6 7 8 9

Acknowledgments

Writing may be a solitary art, but writers need the support of colleagues, friends, and family to accomplish their goals. To list them all would require a coffee table edition of *Heartwood*. Short of that, I'd like to acknowledge the following people whose contributions helped improve this book and kept me (relatively) sane while I wrote it:

Jeanne Cavelos, director of the Odyssey workshop. A terrific teacher, Jeanne's enthusiasm, generosity, and discerning criticism create the perfect environment for writers to learn from each other and hone their skills.

The 2001 and 2002 participants of The Never–Ending Odyssey whose critiques helped shape the book. Special thanks to the following folks who attended both workshops: Daniel Fitzgerald, Marty Hiller, Rita Oakes, Larry Taylor, and Susan Winston.

Laurie Lanzdorf and Michael Samerdyke who critiqued the never–ending first draft of *Heartwood* and remained my friends 180,000 words later.

Susan Herner, loyal agent and friend, who always kept the faith and always kept me going.

Sheila Gilbert for her insight, her patience, and her sense of humor. Every author should be blessed with such an editor and be welcomed so warmly into the world of publishing.

And finally, my husband David Lofink, who read every word of every draft, made invaluable suggestions that changed the course of the story, and offered love and encouragement in good times and bad. He is my heartwood and I dedicate this novel to him.

PART ONE

Winter has come.
It walks the leafless forest and the frost-rimed fields.
It spreads its mantle of snow on the sleeping earth.
It breathes on the waters and locks them in silence.
It whistles on the hilltops, piercing the air with its
  bitter song.
It devours the sun with fangs of icicles.
It clasps my hand with frozen fingers and chuckles
  as I shiver.
Winter has come, wearing a crown of holly leaves.

Wintersong

Chapter 1

FEAR IS THE ENEMY.

Careful not to awaken his brother, Darak flung his mantle over his shoulders and eased aside the bearskin that hung across the doorway. As cold as their hut had been, the frigid air outside stole his breath. Stifling a cough, he swiped his watering eyes with the back of his hand.

Scudding clouds hid the face of the moon goddess, but to the north, pale stars flickered, their light too faint to show more than the smudged shapes of the nearest huts. Old Sim's snores offered a droning counterpoint to the whimper of a babe, quickly muffled as it found its mother's breast in the darkness.

Darak quelled the unexpected rush of resentment the ordinary sounds evoked. He had only himself to blame. When Tinnean declared his intention of becoming the Tree-Father's apprentice, he had dismissed it as a whim. After the ceremony took place at Midsummer, he had convinced himself that his impulsive brother would soon tire of the rigorous training. When his brother remained resolute, he had argued with him. Then came the series of calamities that had devastated the tribe, driving concerns about Tinnean's future from his mind. Autumn found his brother spending every evening with the Tree-Father, leaving him to sit by the fire pit, fighting the emptiness of their hut and the bitterness of his memories. Since then, he had clung to the belief that his brother would realize his error, that like all the men in their line, he would follow the hunter's path.

Foolishly, he had thought time was his ally. Now he knew better.

Control the fear.

He had learned to banish the old fears that stalked his dreams as soon as he awoke. This new fear was harder to conquer. During the day, he held it at bay by driving his mind and body hard, but during the long winter nights, it crept close, a stealthy predator seeking his most vulnerable points. Sleep offered no escape. Better to remain awake, alert, prepared for the inevitable attack.

He paced back and forth, his footsteps crunching too loudly in the hard-packed snow. He would not lose Tinnean. He would not.

Control yourself.

Stillness should come easily to a hunter, yet even when he forced himself to lean against the wall of the hut, his hands kept clenching and unclenching. Silently, he rehearsed the words again. Sling and spear, bow and arrow—those he had mastered, but if he was going to stop Tinnean from ruining his life, words were his only weapons.

He was still trying to find the right ones when he sensed movement. He straightened as the bearskin fell back into place. Of course, Tinnean had come out without his mantle. Darak shrugged off his and wrapped it around his brother.

"I couldn't sleep either," Tinnean said.

Darkness masked his brother's expression. Was that tiny hitch in his voice proof that Tinnean had changed his mind or was he simply nervous about the morrow's ceremony? Darak knew well how doubt could assail a man at night. He would never wish Tinnean to suffer, but it was only one night, after all, and surely worth a little pain to make the right choice. He took a deep breath, readying himself to utter the words he had chosen, the words that would convince Tinnean to abandon his foolhardy path.

Before he could speak, Tinnean grabbed his arm. Taut as a drawn bowstring, Darak searched the village for an enemy.

A sliver of white light pierced the sky. Tinnean's fingers fumbled for his, just as they had when he'd first glimpsed the Northern Dancers as a child. *He's still a child,* Darak thought. *And he still needs me.*

The streamer of light writhed like a snake impaled upon a spear, then exploded into a translucent veil of green and white that filled the northern horizon. The hairs on Darak's neck and arms stood upright as fiery bolts of light shot through the night sky. Beside him, Tinnean's voice shook as he whispered the prayers of protection. The messengers of the gods could herald good as well as evil, but always the appearance of the Northern Dancers foretold change.

The bolts of light grew soft and fluid, curling around each other, twisting into huge, glowing circles as they wove the wild pattern of the dance. Tremulous fingers sprouted from the bottom of the veil and groped earthward, the innocent rose darkening to stain Tinnean's upturned face blood red.

Darak reached for the bag of charms at his neck before he remembered that he no longer wore them. Quickly, he flicked his forefinger against his thumb three times. After that, he could only wait; the dance could last until dawn lightened the sky.

Instead, between one breath and the next, the sky flames simply vanished. Darak blinked, his eyes adjusting to the sudden darkness. Perhaps the gods listened to Tinnean's prayers; in the moons since Midsummer, they had never answered his.

He was still staring skyward when Tinnean tugged his hand free.

"I must go to the Tree-Father."

Before he could stop him, Tinnean raced off. Once, his brother would have looked to him for answers; these days, he was always running to Struath.

Long after Tinnean's figure had disappeared, Darak stared into the darkness. Then, with a muttered curse, he flung back the bearskin. Why ask the shaman to explain the signs? Even an ordinary man knew they foretold disaster.

When the tribe gathered at dawn for the first of the daylong rites, Darak observed the Tree-Father closely. If Tinnean's report had unsettled Struath, he hid it well. His face was as calm as ever, his voice steady as he led the tribe in the chant to honor the dead. Tinnean's shook, though; so did his hands, the knuckles white as he clenched the woven reed basket containing the bones of those who had died since the harvest. Their bodies had lain on stone platforms in the Death Hut for three moons, allowing time and scavengers to eat away the flesh. The priests had gathered the bones at the dark of the moon and scoured them clean in preparation for today's interment.

At least they would receive a proper rite. The bodies of those who had died in the plague—forty-three men, women, and children—had been burned and their bones hastily buried after Struath had discovered dead crows and ravens littering the ground around the Death Hut. Even after death, the plague continued its ravages.

Darak realized he was stroking the pockmarks on

his cheek and let his hand fall to his side. Frowning, he watched the Tree-Father and Grain-Mother as they walked sunwise around the circle of worshipers. Yeorna's unbound hair rippled like ripe barley in the wind, the only bit of brightness on this gray morning. Gortin and Lisula followed, their faces solemn. Gortin's seemed gloomier than usual; Darak wondered if he was smarting at his failure to be elevated to Tree-Brother. After the plague took Cronig, the entire tribe expected Gortin to take his place, but Struath had announced only Tinnean's initiation.

Today.

Darak's voice faltered. Tinnean shot him a quick glance as he passed, his brother's clear tenor ringing out all the louder to make up for his momentary lapse.

It was all happening too quickly. Tinnean had only begun his apprenticeship at Midsummer and today he would become Struath's initiate. So many changes in their lives these last six moons—and all of them bad.

Struath thumped his blackthorn staff on the snow-crusted ground and Nionik led the white bullock forward. Darak amended his previous thought; Nionik's election as Oak-Chief was the only good thing to come from the disasters that had befallen the tribe. Chosen in haste after the plague, he well deserved the three eagle feathers braided in his hair. He had seen the tribe through the hailstorm that had leveled the barley and the foot rot that had carried off half the sheep in their small flock.

Bel's golden face peeped through the clouds. A relieved sigh eased its way around the circle at the sun god's appearance and more than one face turned skyward, smiling at the good omen. His kinfolk were still smiling when the bullock stumbled.

Several people gasped. Fingers moved in covert signs of protection. Even Struath frowned slightly as he nodded to the chief. Nionik took a firmer grip on the bullock's nettle-braid halter. He passed the lead rope to Gortin who yanked it hard, pulling the beast's head back to expose the muscular throat. Struath lifted his bronze dagger high.

"That its blood may feed our dead. That its flesh may feed the living. That its spirit may strengthen the Oak-Lord in tonight's battle." With the expertise of many years, Struath plunged the dagger into the bullock's throat.

The animal staggered to its knees and collapsed, its lifeblood spurting into the basin held by the Grain-Mother. Lisula knelt to catch the last of the offering in the ceremonial cup of polished black stone. Their ancestors had carried it with them when they fled north to escape a horde of invaders. Ten generations of their bones lay in the tribal cairns; only the cup remained, mute testament to their flight.

Before they left the village for the rite at the heart-oak, Struath would remove the heart, lungs, liver, and genitals from the bullock. Yeorna would sew each into a piece of the animal's hide. Struath would carry the heart into the First Forest and offer it to the Oak-Lord. On the morrow, after the tribe returned from the forest, the tender liver would be cast into the lake to thank the goddess Lacha for sharing her bounty. The lungs would be burned, carrying the bullock's breath to the gods of lightning and thunder. The genitals would be buried in the fields to ensure Halam's blessing of fertility for the crops.

Once, Darak had found comfort in these rites, handed down from one generation to the next since the first Tree-Father had sacrificed to the gods. Now, he stared dully at the cooling carcass of the bullock, wondering if the gods even noticed their piety.

A thread of steam rose into the air as Lisula handed the cup to Struath. The shaman proffered the cup to the four directions before raising it to his lips. Yeorna drank next, then Gortin, and finally Lisula who held the cup for Tinnean. Darak saw his lips move in a quick prayer before he lowered his head to drink. That unruly lock of hair fell across his forehead. As he raised his head, Lisula brushed it back, smiling. The gesture clearly surprised Tinnean, but after a moment, he smiled back, ducking his head shyly.

Darak discovered answering smiles on the faces of his kinfolk and found himself recalling the time a bee had stung Tinnean on the lip. Their mam claimed his smile was so sweet, the poor insect had confused his mouth with its honeycomb.

Darak's smile faded. He had gifts, too: the ability to walk silently through a forest, to face a charging boar, to drop a deer with a single arrow. His tribe respected him for those gifts. But had any face ever lit up at the mere sight of him? Only Tinnean's, he realized. And that was long ago.

He marched with the others to the cairn. Watched with the others while Struath ducked into the dark entrance of the barrow, carrying the basket of bones. Sang with the others when he emerged again, proclaiming that those who had gone before had cried out a welcome to their blood-kin. Habit impelled him to pick up a stone and lay it atop the cairn in memory of his dead. A few women wiped their eyes. Tinnean wept openly, apparently unashamed of the tears streaking his cheeks. The only tears in Darak's eyes came from the gusting wind off the lake. He had no tears left to shed for the dead; he hadn't even been able to weep for the dying.

Bel fought a losing battle against the thickening clouds as they marched back to the village for the ritual relighting of fire. While Struath struggled to call forth a spark from his ceremonial firestick, Darak struggled with the words he would say to Tinnean. The speech he had prepared would not suffice, not with the power of today's rite still fresh in his brother's mind and the anticipation of his initiation beckoning. He needed to find new words, better ones. And he had to find them quickly.

Here and there, children blew on numbed fingers and stamped their feet, subsiding into stillness again at a parent's sharp look or pinch. When a spark stubbornly refused to catch, even the adults stirred restively, chafing chapped hands against tunics or clasping them under their woolen mantles. Darak curled and uncurled his toes inside his fur-lined shoes in a vain effort to take away the ache of the cold. He could only imagine the pain Struath must feel, crouched in the snow, forcing fingers gnarled with age and the joint-ill to spin the firestick again and again. He felt a reluctant admiration for the old man whose expression remained impassive.

Finally, a spark flickered and grew strong, drawing a victorious whoop from Red Dugan, quickly stifled when Struath turned that single blue eye on him. Struath and Yeorna lit their torches from the sacred fire. One by one, the head of each household lit a torch from theirs. As Darak dipped his torch toward Struath, the Tree-Father's eye bored into him. Admiration gave way to animosity. He would not let Struath take his brother, no matter what curse the Tree-Father flung at him. Surreptitiously, he flicked his forefinger against his thumb; no sense ill-wishing himself.

The crowd quickly dispersed, each family eager to get out of the wind and relight the household fire. Tinnean lingered beside Struath. Darak waited, his gaze drawn to Krali and Griane. Krali's long gray hair masked her face, but her shoulders shook in silent sobs. Today, she had watched Struath carry her father's bones into the barrow, but surely she was remembering all the others she had lost: her mother to the blood-cough, both sons to the plague, and the niece who was a daughter to her in all but the birthing.

Darak took a deep breath and let it out slowly. He would not think of Maili now.

Griane clasped her aunt's hand. Although her eyes were dry, she·was gnawing her upper lip, a sure sign of distress. Their eyes met. Her chilly stare commanded him to do something, say something, but what words could possibly assuage Krali's grief? Griane had grown up in Krali's hut. She called her "Mam." She was assistant to the tribe's healer. If she couldn't comfort poor Krali, how could he?

As he hesitated, Tinnean broke away from Struath and approached the two women. He touched Krali's shoulder gently. When she turned to look at him, he opened his arms. With a soft cry, she leaned into his embrace. His arms came around her, hugging her hard. His lips moved as he whispered something. When Krali straightened, tears still stained her lined face, but she·managed a smile as she touched Tinnean's cheek. The smile· vanished as Red Dugan approached.

"Stop your sniveling, woman. You're making a spectacle of yourself."

Griane's head snapped up. "You're a fine one to talk, Uncle Dugan. Drunk before midday."

Darak stifled a curse. She should know better than to taunt him when he had been drinking. Without waiting for Dugan's inevitable bellow, he started forward. His shout forestalled the blow, but it was Tinnean who stepped between Griane and her uncle.

"Enough. Please. This day is sacred to the Oak. Would you dishonor his spirit—and those of our ancestors—by quarreling?"

From their truculent expressions, it was clear that both Griane and Dugan were prepared to do just that. Tinnean stared from one to the other. Dugan unclenched his fist. Griane whirled away so abruptly that her long braid slapped her uncle across the chest. Dugan muttered something under his breath, but contented himself with shoving Krali toward their hut.

A great puff of steam filled the air as Tinnean let out his breath. Before Darak could speak, Struath strode forward.

"Forgive me, Tree-Father. I know it was not my place to speak, but . . ."

Struath shook his head, smiling. "It is the duty of every priest to guide his people. You did well, Tinnean."

As Tinnean stammered his thanks, Struath's gaze met Darak's and his gentle smile shifted into one of satisfaction. Darak spun away, narrowly avoiding a collision with Sim. Quickly righting his flaming torch, he seized the Memory-Keeper's arm to steady him. The old man clung to him, wincing, and Darak eased his grip.

"You've a strong hand, Hunter."

"And you're too silent by half, Memory-Keeper."

Four yellowed teeth flashed beneath the long white mustache. "I was a hunter, too, once. Before I found my true path. As Tinnean has."

Darak glanced over his shoulder to find Tinnean staring worshipfully at Struath. "Paths can change."

"For some men." Sim's rheumy blue eyes regarded him steadily. Darak waited, trying to curb his impatience. Perhaps Sim sensed it, for he chuckled. The chuckle turned into a wheezing cough. Darak pounded him on the back until the old man raised a protesting hand. "Some paths change," Sim managed between gasps. "Some are set. Didn't the blackbird sing to him on his vision quest?"

Darak scowled. "And didn't an eagle scream at Jurl?"

"Any creature with sense would scream at Jurl."

Sim chuckled again and hawked a gob of phlegm onto the snow.

"A bird came to them both, aye. But Jurl was no more destined to be a priest than Tinnean."

"Let him go, Darak."

"He's a boy. He doesn't know what—"

"Let him go. Or you'll lose him."

Darak offered Sim a stiff bow. "With respect, Memory-Keeper, I think I'm a better judge of that than you."

With a final glance at Tinnean, he strode back to their hut. Crouching beside the fire pit, he touched his torch to the stack of peat and dried dung. The smoke burned his eyes and he turned away, coughing, to seize a handful of dead twigs.

Let him go or you'll lose him.

With a quick, savage gesture he broke the twigs in half. The last thing he needed today was Old Sim and his homilies. He took several deep breaths, letting each out slowly. Twig by twig, he fed the fire, keeping each movement small and controlled. By the time the spark had grown to a flame, he was calm again.

Sim meant well, of course. And he could forgive the old man's meddling, for he had grown up on the Memory-Keeper's tales, had listened to that reedy voice intoning the ancient legends at every rite. His youngest son shared the title now, but it was Old Sim who held the tribe's heart—and its awe. Who among them had seen sixty summers? Not even Mother Netal and she was as ancient as Eagles Mount. Sim looked like a good breeze would topple him, but the stringy old man had outlived all his children save Sanok. Still, Darak wished he'd stick to the familiar legends and leave off interfering in matters he could not understand.

A draft at his back announced Tinnean's arrival. Without looking up, Darak said, "Close the bearskin before we freeze."

Pale sunlight leaked through the smoke hole in the roof and the chinks in the turf and stone walls, but neither sunlight nor fire could dispel the cold. Darak pulled his mantle closer, scraped the remains of yesterday's porridge into two bowls, and held one out to Tinnean.

"We cannot eat until after the battle, Darak. You know that."

Of course he did. He'd been distracted by thoughts of Old Sim and his hands had moved without thinking. Thankful that drink was not forbidden, he reached for the jug of brogac, sighing as the fiery liquor settled in his belly.

Tinnean's frown deepened, but he merely turned away and pulled off his dusky woolen robe. Beneath it, he wore the tunic their mam had made him. She had scraped and sewed the doeskin herself, presenting it to Tinnean when he had completed his vision quest and been accepted into the tribe as a man. He peeled it off now, shivering. Skinny as a stick, pale skin pebbled with cold, he looked about as manly as a newborn calf.

Darak lowered the jug as his brother crouched beside the stone basin that held their water and broke the ice with his fist. Shivering, Tinnean splashed water on his shoulders, then bent to pick up the chunk of wool-fat soap.

"You must have washed before."

"I cleansed myself with Gortin and Struath." Tinnean glanced at him, then looked away. "I meant to come back, Darak. I wanted to talk to you about . . . about what we saw. But—"

"It doesn't matter." He'd lain awake the rest of the night, waiting for his brother, but that was unimportant now. "Why wash again?"

"I want to be clean. Before . . . the ceremony." Again, that half-fearful look, the inadvertent flinch. *As if he thought I'd strike him.*

With an effort, he kept his voice light. "Well, don't scrub so hard. You'll wear your skin off."

The sudden smile made his breath catch in his throat. He tried to remember the last time his words had brought a smile to his brother's face. Tinnean shot him another sidelong glance, this one mischievous. He whistled, scrubbing his body harder.

"Fine, then. Don't blame me if you catch your death of cold."

"Fine, then. I won't." Tinnean's smile became a grin.

Darak grinned back at him. "Impudent pup."

"Old woman."

Darak flung a stale oatcake at his brother. Tinnean ducked and hurled the soap across the fire pit. Darak caught it one-handed and tossed it back, glimpsing downy fuzz under Tinnean's arm as he reached up to snatch the soap out of the air.

"You throw like a girl," Darak said.

"You drink too much."

"I do not." He took another long pull from the jug. "What else is there to do at Midwinter?"

"Pray."

"The gods don't hear my prayers."

"The Forest-Lord does. Else you wouldn't be the best hunter in the tribe."

"If the gods heard my prayers, you wouldn't be leaving."

Tinnean took a deep breath. "It's what I've always wanted, Darak."

"Two summers ago, you wanted to be a hunter."

"I was a child then."

"You're still a child."

"I am fourteen. Almost."

"At fourteen—almost—you should be thinking about girls, not gods."

"I do think about girls." Tinnean ducked his head. "Sometimes. At night."

Darak frowned. "You're too young to be thinking about girls. And little good it'll do you as a priest."

"Priests are not forbidden the . . . pleasures of the flesh." Despite his solemn voice, Tinnean's beardless cheeks flushed pink

"But they are forbidden to marry. And if you die without children, our family name dies with you."

"You might marry again."

Darak slowly lowered the jug.

"I know it's been scarcely five moons . . ."

"Leave it, Tinnean."

"I grieve for Maili, too. And for Mam. For all those who—"

"I said leave it."

Two small creases appeared between Tinnean's brows, but he just threw handfuls of water across his soap-streaked chest. Darak frowned at the jug dangling from his forefinger. The mood had turned dark, the atmosphere in the hut charged with tension again.

"Will you hand me my mantle, Darak?"

Darak rose and pulled off his own. Hunching to keep from knocking his head on the curving roof stones, he dried Tinnean briskly, ignoring his brother's look of surprise. A drop of water stole down Tinnean's cheek. Darak wiped it away with his thumb, the simple gesture bringing that sweet smile to his brother's face.

Encouraged by its reappearance, Darak said, "All I'm asking is that you wait a bit. Till you're sure."

The smile died. "I am sure."

Tinnean slipped on his tunic again, then spread his woolen mantle across his bed of skins and laid out the ritual garb: white woolen undertunic and leggings, braided leather belt, and the brown woolen robe of the initiate. Before sunset, he would stand with his tribe before the heart-oak, wearing that robe for the first time. He would be blessed by Struath and formally acknowledged as his initiate. And he would never again live in the hut of his birth.

Tinnean smoothed the folds of the robe, the gesture so loving that Darak looked away. This was his last chance. He had to say something. But all he could do was stand there, fists digging into the damp folds of his mantle, as Tinnean added his few personal belongings to the pile of clothes: his bag of charms, his flint dagger, his flute.

Tinnean gathered the ends of the mantle in his fist. "I must go, Darak. I can't keep the Tree-Father waiting."

He'd carved the flute for Tinnean from the bone of a crane's leg. He'd taught him to play it. Struath had sat here, listening to the music, smiling at Tinnean's gift. Now the shaman was stealing him.

"It's not like I'm leaving forever. I'll sleep in the priests' hut, but I'll see you every day. Every day, I promise." Tinnean's blue eyes were soft now and pleading. "Can't you be a little bit happy for me?"

Darak tossed the mantle aside and placed his hands on Tinnean's shoulders. "Give this up. Then I will be happy."

He remained utterly still, as if his brother were a deer he was stalking. Tinnean's eyes searched him for a long moment. When his shoulders slumped, Darak's heart slammed into his chest. He had his brother back. Maybe the gods heard his prayers, after all.

He was still smiling when Tinnean said, "Even if I gave this up, you wouldn't be happy. I'm sorry, Darak." Tinnean stood on tiptoe to press a light kiss on his forehead. "May the Oak-Lord be with you."

Darak shook his head, the unspoken words of the blessing like ashes in his mouth. In the end, Tinnean completed the blessing himself. "And may his spirit fill you with power, with light, and with peace on this Midwinter night."

Tinnean's lips brushed each cheek. He smelled of soap and wool; a hint of peat smoke lingered in his hair. Darak's hands tightened on his shoulders, but he couldn't bring himself to look into his brother's face. Instead, he stared at the rushes, silently willing Tinnean to stay.

With unwonted firmness, Tinnean removed the restraining hands and slipped out of his grasp. Darak only looked up when he heard the shouted greetings from the men carving up the carcass of the bullock. Jurl's bellow rose above the others, hailing his brother as "our new little priest."

Darak picked up the jug of brogac. His brother was the last of his family and the gods had taken him, as surely as they had taken his mother and his wife. He hadn't been able to prevent that, but damned if he would sing their praises. He would march into the forest with the rest of the tribe, but he would offer no gift to the heart-oak. Let the others sing the night away after the priests crossed into the First Forest to witness the battle of the Tree-Lords. Let them shout joyous greetings when Struath returned at dawn to proclaim that the Oak had defeated the Holly.

This year, his voice would remain silent. As silent as the gods who had turned their backs on him.

Chapter 2

STRUATH'S KNEES ACHED. Piety, he reflected, did as little to ease the miseries of old age as the three layers of furs upon which he knelt. He leaned forward and threw another handful of herbs on the fire, quelling the sigh of relief that the brief change in position offered. As he settled back, Tinnean's stomach growled. The boy shot him a quick, guilty look and Struath lowered his head to hide his smile. Next to him, he heard Gortin sigh and his smile changed to a frown.

Perhaps he should have elevated Gortin to Tree-Brother. His initiate was dutiful and devout. It was not his fault that he was also . . . dull. Struath appended a silent prayer of forgiveness to that thought. But to name Gortin Tree-Brother would give his tacit consent for Gortin to follow him as Tree-Father and that honor must go to the boy who knelt on his left.

Five more winters. Maker, grant me that much time to make him ready.

Others had come into their power young. He had been barely twenty summers when he had assumed the title of Tree-Father. Yeorna had risen from initiate to Grain-Mother within one turning of the year. Of course, Muina had to step down when her moon-blood ceased to flow and Aru had died in the plague, but difficult times bred change.

Besides, Tinnean was special; he'd known that even before the boy had returned from his vision quest. He had only to sit before the fire and stare into the flames to fall into the trance state. His nature made him easy to love—and a priest who was loved by his people would be followed without question. He could be impulsive, allowing the beauty of a summer morning to lure him into the forest when he should be honing his skills, but he was learning to curb that aspect of his nature. A few moons ago, he would have aroused the whole tribe when he saw the sky-flames. Last night, Tinnean had come to him.

Struath shifted uncomfortably on the furs. He had withheld the terrible omens from the rest of the tribe, even from the Grain-Mother. Gortin knew, of course. His initiate shared his hut and had heard Tinnean's story, but both had accepted his explanation: the sky-flames represented the red of the Holly-Lord's berries and their sudden disappearance proved the Oak-Lord would triumph in tonight's battle. He could trust Gortin and Tinnean. He'd been less confident about Darak, but Tinnean had assured him that Darak would say nothing.

The boy's face had clouded then, as it always did when his brother's name intruded on their conversations. It infuriated Struath that Darak should steal the joy of this day. Any other man would be proud of the honor shown his brother. And any other man would recognize how important Tinnean's pure faith was to the well-being of the tribe—especially now.

After all his tribe had suffered, he had taken extra precautions to ensure the gods' blessing for the Midwinter rites. He had fasted for the requisite three days. Risen before dawn to cleanse his body in ice-cold water. Braided his hair fifty-two times, one plait for each living member of the tribe, each plait tied off with a finger bone of the tribe's dead. Despite his careful preparations, the bullock had stumbled before the sacrifice, Bel had hidden his golden face behind the clouds, and the ritual fire had taken forever to kindle. Although faith and experience told him balance would be restored, in these last six moons it seemed that the Lord of Chaos would triumph over the Maker for control of the world.

Gortin cleared his throat, jarring Struath from his thoughts. "Aye, Gortin. I know." Seeing his initiate's downcast expression, Struath softened his voice. "Will you fetch the ram's horn?"

Gortin nodded, eager and obedient as a dog.

Gods forgive me. He is a good man, loyal and true. I must be kinder to him.

Struath rose stiffly, waving away Gortin's hand. "Are you ready, Tinnean?"

Tinnean nodded, gazing at him with those shining eyes. Struath wondered if he had possessed such a purity of spirit at that age. He hesitated, then leaned forward to press his lips against the boy's forehead. Belatedly, he offered the same blessing to Gortin, turning away abruptly when he saw tears in his initiate's eyes.

He seized his blackthorn staff and ducked outside the hut. The cold hit him like a blow. He breathed in quick, shallow breaths to keep from coughing, smiling wryly as Tinnean raised his face skyward, sucking in great gulps of the frigid air. Thankfully, Bel had reemerged from the clouds. At last, a good omen.

Gortin sounded the ram's horn three times, its low, mournful call filling the silence of the village. One by one, families emerged from their huts and formed a circle around the fire pit where slabs of meat roasted under hot stones in preparation for the morrow's feast. A few men cast longing glances in that direction. Patches of damp earth showed through the snow where the men had scraped away the blood and entrails; at least this year, Red Dugan had remained sober enough to complete the task properly.

Yeorna approached with Lisula behind her, bearing the leather flask of sacrificial blood. Struath nodded, signaling the Grain-Mother to begin the chant.

A rim of sunlight still haloed Eagles Mount, staining the uppermost branches of the forest orange. The rest of their valley lay in shadow; the circled huts resembled twenty small cairns. Shaking off that disturbing image, Struath walked sunwise around his kinfolk, pressing the back of his left hand to each forehead, blessing each person with the touch of the tattooed acorn. He repressed a pang at the sunken cheeks, the new lines etched by grief. Nearly one hundred people had gathered here at Midsummer; little more than half remained.

He extended his hand to offer his blessing to Darak, then drew back at the mingled reek of stale body odor and brogac. Instead of hanging his head in shame as any decent man would, Darak had the effrontery to stare down at him, his eyes as menacing and gray as storm clouds.

He could no more permit Darak to attend the rite in this condition than he could tolerate such an open challenge. But after all the bad omens, he feared that the absence of even one voice would undermine the Oak-Lord's strength.

As if sensing his quandary, Darak smiled. That decided him. Struath stepped back and raised his voice so all could hear. "Darak, you are an affront to gods and men alike. Go back to your hut. On the morrow, I will choose a fitting punishment for your irreverence."

The strangled cry shattered Darak's veneer of cockiness. As one, their gazes shifted to Tinnean. The boy's lips were pressed together to prevent another outburst, but his eyes pleaded with him to relent. Struath hesitated, knowing how much Darak's absence would wound Tinnean. He turned back to Darak, waiting for some sign of repentance. Instead, his expression hardened into its usual stoniness and he stalked away.

Worried murmurs rose from the rest of the tribe. Struath quelled them with a peremptory gesture. "Only one who is clean in body and mind may stand before our heart-oak. Only then can we help the Oak defeat the Holly."

Tinnean's head drooped. His shoulders rose and fell in a shuddering breath. When he raised his head again, he nodded once. Struath wished he could call Darak back, if only to restore the light to the boy's face, but not even for Tinnean would he allow his authority to be undermined.

Three times, Struath thumped the frozen earth with his blackthorn staff. Three times, Yeorna raised and lowered the dried sheaf of barley, the symbol of the Grain-Mother's power. Tinnean and Lisula broke the circle; tonight, the youngest had the honor of leading the tribe into the forest.

Struath eyed the guttering torches and murmured a brief prayer to strengthen the fire. A balky bullock could be ignored. Even Darak's arrogance could be overlooked; he had refused permission to attend the rites before because of drunkenness. The death of the flames would be disastrous.

The bones in his hair clicked in a gust of wind. Once, wool and piety had been enough to shield him from the cold, but long before the procession reached the forest's verge, Struath was shivering so hard that his staff shook in his numbed fingers. The icy air seared his lungs. As he picked his way along the narrow forest trail, his chants barely rose above a whisper. Yeorna, bless her, chanted all the louder so the others would not notice.

He knew there were whispers in the tribe, though none dared to speak against him openly. After all their troubles, it was only natural that some would wonder if he had lost his power to intercede with the gods. Tonight, he would prove them wrong. And tomorrow, he would humble Darak before the entire tribe.

It had been thirty years since the elders of the Oak Tribe had named him Tree-Father, the youngest ever to be accorded the honor. Thirty years since Brun—may his spirit live on in the sunlit Forever Isles—had stood before him and gouged out his left eye with the point of the ceremonial bronze dagger. The right eye to see this world, the blind one to penetrate the unseen one.

Surreptitiously, Struath wiped his cheek. Thirty years and still the cold made tears ooze from the empty socket. Aching joints he understood, and fingers too swollen to close into a fist. But how could an empty eye weep?

Not that he was ancient, he reminded himself. Mother Netal and the Memory-Keeper were older. Only three of them left who remembered Morgath as a living man, not merely as the central character in a gruesome cautionary tale.

At the thought of his predecessor, Struath forced his numb fingers to make the sign against evil. "That it may not come through earth, through water, through air," he muttered. Relenting, he added a quick prayer that Morgath's spirit might have found light and peace. Power he would not wish him; his mentor had hungered for it too much while he lived.

The words brought on a coughing fit that left him feeling as weak as a newborn lamb. He thrust the weakness aside, along with the resentment of knowing how few rites remained to him. All across the world, tribes were gathering to drive away the dark with songs and shouts and blazing torchlight. Tonight, all his strength, all his power must be concentrated on the battle in the grove.

Tinnean and Lisula stepped aside as they reached

the clearing. The chanting ceased, leaving only the sigh of the wind and the groan of bare branches. Struath closed his eye, allowing the ages-old strength of the forest to fill him, drawing on the power of the earth beneath him and the sky above him to drive out cold and pride and doubt. Only then did he open his eye to find Tinnean watching him. So young, Maker bless him, and so eager, illuminated by an inner light far brighter than the torch's flame. Once, he had possessed that radiance—or so Morgath had said.

Shaking off his memories, he stepped into the glade. Soaring pines reached skyward, dark, jagged silhouettes against the violet sky. The other trees were indistinguishable from one another in the gloom save for the venerable heart-oak. The light from their torches cast strange shadows on the sacred tree, making the runneled bark seem to shift and move, creating a mouth that now smiled, now frowned, and eyes that followed their movements.

Struath nodded to Tinnean who took his place before the heart-oak. Then he hesitated. Belatedly, Struath realized why.

Tradition called for him to pass his torch to the oldest male of his family. That honor should have fallen to Darak. An uncomfortable moment passed before Sim stepped forward. Struath nodded curtly and the Memory-Keeper accepted the torch. When he retreated, Struath stepped forward to stand at Tinnean's side.

"In the time before time, The People came to this land. Our ancestors worshiped the One Tree that is Two—the One Tree that is the Oak and the Holly."

He paused to allow the tribe to intone the traditional response. "May its roots remain ever strong."

"From one People, we became two tribes, forever linked by our common history."

Again, the tribe responded. "May our bond remain ever strong."

"Since the time before time, we have gathered before our heart-oak to honor the gods and to perform our sacred rites. It is fitting that on this holy day, we gather not only to lend our strength to the Oak-Lord in his battle tonight, but to honor this man's commitment to the way of the priest."

"May his path remain ever clear."

Gortin sounded the ram's horn as Struath faced Tinnean. "Tinnean, son of Reinek and Cluran. Before the gods of our people, do you affirm your willingness to be initiated?"

"I do so affirm."

"Before the sacred tree of our tribe, do you affirm your willingness to be initiated?"

"I do so affirm."

"Before the people of your tribe, do you affirm your willingness to be initiated?"

"I do so affirm."

"Kneel, then."

Tinnean knelt between two of the oak's exposed roots. Struath gazed down at him. His vision blurred. Thirty years ago, he had knelt there to cut out Morgath's heart.

Do not taint this sacred place by thinking of him.

Struath paused to gather himself. Tonight of all nights, his mind must be uncluttered.

"Tinnean, son of Reinek and Cluran. Do you vow to honor the gods, worshiping them with your body, your mind, and your spirit?"

"I do so vow."

"Do you vow to honor the Oak and the Holly, worshiping them with your body, your mind, and your spirit?"

"I do so vow."

"Do you vow to honor the laws of our tribe, following them with your body, your mind, and your spirit?"

"I do so vow."

Gortin stepped forward, holding the cluster of acorns.

He raised them toward the naked branches of the heart-oak before pressing them against Tinnean's forehead. "The blessing of the Oak upon you."

Lisula proffered the leather flask. Struath dipped his forefinger into it and daubed Tinnean's cheeks with two spots of blood. "The blessing of the Holly upon you."

The Grain-Mother touched Tinnean's chest with her sheaf of barley. "The blessing of the fruitful earth upon you."

Even in the fading light, Struath could see the awe on the boy's face as he took him by the shoulders. He could still recall the shiver of excitement that had shaken his body so long ago, the swell of pride when he rose to his feet, the comfort of Morgath's hands on his shoulders . . .

Struath shook his head, frowning, and Tinnean's expectant smile died. He offered the boy a quick, reassuring nod and turned him to face the tribe.

"He knelt before us a man. He stands before us a priest. Welcome, Tinnean. Initiate of the Oak Tribe."

"Welcome, Tinnean." The shout rolled through the glade, shattering the forest's stillness. The sound was still fading when Struath raised his hand.

"People of the Oak. The day is waning. On the morrow, we will celebrate the Oak's victory and Tinnean's first battle rite. But now we must make ready."

The Memory-Keeper began the song, his quavering voice quickly supported by others.

> *"Now is the dark time.*
> *The sun's light is ebbing.*
> *The old year is waning.*
> *The earth is asleep.*
>
> *Now at the dark time*
> *The Oak-Lord awakens.*
> *The Holly-Lord threatens.*
> *The battle begins.*

> *Pray for the Oak.*
> *Help him vanquish the Holly.*
> *Pray for the Oak.*
> *Make the darkness retreat.*
>
> *Sing to the Oak*
> *And the earth will awaken.*
> *Sing to the Oak*
> *And the spring will return."*

As they sang, Struath led the procession around the heart-oak. He offered the first gift, sprinkling blood from the flask over the tree's roots. Children crumbled oatcakes, women poured libations of berry wine, men paused to tie arrows and fishhooks to the lowest branches. The last streaks of color were fading from the sky when he motioned the priests aside. It was time.

Only at sunset and sunrise, when the boundary between the worlds was thin, could they make the crossing. The first time, he had expected bolts of lightning or howling winds to mark the passage. Although he knew how it would happen, the wonder was as great as ever when he uttered the ancient words of permission and, between one step and the next, led the priests out of their tribal glade and into the grove of the First Forest.

He heard Tinnean gasp as the shadowy figures of other worshipers appeared. They came alone and in pairs, men and women, even a few who looked to be children. Some wore animal skins, others robes. Some bore elaborate tattoos, others were unmarked. Countless strangers, from all the tribes who worshiped the Oak and the Holly. All came in silence and in darkness, torches extinguished during their passage; the First Forest did not welcome fire.

Gheala emerged, full-bellied and fat, from behind the clouds. Tinnean gasped again as her moonlight revealed a grove so large their entire village could fit within it. And at its center, the living heart of this limitless forest, stood the One Tree.

As always, the sight filled Struath with awe. The One Tree had stood in this grove since the world's first spring, observing the passing of time as a man might mark the passing of seasons. Each root was thicker than the trunk of their heart-oak. Twenty men with their arms outstretched could barely circle the trunk. But the true miracle was that the One Tree was also Two, for from those roots, from that trunk, grew the Oak and the Holly.

Tinnean's eyes were wide, his face as pale as Gheala's. *So I must have looked that first time,* Struath thought. He experienced a vivid sensation just then of his mentor's hand resting on the back of his neck. He hunched his shoulders, shrinking from the memory.

One by one, each tribe laid its offerings among the Oak's roots: blood and water, meat and grain, flint arrowheads and smooth stones. One man carried a brace of hares, another a gourd painted with bold green leaves. The gaunt woman before him in the procession offered a bouquet of dried goldenrod. Struath knelt and placed the bullock's heart next to it.

"It is not the offering that is important, little rook, but the heart of the one who makes it." So Morgath had told him before his first battle rite, the deep voice calming his anxiety, the gentle touch stilling his restlessness. Even as Struath shuddered, he realized he had failed to offer such reassurance to Tinnean. As he moved back from the One Tree, he squeezed the boy's shoulder and was rewarded with a quick, relieved smile.

By the time each gift had been presented, Gheala's light had traveled halfway across the grove. Struath's heartbeat quickened with familiar excitement. In a dozen tongues, they offered the greeting. "Lord of the Oak. Lord of the Holly. We stand before you." In a dozen tongues, they made the affirmation. "Lords of the First Forest, we come to witness." And then they waited.

The air trembled. A shiver ran down Struath's spine as the energy flowed around him and through him, through all of the watchers, human and tree alike—a circle of living power surrounding the Tree. A shudder rippled through the massive trunk. The sweeping boughs of the Holly shook as the Lord of the Waning Year offered the challenge. The Oak rattled its spindly branches, accepting.

"They battle!" Tinnean cried.

The boy should not have spoken, but Struath understood the need to give voice to the wonder. Around the circle of worshipers, the power surged. Through earth and air, the power of the First Forest resonated, filling his senses, making him want to shout like Tinnean with the joy of it.

Then the Holly attacked. The finger-length spikes of its leaves carved long gouges in the Oak's trunk. Struath sang with the others, his voice shaking with cold and apprehension. Each day since Midsummer, the Oak-Lord's strength had dwindled, and with it the strength of the sun. Tonight, his power was at its lowest ebb, yet somehow, the Lord of the Waxing Year must prevail.

A great bulge ran up the trunk of the Tree. Twigs burst out of the Oak's naked limbs. They grew thick and strong, swelling with power. The Oak lashed the Holly, the sharp retort of cracking branches punctuating the singing. Green boughs sagged. Red berries, large as fists, rained down.

Struath flexed his fingers, unaware until now how tightly he'd been clenching his staff. As many times as he had stood here, the battle between the old year and the new was a fearful thing to behold. But all would be well. The Oak-Lord would vanquish his

rival, the dying sun would be reborn, and just as their
ancient song promised, winter would yield to spring.

The Holly's limbs shriveled, retreating before the
burgeoning power of the Oak. Even as relief surged
through him, Struath heard a high-pitched whine. The
chanting faltered. The smooth flow of energy frag-
mented as the worshipers searched the grove for the
origin of the sound.

The whine intensified. Struath peered at the One
Tree. Surely it was a trick of Gheala's waning light
that made the Oak seem to waver. Or was it his aging
vision that created the illusion of a crevice snaking up
the trunk of the Tree? In shocked disbelief, he watched
the crevice widen, revealing a featureless void darker
than the Midwinter night. Before he could puzzle it
out, the Oak split with a horrifying shriek of rending
wood.

Shards of wood, longer than any spear, catapulted
through the air. Men and women fled screaming, trampling those in their path. Struath stood frozen as one
of the flying spears shattered a man's head. Another
impaled a woman on a birch where her body hung,
twitching.

A bearded man shoved Yeorna and she fell. Struath
threw his body over hers, crying out as feet kicked his
ribs and back. The Tree shrieked again. Struath raised
his head as the Oak shuddered and ripped away from
the trunk of the Tree. The great branches fell to the
ground with eerie slowness, the shock of the impact
knocking the few worshipers who still stood off their
feet.

Blackness filled the jagged scar. In the blackness,
stars red as blood. They gleamed with an unholy light
as they swirled, slowly coalescing into a shape. A
hand, Struath realized. An outstretched hand, the fingers curling and uncurling as if reaching for him. Even
as an arm struggled to shape itself, the hand disinte-

grated, melting into a trail of red stars that oozed down the trunk of the Tree like malignant sap. Struath's lips moved in the prayer to avert evil, but no sound would emerge from his mouth.

It was Tinnean who screamed.

Even as Struath reached for him, he knew he was too late. Tinnean raced toward the Tree, unlit torch raised high. It seemed to take forever for the torch to complete its graceful arc toward the trail of bloody slime and only a heartbeat for the torch to shatter.

Tinnean hurtled into the air. He screamed again, the shrill cry of a terrified animal. For a moment, his body was silhouetted against the swirling red stars. Then he plummeted into the branches of the Holly, his scream abruptly cut off.

An owl swooped past. The insistent whine faded. And then, as if Gheala could not bear to witness more, the moon disappeared behind a cloud, plunging the grove into darkness.

Chapter 3

DARAK WOKE WITH a startled curse. A drop of water ran down his cheek. Reluctant to leave the warmth of the wolfskins, he shifted on his pallet. The movement sent pain lancing through his temples, a vivid reminder of the jug of brogac he had drained the night before. Groaning, he lay still.

Another drop spattered on the bedstraw next to his head as melting snow dripped through a hole in the turf. He had meant to repair the roof before the snows came, just as he'd meant to plug the chinks in the walls, but he had more important concerns this autumn than the roof or the walls.

Judging from the light sifting through those selfsame chinks, it was past dawn. They would be back soon. A creeping sense of shame assailed him. No matter what he thought of the gods, he should have stood with his tribe. And no matter what he thought about Tinnean's decision to become a priest, he should have attended his brother's initiation.

Instead, he had made a spectacle of himself. And soon, he'd become a bigger one. When Red Dugan had passed out in his hut before the Midsummer rite, Struath had made him kneel in the center of the village for an entire day, chanting apologies to the gods, to the Tree-Lords, and to each member of the tribe.

The thought intensified the throbbing in his head. Whatever punishment Struath decreed, he would have to accept it. That was the law of the tribe and no man stood outside it.

He crawled out from under the skins, scratching his cheeks; two days' growth of bristles couldn't obscure the plague scars. The fire was nearly dead. His eyes felt gritty. His mouth tasted foul. And he stank.

He stumbled outside, blinking in the watery sunlight. The eerie emptiness of the village made him shudder and the shudder made his head ache. Cursing Tinnean's insistence on dedicating himself to unfeeling gods, he hitched up his tunic and unknotted the thong at the waist of his breeches. The gods hadn't cared when his wife died, screaming as the red plague pustules burst all over her body. They hadn't cared about his mam, too weak to scream, too wasted to move, who simply ceased to exist between one breath and the next. The gods cared only for themselves.

Piss on the gods.

Rearranging his clothing, he peered east to find his kinfolk surging through the stubbled fields. He ducked back inside. When he faced Struath, he wanted to look his best.

He broke the ice in the basin and splashed water on his face. He rolled more water around his mouth to take away the taste of the brogac and spat it out on the rushes. Crouching beside the basin, he lathered his face, stretched the skin taut, and dragged his dagger across his cheeks. A shout outside made his hand slip; he winced as the flint blade nicked him, then resolutely finished the task. He wiped the dagger on his breeches and sheathed it as Griane flung aside the bearskin.

"You better come, Darak."

The last thing he needed this morning was Griane's breathless dramatics. Because she was his wife's sister, he bit back his retort and asked, "What now?"

Judging by the way her lips thinned almost to invisibility, his answer had not been civil enough. Her face grew paler, making the freckles stand out all the more. He knew he should be patient, but he had a wicked headache and little inclination to wheedle information from the girl.

"What?"

Griane tossed that impossibly red braid over her shoulder. For a moment, he thought she might simply run off. All the women in her family had that odd manner, as if they were wild creatures only recently tamed. In Maili, he'd found it endearing.

Just when he was on the point of telling her to speak her mind or get out, he realized she was holding Mother Netal's basket. Perhaps she had brought herbs to ease his pounding head. Regretting his gruffness, he mumbled an apology.

Griane's face crumpled. Before he could do more than gape at her, Nionik ducked inside, cradling Tinnean's limp body in his arms. Fear stabbed Darak, keen as a dagger's blade.

The chief laid Tinnean on his pallet and Darak knelt beside him. Bloody scratches marred his brother's face and hands, but he could see no other marks of violence. He might almost be sleeping, so peaceful did he look. His cheek was cold, though, and the hand that he grasped lay limp between his fingers. Melting snow spattered onto Tinnean's face from another hole in the roof. He hauled the bedding closer to the fire pit.

"What happened?"

Nionik glanced away as Yeorna and Lisula slipped inside, all of them shoulder to shoulder in the close confines of the hut. Their silence terrified him as much as their haunted expressions. It was a relief to hear Mother Netal shouting at those outside to let her through.

He pulled Tinnean into his arms, hugging him hard, just as he had the morning Tinnean returned from the forest after disappearing for an entire day and night. That was the first time he had whipped his brother.

"Stop shaking the boy." Mother Netal's gaze swept past him, her nose wrinkling. Once, this hut had been the kind of place you wanted to come home to, filled with the heavy aroma of peat smoke, the rich, onion-scented smell of simmering stew, and the dusty fragrance of herbs. Now it smelled of musty rushes and his sour body.

For once, the healer kept her opinions to herself. She held out an imperious arm to Griane who helped her squat beside Tinnean. "Give me room," Mother Netal said, punctuating the remark with a sharp elbow.

Darak reluctantly ceded his place to her, but kept his grip on Tinnean's hand.

"Make yourself useful, boy. Tend the fire."

Before he could move, Griane snatched up a peat brick. Nionik cleared his throat. "The Tree-Father and I will talk to the people. Lisula, help the Grain-Mother to your hut." As they turned to leave, Darak noticed the makeshift sling supporting Yeorna's right arm. Shouted questions greeted their appearance. Nionik's voice rose above the cacophony. "Go to your homes. After Mother Netal has seen to Tinnean, we will meet in the longhut in council."

Mother Netal cuffed him. "Don't hover. Fetch some water so I can wash these scratches."

"I'll do it," Griane said. "You see to the fire, Darak. The peat's laid. All you have to do is—"

"I know how to tend a fire."

Griane shouldered the waterskin and sidled past as if she'd be contaminated by any physical contact with him. Darak restacked a few of the peat bricks and stirred the embers into life.

"Add some deadwood," Mother Netal said. "I need more light."

He obeyed, grateful that Mother Netal was too busy laying charms around Tinnean to notice his trembling hands. She dipped into her basket again. One by one, she tossed three small bundles of twigs into the fire pit. "Alder, protect him. Ash, give him will. Rowan, give me vision."

She brushed back Tinnean's hair and peered into his ears before pulling back his eyelids. At her satisfied grunt, Darak let out his breath. She lifted Tinnean's head, gnarled fingers dancing lightly over his scalp, across his forehead, and down his neck. She rested her ear against his chest, then pushed the robe back from his arm and fingered his wrist.

"Is he all right?"

The ever-present frown deepened. "I won't know if you keep interrupting me. Help me strip him."

Again, he obeyed, then crouched beside her as she gently probed Tinnean's ribs, belly, and genitals. At her command, he rolled Tinnean over. Eyes closed, her fingers traced their way down his spine.

"Roll him onto his back again." She sniffed his breath and pulled the wolfskins over him. "Nothing's broken. Eyes are clear. No bleeding from the ears or scalp. Other than the scratches, there are no physical wounds."

"I can see that."

"Are you the healer?"

Hands fisted on his knees, Darak shook his head.

Mother Netal grunted. "I'll make a lotion of yarrow and Maker's mantle for his scratches. As to the rest, we'll have to wait till he wakes."

"What do you mean, 'the rest'?"

Before she could answer, Darak felt a blast of cold

air and turned to see Gortin holding back the bearskin for Struath.

"You're supposed to be in bed," Mother Netal said.

"How is the boy?"

"As he was."

Darak rose. "What happened? What did you do to him?"

"If you had been in the glade instead of drunk in your hut, you would know what happened."

Darak's head jerked back, knocking hard against the roof stones. "Tell me, damn it."

"Hush," Mother Netal said. "You will not speak to the Tree-Father that way. And you . . ." She frowned at Struath. "You need rest and food. Gortin, try and get some hot soup into him."

"Gortin, go to the Grain-Mother's hut. Make sure Yeorna is all right."

"Aye, Tree-Father. But Mother Netal is right. You should—"

"I will remain here until the boy wakes."

Darak returned the shaman's glare. Mother Netal's rudeness, he could tolerate. She had been healer to the tribe all his life and he trusted her absolutely. But he would never forgive Struath. If not for him, Tinnean would be hunkered down by the fire pit right now, ignoring his instructions to let the porridge cool and offering a sheepish smile when the first mouthful burned his tongue. Still, Struath held the secret to what had happened in the grove and for that reason he controlled his temper.

"I don't care about your rites or your magic. Just tell me . . . I need to know what happened to my brother."

Struath remained silent, staring down at Tinnean.

"Struath. The plague took my wife and my mother." His voice shook and he took a moment to master himself. "It took my uncle and his whole family. It left me these." He fingered the pockmarks on his cheeks. "He's all I have."

Before Struath reduced him to begging, Mother Netal said, "Tree-Father. He should know."

Darak managed to listen without interrupting, but when Struath related how Tinnean had been thrown skyward, the air rushed out of his lungs. And when the shaman described his brother hurtling into the Holly, he flinched as if his body felt the impact.

"And after?" he asked, damning his voice for breaking.

"We found him lying beneath the Holly. Scratched, but otherwise unhurt."

"And he's been unconscious since?"

"Aye."

"Can you help him?"

Struath hesitated. "I must wait until he wakes."

Darak studied the shaman. Exhaustion had etched deeper lines around his mouth and eyes, and although he appeared to be leaning casually against the wall, a tremor ran up his arm from the tense, splayed fingers.

"All right. We'll wait."

He crouched beside Tinnean. Behind him, the voices of Mother Netal and Struath rose and fell in a barely audible murmur. Deliberately, he shut them out.

Fear is the enemy.

He wiped a drop of blood from his brother's cheek.

Control the fear and you can control yourself.

He clasped the cold hand.

Don't take him, gods.

Not a prayer, he told himself. A command.

With his free hand, he brushed the lock of hair off Tinnean's forehead. Softer than his. Brighter, too, like their mam's before it went white. All the colors of autumn.

Wake up, Tinnean. Wake up and look at me.

Not a command this time. A plea.

Chapter 4

NOT-FOREST.

A place that was dark and close, but not the darkness of night or the closeness of trees. Inside, a dull tattoo beat, like a woodpecker's drumming or the dripping of rain on leaves, but slower than the bird and steadier than the rain. Not-earth beneath him, but something that shifted. Above, no moon, no stars, only stone and smoke. Smoke meant fire. Fire meant danger. The tattoo thudded, fierce and fast.

Out of the darkness and the smoke, a shape loomed, pale as birch, framed by dark fur. The face of a man, closer than ever before, bigger than the full moon. Two shining eyes blinked. A mouth opened. A voice croaked, deep and harsh as a raven's.

The tattoo grew wild, a hawk's wings beating the air. White claws gripped him, cold and strong. Stars crowded in upon him. The face faded. Then there was only the tattoo and the darkness.

"He opened his eyes," Griane told the others as they crowded around. "Just for a moment." She squeezed Darak's shoulder hard, but he ignored her.

"Let him sleep," Mother Netal said. "That's the best thing for him now."

Darak relinquished his grip on Tinnean's arms long enough to tuck the wolfskins under his chin.

"It'll be all right, Darak." She offered him her most confident smile and received a brief, bleak glance in return before he sank back on his haunches.

Stupid, Griane. Nobody knows if it will be all right.

She squeezed Darak's shoulder again to apologize for her useless words. Then she squatted by the fire pit, snatched up a turtle shell, and started scraping the crusted porridge from their bowls.

When the darkness went away, the same not-so-dark place returned. A new face peered at him, as deeply grooved as the trunk of an elder. This man had only one eye the color of a robin's egg. Twisted vines of gray fur hung from his head.

Another face appeared. The Fox-Fur slipped warm claws under him and raised him up. He had to take refuge in the darkness because the tilting of the world was not-good. When he saw again, the Fox-Fur's face loomed closer and its claws held out a hollow stone. Mist rose from it as it might from a lake on an autumn morning.

The Fox-Fur moved the stone closer. Warm not-water drizzled into him. His upper being heaved and the not-water spewed out. Only after the pouring had been repeated several times did he learn to take the liquid in, little by little. This made the Fox-Fur's mouth turn up.

The hollow ache inside disappeared, replaced by a fullness still lower in his being. He searched his mem-

ory, but like the not-water, this, too, was outside his
knowing. The fullness peaked. Warm wetness soaked
him. He waited for it to roll off. When it did not, he
tried to pull it into himself and failed.

The Fox-Fur rubbed something soft on him. Some
of the wet went away. There was more underneath
him on the prickly, shifting ground. The Fox-Fur and
the Dark-Fur moved him. The tilting was so not-good
that his being heaved again. Heat seared him, gushing
out to spatter the Dark-Fur's claws.

The Dark-Fur's mouth turned down. The Fox-Fur
made soft noises and stroked him with soft claws, like
a vixen cuffing her kits. He wondered why the Fox-
Fur did not lick him. Perhaps men did not do that.
The Fox-Fur was a different sort of man from the
other two, but it was clearly their kind—just as he
was not.

Too agitated to sit, Darak paced. "He doesn't speak.
He throws up his soup. He pisses the bed." Four
strides across the width of the hut. Four strides back.

"It's only been a day," Griane said.

Mother Netal grunted. "Give him time, Darak."

Asleep, his brother looked unchanged. Only the
scratches on his cheeks and the faint shadows under
his eyes spoke to the ordeal he had undergone. Darak
squatted beside the pallet once more. The next time
Tinnean opened his eyes, his brother would know him.

He learned that there were times that were dark and
times that were not-so-dark, but even in the not-so-
dark times, there was no sun or wind or snow. He
learned there were many men and that they were as
varied as the leaves of the trees: some small, some
large, some broad, some slender. Strangest of all, he

learned that he was no longer rooted to the earth, that he could will himself to move, not simply rely on the men to move him.

With that knowing came another that made the inner tattoo beat very fast. Instead of many limbs, he now had only five. Two longer ones grew out of his upper trunk. Two others, longer still, grew from his lower trunk. One, small and limp, grew from his center. All were pale and soft.

The awareness horrified him so he shut out the sight of the not-forest and the men and his own pitiful, pale form. Then he could remember birds and beasts, wind and rain, sun and moon and stars, and everywhere, trees.

He could not shut out the not-forest for very long or the needs of his new form. He learned to move about the small, dark place using the lower limbs, which trembled and folded beneath him until he managed to control them. He learned to cover his limbs with the skins of dead animals to keep out the cold. He learned to scoop up the not-water with a turtle shell. And always, he watched the men who watched him.

Each time he moved, the Dark-Fur's body tensed like a stalking wolf's. The Dark-Fur did not seem to understand how strange and terrifying and enthralling his new form was to him. When he rolled the thick not-water around his mouth, savoring its lumps, the two wings above the Dark-Fur's eyes drew together. When he explored the ridges and hollows of his face with his claws, the Dark-Fur's voice rumbled like distant thunder. When he rubbed the small limb in his center and made it stand upright, the Dark-Fur's face turned as red as a crab apple; even after he stopped rubbing, the Dark-Fur continued to shake him, snarling loudly all the while.

When the Dark-Fur left, the One-Eye would come, or the Fox-Fur, or the small White-Fur with the gentle hands and a face as wrinkled as a dried rowanberry. Often, the One-Eye grasped his face gently and closed his eye. He would feel an odd tingling, like and unlike the energy that flowed among the trees in the forest. When the robin-egg eye finally popped open, the One-Eye shook his head, more grooves sprouting on his face.

Once, the One-Eye brought three other men into the den. They burned dry weeds and rattled turtle shells while the One-Eye held up a little round rock that sparkled as if it held the sun. The One-Eye moved it round and round him until his head ached from watching. Then the One-Eye held the sunstone in his hand, closed his eye, and rocked back and forth on his haunches until he fell over in a heap. He lay there a long while, twitching like a sleeping wolf. When he awoke, he shook his head and all of their faces became deeply grooved.

They always went away when the Dark-Fur returned. The Dark-Fur poked a stick through the dead animals and birds he had brought and laid them over the fire. He did not like to eat the dead creatures, but if he refused, the hollowness came back and the Dark-Fur would snarl. He would finish the eating quickly so he could lie beneath the skins, and close his eyes, and try to recall what had happened to bring him to this place.

"Why is he like this?"

Struath turned away. He disliked having Darak loom over him.

"He's getting better," Mother Netal said. "He responds when you call him now."

"So does a dog." After a long silence, Darak spoke again, his voice flat. "He's going to be like Pol, isn't he?"

"Nay, lad. Pol's addled because he was kicked in the head by the ram."

"Then what is it?" Darak rounded on him again. "Is he possessed by a demon?"

Struath shook his head.

"Folk who've had a great shock react in different ways," Mother Netal said. "Old Sim who swore he saw a portal to Chaos open—his hair turned white overnight and him only four and twenty summers then. Ania has neither moved nor spoken since the bear mauled her. Sometimes, a person's spirit shatters and the fragments flee to the Forever Isles."

"But Struath can find them." The pleading in Darak's eyes belied the challenge in his voice. "Can't you?"

Struath straightened to his full height, but he still had to look up at Darak. "I can."

He had touched Tinnean's spirit many times—at his birth, after his vision quest, before he took the boy on as an apprentice. If Tinnean's spirit had shattered, he would have recognized the fragments left behind. This spirit felt confused, lost, and utterly unfamiliar. To reveal that would only lead to more questions, and he refused to allow Darak to bully an admission of ignorance from him.

He was Tree-Father. He must continue to seek the answers to this mystery. But how would he find them when his visions had deserted him?

Chapter 5

THE DARK-FUR was called "Darak" and the One-Eye "Struath." Little White-Fur was "Mother Netal" and Fox-Fur was "Griane." They were females. Like wolves, they were smaller than the males, but equally fierce.

They all nodded and curled up their mouths when he called them by their not-fur names. Because it seemed to please them, he made an effort to learn the names for the other things in their world, even when the names confused him. The not-water container was called "bowl" although it was clearly a hollow stone. "Pot" was the larger stone container that sat in the fire. "Pot" contained different not-waters, sometimes "porridge," sometimes "stew," sometimes "brose," which was watery porridge, and sometimes "soup," which was watery stew. His favorite not-water was the "hot apple cider" Griane brought in a large pouch named—oddly—"waterskin."

He learned the names of things like "shoes" and "cup" and "bed." He learned the names of not-things like "please" and "thank-you" and "hello" and "good-bye." But he did not know how to ask them why he was here or how he could return to the forest.

Then Griane took him outside the den. The wind stung and the brightness of the sun made his eyes leak water, but it was very good to be out of the darkness and to know that their world was not so different from his.

He saw many small dens like Darak's. He saw very small men playing with small wolves and a herd of curly-furred not-deer called "sheep." Then he saw the line of willows and alders, and beyond them, on the rising slope of a hill, the Oak.

He ran, zigzagging like a mouse through the clusters of men. He heard Griane shout his not-name, but he ran on, his tattoo beating very fast. He reached the trees and splashed across the stream, slipping once on the wet rocks, patting the branches of the willows and the alders, but not stopping, not even for them, until he reached the Oak.

It was smaller than he remembered, but if he should now wear the form of a man, then it might have shriveled into this slender being. If he had been transported to this place, perhaps the Oak had as well. None of that mattered as long as they were together.

Breathless, he stood before the Oak, fog rising from his mouth in great clouds. He touched its trunk with one careful finger and felt nothing. He laid both hands on the tree. This time, it roused to his touch. He closed his eyes, sending his energy to the tree. He poured out his confusion and begged it to tell him why he was here. He stood there until the cold stole the feeling from his fingers and Griane's urgent tug on his arm could no longer be ignored.

The oak had recognized him, waking from its winter drowsiness to hum quietly beneath his fingers. But it was simply a tree, content to doze until spring awakened it. It was not the Oak.

Griane turned him away. His gaze swept across his new world. The heart tattoo thudded wildly. Beyond the stream and the dens and the snow-covered ex-

panses called "fields," he saw the dark silhouettes of
countless trees. He tugged free of Griane's hand. Once
again, he ran.

Darak loosened the snare and removed the rabbit.
Too weak to struggle, the quivering animal stared up
at him, its dark eyes wide with fear and hopelessness.
Instead of breaking its neck, the sinew had looped
around one foreleg, nearly severing it. Judging from
the spots of blood staining the snow, the creature had
hung here only a short while, but the hunter in him
abhorred the messiness of the kill.

He bowed his head. "Little brother, I thank you for
giving your life for us. And I ask your forgiveness for
the suffering I have caused you." With a quick twist
of his hands, he snapped the rabbit's neck.

He spread the limp body on a clean patch of snow,
carefully facing the animal west so that its spirit might
race after the sun. He hoped the cruelly maimed foreleg would not hinder its progress. When he heard a
rustling in the grasses, he knew the rabbit's spirit had
accepted his apology and begun its journey to the
afterworld. Crumbling a bit of oatcake over the snow
in thanks for the kill, he rose and bent the sapling
down to reset his snare.

Even with his eyes focused on his work, he could
feel the forest. The silent trees watching him with their
never-sleeping awareness, trunks shimmering with otherworldly power, naked branches creaking as they
reached out to drag him from the open field into the
gloom of the tangled undergrowth. . . .

Despite himself, he glanced up, then scowled. The
trunks of the closest trees glowed with the ruddy light
of the late afternoon sun and the branches rattled only
through the power of the wind. It was the strain of

dealing with Tinnean's condition that was making him so jumpy.

He was glad now that he'd obeyed the irascible old healer. Mother Netal and Struath both promised to watch over Tinnean; Griane swore that if their duties took them elsewhere, she would remain with him. He'd found her assurances less comforting than Mother Netal's, but he could not neglect his responsibilities forever; everyone—even the children—helped provide food for the village. And now—like the children—his pride had reduced him to setting snares in the fields and along the lakeshore.

He was the best hunter in the tribe. No one knew the forest paths as well, none possessed his skill with the bow. He had been fifteen when he earned the hunter's tattoo, younger even than his father, the only other man in living memory to bring down a stag with one arrow to the heart. He'd been so proud of besting his father that he had scarcely noticed the pain when Struath pierced his skin with the bone needle and created the antler tattoo that branched across his right wrist.

But only a man who performed the necessary rites could hunt the forest and only a man who asked the gods for their blessing could hope for success. The rites he could manage, but he was damned if he would humble himself to the gods who had stolen everyone he had ever loved.

He wasn't sure if his kinfolk blamed him for missing the Midwinter rite or for his refusal to enter the forest now. Perhaps he only imagined the surliness of their replies when he greeted them and the doubt on their faces when he assured them that Tinnean was getting better every day.

He told himself that the strangeness would pass, but it still hurt when his brother flinched at the sound of his voice or shied away when he tried to touch him.

He could scarcely believe this was the same boy who used to tag along behind him like an eager puppy. Tinnean seemed to have forgotten all the things he had taught him: how to build a fire and clean a kill, to strip feathers into fletching and chip an arrowhead from flint. The lessons a father taught a son. The lessons that had fallen to him to teach after their father died from the wasting sickness and Tinnean barely walking.

All those years, all those memories—lost. But Tinnean would remember. He would come back.

Sprinkling a handful of snow over the snare, Darak rose. He still had three more snares to check. If they were full, he could stay home tomorrow. Spend some time with Tinnean. Remind him how to play fox and hare or cast-the-bones. He'd always liked games.

Darak had just slung the hunting sack across his body when he saw the two figures racing across the fields. The flame-colored hair could only belong to Griane, which meant the figure running away from her had to be Tinnean.

Fear changed to relief when he saw his brother's face, alight with joy and excitement. Tinnean flung out his arms. Darak ran toward him, shouting.

His brother froze. Darak's footsteps slowed, stopped. "Tinnean?"

The joy faded, replaced by uncertainty and then desperation.

"Tinnean."

Tinnean backed away, shaking his head. Griane shouted something. Tinnean glanced over his shoulder, then back at him, eyes wild. Darak took one step toward him, hand outstretched.

Tinnean screamed.

Darak watched him lurch off in a new direction. Saw him look over his shoulder to see if they were still pursuing him. Watched him slip, fall, and stagger to his feet again. When he realized his hand was still reaching after his brother, he let it fall to his side.

It was easy to stalk him. Tinnean floundered in the new-fallen snow, exhausting himself unnecessarily. Each time he cut toward the trees, Darak blocked his path. Each time he turned away from the forest, Darak let him run. The third time Tinnean fell, he simply lay there, but as Darak drew close, he rolled over and crawled through the snow on his hands and knees.

Darak seized him by the back of his mantle and spun him around. Tinnean toppled into the snow. Again, he tried to crawl away. Again, Darak flung him back. This time, Tinnean staggered to his feet and stood before him, swaying.

"Please, Darak."

The first time Tinnean had spoken his name.

"Please, Darak. Home."

Relief suffused him. Then he realized that Tinnean meant the forest. A dark, unreasoning fury rose up in him. He shook his head and pointed at the village.

He wasn't sure what he expected Tinnean to do. Plead maybe, or weep, or simply fall to his knees in defeat. The attack took him completely off guard. He fell backward into the snow with Tinnean on top of him, too stunned to do more than raise his arms to shield himself from his brother's ineffectual punches. When he recovered his wits, he seized Tinnean's arms and shoved him off.

Tinnean attacked again. Most of the punches landed harmlessly, but one took him in the eye, momentarily blinding him. As if heartened by his success, Tinnean flailed furiously. Nails raked Darak's cheek and he winced. When had Tinnean stopped biting his nails?

He grabbed his brother's wrist. Tinnean clawed him with his free hand. "Stop." He ducked his head, trying to evade the blows. "Tinnean. Stop it!" He seized his other wrist and spun him around, forcing his brother's arm behind his back, driving him onto his knees. He crouched over him, panting, until he felt Tinnean go limp.

He backed away as Griane stumbled toward them, screaming at him to stop. She threw herself on her knees and wrapped her arms around Tinnean, stroking his snow-dusted hair and crooning soft nonsense, all the while shooting murderous looks his way. Darak watched as long as he could.

"Get up."

"If you hurt him . . ."

"Get up!"

With obvious reluctance, she rose, but hovered close as he circled around to face his brother. He held out his hand. Tinnean started and looked up, his eyes as wide and hopeless as the snared rabbit's. Moving slowly so he would not startle him again, Darak bent down and placed his hands under Tinnean's elbows. When he submitted to the touch, Darak pulled him to his feet. But when he stretched out his hand to brush the snow off Tinnean's shoulders, his brother backed away.

"I won't touch you again. Just tell me why." Darak lowered his voice so Griane would not hear him beg. "Please."

Tinnean's mouth worked, but no words came. Finally, he just shook his head.

Griane pushed him aside and flung her arm around Tinnean's waist. "It's all right, Tinnean. Lean on me."

She turned him toward home. Once, Tinnean paused to look back. Darak felt his brother's gaze pass over him to linger on the trees. Then Griane murmured something and he turned away. Together, they continued their slow walk back to the village, leaving Darak to trail after them, silent and bitter as the cold.

Chapter 6

STRUATH LEANED on his blackthorn staff and stared across the lake. The rolling hills cloaked the western half in twilight, but the rest still shimmered so brightly that his eye narrowed into a squint. Coracles bobbed on the surface, the skin-covered boats looking like children's toys on the shimmering gray-green expanse. A wedge of geese flew overhead, their nasal honks drowning out the lapping of water against the pebbled beach and the faint voices of the men calling to each other as they paddled home. Standing there, shading his eye against the sun's glare, he could almost convince himself that all was well.

Reason told him otherwise. His prayers to the gods had gone unanswered. His efforts to restore Tinnean had failed. Even his spirit guide seemed to have deserted him, and only with Brana's help could he find the answers he sought.

In the first few days after the rite, he had seen fear in the eyes of his tribe. Now, nearly a moon later, those same gazes held suspicion and accusation.

He had offered daily sacrifices at the heart-oak. He had paddled across the lake to discuss the disaster in the grove with the Tree-Father of the Holly Tribe. At the new moon, they had crossed over to the First Forest to make a sacrifice. Fresh offerings nestled at the base of the One Tree, proof that others had preceded them. In the light of day, the damage to the Oak was even more terrible to behold, its great trunk split nearly in two. They spilled their blood on the roots and spent the rest of the day in prayer without daring to speak their fears aloud.

He turned away from the lake to gaze at the three standing stones. Sunlight still bathed the stone guarding the western edge of the burial ground; the easternmost stone was lost in the shadows cast by its brothers. It was the center stone that commanded his attention now.

Two deep grooves bisected its surface, one on the northeast face of the pillar and the other on the southwest face, chiseled ages ago to mark the rising of the sun at Midsummer and the setting of the sun at Midwinter. The stone was nearly twice his height, but each groove was at eye level. A bold slash of charcoal filled the groove on the southwestern face of the pillar. He had drawn it the eve of Midwinter to make the sighting easier. His ability to see into other worlds might have faltered, but everyday vision would give him the answer he sought today.

He took a deep breath and called on the spirits of the Oak and the Holly. Ashamed of the tremor in his voice, he spoke their names again. He called on the gods and goddesses who shared the land: on Lacha, goddess of the lake, and her sister Halam, the earth goddess. On Taran the Thunderer and his brother Nul, Keeper of Lightning. On Bel, the Sun Lord, and his lover Gheala, the Moon Lady whom he chased across the sky. He appealed to Hernan, the god of the forest and protector of the animals, as well as his brother Ardal, the Dark Hunter of spirits. He invoked the Maker and even the Unmaker, the Lord of Chaos.

As always, the familiar litany comforted him. Just as the Oak had the Holly, each god had a counterpart. Just as the Upper World of the gods flourished in the silver branches of the World Tree, so did the Forever Isles of rebirth float among its roots. Here in the Middle World, the same duality prevailed: night yielding to day, winter to summer. Each member of the tribe helped preserve that balance. The shaman offered sacrifices to keep the rival gods content. The fisherman, blessed with a bountiful catch, threw a fish back into the lake. Every debt honored, every favor repaid. Only then could the precarious balance between life and death, order and chaos, be preserved.

He unsheathed the bronze dagger. A treasure crafted by the smiths of the south, he used it only to offer sacrifices: to slit the throat of the first lamb, to gut the first of the season's salmon. To cut out his master's heart.

He shoved back his sleeve. Both arms were crisscrossed with scars; yesterday's wound still leaked blood through the nettle-cloth bandage. He found a patch of unmarked flesh and drew his dagger across his forearm, allowing his blood to drip upon the base of the standing stone.

"I give my blood," he whispered. "I will give my life if you require it. Just give me a sign. Give me the sign I need."

Eye fastened upon the groove, he waited. Even after the sun had disappeared behind the cleft in the western hills and the shadows enveloping the lakeshore had deepened from purple to indigo, he stood before the pillar, his mind refusing to accept what his eye had seen.

The shadow of the western stone had fallen neatly across the groove—exactly as it had at Midwinter. The year was not turning.

It was impossible. Surely, the gods would not permit

the world to die or allow the Oak-Lord to be destroyed.

"Nay." He spoke his denial aloud, repeated it again and yet a third time, his fingers flying in the sign to avert evil. That awful presence in the grove might have disrupted the battle, but the Oak's spirit still lived. Otherwise, the days would be growing shorter. The god must have fled.

A new thought made him gasp. Could the Oak's spirit have found refuge in Tinnean's body? It would explain the strange energy he had touched. And it might mean—merciful Maker, let it be so—that the boy's spirit was safe in the One Tree.

He hurried back to the village, leaning heavily on his staff. He must seek confirmation in a vision. Only then would he share his discovery with the Grain-Mother. He would need her help to retrieve Tinnean's spirit and ease the Oak's back into the One Tree. He had brought lost spirits back from the Forever Isles, but no Tree-Father—not even Morgath—had ever attempted to exchange spirits between two bodies. If he failed, he could lose them both. Awful enough to lose the boy; to lose the Oak meant the death of the world.

Buoyed by hope, he paid no attention to the shouting at first. His footsteps slowed as he reached the huts. Flickering torchlight illuminated the crowd. He made out Darak's tall figure, standing at the doorway of his hut, confronting Jurl. Over the babble of voices, a woman shouted, "It's his fault!" Others took up the cry. A man shouted, "He has cursed us."

Tinnean peeped over Darak's shoulder. Griane flanked the boy, blocking him from the crowd with her body. Red Dugan's voice rose above the others to yell, "Go to the house, girl." Griane shouted back, "I live with Mother Netal. In case the brogac's made you forget."

After that, it all happened very fast. Red Dugan

pushing past Jurl. Darak shouldering Tinnean into their hut, pulling Griane away from Red Dugan's outstretched hands. Another outburst of shouting, punctuated by Red Dugan's curses. And then a sudden silence.

"Let me pass." Struath used his staff to force a way through. "Jurl, Onnig, do you hear me? Dugan, move aside." He halted abruptly when he saw the naked dagger in Darak's hand. Darak's gaze flicked toward him, then immediately returned to Jurl. Struath faced the crowd, summoning his voice of command. "What are you thinking? Tinnean has done nothing to harm you. We are one people. One tribe. We must—"

"The boy is bewitched."

"He has brought down the gods' anger."

"The year is not turning."

"And you do nothing, old man!"

Speechless, he stared at them. Never had any of his tribe dared to speak to him with such disrespect. Never had he seen their familiar faces twisted with such fury and fear. He was still gazing around in shocked silence when he heard Nionik's voice and discovered the chief making his way through the crowd. Although he had neither Jurl's brawniness nor Onnig's silent menace, the brothers stepped back to allow him to pass.

Nionik bowed to him. "Tree-Father."

Struath returned the bow and the formal greeting. "Oak-Chief." He damned his quavering voice. Now more than ever, he must appear strong.

Nionik's gaze shifted to Darak. "Sheathe your dagger."

As if emerging from a trance, Darak obeyed. Griane eased aside to let Nionik stand at Darak's shoulder.

"People of the Oak." Without any visible effort, Nionik's voice carried throughout the silent village. "We have faced plague and famine and, by the grace of the gods, we have survived both. Now we face a new danger—a mystery we cannot fully understand. The year is not turning."

Only now did the words register. They knew. They all knew. And why not? Any one of them could have gone to the standing stones. They needed no shaman to interpret that sign.

"Irdal has taken his boat across the lake to the Holly Tribe," Nionik said. "I have asked their elders to join our council."

Struath heard a few gasps. Only once in his memory had the tribes ever held common council—to judge and condemn Morgath. If Nionik had chosen this course, it could only mean the chief had lost faith in him.

"Tonight, we will determine what steps to take. On the morrow, we will announce our decision. Until then, there will be no more of these outbursts." Nionik cast a sharp glance at Jurl before continuing. "Anyone who seeks to thwart the will of the council will be cast out, never to walk the shores of our lake, never to stand before the heart-oak."

Struath stepped forward. He must speak. He must reassert his authority. "Go to your homes. Pray for the blessing of our gods. For the guidance of the Oak and the Holly. And for the wisdom of your elders."

His heart thudded unevenly when they just stared back at him. Then, slowly, the crowd dispersed. Jurl hawked a gob of phlegm at Darak's feet. Darak's breath hissed in, but he stared Jurl down, as unmoving as one of the standing stones. Only when their kinfolk had retreated did he turn to Nionik and bow. "Oak-Chief. I thank you for interceding for my brother."

"Save your thanks for after the council meeting, Darak." Nionik turned to him, his face stern. "Tree-Father, I would speak with you before the elders of the Holly Tribe arrive."

He nodded, shamed by the implicit criticism. As Nionik strode away, Struath's gaze traveled around the village. Two boys darted in and out among the huts, hurling snowballs at each other. Smoke streamed from the vent holes of the roofs. A sheep bleated. A woman called. The boys mounted one last attack before running home. Just like any other winter evening.

"Struath. Tree-Father. You have my thanks as well." Stiff-necked as always, Darak couldn't bring himself to bow, but he did dip his head. On any other day, Struath would have considered it a victory.

His answering nod was equally curt. Squaring his shoulders, he walked away. Gortin emerged from the shadows. Struath refused his initiate's outstretched hand, just as he disdained to lean on his staff. Only when he was inside his hut did he permit himself to collapse into Gortin's arms.

Once, he would have scoffed at the idea of his people raising their voices against him. But he also would have sworn that the Oak-Lord would always defeat the Holly-Lord at Midwinter, that no power could prevent the year from turning. Now he knew better. He should have taken the chief into his confidence as soon as he detected the strange spirit inside of Tinnean. With Nionik's help, he could have kept the people's fear in check while he waited for the gods-given vision to come.

His fingers crept up his chest to stroke the nettle-cloth pouch that hung around his neck. He tugged open the drawstrings and pulled out the spirit catcher.

The flickering firelight sent tiny orange flames dancing among the crystal's facets. It had taken him more than a moon to shape it, meticulously chipping away the quartz with a tiny flint hammerstone. For thirty years he had used it to recapture the fragments of wandering spirits, sundered from their bodies through shock and grief. He slipped the spirit catcher back into its pouch; tonight, it could not help him.

"Gortin. Build up the fire. Fetch the herbs."

"Tree-Father, you are too tired—"

"I must try. I must."

Tonight, the council would decide Tinnean's fate. He must summon Brana again and hope that this time, his spirit guide would answer.

Chapter 7

DARAK HELD OUT Tinnean's tunic. "Take off that robe and put these on." He told himself that Tinnean could move more freely in tunic and breeches, but he knew the real reason he wanted his brother to discard it.

He shoved the pouch of meal into his hunting sack and examined the supplies he had tossed onto the tanned hide: five suetcakes, some strips of dried venison, and the pheasant he had smoked the day before. He gathered the hide together and tied it with sinew before thrusting it into his hunting sack.

He had made up his mind during his silent supper with Tinnean. If it had been his tribe alone, he might have risked waiting. With the Holly elders sitting in judgment too, the odds against Tinnean were too great.

Even with careful rationing, the meat would last only two or three days. After that, they could live on the barley meal and suetcakes until he made a kill. With or without the gods' permission, he would have to hunt.

He added one of the stone bowls for cooking porridge. The coiled braid of nettle rope. Three snares.

Extra arrowheads and sinew. His sling. He snatched
up a handful of fishhooks, wincing as the sharpened
bone stuck him. He sucked his bleeding thumb, then
grabbed his small net and the twisted strands of deer
gut he used as fishing line.

Only two fire bundles. No time to make more. He'd
have to use his firestick the first night. Then he could
insert a clump of burning cinders into the bundle and
transport fire to their next camp.

"Roll the spare clothes in the skins." When Tinnean
just stared at him, Darak showed him what to do.
Muttering a curse, he threw the discarded robe onto
the pile; the woolen garment would provide added
warmth during the long nights.

He had never been farther east than the sacred
grove or farther west than the mouth of the river and
then only at the Gatherings. But tonight, he must steal
a coracle. Sail up the lake. Find someplace isolated.
Someplace Tinnean would be safe.

He opened his small belt pouch to inspect his supply
of flints, tinder, and straw. He added a handful of
shredded bark for making fire bundles, then yanked
the drawstrings tight.

Perhaps it would be better to sail down the lake.
Follow the traders' route south and lose themselves in
one of the fishing settlements that dotted the coastline.
Then he remembered the autumn Gathering and his
mouth twisted in a grimace.

If one man had told the tale, he might have dis-
counted it, but the leaders of all the coastal tribes
offered the same accounts. The enormous wooden
boats that stretched ten or twelve times a man's
height. The spar of wood that rose like a dead tree
from the body of the boat and the giant woven cloth
attached to it that grew big-bellied when the wind
filled it. The black eye silhouetted on a circle of red
that marked each of the wind cloths. The long paddles
on either side that drove the boats right into their

protected coves. And the blood-chilling screams that tore the sleeping villagers from their slumbers to confront dozens of men armed with long, curving daggers who stole their livestock and their children, killing any who opposed them, before retreating to their boats and vanishing into the dawn mists.

Even if the stories were exaggerated, he couldn't risk their lives by venturing south. And surely winter lay even heavier on the settlements to the north where strangers would be turned away for lack of food and shelter. Somehow, they would have to manage alone.

"There's a shawl under my skins." He examined the arrows in his quiver. Reknotted the sinew on one to secure the flint to the shaft. Shot a quick glance at Tinnean and found him rubbing his cheek against the shawl.

Maili had done the same thing when Krali had given it to her. A wedding gift from the eldest woman of her family and the village's weaver. Soft as a cloud, Maili had said. And the lambswool the same smoky blue of her eyes.

"Roll the wolfskins in it."

"Soft."

"Aye. Leave two ends free to tie around you."

"Yours?"

"Nay."

"Griane's?"

"Nay!" He took a deep breath. "Maili's."

Six moons since he'd spoken her name.

Tinnean cocked his head. "Maili?"

Darak looked away, his mouth twisting. Tinnean had known Maili all his life. He had eaten the food she'd cooked, slept under the same roof, teased her about the way her curly hair always escaped from her braid.

"We've no time for this." He snatched the shawl away from Tinnean, spread it on the rushes, and laid the rolled wolfskins on it. "Put your mantle on."

"We go?"

"Aye. Hold out your arms." He tied the ends of Maili's shawl at Tinnean's shoulder and adjusted the bundle so that it rested snugly against his back.

"Where?"

Darak settled his quiver on his back. "Away."

"Where?"

He slung his hunting sack across his body, shoved his ax in his belt, and picked up his bow. The sack bumped against the ax, the bow bumped against both. He shifted the ax, frowning. Now it bumped against his dagger.

"Damn."

The ancient legends never bothered to describe how the great heroes dealt with these kinds of problems. It was all very well to hear about slaying monsters and crossing the rainbow bridge into the silver branches of the World Tree, but it would have been nice to glean something useful to an ordinary man.

He hefted his spear and took a last look around the hut. The place where his mam had birthed him, where he'd brought his wife, where both had died, and his father and little Milia, all those years ago. His sister would have been seventeen at Midwinter.

When he spied the turtle shells, he added them to the sack. What else was he forgetting? He hesitated when he saw Tinnean's flute. They didn't need it. His sack was already bulging. Still, he snatched it up. He hesitated even longer when he saw the small pouch shoved into a crevice in the wall.

He had gathered the charms as a boy: the pointed tine of the stag's antler; the feather of the golden eagle; the fire-blackened twig in the jagged shape of a lightning bolt; the scaly tail of the salmon. Earth, air, fire, water. He'd worn the bag around his neck day and night until the morning he had laid his mam and Maili in the Death Hut.

Cursing, he yanked the bag free and slipped the

leather thongs over his head. His fingers crept up to stroke the soft doeskin. In spite of all that had happened, the touch comforted him.

He looked up to find Tinnean watching him, a hesitant smile on his face. A little ashamed to be caught clutching his bag of charms, Darak dropped his hand and nodded toward the doorway. Even if the council decided in Tinnean's favor, this act of defiance would make them exiles. They would never see their village again, never stand with the others before the heart-oak, never watch Bel perch for a heartbeat atop Eagles Mount before impaling himself upon the mountain's peak to die and be reborn the next dawn in the eastern forest. They would be alone—without home, without kin—from this night on.

Out of the corner of his eye, he saw the bearskin move. Dropping his spear, he thrust Tinnean behind him, ripped his dagger from its sheath, and fell into a defensive crouch.

Yeorna's eyes widened at the sight of his dagger. Darak sheathed it as Struath bent low to enter. He forced himself to offer the formal words of greeting. "You are welcome in my home."

"Your welcome warms us on this winter's night," the Grain-Mother replied.

Oddly, both Yeorna and Struath offered deep bows to Tinnean. His brother studied them a moment before mimicking the greeting. Darak gestured to the fire pit. "Would you sit?"

The stiff formalities helped him control the fear twisting his guts. There had never been a casting-out in his lifetime, but he had heard the stories told by the Memory-Keeper: the evildoer stripped naked in the center of the village, proclaimed dead by the Tree-Father, and then driven from the village with rocks and dung, his face never seen again, his name never spoken.

He struggled to keep his voice even. "When will you perform the casting-out?"

"It is not a casting-out," Yeorna said.

With her words, fear changed to terror. Every child learned the story of the wicked shaman Morgath. It was a tale whispered around fire pits, warning of the fate that awaited those who subverted nature's order. And now the council had proclaimed the same fate for his brother.

Tinnean would be bent backward over the roots of the heart-oak. Tinnean's still-beating heart would be cut out of his chest. Tinnean's dripping blood would be sprinkled around the glade. Tinnean's body would be hung from the oak's lowest branch. Tinnean's flesh would be devoured by animals. Tinnean's bones would lie in a discarded heap, never to be gathered by his family, never to lie in the tribal cairn.

"You cannot do this."

"Darak . . ."

"I'll not stand by while you sacrifice—"

"Darak!" Struath's voice overrode Yeorna's protestations. "That is not the council's decision."

Relief left him weak. He had to clear his throat twice before he trusted his voice. "What then?"

"No demon possesses Tinnean, but there is another spirit inside him. I've known that for some time, but until today—"

Darak rose out of his crouch, only to be stopped by Yeorna. "Please, Darak. Listen."

He subsided, silently cursing Struath. Each day since they'd brought Tinnean home, he had asked—begged—for answers. And the shaman had withheld them.

"Today I had a vision. I now understand what happened in the grove and why the year is not turning. The spirit of the Oak fled the One Tree—and took refuge in your brother's body."

As one, they looked at Tinnean. His brother's puzzled expression gave way to a fierce intensity, as if he understood that something important was happening.

Darak touched his arm and Tinnean started, wariness transforming his face into that of a stranger again.

"It's not possible," Darak said, looking at Yeorna for confirmation.

"Who can say what is possible for a god?"

"But how can you be sure? Struath, you've said yourself that visions are hard to interpret."

"I have never touched a spirit like this one. It is . . . it is not the spirit of a man."

That silenced him. Visions were beyond his realm of understanding, but he knew the power of Struath's touch.

"The council would have voted to sacrifice Tinnean if the Tree-Father had not convinced them. As he convinced me." Yeorna's smile was so eager that Darak found himself nodding.

"But Tinnean's spirit is still here? Inside him, I mean."

"I believe Tinnean's spirit is in the One Tree," Struath said.

"But you don't know?"

Struath opened his mouth and closed it, visibly reining in his temper.

"We will only know the truth if we take Tinnean to the First Forest," Yeorna said.

"And do what?"

"With the Grain-Mother's help, I will try to restore both spirits."

"You can do that? Without harming Tinnean?" When Struath hesitated, Darak shook his head. "Nay."

"Darak . . ."

"The last time you took my brother into the First Forest, you brought back a stranger. This time, you might not bring him back at all."

"There is more at stake here than the life of one boy."

"Not for me."

"Then you're a fool." Struath pushed himself to his feet. Darak did the same, facing the shaman across the fire pit. "If the Oak's spirit is not restored to the One Tree, the battle cannot be completed. The year will not turn. And everything in the world—including Tinnean—will die."

"Darak." Yeorna rose and laid her hand on his arm. "You are right to protect Tinnean. He is a dear boy and we would never wish him to be harmed." Her fingers dug into his arm, silently demanding that he look at her. "I will not lie. There is risk in what we will attempt. But I see no other way to restore your brother and the Oak."

Darak forced open his clenched fingers. He hated feeling so helpless. But if this was the only way to get his brother back, he had no choice. "I'm going with you."

Struath glared at him. "That is out of the question."

"I can't just sit here and wait."

"Then pray."

He refused to rise to that bait. "Tinnean needs me."

"The First Forest is not for the uninitiated," Yeorna said.

"And it is not for a man who has turned his back on the gods," Struath added. "You will not even pray so that you may hunt in our own forest. Do you think the Forest-Lord will permit you to trespass in his sacred grove?"

"Then give me a rite to perform." On his knees if necessary. As long as he could be with Tinnean.

"I will not permit it."

With an effort, Darak restrained the urge to curse Struath as a stubborn old tyrant. That thought led to another. "You're too old to be daring the forest at night with a woman and an addled boy."

"Gortin will come with us."

"Gortin?" Darak saw Struath's frown deepen at the

scorn in his voice. "Gortin's a good man, but he's a shepherd. Was, I mean, before he became a priest. Nay—hear me out." He kept his voice respectful, but made no effort to mask his urgency. "Gortin's no hunter. He cannot protect you from wildcats or wolves."

Struath started. Before the shaman could recover, Darak pressed his advantage. "I know the forest. I can watch your backs."

Struath and Yeorna exchanged glances. After a long moment, Struath nodded. "You may come. But only as far as the grove of the heart-oak."

He was still seeking the words to wring a greater concession when Yeorna added, "You must make a sacrifice at the heart-oak. And ask the gods' permission to enter the First Forest." Yeorna held up her hand, forestalling Struath's objection. "These are extraordinary times, Tree-Father. If the gods are willing to accept Darak's presence in their grove, it is not for us to deny him."

He hardly breathed as he waited for Struath's response. Finally, the Tree-Father nodded again. "As always, you are wise, Grain-Mother." The grudging tone of his voice belied the words, but Yeorna accepted them with a gracious smile. Darak resisted the urge to hug her, choosing instead to bow to both of them. Struath's words caught him as he straightened.

"You cannot command the gods, Darak. You must humble yourself before them. They will know if your gestures are empty."

That single blue eye raked him, just as it had that spring morning nine years ago. He had stumbled out of the forest after sitting three days and three nights in a thicket, starting at every rustle in the undergrowth, battling hunger and thirst and fear as he waited for his vision to come. He could still remember racing across the fields, exhilaration banishing exhaustion. Finding Struath waiting in the center of the village. Feeling the shaman's hands cupping his face, the sightless eye probing him, searching for confirmation of the vision. And swaying with relief and triumph when Struath called out, "Today, a man walks among us."

Darak knew then that Struath had seen the she-wolf, had heard the animal's howl, just as he had when she called him in the dark. While his kinfolk surged forward, laughing and shouting his name, the shaman whispered, "She hunts with the pack and will kill to defend her pups." He had been honored by the wolf's choice, but it still puzzled him. Certainly, he would kill to defend Tinnean, but even as a child, he'd always been a loner.

Struath was watching him, awaiting his decision. Darak rose and walked around the fire pit. He seized the shaman's hands and laid the palms against his pitted cheeks. "I will do anything."

"Even beg, Darak?"

Struath's inexorable gaze bore into him. Darak met it without flinching. "Anything."

Chapter 8

WHEN MOTHER NETAL'S breathing subsided into soft snores, Griane slipped out from under the rabbitfurs. The dying embers provided little illumination, but she had lived in the healer's hut for more than a year now and knew where everything was stored.

She shoved a few oatcakes into her healing bag, added two smoked trout, and flung her mantle around her. She eyed the other, still hanging from the bone hook by the doorway as if expecting its owner's imminent return. Until the plague, each mantle in the village was patched and preserved with care, handed down from father to son, mother to daughter. Now there were mantles to spare, but this one, she could not take. Not even for Tinnean.

"You could wait."

She whirled around to find Mother Netal lying on her side, watching her.

"For the council's decision, child."

"Darak won't."

Mother Netal grunted.

"He won't risk a casting-out. He'll pack weapons and food, but men never think of things like healing herbs or bone needle and sinew for sewing or—"

"Don't get caught."

She resisted the urge to hug the old healer.

"Take it."

"What?"

"Umi's mantle."

It was the first time Griane had heard Mother Netal speak her companion's name since they had carried Umi to the Death Hut. She started to stammer out her thanks, but Mother Netal just pulled the furs over her head and rolled over.

She bundled her healing bag inside Umi's mantle and slipped outside. Too bad she couldn't risk creeping into her uncle's hut. She'd enjoy stealing his mantle; small enough repayment for all the whippings he had given her.

Darting from shadow to shadow, she made her way around the circled huts. She froze when she heard men's voices, then crept closer when she realized they came from Jurl's hut.

"It's the only way to be sure." Jurl's voice, low and urgent.

"But shouldn't we wait till after the council?" Onnig, for once questioning his brother.

"Darak won't. If we don't move now, he'll hide Tinnean."

"But still . . ."

"It's not like we're going to hurt the boy. Just hold him till the morrow."

"That's right." No mistaking her uncle's drunken bellow, quickly hushed by the others. "It's our duty. To the tribe and all."

"Onnig, we'll see to Darak. Dugan, you grab the boy."

"Sure, Jurl, sure. How 'bout a drink to seal the bargain?"

Abandoning the safety of the shadows, Griane ran the rest of the way to Darak's hut. She threw back the bearskin and caught her breath. The hut was empty, the fire banked to mere embers. She couldn't warn them. She couldn't give them her gifts. She couldn't even say good-bye.

She swallowed down the lump of disappointment and peered outside. No sign of Jurl or the others yet. At least Darak and Tinnean would have a good start. There was no better hunter than Darak, no fiercer fighter when roused. For all that he infuriated her, she knew he would die before he'd let Tinnean come to harm.

Clutching her bundle, she raced down to the lake, hoping for a last glimpse of them. Gheala's moonlight cut a silvery path across the dark surface of the water. She stared west, then east, comforting herself that if she could spy no coracle, neither would the others.

She gazed at the neat row of boats lining the shore. With their skin bottoms facing skyward, they looked like ten sleeping turtles. She was turning back to the village when her mind registered what her eyes had seen. Ten coracles. Just like always. Darak and Tinnean had left on foot.

It made no sense. Even Darak wouldn't risk the pass over Eagles Mount in winter, but she couldn't believe he would take Tinnean into the forest.

A shout from the village made her whirl around. Another answered. She spun west toward Eagles Mount, then east again. More shouts, closer this time, and the flicker of torchlight, heading her way.

No matter what Darak wanted, Tinnean would go to the forest.

She knew the trail. She had followed it countless times with Mother Netal, gathering roots and berries and healing plants. But never alone—and never at night. The night belonged to the Forest-Lord and his creatures—the wolf, the owl, the wildcat. And to unseen creatures as well—spirits of the uneasy dead,

demons who envied the living. She had her sling in
her belt, but stones offered precious little protection
from demons.

Someone shouted her name. Mother Netal would
never have betrayed her. Had her uncle guessed her
plan? Or Jurl? Breathing a quick prayer, she sprinted
toward the trees.

Please Maker, let me find them before the others do.

The trees were everywhere. Although the boy's eyes
could make out only shadows, he felt them all around:
oak and hazel, birch and pine, rowan and elder. He
reached out his hands to brush overhanging branches,
laughing at the soft slap of fir boughs. The thrum of
recognition tingled his palms. The energy circled out,
wider and wider, until the whole forest sang its welcome. The power made him reel.

A strong hand seized his arm and steadied him.

"Are you all right?"

"Aye, Darak."

"Stay close, then. You hear me?"

"Aye, Darak."

He did not understand why Darak wanted him to
come to the forest now when so short a while before,
the big man had prevented his escape. He did not
care. Finally, he was home.

He followed Darak obediently, sucking in great
gulps of the sweet, clean air. It burned his throat and
tasted even better than Griane's hot apple cider.

Thinking of Griane drove away some of the sweetness of the air. A lump formed in his throat as if a
small stone had lodged there. He swallowed hard and
it grew larger. Stroking his throat only made it worse,
for then he remembered Griane's·hands patting his
face, light as moths. He would miss her hands. And
her voice, soft and growly when she was happy, yippy

like a fox when she was not. And the many smells of her—sheep and apples and green plants and a musky scent that all combined to make his nose quiver.

But he did not belong with Griane. He belonged here. The trees knew it. They called him, their energy as eager as his, beckoning him. Abandoning the trail, he ran.

Darak shouted his not-name, but this time, he could not obey. He wove in and out among the trees, staggering against them, laughing. He fell to his knees to trace curving roots. He clawed through snow and pine needles to breathe in the cold, rich, wondrous scent of earth. He touched rough bark and sticky sap. That tang came from the pine. He licked his fingers. He had never known its taste, but now he would carry the knowledge with him forever. He closed his eyes, his senses overwhelmed. Then he heard Darak shouting.

He was close now, but he still needed them to reach his grove. Summoning his ages-old patience, he rose and turned toward the sound of Darak's voice.

Darak seized Tinnean's shoulders and shook him. "Don't do that again. You must stay with us."

"Aye, Darak."

Keeping a firm grip on Tinnean's arm, he led him back to the trail, willing his heart to stop pounding, willing his mind to stop imagining how easily he could have lost him.

He kept his pace slow, guiding himself with memory and touch as much as sight, head cocked to catch any sounds that might mean danger or that his brother had strayed from the trail again. Even at midday, the forest was a place of shadows. In the heart of the night, each shadow seemed to hold the thing that had attacked Tinnean.

Every hunt held fear: the quarry could elude you,

you could be injured, you could surprise a predator. You had to accept the fear. Only then could you conquer it. Control fear and you could control anything. Even yourself.

Something brushed against his forehead and he pulled up short, clawing at his face. A vine. Only a vine. His heart thudded loudly enough for the whole forest to hear. He shook his head in disgust. The great hunter—trembling before a vine.

Even in the dark, he recognized the looming mass of the boulder on the little outcropping, the birch with the broken limb. With a sigh of relief, he skirted the birch and walked into the glade.

After the close-packed trees, he felt exposed and vulnerable in Gheala's creamy light—and utterly insignificant before the heart-oak. He knew that the slight rise the oak straddled made it seem even taller, that the shadows cloaking its lower branches lent a greater air of mystery. As always, awe conquered logic, the same awe he had felt as a child, head thrown back to look at the soaring trunk that made the tallest of the pines seem as small as his first spear.

Tinnean edged past him, moving like a dreamwalker. He stretched out his hands and laid his palms against the trunk. His body slumped. "Not the oak."

"Your Oak is in another forest," Struath said.

"Close?"

"Very close." Struath took Tinnean's arm and led him to the edge of the glade where Yeorna and Gortin waited. At least the shaman would not hear his prayers. He could humble himself before the gods, but humbling himself before Struath would be intolerable.

Darak gazed around the glade, uncertain how to begin. The shadowy trees held no answer; they simply waited, a silent black mass. Finally, he squared his shoulders.

"Hernan. Lord of the Forest." His whisper sounded loud in the stillness. "You know me. I'm a hunter, not a shaman. But I ask your permission to enter your sacred forest. I intend no harm to any of your creatures. I just want to accompany my brother and help him find his way home."

If the Forest-Lord heard, he gave no sign.

"Oak-Brother." He stroked the heart-oak's runneled trunk, just as Tinnean had. "My people have always revered you and your tree-kin. We clear only the ground we need to sustain us. We cut no limb from a living tree without offering a sacrifice in return. Help me. Please. Not for my sake, but for my brother's. He's a good boy and he loves you and he is lost."

He had offered many prayers to the Forest-Lord over the years, but tonight he found it easier to speak to the heart-oak. It had stood with his tribe since the beginning. It was as mortal as he was and knew what it was to suffer loss. He found himself telling the tree how Tinnean used to sneak off to the forest long before his vision quest, driving them all near frantic with worry until they'd spy him running through the fields, laughing and breathless with the excitement of some new discovery.

Darak shook his head. Maybe there had always been something different about Tinnean. Else how could a child wander the forest and never come to harm?

His father would have known; he'd always had the answers.

Gheala's oval of light had crept to the far side of the glade. The night was waning. He slipped his bow off his shoulder and drew his dagger. Then he hesitated, staring at the squat quickthorn that grew in the shadow of the heart-oak. Its dense tangle of branches reached away from the oak, seeking the light and space denied to it by its giant brother. Sheathing his dagger, he shrugged his mantle off his shoulder and pushed back his sleeve. Then he plunged his arm into the branches.

He winced as the thorns pierced him, but jerked his

arm back to allow more to claw a fiery path down his forearm. Fist clenched, he shoved his arm deeper into the branches, twisting it back and forth to expose more of his flesh. Sweat broke out on his forehead, but he pressed his lips together, mastering the pain. Finally he pulled his arm free, grimacing as a thorn caught the flesh inside his elbow and ripped him open to the wrist.

He crouched before the heart-oak and let his blood drip onto the exposed roots, squeezing the flesh around the shallower cuts so that they, too, spilled their offering. When he finished, he scooped up a handful of snow and rubbed it against his wounds. The fire flared briefly, then receded to a dull throb.

"Struath said I must humble myself. And so I will. I cursed you after the plague. I know that was wrong. But they suffered so, Mam and Maili. Six days and nights, burning up with fever, screaming as the sores burst . . ."

The grief caught him unprepared, choking him. He thought he had conquered it by now. He rested his head against the heart-oak, waiting for it to subside. When it didn't, he beat his forehead against the trunk of the tree, again and again and again, until finally, pain banished grief. Weary now, he addressed the gods one last time.

"I blamed you for their suffering. And for what happened to my brother. Maker help me, I cannot forgive what you did to my folk and 'twould be a lie if I pretended otherwise. So punish me. Not Tinnean. Bring him back. I . . I beg you."

He rose. Whatever sign the gods sent, he would meet it on his feet like a man.

Please don't let my punishment be to lose him.

He heard a gasp behind him and spun around, automatically reaching for his dagger.

A wolf stood at the edge of the trees. A huge beast, twice the size of any he'd killed. Impossible that it could have crept up on him. Years of hunting had taught him to stay alert at all times. Even when the awful grief had seized him, one part of him had remained attuned to the forest. Briefly, he wondered if his vision mate had somehow materialized, but he dismissed the idea when the animal stepped into Gheala's light; this wolf was silver, not black.

Never taking his eyes off the beast, he slowly bent and retrieved his bow, right hand already reaching over his shoulder. As he straightened, he nocked the arrow in his bowstring. Even in the predawn gloom, he could see Yeorna's fingers flying. Gortin was trying to pull Struath behind him, but the shaman just stared at the wolf, transfixed.

The wolf shambled toward the others, weaving like Crel's dog when it had the water sickness last summer. It came to a halt before Struath. Edging left, Darak drew the bowstring back, but the wolf just stood there, swaying slightly with the effort to keep its footing.

"Struath?" He kept his voice soft, but the animal's ears pricked up. "Move right. Now."

The wolf crouched. Struath cried out and pushed Tinnean into the brush. Darak loosed the arrow as the wolf leaped. The animal yelped and spun toward him. For a moment, they were face-to-face. He was reaching for another arrow when the wolf bolted. Its legs buckled once, but it recovered and staggered into the underbrush, the cracking of twigs and branches testifying to its headlong flight.

Darak raced across the glade. "Are you all right? Tinnean?"

"Aye, Darak."

Struath clutched his staff as if it were the only thing keeping him on his feet. Darak peered at his face, stunned by the stark terror he found there.

"He saw the wolf," Gortin said. "In his vision today."

Darak retraced his steps, bending low to examine

the snow-dusted ground. His fingertips and nose confirmed what his eyes found: the wolf might have appeared in a vision, but it shed real blood.

A quick glance overhead showed the circle of sky had lightened to deep blue. Whatever the creature was, he had no time to track it. He walked back to the others. Struath was still staring after the wolf, visibly shaking. What in Chaos had the old man seen in his vision?

Yeorna gave a helpless shrug. "The wolf is . . . part of this. Somehow. And so are you, Darak. The gods must value honesty over humility." Her rueful smile made heat flare in his cheeks. Silently, he took her proffered hand.

"Tree-Father," Gortin said in a gentle voice. "It is time."

As if waking from a dream, Struath took Tinnean's hand.

"Darak. My hand." Yeorna's voice was gentle, but a hint of amusement lingered. It took him a moment to realize he was crushing her fingers. The embarrassing heat flushed his face again. Yeorna's small smile only made it fiercer.

Struath led them sunwise, his lips moving in secret words too soft to hear. A blackbird greeted the dawn, its melodious warble drowned out by crashing in the underbrush. Yeorna's fingers tightened on his. The clump of elders shook. Griane stumbled into the glade. Without thinking, he reached out his free hand to steady her. Ice-cold fingers clasped his. And then the glade disappeared.

Chapter 9

STRUATH GLANCED AROUND wildly, letting out his breath when he realized the wolf had not followed them. He wheezed out a shaky prayer, staring at the gaping wound that split the Oak nearly in two. Ragged shards of heartwood reared up, as sharp and menacing as the wolf's fangs.

"Nay."

"Tree-Father?" Gortin grasped his arm, his kind, homely face twisted with concern. "Are you all right?"

"I am fine." A lie. But not as awful as the others he had spoken this night.

"Tree-Father. What is it?"

He had lied to Gortin. He had lied to Yeorna. He had lied to the council. When the wolf appeared in the glade, he was certain it had come to punish him.

Tinnean's strangled cry startled him out of his thoughts. The boy tottered forward, picking his way through the branches that littered the ground. Struath flung off Gortin's hand and stumbled after him, but Darak reached him first. He grabbed Tinnean's hand as he reached for one of the Holly's branches, so heavy with leaves and berries that it brushed the ground.

"Don't touch it, Tinnean. It could hurt you."

Of course, Darak didn't understand. He saw only the boy's form, not the spirit inside. He saw only what he wanted to see.

Struath shuddered. Was he doing the same? He had seen the wolf in the vision that had come to him before the council meeting, but the rest was sheer invention: the mist-shrouded island, the wolf threatening Tinnean, the green-boughed Oak that rose from the heart of the island to protect the boy. It was the only way he could save him—and the ancient spirit that now inhabited his body.

The boy stroked one shiny green leaf with his forefinger. His eyes closed. He swayed, might have fallen if Darak hadn't steadied him. He reached for another leaf and jerked back with a gasp, staring at the blood welling up on his fingertip.

"You see? It can hurt." Darak grabbed his hand and sucked the blood away. Seeing Tinnean's mystified expression, he said, "To keep it clean." He raised the finger to Tinnean's lips and the boy obediently sucked at it, then rolled the blood on his tongue, tasting it.

When he looked up, his face was serious. He bowed to Yeorna and to Gortin. He smoothed Griane's hair. Cold palms clasped his cheeks. It took Struath a moment to realize the Oak-Lord was imitating the gesture he had used so often when trying to reach his spirit. Struath stared into those blue eyes, humbled by the knowledge of the spirit that looked out from them.

Finally, the boy turned to Darak. He hesitated, then seized him by the shoulders and shook him. After a moment of stunned surprise, Darak's arms went around him. He hugged him hard and abruptly pulled away. "Aye. Well. That's fine. Everything'll be all right now."

Tinnean smiled. That errant lock of hair fell across his forehead. Struath resisted the urge to brush it back.

"So. We're here." Darak's voice still sounded a bit thick, but his expression had settled into its usual sternness. "What happens now, Struath?"

The boy turned back to the Tree and laid his palms against the trunk. His head fell back, his mouth half open in a smile. Still smiling, he sank slowly to his knees and fell to the ground.

The boy's body fell away. The faint thrum that he had sensed upon entering the grove became a roar as the energy flowed around him and through him and into him, no longer tugging at the periphery of his awareness, but becoming a vital, throbbing power that *was* awareness.

He stood rooted once again to earth, branches touching sky and ground. He observed each of the tiny creatures that wriggled among his roots, the wren perched on one branch. He felt the small tremor that quivered through the branch as the bird shifted its weight, the scratch of its claws on his bark, the lightest brush of air as it fluttered its wings.

He drew strength from the soil beneath him and energy from the newly risen sun above. He was the center, linking earth and sky. The energy pulsed with the same urgency as the tattoo he had known in the boy's body. Each pulse carried the memory of countless seasons unfolding with slow inevitability: spring's sap rising inside him, summer's heat metamorphosed into flowers, autumn's frost riming his branches, winter's ice scoring his bark.

He was Holly and he was home.

The thrum of recognition raced through the forest as the others welcomed him. He touched hazel, willow, elder, sensed the eagerness of the birch, the defensiveness of the quickthorn. Only the Oak was silent.

He had seen its shattered limbs, but many of his

had been sundered as well. Never, in all their cold-time battles, had he defeated the Oak. Yet when he brought his awareness to bear upon the other half of himself, he discovered only an empty shell.

He allowed his consciousness to expand until it encompassed the whole of the First Forest. He knew the wolf packs that prowled its shadowy depths, the eagles that circled its canopy, the fish that swam in the dark pools. He found the rootless ones whose spirits guarded the forest. He found Hernan, protector of the beasts, antlered head cocked as if sensing his return.

A fox scented the wind. Its sleek, small body stretched, grew a man's torso, a man's arms and legs. A long tongue lolled out as the Trickster smiled. With a quick swish of his brush, the god shifted back into fox-form and darted into the shadows.

His awareness soared farther. He tasted sun. He smelled wind. He touched cold. Nowhere could he feel the Oak.

The others echoed back his sense of wrongness; it drifted around him like mist. Out of the mist, he drew their memories of the darkness that had invaded the grove and the boy whose spirit had collided with his.

Another sensation, dim but discernible, intruded on his consciousness. It emanated from the outsiders. The big man was on his knees, cradling the body that had sheltered his spirit. The girl with the fox-fur hair knelt beside him, fingers pressed against the boy's wrist. The others stood near them, making those strange gestures with their fingers.

The agitated pulse of their energies was not-good. He withdrew his awareness, only to have it pulled back when the old one began chanting. The sound tugged at him, urging him to abandon his Tree and walk again among men. The trees added their collective energy, reminding him that the Tree-Lords had always had a responsibility to the world of Men, the youngest and most helpless of the Maker's creations.

He resisted the call. He belonged here. His being felt complete, connected, whole. His power was undisputed, his ancient rival vanquished, never again to challenge him for supremacy.

But it was not enough. It would never be enough. During the dark half of the year, he reigned supreme, but the bright half belonged to the Oak. It had always been the way. It would always be the way. To destroy that balance was to destroy the world the Maker had created.

It was not-right.

From the trees' vast store of knowledge, he gleaned the words to communicate with them and shaped the memories of the path he had taken once before. Then he gathered his strength and sent his spirit back into the body of the boy called Tinnean.

Struath gripped Darak's shoulder, forcing him to see what he saw. The boy's chest heaved again, then rose and fell in a slow, steady rhythm. His eyes fluttered open. He stared up at them, searching their faces as if he had never seen them before.

Darak hugged him so hard Struath could hear the breath whoosh out of that slender body.

"You scared the life out of me." Then he seemed to remember himself and added, "What happened, lad? Did you faint? Was it the shock of being here again?"

"Darak, one question at a time," Yeorna said.

"I know. I'm sorry." He kept shaking his head, grinning foolishly. "You're not hurt? Can you stand, do you think? Nay, best wait till you've got your strength back."

Struath held up his hand and Darak subsided, but he kept touching Tinnean as if he couldn't believe he was real. "What happened?"

"I went into the Tree."

"On your own?" Darak interrupted. "Just like that?"

Struath silenced him with a brusque gesture. "Why did you go into the Tree?"

"I am the Tree."

Struath let out his breath. The vision may have been a lie, but his intuition had been correct. Why, then, had his spirit returned to Tinnean's body? Before he could ask, Darak pulled the Oak-Lord to his feet.

"He's still a little muddled. But he's back. You can see that. He'll be fine once we get him home."

"This is my home, Darak."

"This is not your home!"

"Be silent!" Struath held Darak with his gaze until he was certain the younger man had regained his control. "Why did you come back to us, my lord?"

"To find the Oak."

Struath swayed, would have fallen if Gortin hadn't steadied him. In his initiate's stricken expression, he saw his own sick fear. The Oak's spirit had not taken refuge in the boy. It was gone. Lost.

Yeorna recovered first. "You . . . you are not the Oak?"

"Nay."

"You see?" Even through his haze of fear, Struath could hear the relief in Darak's voice.

"I am the Holly."

Struath's legs folded under him. Somewhere close by, a wren warbled, its song a sweet counterpoint to Darak's harsh breathing. Closer still, Griane's voice, asking if he was in pain. The bones in his back cracked in protest as he bent his head to the forest floor. The musty scent of dead leaves and cold earth filled his nostrils.

"My lord. Forgive me for not knowing you."

Chapter 10

DARAK DRAGGED STRUATH to his feet, ignoring his grunt of pain. "How can you do this?"

"Take your hands off of me."

He released him, but returned the shaman's glare. "I trusted you. I brought him here because you told me you could restore him. And when he comes back—with no help from any of you priests—you fall on your knees and feed his madness."

"He is not mad. He is the Holly."

"First he was the Oak. Now the Holly. Who'll you decide he is next—the Trickster?"

Struath's head snapped back as if he had struck him.

"How dare you speak to the Tree-Father that way?" Gortin's face was flushed with outrage.

"You heard him yourself," Yeorna said. "Why won't you believe him?"

"Because I'd have to accept that my brother is gone!"

The sympathy on Yeorna's face was more unbearable than the awe he'd seen on Struath's. He spun away from her outstretched hand to face his brother. Tinnean backed away from him, wary as a deer.

"I won't hurt you. I won't even touch you. Do you understand me?"

A cautious nod.

"You say you're . . . the Holly?" Just speaking the words made him sick.

Another nod.

"Then go back into the Tree where you belong and send Tinnean's spirit back to his body."

"I cannot go back. I must find the Oak."

"Damn the Oak." Even Griane gasped at his sacrilege, but Darak was beyond caring. "I want my brother."

"His spirit is not in the Tree."

Darak's gut clenched as if he'd been punched. His lips managed to shape the question, but it took three attempts before sound emerged. "Where?"

"I do not know."

So utterly, inhumanly calm. He might have been talking about a missing fishhook. This could not be his brother. Surely, even in the depths of madness, something of Tinnean would remain.

"Perhaps he is with the Oak," the Holly-Lord said.

"You know where the Oak is?" Struath asked even as Darak demanded, "Why?"

The Holly-Lord looked from one to the other as if trying to decide which question to answer first. "They were together that night." He winced. Perhaps he felt some emotion, after all.

"What happened?" Struath's voice was little more than a whisper. "Do you remember?"

"The others helped me understand."

"The others?" Struath asked.

The Holly-Lord gestured to the surrounding trees, his expression softening. Darak clenched his fists. He could feel tenderness for the trees and nothing at all for Tinnean.

"Tell us," Struath said. "Please."

The Holly-Lord's face went blank, as if his spirit had left his body again or he was looking at something none of them could see. Then he nodded. "It was like a great storm ripped the Tree apart. I was not-rooted. Drifting like . . . like smoke from a fire. I saw the small man running. And there was another . . . more . . . ripping. I touched another spirit. It was not a tree. I think it was the small man."

"Tinnean," Darak said. "His name is Tinnean."

Ever since the battle, he had been haunted by the image of that slender body hurtling through the air, imagined the spikes on the holly leaves that had left such long, bloody scratches. He'd seen the spikes for himself now. Twice as long as those of the quickthorn that had ripped open his arm. And Tinnean's arms so much skinnier than his. The small man who wasn't even a man yet.

The Holly-Lord was studying him. Darak let out his breath slowly, forcing himself to appear just as dispassionate.

"And then?"

"The Oak disappeared." He closed his eyes, one hand fisted against his chest. But when he opened them a moment later, his voice was as calm as ever. "The small . . . Tinnean . . . he disappeared. I was rooted again, but not in the earth. I fell. It was dark. And then I woke in this body."

"Tinnean's body." Darak ground out the words between clenched teeth.

"Tinnean's body," the Holly-Lord agreed.

"Do you know where they are?" Struath asked. "The Oak and Tinnean?"

"There is a place . . ." He frowned. "The words are hard to find." Again, his face went blank. "There is a place where the Oak rests in the warm-time. Where the trees are always green."

"The Summerlands." Gortin breathed the words on a soft exhalation of wonder.

"Of course." Yeorna's voice was breathless with hope. "That was your vision, Tree-Father. The Oak. The island."

Struath nodded, but he looked troubled. Darak was, too. "The legends say the Maker carries the spirit of the Oak to the Summerlands after his defeat at Midsummer. Why would he go there now?"

"Because that is where his spirit always goes when he leaves the One Tree," Gortin said.

"But not at—"

"And the Tree-Father has seen it."

Darak caught Struath's eye. The shaman stiffened, but all he said was, "Can you lead us to the Summerlands, Holly-Lord?" The Holly-Lord nodded. "Then we must go." The shaman's voice sounded as decisive as ever, but his frown lingered.

"What?" Darak asked. "What troubles you?"

Struath glared at him. "The Oak's spirit is gone. Your brother is gone. I am about to embark on a journey no mortal has ever undertaken. Surely, that is enough to trouble any man."

Darak bit back a retort and turned to the Holly-Lord. "Which way?"

He pointed. Hard to gauge the position of the sun through the trees, but Darak judged the direction as roughly southeast. "You can . . . feel the Summerlands?"

"It is the one place in the forest I cannot feel. That is how I know it is there."

Struath squared his shoulders. "Gortin, you must return to the village."

"But Tree-Father—"

"Someone must bring word. And they will need your guidance in the days to come."

Gortin's head drooped. "As you command, Tree-Father."

"Prepare yourself well. The first crossing is difficult. More so when you attempt it alone."

"But the Grain-Mother . . ." Darak darted a quick look at Yeorna. "Surely you can help Gortin."

"The Tree-Father needs my help to restore the Oak

and Tinnean. Lisula must fulfill my duties until I return."

"But you're—"

"Only a woman. I know, Darak."

"With respect, Grain-Mother, I was going to say that you don't know the forest."

"No one knows this forest."

She was right. The First Forest was a world where the gods walked, where an alder and a rowan had dragged their roots from the earth and crossed the boundary between the worlds to become the first man and woman. The priests had never ventured beyond this grove. The trails were unknown, unmarked by human footprints. His skills would be valuable, but only the Holly-Lord could guide them to their destination.

He blessed the foresight that had made him bring along his hunting sack and their bundles of clothes. Struath had insisted they would return at sunset, but he had wanted to be prepared in case it took the priests more than a day to work their magic. Only the gods knew how long this journey would take. They had little food, no shelter. It would be a miracle if they lasted the night.

Struath's brisk instructions interrupted his thoughts. "Gortin, I believe you and Griane will be safe, but ward yourselves until you cross back."

"I'm not going with Gortin," Griane said. "I'm coming with you."

"Nay." He and Struath spoke at once, exchanging surprised glances at finding themselves in agreement.

"It's too dangerous," Darak added.

"All the more reason to have a healer with you." She cast a pointed look at his bloodstained sleeve.

"I can tend to that later."

"And can you make a poultice to keep the wound from turning putrid? Or brew a drink to drive away a fever? Or—"

"You're not coming." She closed her mouth, but her chin thrust out at a mutinous angle. "You've no business being here in the first place. What were you thinking, wandering around the forest at night?"

"I wasn't wandering," she said, flushing. "I came to warn you. They were coming for Tinnean."

"Who?"

"Jurl. Onnig. My uncle. I heard them talking. I was coming to your hut—with these." She thrust out the lumpy bundle she'd been clutching. "Warm clothes. Herbs. And some food. Just oatcakes and fish. There wasn't much to spare."

"Griane, I . . ." He didn't know whether to shake her or hug her. Twice in the space of a day, she'd stood with him, defying her uncle, defying the whole tribe.

"So I can't go back." Her pointed little chin trembled. "The council would cast me out along with Tinnean."

"Griane, the council did not vote for a casting-out," Yeorna said. "The elders agreed to allow us to attempt a restoration."

Her resolute expression leached away. "Then . . . you weren't in any danger at all?"

"That is correct," Struath said. "If you had waited—"

"The Maker only knows what Jurl might have done," Darak said.

"They said . . ." Her voice sounded so soft and small that Darak felt a reluctant tug of sympathy. "They weren't going to hurt Tinnean. Just keep you from taking him away." In an even smaller voice, she added, "I listened outside their hut."

Struath made an inarticulate sound of disgust. "By now, the whole village will be roused."

"She was trying to help," Darak said.

"So now you condone her behavior?"

"She might have acted rashly, but only because she

was worried about Tinnean. Even you can't condemn her for that."

"If I may . . ." Yeorna ventured.

Struath frowned, but nodded.

"Griane is not a child. She deserves the right to choose for herself." Before any of them could interrupt, she added, "None of us knows what danger we might encounter in the days ahead. Griane's gift of healing may prove as important as your skills as a hunter, Darak. Or your knowledge of the spirit catcher, Tree-Father."

The Holly-Lord smiled. "Come, Griane."

She smiled back and laid her palm against his cheek. Then her face changed and her hand fell to her side. "I will come, Holly-Lord."

Darak and Struath turned to Yeorna. Darak hoped he didn't look as helpless as the shaman.

"Everything happens for a reason," Yeorna said.

Whether or not that was true, impulsive acts surely led to disaster. If Griane had waited for the council's decision, she would be safe at home. If Tinnean had not charged the Tree . . . His gaze fell on the Holly-Lord who was helping Griane retie her bundle. As soon as he turned back to the Tree, her brave smile faded. She gazed at the giant trees, gnawing her upper lip. When she caught him watching her, she scowled.

Struath motioned Gortin aside to murmur some priestly instructions. He touched the back of his hand to his initiate's forehead, then drew back, frowning, when Gortin seized his hand and pressed a kiss to the acorn tattoo. Poor Gortin looked crestfallen. He returned Yeorna's hug, but pulled away to retrieve Struath's staff and hand it to him.

"Gortin, watch your back after you cross," Darak offered by way of farewell. "The wolf may still be lurking about."

Darak's gaze locked with Struath's. The shaman was the first to look away.

"How far?" he asked the Holly-Lord.

"Far."

When it was clear he would get nothing more, Darak nodded. "Right, then. We'll take it slow. No running ahead, Holly-Lord. Do you understand?"

He nodded, his gaze lingering on the Tree. Darak took him by the shoulder and spun him southeast.

He was not Tinnean. Tinnean was lost. But he would find him. In the Summerlands, in the Forever Isles, in Chaos itself if that's where he had to search. Meanwhile, he would keep his brother's body safe until the one who stole it could be sent back into his Tree forever.

Chapter 11

MORGATH LAY in the thicket, worrying the broken shaft of the arrow protruding from his flank. He had watched the girl stumble into the grove and vanish with the others. Strangers, all of them— except for the old one. Too weak from the crossing to probe his spirit, he might not have known him at all if the Hunter hadn't spoken the name.

Struath.

His lips drew back in a silent snarl. Time moved differently in Chaos, but he had never imagined that so many years had gone by in the world of men. How many had he lost—twenty? thirty? Half a lifetime stolen by the one who had betrayed him and cast his spirit into Chaos.

Somehow he had escaped. Perhaps his little apprentice had inadvertently drawn him through the portal. Joy had changed to terror when he felt his spirit drifting away. When the owl flew past, he threw all his power at it and pushed the bird's spirit out. He had done it many times when he had worn a man's body, sometimes spending half a day in his temporary host, testing his magical powers just as he stretched his newly acquired wings. Expecting to soar with that same effortless skill, he had collided with a low-hanging branch, injuring one wing.

Remembering the rage and helplessness of that moment, Morgath growled. He'd had to roost in an elder for an entire day before he found the strength to look for a new host. This time, he chose carefully. Sluggish with sleep, the bear barely stirred when he usurped its body. The act, coming so soon after stealing the owl, drained what little magical reserves he possessed.

Fat from last summer's foraging, the bear provided an ideal host for his recovery, but he had not escaped Chaos to drowse away the winter. He had lumbered out of the den, delighting in the feel of blood pumping through his body, the sweet taste of air in his lungs, the delicious reek of his fur. His limbs moved with heavy grace and he loved them. The excitement of seeing out of both eyes again more than made up for the colorless world he beheld.

He found a cluster of elderberries, overlooked by the birds; if he'd still worn a man's form, he would have wept as the tartness of the shriveled black berries exploded on his tongue. Even more satisfying was the mouse he trapped under his paw: the delicate crunch of its small bones, the tickle of fur as it slid down his throat.

A thick thread of saliva oozed between his half-open jaws. Had the act of eating ever been so satisfying when he was a man?

The mouse had awakened a desire for more flesh. He chased a fox away from its kill, savoring the rabbit's still-warm flesh and rich, heavy blood before roaring his satisfaction to the forest. The wolf pack had been less willing to surrender its kill. Bodies low to the ground, fangs bared, they waited for him to retreat. When he refused, several of them slunk away from the others to flank him.

He quickly decided to assault the smaller male. The

attack followed the same lines as the others: the sudden
invasion; the brief but impossible battle to repel him;
and finally, that ecstatic moment when the host's spirit
hurtled out of its body, leaving him in possession.

The silver-muzzled male circled the lifeless bear several times before padding toward him. This time, the
release of magic had left him barely conscious. If the
wolf had chosen to attack, he would have been helpless. Tail lowered, eyes averted, Morgath whined as
the pack leader sniffed him. Finally, the male licked
him and led the others back to gorge.

He remained with them several nights, gathering his
strength and honing his skills. But wolves are wise;
they sensed something wrong. Before they could turn
on him, he left the pack and made his way back to
the grove.

He'd had no time to observe the devastation when
he first escaped. He remembered little more than
screams and that dizzying flight through the trees.
Standing before the One Tree, he wondered if the
Tree-Lords had finished their battle. And if not, what
consequences did that hold for the world?

That must be the reason the Betrayer had come to
the heart-oak—to offer prayers and sacrifices. His lip
curled. It would take more than prayers to restore the
One Tree. If the Betrayer needed proof of his master's
power, he had only to look at the devastation he
had wrought.

Morgath rose and limped into the glade, whimpering as the arrowhead ground deeper into his flank.
He had a new enemy now. The Hunter, too, must
be punished.

He wove his way toward the heart-oak. The crossing
had drained him, but now he was home, standing before the heart-oak to which he had offered so many
sacrifices. Blood spattered the tree's roots. He sniffed
eagerly, tongue flicking out to savor the Hunter's es-

sence. Sacrificial blood was richer than ordinary blood. He wondered if the animals that had feasted upon him so many years ago had recognized the difference.

He nosed through the dead leaves, half-hoping to discover some piece of himself, but of course, there was nothing. His blood had long since soaked into the earth, his flesh devoured by scavengers, his bones scattered. Only his spirit remained to bear witness to the murder.

He raised his muzzle and howled. Roosting doves fled skyward with a noisy flapping of wings. His legs collapsed under him and his vision clouded. He dragged himself back to the thicket and laid his head down on his paws.

They could not return until sunset. When they did, he would be waiting.

PART TWO

In the springtime of the world, the One Tree stood alone.
And the Maker created the sacred trees to stand with
 the One Tree.
And the trees became the First Forest and it covered
 the earth.
And among the trees roamed the beasts of the
 woodlands.
And above the trees soared the birds of the air.
And between the trees swam the fish of the rivers.
And beneath the trees crawled the creatures of the
 earth.
But no people walked here . . .

—Legend of the First Forest

Chapter 12

AT FIRST, DARAK THOUGHT the giant trees were making him uneasy; even the smallest birch loomed above them. By midmorning, he realized it was more. Out of the corner of his eye, he'd catch a flicker of movement, a shadow flitting from trunk to trunk. Once he noticed the shadows, he saw more, as if his very awareness drew them closer. He had spent too many years in the forest to dismiss the sensation.

He let his gaze drift across the trees, hoping to spot a break in the pattern of color and light and motion. Struath watched him, two vertical creases forming between his brows. "What is it?"

"There's . . . something." Struath nodded; he must have noticed the shadows, too. Darak lowered his voice. "The wolf couldn't cross over until sunset, could it?"

"Nay. At least . . ." Struath swallowed, then turned to the Holly-Lord. "There is a strange presence in the forest."

"It is only the rootless ones."

Struath's breath hissed in. "So the story is true."

"What story?" Darak asked.

"About the trees who have died—struck by lightning, killed by rot. Their spirits live on in the First Forest, guarding the living trees."

"Are they dangerous?"

"My . . . the man who told me the story . . . he said the Watchers are not malevolent. As long as we do no harm to the trees, I think they will leave us alone."

"And you trust the man who told you this?"

Struath looked away. "I believe the story."

Darak estimated it was only midafternoon—it was impossible to tell in the dimness of the forest—but he called a halt when they reached a clearing. Harmless or not, he preferred to keep the Watchers at a distance. Besides, Struath looked utterly drained. If a day's easy march exhausted him, how would he ever reach the Summerlands?

While Griane showed the Holly-Lord how to scoop up fallen leaves and pine needles for bedding, Darak squatted down to clear a space for the fire pit. "Yeorna, gather fuel, please. Twigs, pinecones . . ."

"Darak."

"A moment, Struath. Bigger branches, too, if you find them. Struath, we'll need stones for the fire pit."

"Darak, you cannot light a fire."

Darak examined the clearing again. The lowest branches were easily ten times a man's height. Even if an errant spark flew that high, the wood was too wet to catch.

"There's little danger. Griane, that'll do for bedding—we've got the wolfskins as well."

"That's not what I mean."

Darak swiveled toward the shaman. "Then speak plain."

"This is the First Forest. To light a fire here is an act of disrespect."

"You expect us to survive without fire?"

"Fire is anathema to the forest. To build one can only incur its wrath."

"So we're damned if we build a fire and we freeze to death if we don't. That's our choice?"

"We have no choice, Darak."

Darak rose. "Are you telling me you will not permit me to light a fire?"

"I am telling you that the First Forest will not permit it."

"Tree-Father. Darak." Yeorna dropped the dead branch she was dragging and walked toward them. "When a hunter cuts ash to make a bow, he asks permission of the tree first. When we clear trees for a field, we offer a sacrifice. We've always done this and the trees have never punished us."

Struath hesitated, then turned to the Holly-Lord. "Can you explain our need?"

The Holly-Lord looked troubled, but he walked among the trees, pausing to lay his palms against their trunks. When he turned back to them, he shook his head. "It is hard. Fire is the destroyer. They fear it."

"Then I'll build it," Darak said. "And I'll make the sacrifice. If the forest seeks vengeance, let it fall upon me and me alone." He stared from his bloodstained sleeve to the dagger in his hand.

"Water," Struath said.

"We need the water for ourselves."

"Then it is a greater sacrifice than blood."

After a moment, Darak nodded. He circled the clearing, sprinkling water on the ground while Struath and Yeorna chanted, "Water of life, we offer you. Fire, we ask in return."

Even with a flint dagger, it was hard work digging up the frozen earth; despite the cold, he was sweating by the time he finished. After smoothing the furrowed earth with his fingers, he laid the rocks Griane had gathered in a circle. He dug into his belt pouch and dropped a handful of tinder into the shallow pit, then placed his notched fireboard over it to catch the first spark. Finally, he reached for his firestick.

He had crafted it from an ash branch, scraping it with the sharpened tine of an antler until it was only the thickness of his forefinger. Most men made a new firestick each winter; he had clung to his for three. In all their years together, it had never failed him.

He placed the blunt end of the firestick into one of the notches in the fireboard and whispered the simple prayer his father had taught him: "Ash-brother, give us fire." Arching his fingers stiffly, he placed his palms at the top of the firestick and twirled it quickly. When his hands reached the bottom of the firestick, he began the ritual again.

It was slow work, but strangely soothing. He spun the firestick, his body swaying slightly with the rhythm of the movements. As he worked, he hummed the hunter's song, a blessing for the smooth path, the clear shot, the true-flying arrow. Black dust collected beside the notch. His hands moved automatically while he watched for the first sign of smoke, the first glow of a spark.

He felt the others around him, and behind them, the unseen Watchers. Were they the ones preventing the fire from lighting? He shifted position without losing the rhythm. A gust of wind tugged at his mantle. A snowflake fell. His voice faltered. Struath took up the hunter's song, weaving it into his chant for fire.

He repeated the prayer for fire, silently this time. One prayer each time his palms journeyed down the firestick.

Ten journeys.

Twenty.

Fifty.

Blisters formed and burst open on his raw palms. He spun the firestick faster to keep it from sticking to his oozing flesh. Griane's hands appeared at the top of the firestick, beginning the twirling as his reached the bottom.

Ten more journeys and ten more after that. Yeorna's voice was hoarse from chanting. A hand came down on his shoulder.

"Darak."

He lost the rhythm. Found it again.

"Darak. Stop."

He spun the firestick furiously and heard a sharp crack. He sat back, holding the shattered pieces of ash in his hands.

"It is not you," Struath said. "It is the forest."

He cleaned the fireboard and returned it to his pack. He gathered the tinder and sprinkled it into the pouch. He moved slowly, carefully. By the time he rose, he had conquered the helpless frustration that had threatened to overwhelm him.

He thrust the broken halves of the firestick in his belt. "Heap the leaves there." He pointed to the overarching roots of an oak. The hollow beneath was nearly the size of his hut. "Griane, help me unpack the wolfskins."

"After I see to your arm."

"Later."

"That's what you said in the grove."

"They're just scratches."

Griane glared at him, hands on hips. "Now. But when the wound starts to stink and your arm swells up and turns black and—"

Silently, Darak pushed back his sleeve. Griane winced and no wonder; his arm was a bloody mess. She squatted down and unwrapped her bundle. A mantle, he realized. She opened a large doeskin bag and laid out an astonishing assortment of leather pouches, clay flasks and jars, a small stone bowl, a mortar and pestle, and several neat rolls of nettle-cloth.

"What did you do—raid Mother Netal's hut?"

He could have cut himself on the look she gave him.

"What did you do—arm wrestle a bramble bush?"

"A quickthorn, actually." It might have been her little snort that made him add, "I needed a blood sacrifice."

Her hands went still for a moment, then busied themselves pouring water into the bowl. Her brisk but gentle touch surprised him. Although she was Mother Netal's assistant, he still thought of her as his wife's annoying little sister, the child who had once filled his shoes with porridge, the girl who had called him a brute and a bully just—gods, was it only yesterday?

"Keep your arm out," she said, tossing out the bloody water. "Wrist up."

She poured fresh water into the bowl, adding a pinch of herbs from one packet, a generous handful of dried leaves from another. "Yarrow and Maker's mantle." She stirred it into a paste, sending him another chilly blue-eyed blast. "I do know what I'm doing."

"I didn't say anything."

She contented herself with unrolling one of the nettle-cloth bundles. With the same briskness, she sliced off several long strips of cloth, spread the paste on his cuts, and wound the bandage around his arm.

"Thank you."

"I haven't finished yet."

"Not just for this. For standing with us the other day. For coming to warn us."

Her fingers fumbled the roll of nettle-cloth. He caught it and pressed it back into her palm. She jerked her hand away and bent lower to tie the bandage at his wrist. Her long braid fell over her shoulder, the feathery tip tickling the inside of his elbow. He lifted the braid, intending only to swing it back over her shoulder, but she glared at him so fiercely that he dropped it.

"I'm done."

"Thank you. Again."

"They're just scratches."

She had always been a fierce child, moods blowing this way and that like a flame in a breeze. Tinnean had always understood her, though. She'd spent as much time in their hut as Red Dugan's, sometimes even sleeping next to Tinnean, the two of them curled up like puppies. Some of his kinfolk had even speculated that they would marry someday, although she was a year older than Tinnean. He'd gotten plenty of elbows and giggles from the women, along with comments about how sweet it would be, the two brothers marrying the two sisters.

Frowning, he watched her help the Holly-Lord spread the wolfskins. Was that why she had followed them? Because she was in love with Tinnean?

Surely not. After he married Maili, Griane rarely visited their hut, devoting herself to the path of the healer. Still, she clearly cared for Tinnean. She had scarcely left his side while he was ill, teaching him words, bringing him hot apple cider, fussing over him. Just like she was fussing over him now.

But that wasn't Tinnean. He'd have to remind her of that.

He motioned the others under the roots, seating himself between Griane and the Holly-Lord while they shared the pheasant and two of Griane's oatcakes. They passed the waterskin around, each person taking a small sip. When they curled up to sleep, he covered them with the spare mantle and Tinnean's robe, then settled himself with his back against a root.

Night fell fast at Midwinter, the light fading from cream to gray to charcoal in moments. As the hard edges of the tree trunks melted into the darkness, the shadowy Watchers took on greater substance. They circled the clearing, darting from tree to tree, pausing now and then as if observing him. The forest was oddly silent, though now and then he heard a furtive rustling among the trees as though the Watchers plotted among themselves. If the First Forest did not welcome fire, neither did it welcome strangers.

Dagger in hand, he kept watch. Only when he glimpsed the first patches of gray between the lattice-work of naked branches did he allow himself the luxury of sleep.

Chapter 13

GRIANE'S STOMACH GROWLED as Yeorna carefully broke their last two oatcakes in half. Only four days from the grove and their food was almost gone. She should have brought more, planned better. No wonder Darak always chided her for being impulsive.

He was frowning at her now. Before he could berate her for her oversight, she thrust out his portion of oatcake. He just shook his head and crawled out from under the slab of rock that had sheltered them the night before. Muttering a curse, she followed.

She found him blowing on his fingers, still frowning. He shot her a quick glance as she stamped feeling back into her feet, then turned away. When the numbness in her toes gave way to an unpleasant prickling, she held out the oatcake. Again, he shook his head.

"You should eat."

"I'm not hungry."

"Don't be silly. We're all hungry."

"You think I don't know that?"

She recoiled before the anger in his face.

"Griane." His breath blew out in a great billow of steam. "I didn't mean to bite your head off."

He met her gaze calmly enough; only the muscle twitching in his jaw betrayed his tension. She threw back her mantle and bared her throat. "It may be skinny, but it'd take more than one bite to sever it."

His mouth twisted in a reluctant smile and she caught her breath. He smiled so seldom that she forgot how much he resembled Tinnean.

"Aye. Well. I'm sorry all the same." The smile faded as quickly as it had come.

"It's not your fault."

"I shouldn't have snapped at you."

"I meant the fire."

Darak had spent their brief rest periods crafting a new firestick. Each evening since he had completed it, he tried to call forth fire. Each time, he failed.

"I just . . ." His hands clenched convulsively at his sides. He shoved his fists under his armpits as if to prevent them from betraying him further. "I feel so damned helpless."

It was the first time in her life she'd ever heard him admit to that. Somehow, that scared her more than the towering trees or the ever-present Watchers. He must have seen her fear, for he gave her a quick, forced smile. "You wouldn't have anything in your magic bag for that, I suppose."

"Nay. But if you're costive, I could brew you up a draught of dandelion root and yellow dock that'll have your bowels moving in no time." This time, his grin was genuine, encouraging her to add, "Or if it's a bad case, there's some suetcake left. I'd be happy to mix the herbs with the suet and then—" She put her fingers together and shoved them upward.

Darak backed away, laughing. "With your cold fingers? I'd be bound up tighter than an owl."

She gave him her sweetest smile and held out the oatcake. "Try the oats, then. Very good for the bowels."

"You're as bad as Mother Netal. Both of you convinced a man's fate depends on the state of his bowels."

He took the halved oatcake, broke it in half again, and gave one portion back to her. They munched in silence, chewing each mouthful as long as possible to savor it. The brooding look descended on his face again.

"I never understood it," he said.

"What?"

"Tinnean's fascination with magic." He kicked at an inoffensive pile of leaves, before adding, "Did you?"

She shook her head. The lines in his face relaxed just a bit. "That's what I like about healing. Not so much the charms and the prayers, but knowing that yellow dock and dandelion root are good for the bowels, coltsfoot'll soothe a cough, and elder leaves'll take the fire out of a burn. Things you can see and touch."

"Aye. Like knowing if you strike the flint just right, you'll chip out an arrowhead." His eager expression died. "Or if you spin the firestick, you'll make fire." He raised a hand, cutting off her protest. "I'd best fetch Struath. I'll need his blessing before I hunt. And the Forest-Lord's if I'm to be successful."

"The Forest-Lord has always brought you game."

"That was before."

She wasn't sure if he meant before Tinnean had been lost or before they'd come to the First Forest. "He may be a god, but he's as much a part of nature as we are. I cannot believe he wants us to die." When Darak remained silent, she added, "And if you think that, then you might as well give up now and go home."

"Don't worry, girl. I'm not giving up. I'll defy the Lord of Chaos himself if that's what it takes to get Tinnean back."

Darak knelt before the shaman. Together, they in-
toned the prayer to the Forest-Lord. Yeorna dribbled
some of their precious water over his hands and he
splashed it on his face, hoping the meager ablutions
would suffice. With one of his arrows, he etched crude
pictures of squirrels, rabbits, and birds in the hard
earth. The Tree-Father blessed his bow and arrows,
his sling and snares. Finally, he cut open his unscarred
arm, and painted each stone, each arrowhead, feeding
the weapons with his blood.

It was a relief to focus his senses on the hunt, to
relinquish his thinking self to his physical one, aware
of each footfall and breath, attentive to each small
shift in wind and landscape. For the first time, he felt
in control again and—at least for a little while—he
could put aside his fears for Tinnean and forget the
momentary weakness that had led him to confide in
Griane. A man should bear his fears in silence. It was
one of the first lessons his father had taught him.

Only yesterday, Struath had remarked that a winter
forest was an empty, lonely place. Darak could not
understand how a man who could see into other
worlds could be so blind to his own. Everywhere, he
found signs of life. Wood pigeons cooed overhead.
Squirrels skittered through the branches with a noisy
scratching of claws. Powdery pockmarks in the snow
pointed to a small community of hares.

He found signs of other hunters in the forest: a
weasel's burrow under a rotted log; black and scabby
slashes on an ash where a bear had clawed it moons
ago; the pungent scent markings of a male fox on a
tree stump.

He almost missed the squirrel, its fur the same mottled white as the birch it was climbing. It leaped onto
an oak and he blinked as the color of its fur deepened
to a dark gray. Could all the animals in the First Forest change their coloration as easily as the ermine shed
its summer coat for winter white?

He thrust aside his wonder and slipped a stone into the sling's pouch. Deliberately, he slowed his breathing, allowing the familiar calm to steal over him.

Forest-Lord, guide my arm.

Eyes fixed on the squirrel, Darak whipped the sling behind his body and over his head.

Stone, fly true.

His body flowed forward in one smooth, powerful motion as he released. He caught his breath as the stone soared through the air, let it out again as the stone smashed into the squirrel's skull. It tumbled out of the tree, landing with a rustle of leaves.

Only when he felt his muscles relax, did Darak realize how tense he had been. He mounded the leaves into a small pile and carefully laid the dead squirrel atop them. Then he knelt beside his offering and bowed his head.

"Forest-Lord, to you I offer the first kill." He abandoned the rest of the ritual words and simply added, "Hernan. I don't know why the gods sent the plague to our village, but I know it was not your doing. My curses were never meant for you. You have always been good to me. Never more so than now. Thank you for not abandoning me."

For a long moment, he knelt there, savoring the peace that filled him. Then he raised his head and found himself staring into a pair of golden eyes.

The fox was easily as large as a wolf. It sat so close he could have reached out and touched it if he'd dared. The utter silence of its approach made him wonder if it was real, but the breeze ruffled the ruddy fur on its shoulders and there was no mistaking its gamy scent. Surely apparitions didn't smell. But just as surely, no ordinary fox bore the unmistakable fragrance of honeysuckle.

He sank back on his haunches. The fox observed him with a single twitch of its black whiskers. His fingers closed on the haft of his spear, then relaxed.

Denizen of the First Forest or sign from the gods, he was loath to kill it.

"Gods, you're beautiful."

Its tongue lolled out as if the creature were grinning at him, the friendliness of its expression considerably lessened by the two long shears on its upper jaw.

"You're real. Aren't you?"

The fox blinked. And then, without even seeming to move, it was on him.

He might have been sinking into the deep waters of the lake, so slowly did he fall. Sprawled full-length on the ground, he stared up into eyes the color of clover honey. Bees buzzed all around him, although reason told him that was impossible. He tried to grope for his spear, but he seemed to have lost control of his limbs.

The somnolent drone of the bees filled his ears, just as the golden eyes filled his vision. The slitted black pupils opened wide. Flames erupted in the two dark pools. The flames coalesced into images: a child crouching beside a fire pit, a man standing over him.

Although he only saw him from the back, he knew the man was his father, watching the child struggle to call forth a spark with his firestick. The child's mouth—his mouth—was clamped tight. As the small fingers spun the firestick, a grimace of pain replaced the frown of concentration. His fingers moved faster— too fast. The firestick shattered. Mouth twisting, he hurled the broken halves across the hut.

The child's shame washed over Darak like a sudden sweat. His father removed his belt and walked away. Head bowed, the child followed.

Then they were both standing outside the hut, the child bent over against the turf wall, the man behind him, arm upraised. Darak would always remember that whipping; it was the first he'd ever received from his father. And he would always remember the words that accompanied it: "The whipping is not for breaking the firestick, but for cursing it and throwing it away. Until you learn to control yourself, you will never be a man."

The child's fingers dug into the crevices in the wall, his body flinching with each of the ten blows. When it was over, he straightened slowly and turned. A low moan escaped Darak when he beheld Tinnean's tear-streaked face.

Even before the man turned, Darak knew whose face he would see. Even before the man spoke, he knew what words he would say: "You cannot be running off into the forest whenever the whim strikes you, Tinnean. You must learn to control your impulses."

Darak's throat closed in silent protest, but he could only observe his dream-self, staring after Tinnean: the tight mouth, the slanting cheekbones, eyes gray as a winter sky and just as bleak.

Gods, I look just like my father.

It was his last conscious thought before darkness engulfed him.

When he returned to himself, the sun stood mid-sky. His head ached and his arse was cold from the damp seeping through his breeches. He sat up carefully and looked around. The fox was gone, but where it had sat, a small fire blazed.

He pushed himself to his knees. The fire burned atop a perfect oval of naked earth. He stretched out shaking hands; if the fire's origin was otherworldly, its heat was completely real. The flames curled like beckoning fingers and a shiver raced down his back.

Fire was warmth against the cold, light in the darkness. Fire was a gift of life. But did he dare accept a gift from the Trickster-God? For that was surely who he had just encountered. The legends spoke of the Trickster taking the form of a fox to charm hunter and prey alike. And only the Trickster would have taunted him with those visions of his past.

No sane man wanted to be in the Trickster's debt,

but neither could he afford to offend the god by refusing his gift. They had survived four nights without fire, but if a storm blew in, if they could not find adequate shelter, they would suffer more than frostnipped fingers and toes.

In the end, he brought down two wood pigeons with his sling and laid them on a rock as an offering. Then he hacked a fallen branch into a stave and touched it to the fire. As soon as it caught, the fire vanished without a trace of smoke or ash.

He headed back to camp, stopping twice to set spring pole snares near the hare runs. He tried not to think about the vision the Trickster had sent, but he could not help wondering why the god would help them—and whether he would demand a much higher price than two dead birds.

Chapter 14

STRUATH LISTENED to Darak's tale with mingled awe and resentment. He was grateful for Griane's interruptions; it would have been undignified for him to ply Darak with such an endless stream of questions. All his life, he had dreamed of meeting a god face-to-face. And now, Darak had been chosen. Darak, who had cursed the gods. It was just the sort of irony the Trickster would enjoy.

He told himself it was caution that urged him to temper Griane's excitement by noting that it might have been a powerful animal spirit that Darak had encountered. When Darak revealed what the god had shown him, he told himself it was his skill in interpreting visions that made him press Darak for details that the younger man was clearly reluctant to provide. Yeorna surprised him by interrupting.

"Tree-Father, Darak's vision seems a personal one with no bearing on our quest. I don't think we need to hear all the details. Unless . . ." She turned to Darak who shrugged uncomfortably.

"As you say, Grain-Mother, the vision was personal."

"The Trickster's interest worries me. Your offering was generous, but . . ."

"You think I should return the fire?"

Yeorna's brow wrinkled in thought. "Tree-Father, what do you advise?"

Struath had to admire her diplomacy, saving Darak's pride in one breath and soothing his in the next. He envied Yeorna's gift all the more because he believed it to be unconscious, born of concern for her kinfolk. Humbled, he vowed to be more like her.

Aloud, he simply said, "We need fire if we are to survive. The gods must know that. As to the Trickster, perhaps Brana can offer some clue as to his part in all of this."

"Brana?"

He glanced quickly at Darak, but found only confusion in his face. "My spirit guide." He shook his head in exasperation; how quickly he forgot his vow to be understanding.

"Forgive me, Tree-Father. I didn't know." The title surprised him as much as the apology, but magic always humbled Darak. He waved away the apology and even managed a smile. It was ridiculous, this constant striving with Darak. Worse, it was beneath him.

The wolf had tainted his perceptions. The animal haunted him—both the malevolent creature he had seen in his vision and the hulking beast they had encountered in the grove. The meaning of both encounters still eluded him. Darak had seen a she-wolf on his vision quest. Could the vision have been warning him that Darak was a threat?

Struath shook his head. Darak might challenge his authority, but he was committed to finding Tinnean.

"Tree-Father?"

Yeorna's voice interrupted his thoughts. He looked up to find all of them watching him.

"I was just thinking. About the Trickster."

Darak rose. "With respect, Struath, think about him

while we move camp." Griane groaned. "I passed a grotto under an embankment less than half a mile on. If we hurry, we can be settled in before dark."

Struath waited impatiently for the others to fall asleep. So far, he had been useless on this quest, his aging body slowing their progress and leaving him too exhausted at night to attempt a vision. Tonight, he had all but promised one.

He stared into the flames.

Please gods, give me the strength.

Without Gortin's chants or the drum or the dreamherbs, he could rely only on his years of training—and on his spirit guide.

Please, Brana, heed my call.

Once, his spirit had been able to slip from his body between one breath and the next. Once, he had only to call Brana's name for her to appear. For the last six moons, he had struggled like an apprentice, the vision of the wolf his only reward.

Please, Maker, let me See.

He breathed deeply, willing his body to relax. Breathing. Stillness. Emptiness. The first lessons an apprentice learned. Opening the mind. Surrendering the spirit.

The firelight danced. The familiar paralysis crept into his limbs. Stone and earth fell away. A roaring filled his ears. The flames stretched into a fiery tunnel and he followed it, through light into rushing darkness.

He stood alone on a vast plain. The grasses stirred, but not from any wind known to men. They swirled in a slow spiral, rich green changing to yellow, then orange, then deepening to dark red. A tree thrust out of the grass. Branches shot skyward, green leaves fluttering. The seven-lobed leaves of the blood-oak, he realized. It grew taller, wide-spreading branches arcing above his head. On the lowest branch perched a robin.

Tears of gratitude spilled down his face. The Oak was alive. Its sacred bird still sang in its branches. As he bowed his head to whisper a prayer of thanks, the robin's song died.

He looked up to find that the grass around the Oak had withered, revealing patches of parched earth. The Oak's branches shriveled. Green leaves turned brown. Thorns erupted on twisted limbs. The robin screamed with Tinnean's voice as the thorns pierced its breast.

Struath reached for it, only to be driven back by the blood. Impossible gouts of it, gushing out of the small bird, drenching his robe, soaking the grass until the plain lay flooded in a seething red torrent. And then it vanished, leaving an endless expanse of snow and ice.

The robin fell from the branch. He bent to lift it in cupped hands, bloody braids brushing its mauled body.

"Forgive me," he whispered. "Forgive me."

One glazed eye winked at him.

Struath gasped. The robin slipped from his grasp. Claws scrabbled on ice as it hopped erect with an agitated flutter of wings. The dainty beak grew thick and hooked. The wings stretched. The tail widened into a wedge. The blue and gold of the robin's feathers transformed into iridescent black.

His spirit guide winked again.

"You are cruel, Brana."

"So is the world."

It was the first time his raven had appeared to him since the plague. He had never been without her so long, not since he had first heard her gruff voice as a child of ten, speaking to him in his dreams.

"Why did you desert me?"

"I didn't desert you."

"You didn't come when I called."

The shaggy feathers at her neck rose. "I am not a dog."

"I didn't mean that."

She croaked, either in dismissal or acceptance. Acceptance, he decided, as the feathers subsided. "You were asking the wrong questions. Looking in the wrong places."

"I didn't know what to ask. Or where to look."

"Obviously."

Always she spoke in riddles, teasing him, testing him. No one knew him as well, his strengths, his weaknesses, his hidden fears, his secret desires. It was why he loved her—and hated her sometimes.

"Is the Oak dead?"

"The Oak's spirit is immortal."

"But its body?"

"Well." Brana cocked her head, regarding him with beady, black eyes. "Bodies may be destroyed. Or exchanged."

"Exchanged?"

"Robin to raven. Tree to boy."

Green-boughed oak to twisted thorn tree.

"Will you fly with me?"

Struath stared at her, aghast. "There is more?"

"If you will See."

"I have tried to See. My visions are unclear."

"Because you do not wish to See the truth. Will you fly with me?"

He sighed and gave her the ritual answer. "I will fly."

With a little hop and a powerful flap of wings, she ascended. He shrugged his shoulders. His wings sprouted and opened. He closed his eyes and leaped into the air, flapping frantically. No matter how many times they flew together, he always feared he would fall.

The ice-covered plain vanished, replaced by the dark expanse of a forest. The moon rode on his shoulder as he flew. Despite his fear, he reveled in the ease of their journey. If only Brana could carry them all to the Summerlands.

She dove earthward and he followed, wincing as he dodged through the maze of branches. He finally spotted her, perched on the broken spar of a pine. Wings spread to slow his flight, he landed with a graceless skitter of talons. Brana greeted him with a derisive caw.

He always felt clumsy next to her, once more the apprentice struggling to master the gifts of vision, desperate to please the man who had chosen him. But he had persevered; in the end, he had mastered the master and become Tree-Father, respected and admired by his entire tribe.

Brana gave him a sharp peck. "Stop congratulating yourself and See."

He recognized the clearing where they had camped the first night. The feathers on his neck rose when he beheld the wolf, gnawing the bones of some small animal. Then the wolf raised its head and he realized his error. Although the moon leached the ruddiness from its fur, there was no mistaking that narrow muzzle and white ruff. He teetered on his perch, would have fallen if Brana hadn't seized him by the back of the neck and pulled him upright again.

"Lord Trickster," he whispered.

The fox inclined his head, but did not deign to answer. Instead, he returned to his kill. Even from his perch, Struath could hear the crunch of bones.

The Trickster's head came up. A form limped out of the shadows. This time, there was no mistaking the wolf; the broken shaft of Darak's arrow protruded from its haunch.

The wolf crouched, growling. A single yip from the Trickster changed the growl into a whine. Tail curled under, the wolf bellied forward to expose its throat. It trembled in fearful submission when the Trickster nipped its neck. Stiff-legged, the Trickster circled the wolf. His tongue flicked out to touch the broken arrow. It vanished. Another lick closed the wound. The wolf bounded to its feet, racing in frenzied circles around the Trickster. The god yawned. Finally, as if tiring of the antics, the Trickster yipped again and the wolf trotted back to him, panting.

They sat in the clearing, facing each other. The wolf stared intently at the Trickster, but if words passed between them, Struath could not hear them. Beside him, Brana shook herself irritably; she, too, must be excluded from their conversation.

The Trickster looked up, fixing him with his gaze. At once the wolf rose, fur bristling. A low growl rumbled in its chest. Malevolent yellow eyes searched the trees and Struath shrank back.

Brana croaked and flapped her wings, urging him to fly, but the Trickster's eyes held him. With a harsh caw, Brana hopped off the perch and rose. His heart thudded wildly, but even the terror of abandonment could not break the Trickster's spell. Helpless, he felt himself falling into those eyes, just as Darak had.

The wolf paced back and forth beneath him. Exerting all his power, Struath managed to slow his descent, but still he fell. The wolf's eyes met his. Its lips curled back in a snarl. The hatred he had encountered in that first vision assaulted him. Struath commanded his wings to spread, to lift him out of danger, but they hung useless. He drifted downward, close enough to see the muscles bunch in the wolf's haunches, close enough to see the jaws gape open, revealing saliva-slick fangs.

The wolf leaped.

His wandering spirit slammed back into his body with a physical jolt that left his heart pounding so fiercely he feared he would die. He writhed on the wolfskins, racked by the convulsions that always followed a precipitous return from the other world. Strong arms seized him, held him tightly as he wheezed out his name, once, twice, three times, to reestablish the boundaries of his spirit. When the convulsions ceased, he patted his head, trembling hands moving down his body to reestablish the boundaries of his physical self.

He looked up into Darak's eyes. Whatever the flickering firelight revealed, it made the younger man grab his hands. Struath clutched them, grateful for their strength.

"Shall I wake Yeorna?" Darak whispered.

Struath shook his head. Darak eased him back on the wolfskins. He held back a soft moan when those strong hands left him, but they returned moments later, lifting his head to dribble water into his mouth. "Can you tell me?"

Darak listened without interruption, but his grip tightened when he described his narrow escape.

"The place you saw the Oak. It doesn't sound like the Summerlands."

"It may not be a real place at all. Visions are like that."

"But the Oak is alive?"

"Its spirit is immortal. Those were Brana's words." Darak hesitated. "You . . . you didn't see Tinnean?"

"Nay, Darak. I'm sorry."

Darak shook his head as if ashamed for asking. "And the wolf?"

Struath made himself speak the words aloud. "The wolf is my death."

"Not if I kill it first." Darak gave him a tight-lipped smile. Though the eyes were gray, they glittered as ferociously as the wolf's.

Struath shuddered. Darak squeezed his hand again, gently this time. "Try to sleep." When Struath just stared at him, he added, "Aye. Well. It'll be dawn soon anyway."

Darak settled back, arms folded atop his upraised knees. After a long moment, he said, "Now we know the price of fire."

Chapter 15

DETERMINED TO PUT as much distance as possible between them and the wolf, Darak pushed the others hard. Although they now had the luxury of fire to warm them at night, they found themselves facing another obstacle during the day: the forest was changing. The trees were still tall, but not as huge as the ancient ones near the grove, giving credence to the legend that the First Forest had sprung up around the One Tree.

Without the giants blocking out the sun, smaller saplings and shrubs could exist. Instead of an open path between the trees, the underbrush grew thick. But it was more than the tangled vegetation that impeded their progress. Bushes seemed to spread wider to block the way. Trees leaned toward them, branches slapping their faces and snagging their mantles. Sharp-toothed brambles tore breeches and robes. Vines wove impenetrable barriers between the trees.

The forest was fighting them—and it was winning. Slowly, inexorably, it forced them north.

Reluctantly, Darak confronted the Holly-Lord. "We're going the wrong way."

The Holly-Lord nodded.

"Why?"

"It is the way I always go."

"When?"

"After the cold-time battle."

Struath raised his head. Lines of exhaustion etched the shaman's face but his voice was as strong as ever. "To the Mountain, you mean?"

"Aye."

"We can't go north," Darak said. "If we do, we'll never reach the Summerlands."

The Holly-Lord watched him, tense and wary. Belatedly, Darak realized he had clenched his fists. He forced them open and kept his voice low. "We have to change direction. Can you make the forest understand?"

"It is not-right. The trees know that."

"You're the Holly-Lord. Command them."

The Holly-Lord cocked his head, frowning. "I do not understand."

Through gritted teeth, Darak ground out the words. "Tell them to let us go south."

Silently, the Holly-Lord rose. He passed among the trees, touching trunks, stroking branches, then turned back to them and shook his head.

"All right. I'll lead."

"The forest will not let us pass."

"We'll see."

He bulled his way through the underbrush, shoving back branches that pressed against him with an all-too-real malevolence, using his body to open a way for the others. Occasionally, he would see an opening between the trees, but by the time they fought their way to it, the brush had choked off the path, leaving only that clear trail snaking north. It was as if the forest were taunting them.

Finally, he stopped. Alone, he might have persevered, but he couldn't risk the others. He wiped his streaming face and forced his gaze to meet the Holly-Lord's.

"Can you do anything?"

He shrugged helplessly.

Darak surrendered to the forest and turned north.

The Holly-Lord heard the whispers racing through the trees, although he knew the others heard only the rustle of branches. There was no triumph in the sound. The forest did not know that emotion; it only knew the rightness of their new path, just as it had known that their attempt to travel toward the hidden place the others called the Summerlands had been not-right.

Always before, the journey had passed so quickly. After the cold-time battle—winter, they called it winter—there was a rush of air and darkness and always the presence of his Maker, shielding his fragile spirit until he was safe in the ice cavern at the heart of the Mountain. While he rested and grew strong, he maintained his connection to the Holly, existing in both places at once. He could never explain that in words, not even to Struath who trusted him.

Darak clearly did not. He often caught the big man studying him, deep furrows between his eye wings. Eyebrows. He was glad Darak led the way; the feel of those eyes had made unpleasant shivers run up and down his back.

They all treated him differently now. He missed Struath holding his face and Yeorna clasping his hand and Griane's gentle fingers pushing the hair off his forehead. He had known touch in his other life—the brush of leaves, the scratch of a bird's claws on his branch—but leaves and claws held far less power than human hands. While he regretted the lost pleasure of physical touch, his daily struggle to reach the other trees with his spirit left him trembling with exhaustion.

Worst of all, his connection to the Holly grew weaker
with each step away from the grove.

That made the boy's heart tattoo beat very fast. He
knew the Tree had been hurt. He knew it was not-
right for him to be separated from it, just as it was
not-right for him to go to the Oak's resting place. But
somehow, he must convince the forest to allow them
to pass, to recognize that as long as the Oak was lost,
nothing was right in the world.

Despite his reluctance to leave his folk unprotected,
Darak took to ranging ahead to scout for shelter and
bait springpole snares with bits of suetcake. He knew
he risked exhausting his reserves of strength, but his
folk needed more than a few squirrels or wood pigeons each day to maintain the relentless pace he set.
And as long as the wolf trailed them, they must maintain it.

The first time the trail turned east, he exulted in
the belief that the forest was relenting. After several
days of winding east, then circling northwest, he realized it was simply choosing the easiest route for them,
as if it understood the limits of human endurance.

Oak and ash gave way to spruce and pine. The air
felt noticeably colder and the frost-covered compost
crunched underfoot where before it had felt soft and
spongy. Game grew scarcer; some evenings, he returned with only two or three squirrels to share among
five people. After one bone-chilling night when their
fire was reduced to mere embers, they began collecting
deadwood as they hiked and ripping up golden clumps
of deer's hair that grew beside the trail.

None of his folk complained. Not Struath when Griane bandaged his blistered, bleeding feet. Not Yeorna
when she tumbled down a slope. Not Griane who was
always digging into her magic bag for a mortar and
pestle to smash icicles for water, for pouches of roots

and bark to brew a lukewarm tea, for ointments to bring the feeling back into numb fingers and toes. As for the Holly-Lord, he grew more silent every day.

Their battles were less glorious than those of legend, in which heroes slew shape-shifters with lightning bolts and wrestled three-headed demons unleashed by Chaos. But they were just as valiant as Struath dragging deadwood to camp when he could hardly stand or Yeorna and Griane working halfway through the nights to fashion mittens and socks from Tinnean's robe. With her supply of nettle-cloths dwindling, Griane cut up her doeskin skirt for bandages and wore Tinnean's spare breeches.

They fought the triple nemesis of cold and hunger and exhaustion—and their enemies were winning. Each day, the trail grew steeper, the wind crueler. Each night, Darak fell asleep, worrying how he would keep his folk alive.

Then one morning, he rounded a bend in the trail to find sunlight streaming through a break in the trees. He raced ahead, drawing up short when he burst into the open.

The rolling highlands seemed to stretch on forever, as limitless as the sky crouching over them. Earth and sky seemed to have changed places, transporting him to a boundless wilderness of clouds: undulating gray hills, vast purple plains, and towering ranges of silver-white mountains.

Shaking off the sky's spell, he skirted the stunted firs to pick his way over a lichen-covered ledge of rock. Bracing himself against the wind's ferocity, he peered down.

He blinked, afraid his eyes had misled him. After so many days in the forest, the watery sunlight made them tear. When he saw another flash of white at the bottom of the gorge, he threw back his head and gave a hoarse bellow of triumph.

"Have you gone mad?" Griane's breath steamed in great puffs as she drew up to him. He pulled her into his arms and kissed her hard. She shoved him away, gasping. "Merciful Maker, you have."

"Nay, girl. Look." He pointed at the foaming water tumbling through the rocks below.

"Is it . . . could it be the river that leads to the Summerlands?"

"I don't know." The legends said the Summerlands floated between two rivers carved from the earth by the Maker's tears. This one looked like an ordinary mountain stream, but it did wind south through a sea of evergreens. "No more melting icicles for water, girl."

"And no more stringy squirrels. Not that they weren't delicious," she added with a quick glance at him. "But fish . . ." She breathed the words with prayerful reverence, then frowned, gnawing at her upper lip. "It's awful steep, Darak."

"I'll make it down."

"Getting back up is the trick."

"I'll make it."

He grinned at her and she rolled her eyes. "Just don't break your neck. I've nothing in my magic bag to cure that."

Darak turned to call to the others, but the words died when he saw the Holly-Lord gazing north, his body rigid. Following the direction of his gaze, Darak understood why.

The edge of the gorge had seemed like the top of the world. Now he realized that the top of the world was that distant peak of snow and ice and stone, so high that wind-driven clouds obscured the summit. The morning sun tinged the snow on its upper slopes gold, while violet shadows clung to its flanks. It was as beautiful as it was terrifying.

The Holly-Lord smiled. He took a step toward the

mountain. Yeorna plucked at his mantle. When he ignored her and took another step, Darak seized his arm and swung him around. "You can't go there."

"I must."

"Do you want to find the Oak-Lord?"

"Aye, Darak."

"Well, you won't if you freeze to death."

"But the forest—"

"Damn the forest. You're not going there."

"It is where I belong."

"But not where my brother's body belongs. And as long as you've got it, I won't let you do anything to harm it. Do you understand me?"

The Holly-Lord stared up at him, his eyes as soft and pleading as Tinnean's that last morning. He banished the thought and stepped closer. "Do you understand?"

The Holly-Lord bowed his head. "I understand, Darak."

He whirled around. As one, the others backed away from him, even Griane with whom he'd been laughing only moments before. He stalked back to the gorge and stared at the endless expanse of trees.

"Do you want us to die?" he whispered. "Who will find the Oak-Lord then?"

A thin, dry cough tore at his lungs. He wiped the blood from his lips and raised his voice. "Hear me, forest. I am Darak, son of Reinek and Cluran. I am Darak the Hunter. I am Darak, who was given fire by the Trickster God himself. And I say it is enough. I won't allow it. Do you hear me? These are my folk and I will not allow it."

The coughing took him again, worse this time. He bent over, clutching his chest until the spasms stopped. Blood flecked the wind-scoured rocks at his feet. On his hands and knees, he crawled to the very edge of the precipice and hawked a bloody gob of phlegm at the evergreens far below. "My oath. With blood and water, I seal it."

A hard knot of pain swelled inside his chest. Perhaps his Mountain knew. Perhaps that was why the clouds on its summit roiled like his belly and turned as gray and forbidding as Darak's eyes.

A hot flush suffused his body and quickly ebbed. Was this what it meant to be human? These sickening, blood-pounding changes? If all men experienced this drain of energy, he could understand why they lived such short lives.

Darak made him lead the way south along the edge of the gorge. All that day, he felt those storm-cloud eyes on his back, just as he could feel his Mountain's presence through the earth. A deeper thrum than the trees, it felt like the echo of thunder beneath his feet. With each step, it faded, just as his connection to the trees was fading. They made no effort to stop their journey south. He wanted to believe that they had heard Darak's oath or had grown too sluggish to fight, but he feared they no longer recognized him.

He lagged behind the others to rest his hand against the low-hanging bough of a fir. Panic seized him when he felt no response to his questing energy. He closed his eyes, desperately seeking a connection. Long moments passed before he felt a faint answering thrum, followed by a stab of pain in his palm.

He snatched his hand back. The tip of a thorn poked through his woolen mitten. Dazed, he looked about him, searching for a bramble bush or a quickthorn. Finally, he yanked the mitten off.

He carefully sucked the blood away as Darak had taught him and stared down at his hand. Sharp and beautiful and achingly familiar, the slender, green spike of a holly leaf sprouted from the boy's palm.

He heard Darak shouting, saw Griane turn and trot back to him. Quickly, he severed the thorn with his teeth and pulled the mitten on again. When Griane saw him shivering, she pulled his mantle closer and scolded him for letting himself get chilled. Then she smiled and patted his cheek. For the first time, neither her smile nor her touch gave him comfort.

Chapter 16

DARAK'S SATISFACTION at defeating the trees soon leached away. It took most of the day to reach the stream and by then, the gushing torrent he had seen from the precipice had dwindled to a leaf-clogged creek. Evergreens gave way to stands of sedge and high bush blueberries, barren of fruit. When he caught the overwhelming scent of peat, his shoulders sagged. He shoved his way through the sedge, only to draw up short.

If he were a god, he could have dropped their entire valley into the bog and still had room to spare. Hummocks of sphagnum moss sealed off most of it, but the frozen line of the creek ran through the middle. Here and there, a dead tree rose above the surface, leaning drunkenly toward the shore.

"It's not so big," Griane said, with a defiant tilt of her chin that made him smile.

"It's big enough."

"Can we cross?" Yeorna asked. "Or should we go around?"

Lose your footing on the slick hummocks and you'd plunge into the slurry of peat and icy water beneath. Yet going around would cost them half a day, maybe more. The prospect of slogging through the tangled underbrush only made the bog more tempting. Besides, no wolf in the world would attempt to cross that shifting surface. If they managed it, they would increase the distance between them, maybe even lose the beast altogether.

Darak muttered a curse. Where was the damn wolf? Ever since Struath's vision, he'd been looking over his shoulder. It had picked up their trail. It could certainly outdistance them. By now, it had to be close. What was it waiting for?

He forced his mind to return to the problem at hand. Hoping he was making the right choice, he dropped his hunting sack and handed his bow and quiver to Griane. "I'll try it. If I make it through, I'll come back and lead you across."

"And if you don't make it through?" she asked.

"I'll get wet."

"You'll catch your death."

"You're the one who said it wasn't so big."

"It's big enough."

"It's not the first bog I've crossed, Griane."

"Fine. Go. Serve you right if you fall in and lose your toes to frostbite."

His exasperated sigh earned him an offended sniff.

He pulled the precious fire bundle from his belt and handed it to Struath before shrugging off his mantle. As an afterthought, he removed his bearskin shoes as well; if they got wet, it would take them days to dry.

Carefully, he tested the closest hummock. The frost-hardened grass crunched beneath his toes, but it seemed sturdy enough. Judging from the line on his spear, the water was only ankle-deep. As long as they stayed close to shore, they could avoid the soggier masses in the middle.

He felt slightly ridiculous, leaping from hummock to hummock like a child playing hop-frog. Griane would probably tease him about his awkwardness, but better to be dry than graceful.

He glanced over his shoulder, checking his progress. More than a dozen hummocks so far. At least three times that many to reach the far side. A tangle of sedge and laurel hid the others from sight, so he shouted out that he was fine.

He was gathering himself for another leap when he felt something, like and unlike the gaze of the Watchers. A quick glance around the bog showed nothing unusual, but the sensation lingered. Then he heard the high-pitched whining. He was still trying to figure out how mosquitoes could be here in the middle of winter when the hummock shuddered.

He gripped the spear, steadying himself. The whine crescendoed to a painful shrill. The rest of the bog was utterly still. Whatever had awakened lay directly beneath him. He glanced down and caught his breath. Between his bare feet, the hummock had grown opaque.

Before he could move, the hummock lurched. He clung to his spear, fighting for balance. The crusty surface split open, spewing cold muck over his feet. The sickly sweet odor of rotting meat assailed him and he fought back the urge to retch.

A fissure snaked between his feet. Ghastly green light spilled out. Two tiny lights flickered. Stars, he thought. Stars shining in the depths of the bog. Then the stars blinked.

He froze, his mind denying what his senses told him. Even when he made out a nose and a mouth and a wild tangle of hair, he couldn't move. The creature—man? demon?—stared back at him. Its mouth opened, rounded with surprise. A hand reached up.

That broke the spell. He tugged at his spear, but the muck held it fast. Translucent fingers groped for him, the brown water of the bog clearly visible through them. With an oath, he wrenched his spear free. Clods of mud and peat showered him. He twisted the spear and brought it arcing downward. The hand remained upraised as he sliced through air.

The apparition's mouth moved, but Darak didn't wait to hear its words. He thrust the shaft of the spear through the quaking bog, then reared back and vaulted toward another hummock. The slick mound disintegrated, plunging him into the muck. The shock of the freezing water made him gasp. He staggered to his feet, tugging at his spear.

A head rose out of the fissure. Two hands grasped the edge of the hummock. His spear burst free of the bog and he reeled backward, cursing as his ankle twisted. Ignoring the pain, he planted his feet and drew the spear back.

If not for the otherworldly translucency of its flesh, it might have been an ordinary man kneeling at the edge of the fissure, dressed in what appeared to be an ordinary tunic. Even as it raised its arms skyward, its hands dissolved. Then the arms. Its face shattered into a shower of green mist. The headless torso swayed, eddying around the disembodied legs that still knelt as if in prayer. Then, they too, vanished.

The shrill whine ceased. The hummock settled with an obscene belch. In a moment, the bog was as still as ever.

Discovering his arm still poised to hurl the spear, he let it fall to his side, only to raise it again when he heard a crash in the underbrush behind him. He was still struggling to turn in the imprisoning muck when Griane shoved her way through the sedge, her face as wild as her hair.

"Darak? Are you all right?"

Unable to trust his voice, he nodded and waded toward shore, sinking ankle-deep into mud that only reluctantly released him for his next step. Heedless of

the slime dripping from his fingers, Griane seized his
hand and pulled him to shore. Her arms went around
him, skinny and strong and warm.

A wave of shivering racked him. She whipped off
her mantle to wipe his hands.

"Do you have a pair of spare breeches in your
pack?"

Looking down, he realized he was soaked to the
thighs. He nodded toward the wolfskin bundle she had
dropped at his feet.

"Take off your breeches."

"Griane . . ."

"Do as I say."

When he fumbled with the knotted thong, she
asked, "Are your fingers numb?"

"Nay. But my feet are."

In the end, he had to let her peel off the breeches.
She knelt beside him, wiping his legs clean and steadying him as he pulled the new pair on. At her command, he sat and let her dry his feet.

"How long were you in the bog?"

The skin looked very white. Frostnip, probably. Too
soon for frostbite.

"Darak?"

"Not long."

"A count of ten? A count of fifty?"

"Less than fifty."

She pressed his big toe very gently. "Did you feel
that?"

"Nay."

"It gives. Still soft inside." She slid his shoes on.
With the same strange detachment, he noted that his
toes were too numb to feel the fur inside. "I don't
want to rewarm your feet now."

He nodded. If the sensitive flesh thawed and re-
froze, it would be even worse.

They both looked up when they heard the others

calling. Griane shouted back. Moments later, they emerged from the underbrush. "What happened?" Struath asked. "We heard the whining . . ."

"Later, Tree-Father." Griane's voice, though respectful, was firm. "We must find a place to camp."

Darak rose and pulled her to her feet. She clung to his hand for a moment, darting a quick glance back at the bog. "I think we should go around."

Through his chattering teeth, he managed a shaky laugh.

Long after they disappeared, Morgath crouched in the thicket of sedge. It had taken all his willpower to keep from bolting when the portal opened. He had conquered the wolf's terror and watched in horrified fascination as the spirit vanished like mist before the sun.

That fate might have been his. His body trembled as he recalled those first moments after emerging from the portal, triumph giving way to helpless terror and then to the wild desperation that had led him to fling his power at the first creature he encountered.

Now he reminded himself that he was Morgath, the most powerful shaman in the world. If the owl had not flown past, he could have taken one of the priests in the grove. He controlled his fate, not chance or luck or the Trickster God.

He whined softly. He must guard his thoughts. The Trickster knew everything, heard everything. If he offended the god, no den was secret enough to hide him. And the Trickster's moods changed quickly. He had removed the Hunter's feathered stick—what was it called?—only to allow the Betrayer to escape, yipping delightedly when his jaws snapped shut on empty air.

The frustration and rage he had experienced at that moment surpassed even that of his first sunset in the glade of the heart-oak. Haunches quivering, he awaited the Betrayer's return. Instead, the thickset man had staggered into the clearing alone, so drained from the passage that he managed only a few steps before collapsing. Still he waited, anticipation changing to disbelief and finally to unreasoning fury when he realized that neither the Hunter nor the Betrayer would follow.

After that, there was only the overwhelming need to kill. He gathered himself for the leap, anticipating that soft flesh between his jaws, the snap of the neck, the first hot gush of blood flooding his mouth. He exploded from the thicket, crossing the distance between them in four bounds. He had only a few heartbeats to glimpse the terrified eyes, the mouth open in a silent scream. Then he heard the shout.

He skidded to a halt as the men poured into the clearing. Thwarted, he could only flee, dodging more of the feathered sticks that hissed past his flattened ears. Only later, under cover of darkness, did he follow the trail to their dens. Their huts.

From the shadow of the trees, he stared at the place where he had been born and felt only loathing. The night breeze carried the aroma of peat smoke and the far more enticing scent of sheep, but when he slunk closer, the furious barking of dogs sent him racing back to the protection of the forest.

Three sunrises he waited, too restless to sleep, too anxious to hunt, haunted by the fear that the Betrayer had escaped him. When he crossed at sunset and picked up the old man's faint but musty scent, he whimpered with relief.

It was easy to follow their wandering trail. The wolf's thick pelt protected him from the cold, its strong legs let him lope for miles. The humans moved slowly, allowing him ample time to hunt and to anticipate the pleasure of the kill.

The Hunter first. Then he would pick off the others one at a time until only the Betrayer remained. Post-

poning pleasure made it all the sweeter. He wondered
if his little apprentice remembered that lesson.

Arrow. That was the name of the feathered stick.

With a final glance at the bog, Morgath rose and
trotted after his prey.

Chapter 17

WHEN GRIANE ANNOUNCED they were making camp in the lea of an embankment, Darak protested that he could go on. For answer, she spread a wolfskin and shoved him onto it, then proceeded to order the others about with a brusqueness that would have made Mother Netal proud. Even before Struath got the fire started, she was kneeling beside him to remove his shoe. She peered at his foot, then yanked her tunic out of her belt. "Lie back."

"Couldn't you just breathe on it? Or put them in warm water?"

"Hush."

He subsided with a sigh. She grabbed him by the ankle and thrust his foot under her tunic, yelping when his cold flesh touched her armpit.

"Sure you don't want to breathe on it?"

"Grain-Mother, would you please brew some tea? You'll find a pouch of elderflowers and dandelion root in my bag. Holly-Lord, please take off Darak's other shoe and put his foot under your arm."

Without adequate water or bowls big enough for his feet, it was the best way to treat frostnip, but he still felt like a damned fool lying there with his feet stuck under their armpits. The numbness gave way to painful tingling, like someone was sticking dozens of hot needles in his feet. With the return of feeling, he became uncomfortably aware of the swell of Griane's small breast. He yanked his foot away and promptly tangled it in her tunic. New needles of pain shot through it.

Griane freed his foot and peered at it. "Oh, lovely. Nice and red," she said, with the same ghoulish delight Mother Netal always showed at scabs, crusted sores, and other evidence of healing. She examined his other foot and nodded. "I don't think the skin will blister, but it will probably peel over the next few days."

"You should enjoy that."

"Oh, aye." She wrapped his toes lightly in nettle-cloth before slipping on his shoes. Only when she had settled him by the fire with a cup of herb tea cradled between his hands did she permit Struath to question him. Enough time had passed that he could relate what he had seen without emotion, but the expressions of the others rekindled his dread.

"Describe the creature again," Struath said.

"I told you. It looked like a man."

"A young man? An old one?"

"A green one. Damn it, Struath, it happened so fast."

"With such powers of observation, it's little wonder you're the best hunter in the tribe."

Darak took in a deep breath and let it out slowly. "A man of middle years, I'd say. Long hair. Unbraided. No tattoos that I could see."

"And his expression? Did he seem angry? Terrified?"

Darak frowned, considering. "Surprised. Shocked, even. To see me staring down at him. I thought . . . when he reached up, I thought he meant to attack me, but now . . ."

"What?"

"When he looked at me, before he . . . dissolved . . . I could swear he smiled. Not a wicked smile or a triumphant one, like you'd expect from a demon. But . . . joyful." He shook his head. "Perhaps I'm remembering it wrong."

Struath just stared into the fire as if willing the apparition to reappear and explain itself.

"You've never seen anything like it before?" Darak asked.

"Nay," Yeorna replied. "But that awful whining . . ." Her voice dropped to a whisper. "We heard it the night of the Midwinter battle."

Griane gave a little gasp. "You mean the thing Darak saw in the bog . . . he attacked the One Tree?"

Struath shook his head. "But perhaps it was someone like that."

"Talk straight, Struath."

"I cannot be sure," Struath said. "But I think what we saw the night of the battle—and what you saw today—was a portal."

"A portal to what?"

"Chaos."

Even as he spoke, Struath's fingers moved in the sign to avert evil. Darak found his hand creeping up his chest to clutch his bag of charms. Like every child, he had listened, horrified and enthralled, as Old Sim described how the Lord of Chaos opened gateways into other worlds, allowing his creatures out to wreak havoc, pulling unsuspecting people into his shadowy realm. He'd had nightmares for a moon and his mam had forbidden the Memory-Keeper ever to tell such stories in her hut again. Bad enough to hear the tale, sitting safe beside the fire. Far worse to see an otherworldly hand reaching for you.

"I should have realized," Struath said. "After the battle. But it was only when I heard the sound again . . ." The shaman's shoulders slumped. "Who else would wish to disrupt the turning of the seasons if not the Unmaker?"

"You mean the Lord of Chaos is here?" Griane's voice was very small. "In the First Forest?"

"Nay, child. But it might explain the wolf."

"The wolf was no spirit, Struath. I wounded it. I saw the blood."

It was Yeorna who answered. "There is much we don't understand. The wolf. The Trickster. And now this portal. Somehow they are all linked to what happened in the grove."

Darak took a deep, shaking breath. "If what you saw during the battle was a portal, then Tinnean and the Oak . . ."

Struath finished his unspoken thought. "Their spirits might have been drawn into Chaos."

Darak's fingers tightened convulsively around the bag of charms. The Summerlands at least offered the hope of light and warmth and safety, but if his brother had been dragged into Chaos . . .

Yeorna touched his arm. "We can't be certain, Darak. They might have already fled." Her eyes pleaded with him not to lose hope. Struath's bleak expression offered no such comfort.

"Please," the Holly-Lord said. "I do not understand. What is this Chaos?"

Yeorna glanced at Struath, but he was staring into the fire. "Chaos is the beginning and the end, Holly-Lord. The place out of which all life arose and the place where some spirits go after . . . at the end of life."

"Why do they go there?"

"Some spirits lose their way to the Forever Isles. Some are unwilling to go to the Blessed Isles of Rebirth because they cannot let go of mortal concerns. Others are condemned to Chaos because of their evil deeds and some—those who are torn from their bodies like the Oak and Tinnean . . ."

Her voice faltered.

"They go to Chaos, too. I see."

The Holly-Lord's voice was calm, his expression thoughtful but undisturbed. Fury welled up in Darak so suddenly that he shook with the effort to control it. Reminding himself that the Holly-Lord could not feel emotions as they did only made him think about the terror Tinnean must have felt in the grove, the terror he might be experiencing now.

"Struath?"

The shaman turned on him, suddenly fierce. "I don't know, Darak!"

Then what good are you, he wanted to shout. He bit back the words, but even with one eye, Struath could read his face. The shaman flushed and looked away.

"The Tree-Father will seek his spirit guide," Yeorna said, "and on the morrow, we will seek the gods' guidance as well. Then we will know what to do."

Somehow, Yeorna's quiet confidence was worse than the Holly-Lord's serenity. Awkwardly, Darak rose, ignoring the stabbing pains in his feet.

"What do you think you're doing?" Griane asked.

"I'm going to set some snares."

"You are not."

"Griane . . ."

"You need to stay off your feet. If your toes freeze again—"

"I must do something!"

The sympathy in her eyes nearly unmanned him. Without a word, she handed him his hunting sack. On impulse, he touched her cheek, then hobbled away from the fire.

Fear is the enemy.

He would not think about the face of the man he

saw emerging from the bog. He would not consider the horrors he must have faced in Chaos that would make him joyful simply to cease existing. He would not think about Tinnean's spirit trapped in such a place.

Control the fear.

He concentrated on taking one slow step after another. He scanned the ground for tracks and other game signs. He bent a sapling to set a spring snare, then crouched down to set a deadfall under a slab of rock. Only when he had finished did his hands start to shake.

Control yourself.

He knelt on the forest floor until the shaking stopped and the knot of pain in his chest receded. He rose, noting with dull surprise that twilight had fallen. He had lingered too long. The others would be worried.

He turned toward camp and froze as the hairs on the back of his neck rose. Not the Watchers or the opening of another portal. This sensation he knew even better. A predator lurked in the shadows, one menacing enough to cause the forest to go utterly silent.

In his haste to escape the others, he had ventured out with only his dagger. He drew it now, turning in a slow circle to scan the shadowy underbrush. A light flickered among the trees. Torchlight, he realized. Griane called his name.

He ran toward the light, shouting at her to get back. Twigs snapped behind him. He whirled around as one of the shadows leaped. Hurling himself to the left, he stabbed blindly and felt his dagger rip through skin and flesh. Fur brushed his wrist. A sharp yelp mingled with Griane's scream, the tang of blood with a rank animal scent. He rolled, cursing as his mantle twisted around his arm.

Suddenly, there was light everywhere—red, blue, green, silver. A spiderweb of light and color surrounding him. Surrounding Griane, who loomed over him, waving her torch and screaming curses. Surrounding Yeorna and Struath who stood with their hands upraised, chanting, as light streamed from their fingertips.

He staggered to his feet. The cacophony of snapping branches grew steadily fainter. He seized Griane's arm and pulled her toward camp. The spiderweb followed them as Struath and Yeorna slowly retreated, guarding their flanks. Only when they had both collapsed by the fire did Struath nod. Yeorna ceased chanting and lowered her arms. The spiderweb flickered but grew bright again as Struath spread his hands, sending the wards out in a semicircle from the embankment. The shaman stopped chanting and slowly sank to the ground.

Griane shook in the shelter of his arm. "Are you hurt, girl?"

"Nay." Her teeth chattered. Shock, then. "You?"

Only now did he note the pain and feel the warm trickle of blood. "My arm."

Silently, the Holly-Lord held out her magic bag. When she just stared into the darkness, he pulled out a roll of bandages. "Griane? Darak is hurt. He needs you."

Those words seemed to reach her. She twisted out of his grasp and peeled back the shredded sleeve of his tunic.

"What was it?" Yeorna's voice sounded ragged, either from the magic or the shock of the attack.

"I think . . . it had to be the wolf."

The wards trembled. Struath made a small gesture with his fingers and they shone as brightly as ever, illuminating the bloody claw marks that gouged Darak's arm from wrist to elbow.

"My fault. I shouldn't have left camp unarmed."

"Hush. Pour some water in the bowl, Holly-Lord."

No one spoke as Griane cleaned and bandaged his

arm. Even after she finished, they just sat there, staring into the fire. Finally, Struath broke the silence.

"Grain-Mother, I will take the first watch."

"You need to save your strength—"

"I will wake you when I need rest so that you can maintain the wards."

"Aye, Tree-Father."

"Darak, do we have enough fuel for the night?"

"Aye. I can take a turn—"

"You will need your strength for the morrow. We'll have to find a better shelter. One that is more easily guarded."

"Aye, Tree-Father."

"I will feed the fire," the Holly-Lord said.

They all stared at him. The Holly-Lord gathered leaves for their bedding, he helped carry the supplies, but he could not even bring himself to gather deadwood. He tried to smile, but his face twisted into a helpless grimace of distaste as he eyed the flames.

"I thank you, Holly-Lord, but I can tend the fire." Despite the gentleness of Struath's voice, the Holly-Lord's shoulders slumped. "But perhaps you could sit with me while I keep watch and brew some tea to help me stay awake."

Darak leaned against the embankment and closed his eyes, unwilling to witness the Holly-Lord's eager gratitude. He opened them again when he felt Griane shudder. Ignoring the pain, he eased his arm around her.

"What were you thinking, charging out there like that?"

"I wasn't thinking. I was too scared for you."

"Aye. Well. It was bravely done." He closed his eyes. "And if you ever do it again, I'll wallop you."

She poked him in the ribs. He tugged her braid. Her head plunked down on his shoulder. She was all bony elbows and sharp shoulder blades and jutting knees. He might have been cradling a rack of antlers. Darak pulled her closer.

Strange, the comfort of holding her, sharing her warmth, feeling the gentle rise and fall of her chest. He had almost forgotten what it was like, the feel of a woman's body next to his in the night. His throat tightened.

Please gods, don't let me dream of Maili tonight.

Chapter 18

THE HOLLY-LORD flinched as Struath cut open the throat of the dead rabbit. Yeorna said its blood would appease the gods. He smeared acorn oil on his shoes. Darak said this would disguise his scent. He ate Griane's brose, so watery that the grains floated in the bowl. She said it was not fit for a human to eat, but he sipped his portion gratefully; perhaps it made a difference that he was not really human.

No one spoke of the wolf, but all that morning, Struath and Yeorna kept the pretty spiderweb glowing around them, Darak ceaselessly scanned the trees, and Griane gave a little squeak each time a twig snapped.

He tried to watch the trees as Darak did, but by midday, it took all his concentration simply to make his feet take another step. As the shadows grew longer, he heard a dull roaring in his ears. He was still wondering what could have caused it when Darak came to an abrupt halt, frowning.

Peering over Struath's shoulder, the Holly-Lord frowned, too. The ground fell away sharply to a narrow ledge. Below it, gnarled shrubs gave way to alders and birch. Lower still, he made out a green-white torrent of water. Belatedly, he realized this was the roaring he had heard.

"Can you make it?" Darak asked Struath.

"Aye."

Struath always said that, no matter how many times he fell, no matter how badly he limped. Once, he had believed that men, unlike trees, grew weaker with age. After so many days of observing Struath, he was no longer so sure.

Darak's frown deepened. "It might not be so steep farther south."

"It will be dark by then."

And darkness brought the wolf.

He studied the sheer drop. Perhaps a squirrel could climb down those rocks, but a wolf could not. He doubted that a man could either, but Darak and Struath were nodding, so it seemed they were going to try.

Darak removed the coiled snake called rope from his hunting sack. He tied one end around his waist, then looped another section around Struath's. "Tie Yeorna to you. Griane, you tie the Holly-Lord on next."

When they were done, the rope stretched out between each of them almost two man lengths. Darak inspected each knot, nearly pulling him off his feet when he jerked on the rope.

"Watch the person before you. Follow the same path down. Take off your mittens so you can get a better grip. We'll each take a turn resting on that ledge there. If you need to stop for any other reason, call out."

Darak lowered himself over the side. He might have been a marmot, so quickly did he scramble down the rocks. The Holly-Lord let out his breath. Perhaps it would not be so difficult, after all. When Darak reached the ledge, he shouted up to Struath who tossed down the spear and then his staff. Yeorna murmured a prayer as he descended, smiling weakly as he reached safety.

"I'm going on," Darak called. "Wait until the person behind you reaches the ledge, then continue down."

Once Yeorna was safe, the Holly-Lord removed his mittens and tucked them in his belt; Griane would yip at him if he lost one. Crouching down, he wrapped his hands around the trunk of a sprawling bearberry willow, reminding himself that he must be as strong and brave as the others. Still, it took all his willpower to ignore his shaking legs and his fluttering belly and lower himself over the edge.

For one terrifying instant, he hung in the air, clinging to the shrub's slender trunk. His right foot finally found a small crevice in the rock; his left slid into another. His heart tattoo pounded so fiercely, he thought his chest would burst. He was still waiting for it to ease when his fingers slipped.

Cold hands grasped his wrists. "I've got you," Griane said. "Just slide your fingers down the trunk a little. That's better. Are you all right?"

He nodded.

"Look at me." She lay belly-down at the top of the slope, frowning down at him. "You can do this. Say it."

"I can do this."

"Just pretend you're a squirrel."

He considered reminding her that squirrels faced the ground when they climbed down tree trunks, but her face pleaded with him to agree with her, so he nodded again. Below him, Yeorna called, "Holly-Lord? Can you make it?"

He glanced down. The world began to wobble and spin. Griane's fingers tightened on his wrists. "Don't look down. Remember how Yeorna went. Feel your way with your hands and feet."

"Aye, Griane."

She squeezed his wrists hard and released him. Balancing on his toes, he bent his knees. His cheek scraped rock as he reached for a thick tuft of grass sprouting from a narrow crack. Afraid to turn his head, his fingers scrabbled over the rock, searching blindly for a new handhold on the left. Then he had to move his feet again. The damp grass slid through his fingers, rough blades slicing his palm. His right foot brushed a narrow ridge of stone. He eased his left foot down. By balancing on his toes, he could ease the strain in his arms. Resting his cheek against the rock, he let out his breath.

He had counted each of Yeorna's steps on his fingers the way Griane had taught him. It had taken Yeorna eight fingers to reach the ledge; so far, he had only managed two.

From far below, Darak's voice floated up to him. "What's taking so long?"

"Shut up," Griane yelled. In a softer tone, she added, "Don't pay any attention to him, Holly-Lord. You're doing fine."

Six more fingers, he told himself. He counted off each one on that long journey down the rocks, until finally, he lowered himself onto the ledge next to Yeorna. Her firm hands steadied him until his legs stopped shaking.

"You wait here for Griane, Holly-Lord."

"Aye, Yeorna."

"Don't worry. We'll all be at the river soon."

"I hope so."

He watched Griane skitter down the cliff face, as nimble as the squirrel she had wanted him to pretend to be. Before his heart had stopped thudding, she was next to him.

"There. That wasn't so bad." She actually took her hands off the rocks to hug him. She was amazing. "The next part will be easier. Truly."

"Aye, Griane."

"We'll go together. Just turn around and swing your legs over the ledge. Like this." He gasped as she spun around and plopped down on the ledge, legs dangling in the air. "Lean on my shoulder. That's it. Now just crouch down. A little more. Good."

He collapsed beside her, breathing hard.

"Now we'll just slip over the side. It's not far. And think how good it will feel to have the ground beneath your feet again."

He nodded. So long rooted in the soil, he could imagine nothing worse than hanging in the air. Then he heard Yeorna scream.

Darak whirled around to glimpse Yeorna careening through the trees. He heard another cry as Struath was jerked off his feet. Throwing one arm around a pine, he flung out his hand, shouting Struath's name. The shaman's fingers brushed his as he slid past.

He barely had time to brace himself before the rope snapped taut, wrenching his back and nearly tearing his arm from its socket. Ignoring the pain, he lunged for Yeorna, only to watch her tumble past, still screaming. Scrabbling through wet pine needles and leaves, he dove for the rope. It burned through his hands, then went limp as Yeorna collided with a birch.

At first he thought she was still screaming, then realized it was Griane. He threw his body in front of her. Her feet caught him in the ribs, sending them both sliding down the hill. Somehow he managed to keep his grip on the rope even as something struck him in the eye. Half-blinded, he hung on, grunting as another violent tug tore at his shoulders and twisted him to a sudden stop.

For a moment, he could only lie there. Pain shot through his side with every breath. He pushed himself

to his knees and bent over Griane. Her eyes held that
faraway look he'd seen in dying men, but when she
sat up, he realized it was only the expression a healer
gets when diagnosing a patient. "I'm fine. A bit sore,
is all. Help me up."

She caught his wince. Before she could ask, he said,
"It'll wait."

He untied the rope and threw off his hunting sack,
grimacing at the fresh stab of pain. As he approached
Yeorna, she gave him a weary smile and waved him
toward Struath. The shaman had dragged himself onto
a log. He rocked back and forth in pain. His right
shoulder was hunched and the arm hung at an odd
angle. Careful not to jar the injured shoulder, he eased
Struath's mantle off, glancing up as Griane squatted
beside him.

"Out of joint," she said.

"Jammed my hand into a tree," Struath wheezed.
"Stupid."

"Hush, Tree-Father."

"The Holly-Lord? Is he—?"

"Just bruised. Yeorna's twisted her ankle, but if she
stays off it for few days, she should be fine."

"The gods are kind."

Darak thought it would have been kinder if the gods
had protected them from injury in the first place, but
all he said was, "Do you want to set this now,
Griane?"

"I haven't the strength. You'd best do it."

At Struath's skeptical look, Darak said, "Who do
you think put Nionik's shoulder to rights that time we
were out hunting? The Forest-Lord?"

He took hold of Struath's wrist and lifted his arm.
The shaman had always been slender, but his wrist
was as thin as a child's now. Griane adjusted his grip
on Struath's elbow and moved behind Struath to
brace him.

"This might hurt," he said.

Despite his pain, Struath managed a sour smile. "You're a comfort."

He had to admire the old man. Nionik had been in such pain when he put his shoulder out that he hadn't been able to speak.

"Are you ready?"

"Just get on with—"

Struath broke off as Darak whipped the elbow up and in. Darak gasped at his broken ribs stabbed him. Sweat poured down Struath's face. The arm, which had seemed so light when he lifted it, felt as heavy as stone. Darak was about to give up the effort when the shoulder slid into place with a soft crunch.

Struath stared up at him in amazement. "It doesn't hurt."

"It will. We'll have to strap it for a day or two and after that, you'll need to go slow."

"You are not to move your arm at all until I give you leave," Griane said. "I'll fashion a sling for you, Tree-Father. And Darak, I want to look at your ribs. And your back. Don't gape at me. I can see how you're moving." She rummaged in her magic bag. "And I need to put a compress on that eye. It's already swelling."

He shook his head, staring up the slope. "I shouldn't have risked it."

"We were all willing to risk it," Struath said.

"Still."

"Stop it." Griane glared at him. "Yeorna slipped on some wet leaves. It happens."

"One mistake. That's all it takes." Like a hunter leaving camp without his bow. Or a boy rushing to protect his tribe's sacred tree.

"You cannot foresee every accident."

"I must try."

"People slip, Darak. They twist their ankles. They put their shoulders out. You cannot control it. Any more than you can control a storm. We're alive. Bruised and battered, aye, but alive."

He nodded, too tired to argue. "See to Struath. I'll scout the river for a place to camp."

"Not before I've seen to you."

He captured her hands as they seized the hem of his tunic. "I'll do, girl."

"You'll do what I tell you. Stumbling around like a half-blind bullock. Serve you right if you fell in the river and drowned."

Darak snatched at the air, capturing the words before they reached the ears of the gods. "Last time you said that, I ended up in the bog." Stricken, Griane opened her mouth, looking for all the world like a baby bird waiting to be fed. He opened his fist, keeping his palm flat against her lips until she had swallowed her words.

"I'll be back before dark. I promise."

She brandished the doeskin bandages. "I'll just strap your ribs. That's all."

He surrendered. Some forces of nature were beyond any man's control. Griane was one of them.

Chapter 19

PERHAPS THE GODS heard prayers after all, else he might never have found the cave. Screened by tumbled boulders and brush, it was larger inside than he would have guessed from the narrow cleft in the hillside. It was full dark by the time he got them safely inside. Griane chittered like an angry squirrel when he carried Yeorna up the embankment and his ribs didn't thank him either, but the Grain-Mother was tight-lipped from limping along the riverbank.

The next day, he stayed close to the cave, daring Griane's wrath to help her collect deadwood for the fire and fill their waterskins. He used the rest of his time to tend to his weapons, chipping the flint of his dagger to an even sharper point, restringing his bow, and inspecting every arrow in his quiver. The few blood spatters he'd found after the wolf attack told him the beast's injuries were minor. He might have slowed it down, but if the wolf could find a way out of Chaos, it would surely find their trail.

On the second morning, watching his folk make do with half a suetcake each, he unpacked his fishing gear.

"Nay," Griane said.

"We need food."

"You need to rest."

"Griane . . ."

"Your eye's swollen shut."

"I've got another one."

"And your ribs—"

"Hardly hurt at all."

Her snort told him she didn't believe that lie. "I'm coming with you."

"You need to tend to Yeorna and Struath."

"What if the wolf's about?"

"I'll have my spear."

"I won't have you going alone."

Before he could tell her to hush, the Holly-Lord said, "I will go."

This time, Darak was the one to snort. "You're going to protect me from the wolf?"

"Nay. But I could fish."

"You don't know how to fish."

"You could teach him," Griane said.

He could hardly bear to be in the Holly-Lord's presence. The last thing he wanted was to teach him to fish. "Everyone helps but me," the Holly-Lord said. "Please, Darak. Take me with you."

The breath leaked out of him. The same pleading look, even the same words Tinnean had spoken the first time he had allowed his brother to hunt with him.

They were all watching him now. He rose with a curt nod, waiting impatiently while Griane pulled the Holly-Lord's mantle up around his chin and tied his mittens tightly. He blew out his breath. A moment ago, she'd been fussing at him and now he was acting like some jealous boy because she did the same for the Holly-Lord.

He crawled outside and waited for the Holly-Lord to join him. "Stay here until I signal you. And go slow down the embankment. The pebbles are tricky underfoot."

He chose a spot downstream where the thin brush offered little cover. Although he had yet to spot wolf spoor, there were other predators in the forest. He allowed the Holly-Lord to rummage through his selection of lures. "Nay. Those are duck feathers; they'll only lure lake fish." He held up another, the iridescent blue-green feathers of the daggerbird tied to a tiny piece of quartz. "See how the rock sparkles? That'll attract the fish. And since the daggerbird is a river feeder, its feathers'll ensure a good catch."

The Holly-Lord nodded solemnly, just as Tinnean had so many years ago. He showed him how to bait the bone hooks with bits of suetcake, how to tie on the lures, how to secure the hooks to the line with a bit of sinew, correcting him with a word or a shake of his head. He refused to touch him; it brought back too many memories of guiding Tinnean's grubby fingers as he fumbled with hook and lure. The fingers were just as grubby now, but long and slender. So much more graceful than his. The nails had grown. He found himself missing his brother's bloody hangnails and shook his head.

"Is it wrong?"

He looked up to find the Holly-Lord watching him. "It's fine."

"You shook your head."

"I was . . . it doesn't matter. Now we must ask Lacha, goddess of lakes and rivers, to share her bounty with us."

"What do we say?"

"Lacha, goddess of lakes and rivers, share your bounty with us."

"Oh."

The Holly-Lord dutifully repeated the prayer. Darak tied the line to an alder. "Watch the branch, not the water. If the branch bends, you've caught a fish."

Hefting his spear, he picked his way across the wet rocks to a boulder midstream where the foaming water broke into two smaller streams that created a pool. He breathed another prayer, this one for his brother. It seemed he was always praying these days—for fire, for fish, for Tinnean to be safe.

The Holly-Lord crouched on the riverbank, brows drawn together in concentration as he gazed up at the alder's low-hanging branch. "You needn't stare at it all the time," Darak called. "You'll see it move out of the corner of your eye."

The Holly-Lord nodded. He faced the river, whipping his head around every few moments to stare at the alder. Darak smiled, realized he was smiling, and frowned.

Tinnean had been six or seven the first time he had taken him upriver to fish. Darak had spent most of that time hushing his excited chatter, warning him that he would scare off the fish. Watching the Holly-Lord, so still and silent on the bank, he realized how much he missed that chatter and the good-natured grin that had always followed the scolding.

I scolded him too much. I should have let him be.

His father had always managed to silence him with a frosty stare that told him plainer than any words that he had failed to meet his expectations. Recalling the way his spirit had shriveled under that gray-eyed gaze, he decided a scolding would have been far easier to endure.

A shout from the Holly-Lord interrupted his thoughts. "Darak! A fish. I caught a fish."

His vision blurred. The Holly-Lord's figure became the child, staggering under the weight of a trout, squealing when the tail slapped his belly. He blinked hard and shouted, "Haul the line up."

Hopping from stone to stone, he made his way back to the bank in time to see the fish fly over the Holly-Lord's head. Standing on his toes, he managed to hook his forefinger through the gills while he cut the snagged line. He held it up, marveling at its size. When a shaft of sunlight struck it, he caught the iridescent flash of a rainbow amid the dark speckles on its side.

"It is beautiful."

"Aye." He eased the hook free and tossed the fish onto the bank. "Next time, try not to haul it into the trees."

"Darak."

"What?"

The Holly-Lord pointed at the trout. It flopped on the bank, gills fluttering weakly. "Make it stop."

Darak picked the fish up by the tail and slammed its head on a rock. When he glanced up, he found the Holly-Lord staring at him. "What?"

"You killed it."

The Holly-Lord's horrified expression made his voice harsh. "You've seen the game I've brought to camp."

"Aye."

"Well?"

"It is different. To watch them die. To kill."

"Men hunt. Just like animals. The wolf kills the deer. The owl kills the mouse."

The Holly-Lord nodded, but his face was still troubled. Darak squatted opposite him. "When a wolf kills or an owl, it's neither good nor bad. It's how they survive. We will survive because this fish gives us strength. Can you understand that?"

"Aye, Darak. I understand."

"Good."

"But I do not want to kill again." The Holly-Lord looked away. "I cannot help after all."

Against his will, Darak sympathized. He knew what it was like to feel helpless. "Say a prayer, then."

"To Lacha?"

"To the fish. Thank it for giving up its life for us."

"This is what the wolf does? And the owl?"

"It's what a man does."

"What do I say?"

"Whatever seems right."

The Holly-Lord crouched beside the trout and stroked its gleaming scales. "Fish. I did not want you to be dead. But I thank you for helping us live. Because of you, we will be strong and we will find the Oak." He looked up, a question in his eyes.

Darak nodded and rose; barely midmorning and already he was tired. "Do you want to go back?"

"I will stay. I will say a prayer for the fish you catch."

Chapter 20

BY THE FOURTH DAY in the cave, the Holly-Lord noticed that the ugly colors—bruises, Griane called them—were fading from the boy's body. Yeorna could limp around the cave, but Struath still dozed most of the day. Darak could see out of both eyes now, but his movements were slow and careful. Even so, he always left at first light, returning at day's end with fresh game or fish.

The Holly-Lord no longer asked to accompany him, but the women found tasks for him. Griane showed him how to rub a fish with herbs and bury it in the embers in a little den of clay. Yeorna showed him how to cut off the tails and fins with her dagger and grind them into a magic powder that would save a man from drowning. He had no idea that fish were so useful; he had just thought them beautiful.

He learned many other things during their days together. Caves were damper than huts. Catching fish was easier than mending clothes. Being a female was much harder than being a male.

Yeorna laughed when he told her that. "That just shows how wise you are, Holly-Lord. Women have been telling men that for ages. And men never believe them."

"I do." He pushed the bone needle at the strand of sinew again. Griane took the sinew from him, sucked one end, and poked it through the hole in the needle. She was a wonder.

She could even play the long bone in Darak's pack. Just by blowing into one end and twiddling her fingers over the holes, she made sounds as beautiful as birdsong. When he tried, it sounded like the wheezes Struath made while he slept.

"Blow a little harder, Holly-Lord."

"What is a lord?"

"A lord is like a chief," Yeorna said, which did not explain anything.

Struath grunted as he sat up. "It is a title of respect. To show how important you are to us. Just as I am called Tree-Father."

"What is a father?"

Struath blinked very fast as he did when he was surprised. "A father . . . well, in my case, of course, the word is used to convey respect rather than paternity . . ."

Griane interrupted, her voice brisk. "When a dog fox and a vixen mate, they have kits."

"Aye."

"When a man and a woman mate, they have children. Babies."

"Aye."

"When a woman births children, she is a mother. And the man is called a father."

"Ah." He regarded Struath for a moment. "Do you have many children?"

Struath blinked even faster. This time, Yeorna answered. "Our people call Struath father because he protects us and teaches us. Just as a fox teaches his kits how to survive."

"So you have a name of wiseness—Tree-Father. And a name for yourself. Struath."

"That is right, Holly-Lord."

"Your names are strange to me. When I first saw you—before I knew your other names—I called you One-Eye and Fox-Fur and Fur like Autumn Birch-Leaves."

"Then choose a name that describes you," Griane said.

"I cannot see myself to . . . describe." He repeated that word, savoring the way it made his mouth twist and pucker. "Even if I could, I would describe Tinnean for it is his body that I wear. It does not belong to me."

"The holly tree does not belong to you either," Yeorna said. "But it is part of you. Just as Tinnean's body is part of you for now."

Darak would not like to hear that; Darak would not want any part of Tinnean to be his.

"But I think I understand," Yeorna continued. "You need a name like ours—a name that sets you apart from all others."

He nodded. "Choose one, Griane."

"The Tree-Father would be better. Or the Grain-Mother—"

"You choose."

"Well . . . all right."

"What name is it?"

"Well, I can't come up with something just like that." She snapped her fingers and gave him the look that said a scolding was on the way. "A name's not like threading a needle or gutting a fish, you know. It takes a lot of thought. You don't want to get stuck with something awful just because you rushed me, do you?"

"Nay, Griane."

"You'll just have to be patient. And don't start pestering me about it twenty times a day, either."

"Griane. You are speaking to the Holly-Lord."

She got red in the face when Struath said that and
started apologizing. He did not like it when she
scolded him, but it made him feel that he belonged.
"I will not pester, Griane. My oath." He spat into the
fire just as Darak had spat into the gorge. Griane
looked startled; he wondered if he had done it wrong.
Perhaps spitting into gorges was permitted and spitting
into fire was not. He sighed. There were so many
things to remember, so many things to try and get
right. No wonder Darak frowned so much.

Darak did more than frown when he returned from
hunting and heard the music. He strode around the
fire pit and ripped the flute out of his fingers.

In the silence that followed, only the fire dared to
make a sound, crackling just as it always did. Then
Yeorna, Struath, and Griane all began talking at once.
Darak just stood there, staring down at him. The others always smiled and clapped when he blew into the
flute. He was still trying to guess why Darak was so
angry when his voice rose above theirs.

"You have no right."

That silenced the others again, although the words
made no sense to him.

"Why shouldn't he play the flute?" Yeorna asked.

Darak's voice shook. "Because it was—it is—
Tinnean's."

Now the clenched fists and the narrowed eyes made
sense. He rose, a little afraid that Darak would throw
him to the ground, but the big man just watched him,
breathing like a winded deer. Before he could speak,
Griane shoved between them.

"It's not his fault. I gave him the flute."

"You always find an excuse for him, don't you?
And you." Darak glanced at Struath who was on his
feet as well.

"He is the Holly-Lord. He needs no excuses from me—nor insolence from you."

"Is that what you call it?"

"Do you think it's easy for him?" Hands on hips, Griane scowled up at Darak, fearless as a she-wolf protecting her pups. "Do you think he wants to be here? Far from his home, cold and tired and hungry all the time, not knowing where the Oak-Lord is or whether he's safe."

"I can imagine how that feels."

Griane flinched. When she spoke again, her voice was softer. "I know you can. Better than any of us. So why are you unkind to him?"

A muscle twitched in his jaw. He stared at the dirt.

"He has lost everything, Darak."

His eyes snapped back to hers, the anger burning hotter than ever. "And gained my brother's body."

Struath took his place next to Griane. "That was not his fault."

"How do you know? How do you know he didn't steal it? That he didn't push Tinnean's spirit out so his would be safe? Why are you so willing to trust him?"

"Why are you so willing to doubt? The Tree-Lords have always been our friends. Why should they turn on us now?"

Darak pushed Griane aside. "What happened that night?"

"He's already told you."

"Tell me again."

"Stop bullying him."

Darak seized the front of his tunic and shoved him up against the wall of the cave. The blows Griane rained on his back and arm made him wince, but he ignored Struath's shouts and Yeorna's pleading. Staring up into those glittering eyes, the Holly-Lord wondered if this was how a rabbit felt when a wolf caught it.

"Where is my brother? What happened to him?"
Darak raised his fist and froze.

"Aye, that's my dagger you feel at your back."

He hardly recognized Griane's cold, flat voice.

"You'd defend him? You? Who loved Tinnean?"

"Aye, I will defend him. Just as I defended Tinnean
when you bullied him. And tried to defend Maili when
you brutalized her."

Darak whirled around so fast that Griane stumbled
backward. "Aye, go on. Hit me. That's what you want,
isn't it?"

He gazed at his upraised fist for a long moment
before slowly lowering his hand. "I have never hit a
woman. Including my wife."

Head down and shoulders hunched, Darak stalked
to the cave's entrance. When he knelt down to shove
aside the branches, the Holly-Lord stepped forward.
The last time Darak had walked away from their
camp, the wolf had attacked; he could not let that
happen again.

"The Oak disappeared."

Darak went very still. Slowly, he rose.

"I felt his fear. Not as you feel it. For us, it is . . ."
He tapped his chest. It was so hard with words. "A
shift. A change . . . inside us . . . in the part we all
share. The energy."

Darak nodded; that was good.

"When we are frightened or hurt—if lightning should
strike one of us—the hurt one's energy changes. It grows
fast and loud and shrill. Like the flute."

"Like a scream," Yeorna whispered.

"It was like that when the Oak disappeared. He . . .
screamed. We all felt it. I lost the Holly. I was in a
dark place. Uprooted. And then I felt . . . I think I
felt Tinnean."

"What did you feel?" Darak's voice was low and
hoarse.

"We touched. Not flesh but . . .." Helplessly, he looked up at Darak who kept swallowing as if something had lodged in his throat.

Struath spoke first. "You touched him the way you can touch the other trees?"

"Aye. Like that. I felt him. He screamed like the Oak."

Darak's head jerked back, slamming into the rocks at the top of the cave. He hunched over again, breathing hard, hands fisted at his sides. Without looking up, he said, "Go on."

"I am sor—"

"Go on, damn you."

"The Oak disappeared. Tinnean disappeared. It all happened very fast. I cannot say which happened first. They were just gone. I tried to go back. And then I felt rooted again. I did not understand why until I woke up inside Tinnean's body." He sighed. "I am sorry. I do not tell it right."

Darak raised his head. When the Holly-Lord saw his hard eyes and grim mouth, he knew he must find other words.

"You said I drove out Tinnean's spirit. To . . . steal his body. I think to steal must be a bad thing."

"It means to take something that does not belong to you," Yeorna said.

"Ah. Then I did steal. I did not mean to, but I did." Although he wanted to look away, he forced himself to meet Darak's cold, gray eyes. "But I did not push out his spirit. It was gone. He was . . . empty."

"And that's why you took his body?"

"Any spirit—tree or man—needs a body to shelter it," Struath said. "If it loses one, it must find another or . . . disappear. The Holly-Lord's spirit found Tinnean's body and he clung to it."

Something changed in Darak's face, the softening he rarely saw.

"Are you sure he's gone? Are you sure he's not still inside?"

Struath shook his head. "I would have felt him."

"When Jeok had those fits, you forced the demon out. And Jeok was there."

"You wish me to force the Holly-Lord's spirit out of Tinnean's body?"

"I'm only asking—"

"Tinnean is not here." Darak's head jerked back toward the Holly-Lord. "I would know. But if you want Struath to make the test, I will let him."

"Make the test, Struath."

"Darak—"

"Make the test."

"Nay." Struath's voice was as loud as Darak's. "Do you admit that he is the Holly-Lord?"

"Aye."

"Do you believe that he cast out your brother's spirit and stole his body?"

Darak hesitated, then shook his head.

"And yet you want me to commit this . . . this sacrilege? To force his spirit out? And risk losing it forever?"

"Do you have the power?"

"I don't know. Aye. I think so."

Darak's eyes widened. "You've done it before."

Struath bowed his head. "It was a wren." His voice was little more than a whisper. "A small, brown, beautiful wren. I pushed its spirit out. For a moment, I was the wren. I felt with its body. Saw through its eyes. And then I fled back to my body."

Struath shuddered. After a long time, he raised his head. "The wren died. Such a tiny creature—I could hold it in the palm of my hand. And I killed it. Through pride. Through arrogance. Through my eagerness to test the limits of my knowledge. I vowed I would never commit such a sacrilege again." Slowly,

Struath turned and walked to the back of the cave, his figure lost among the shadows.

When Darak reached for the branches again, the Holly-Lord said, "Please. Do not go. I do not want the wolf to kill you."

He heard Darak's quick intake of breath, but all he said was, "I will not go far, Holly-Lord."

Darak crouched outside the cave, staring into the darkness.

Stupid. Stupid to attack the one person who could help him find Tinnean. The Holly-Lord wasn't his enemy. The wolf, the one who had destroyed the Tree and cast out his brother's spirit—those were his enemies.

Ever since this quest had begun, he'd had to struggle to contain the frustration of not knowing where Tinnean was, the fear that he might be suffering—and the guilt that his refusal to attend the Midwinter rite had caused it. When he'd heard the music and seen the Holly-Lord playing Tinnean's flute, frustration and fear and guilt had coalesced into rage.

It was like and unlike the thrill of the hunt: that same burst of excitement when he spotted his prey, the same pounding of heart and pulse that climaxed at the kill. But always during the hunt, there was the center of calm, the strange separateness of being in the moment and yet standing apart, observing the quarry, the surroundings, and his reactions from a distance.

This time, there had only been the pounding of his blood, and the roaring in his ears, and the saliva thick in his mouth. And then he'd heard Griane's voice, accusing him of brutalizing his brother and his wife. He'd seen himself through her eyes, standing there with his fist upraised for a blow. His mouth had gone dry as if he'd swallowed ashes. Even now, the taste lingered.

During the day, he could keep his senses focused on hunting, on searching for signs of the wolf. Only at night did the fear return. During the darkest time of the night—after the moon had disappeared below the treetops and the sky to the east refused to brighten with the hope of a new day—that was when despair threatened to overwhelm him. When he thought of Tinnean, lost forever, with no hope of forgiveness or farewell. And Maili, safe in the Forever Isles but just as lost to him, with no chance to make amends for those nights when he'd gone a moon without touching her and the need was on him so bad that he wouldn't let her turn away but poured his lust into her while she lay still and silent beneath him.

He told himself that he had been a good provider, that he had only tried to protect Tinnean from his boyish impulses, that he had always tried to be patient with Maili, no matter how many times she flinched from his touch. But he had only to remember the cold accusation in Griane's eyes for those beliefs to leach away like rain seeping into soft, summer earth.

Long after the others had curled up around the fire, the Holly-Lord watched Darak. He sat against the wall of the cave, knees pulled up to his chest. Although his head was lowered on his forearms, the Holly-Lord knew he was waiting. Helpless, he waited, too.

Finally, Darak's head came up. He rose into a crouch. Struath's eye snapped open. Griane's hand slid out from under her mantle, but froze when Yeorna seized her wrist.

Darak must have seen. He saw everything. Picking his way around their still figures, he approached slowly. The Holly-Lord found that comforting until he remembered that Darak moved the same way when he was stalking an animal he intended to kill.

Darak broke a dead branch into smaller pieces. One by one, he threw them on the fire. He poked the flames with a longer branch until they crackled and hissed. Only then did he squat down just out of reach as if to assure him there was no danger of attack.

Darak poked the fire again, although the flames were already high. "I won't lay hands on you again," he said in a soft voice. "You've my oath on that."

"Thank you."

Darak frowned, even though he had spoken politely. Remembering that the giving of the oath was important, he added, "You have my oath that I did not cast out Tinnean's spirit."

Darak crouched there, still and silent. Then he nodded.

"Shall we spit?"

For the first time, Darak looked at him, clearly surprised. "If you like."

Rather than spitting into the fire as he expected, Darak spat into his palm. He did the same. He hesitated a moment when Darak held out his hand, then crawled closer to allow the big man to clasp his. He flexed his fingers until the ache went away.

Darak did not notice; he was staring into the fire again. He knew that expression almost as well as the angry one. This was the look that always came over him when he was thinking of Tinnean. He did not know the words to make that expression go away, but he knew the comfort of touch; Griane had taught him that.

Darak tensed as he reached toward him. He hesitated, his hand hanging in the air between them. Then he leaned forward and patted Darak's leg. It was a very hard leg.

"We will find him."

Darak's breath leaked out of his body. "I'm sorry. That I shoved you. I don't . . . I usually have better control of my temper."

"You were angry. And frightened."

Darak's scowl reminded him, too late, that Griane had told him men did not like to admit to fear. He sighed. It was so much easier to be a tree. Perhaps if he offered sorry for sorry—just like oath for oath—it would make up for his mistake.

"I am sorry that I blew on Tinnean's flute."

Darak closed his eyes. His throat moved. That was not good. He had made another mistake. He should not speak of Tinnean unless Darak did.

Before he could offer another sorry, Darak opened his eyes. "I wasn't ready for it." His large, blunt fingers clenched and unclenched. "Hearing the music. Seeing you . . ." Just for a moment, their gazes met. "It's so hard . . . to have you look at me. With his eyes."

He lowered his head so Darak would not have to see his eyes. "If I left . . ."

"Nay. We must stay together. This . . . I'll be fine."

"Who is Tinnean that you would kill to have him back?"

Darak's head jerked up. "He's my brother."

"Aye. But what is that?"

"He's . . . I thought you understood. Tinnean and I, we're the same blood. The same father and mother."

"The same litter?"

"Aye. But more than that. He's . . . part of me. Like . . ." Darak hesitated, frowning. It was the thinking frown, not the angry one. After a moment, his face smoothed out. "Like two trees growing from the same roots."

For the first time, he understood. Darak felt the same incompleteness, the same loss he did. Of course the big man expressed those feelings in strange and often frightening outbursts. That was the way of all humans, it seemed. They were so very young, so raw and fragile despite their fierceness. No wonder the Maker loved them.

He got to his knees and waited for Darak to look at him. He had spent much time studying that face. He knew that the two vertical lines between the brows could mean anger if the lips were pressed together and the brows went down. Those same lines could mean sorrow if the brows went up and the throat went up and down, or puzzlement if the mouth turned up on one side.

He saw expectation on the face now—brows up, forehead creased, lips parted. When he took Darak's big hand between his, expectation changed to surprise.

"The Oak is my brother."

He watched the hard lines ease and the eyes widen. For once, his words had been right.

Darak's hand gripped his hard. "We will find him."

"We will find both of them."

Although no spit was exchanged, this oath felt even more powerful than the other.

Chapter 21

WHEN HE ROLLED OVER the next morning, he discovered Darak crawling into the cave, brushing snow off his back and shoulders. The Holly-Lord sighed; if the weather was bad enough to keep Darak inside, there would be no escape for any of them.

Struath and Yeorna treated Darak as they always did, but Griane did not speak to him at all, just stabbed her needle in and out of the shoe she was mending for Struath. He found her silence strange, for surely she had heard their words the previous night, just as she could observe Darak teaching him to chip flint with the rock called "hammerstone." Darak even moved his fingers so they gripped it correctly when he had always avoided touching him before. She must understand that he and Darak had exchanged sorries and that everything was all right now.

Sometimes, he would catch Darak watching Griane. She watched him, too, when she thought he was not looking. When they both looked up at the same time, Griane's face flushed red and she would stab the shoe again. Darak just frowned; once he muttered something under his breath.

He decided the flushing and frowning was caused by something other than Darak pushing him or Griane drawing her dagger. He was not sure what it was, but since his flute playing had started the bad feelings, he felt he must do something to make them go away.

"Yeorna, would you please tell the story about the rowan-woman and the alder-man?"

She smiled and the unpleasant fluttering in his belly eased. "You've heard that twice since we've been here."

"It is my favorite."

He had been surprised to learn that people had once been trees. Always, he had thought of them as wolf-kin because of their fierceness and their meat-loving and their habit of traveling in packs. When Yeorna told about the rowan that lifted up its roots and walked out of the forest to become the first woman, the story began to make sense. If Griane had grown weary of standing in the forest, she would have done that.

"Perhaps Griane could tell a story," Yeorna said.

Griane's voice was not as sweet as Yeorna's, nor did it fill the cave as Struath's did, but her stories were very exciting. Like the time she and Tinnean had leaped over the Midsummer bonfire and their tunics caught fire and Darak rolled them both on the ground and nearly squashed them and shouted that they had no more sense than mayflies to be leaping the bonfire when the flames were so high. Or the time she stayed out all night in the forest because she wanted to find a vision mate like the boys did, but she was afraid to close her eyes, because as soon as she did, she heard all sorts of scary sounds, and she wanted to go home, but she was too afraid to move, and then Darak found her and carried her home and put her to sleep with Tinnean, and stopped her father from beating her with a leather strap the next morning.

"Tell about the time you filled Darak's shoes with

porridge," he said. "And you could hear him shouting all the way across the village and he smacked your arse and—"

"Nay." Darak's voice was very quiet.

He caught his breath. He should not have spoken of the arse smacking. He was making things worse. Yeorna must have understood, for she said, "Griane, have you come up with a name yet?"

Darak looked up. "A name?"

Griane glanced at him, then flushed and looked down at her mending. "The Holly-Lord asked me to choose one for him."

"What have you chosen?"

"I was thinking . . . I don't know. I thought of one, but . . ."

The Holly-Lord leaned forward. "What is it, Griane?"

"Cuillonoc."

He repeated the name, slowly shaping it with his tongue and letting it roll off his lips. Yeorna clapped her hands, just as she did when he blew on the flute. "It's perfect. That was the name of the very first chief of the Holly Tribe. Isn't that right, Tree-Father?"

Struath stared at the roof of the cave, stroking the underside of his chin. Recognizing the beginning of a story, the Holly-Lord stretched out his legs; Struath's stories were usually long.

"Long, long ago, before my father's father's father was born, before there was an Oak Tribe or a Holly Tribe, there were The People."

He sighed. It was not only going to be a long story, but one about people he did not know.

"The People came from the south where the soil was rich and black, and the rivers teemed with fish, and the barley grew taller than a man. The summers were long and warm, and in winter, the snows only lingered for a moon before melting away."

The Oak would have liked this place. "Did they have forests?"

"Aye, Holly-Lord. And they worshiped in the sacred grove of the First Forest and witnessed the battle of the Oak and the Holly at Midsummer and Midwinter."

Now the story began to interest him. He must know these People, after all. In the beginning, only the trees and the birds and the beasts had observed the battles. Then came a strange creature, no larger than a bear cub, which fell to its knees when it entered the grove. He wondered if this was one of Struath's People or if they had come later.

"The People had lived many generations in this place when a new people arrived. At first, the two tribes lived in peace, trading with each other, sharing knowledge, even intermarrying. However, each spring brought more of the strangers and in time, there were too many for the land to support. These newcomers dug stone out of the earth for their places of worship. They cut down the forests for their fields. They stole the children of The People to sacrifice to their—"

"They cut down the trees? All of them?" Surely, Struath was mistaken.

"They did not worship the Holly and the Oak. They did not believe that we share this land with our tree-brothers and with the birds and beasts of the forests and the fish of the rivers."

He shook his head, unable to imagine such a people or such a world.

"And so The People fled to their boats and journeyed down the river until they came to a great sea."

"What is a sea?"

"It is a large expanse of water, as big as the First Forest."

This seemed as improbable as the existence of a people who wished to cut down all the trees, but Struath nodded firmly, so it must be true.

"The People journeyed for many days. Each morning, they watched the sun rise over the forests to the east and each evening, they watched it sink into the great sea. Some of The People grew afraid and wanted to turn back. Others wanted to drag their boats to the shore and build their new village right there. But many voices were raised against this idea, because the village would be far from the forest."

He nodded at The People's wisdom; who would want to live far from the forest?

"Their shaman said they must go on and they obeyed him because he was the wisest of men."

Darak made a little snorting sound and Struath frowned.

"And in time they came to another river," Yeorna said. "Isn't that right, Tree-Father?"

"Aye. After many days and nights of travel. The People decided to follow the river. As their shaman advised."

Without looking up from his hammerstone, Darak said, "Who—being the wisest of men—knew that winter was coming on and if they didn't find a place to build their homes soon, they'd freeze their arses off."

This time, Griane snorted. Her face flushed when she caught Darak's glance, but this time, she did not look away.

Struath cleared his throat. "The People followed the river east for two days and two nights until they reached a lake."

"Your lake?"

"Aye. And when they paddled up the lake, they saw the sign that their shaman—with his farseeing wisdom—had promised." Struath paused, looking around the cave. He wondered if he was supposed to guess what the sign was.

Fortunately, Griane blurted out, "The oak. He saw the oak."

"The oak on the hill?"

"Aye, Holly-Lord."

"Tell him about Cuillonoc, Tree-Father."

Yeorna's interruption reminded him of the reason

Struath had begun this story. He sounded out the name softly. The first part rolled around his tongue nicely, but the last part felt like he had something caught in his throat and was trying to cough it out.

"Well, after a time, the Oak Tribe—for so they called themselves now—grew so large that there was not enough grain in the fields to feed them."

The People must have bred like rabbits. Yet, he had not seen so many of them during his time in Darak's hut. Less than the leaves on one branch of a small sapling. Perhaps their breeding habits had changed over time.

"It was decided that half of the tribe would find a new home. And so—and this is the wondrous thing— they sailed across the lake, and on the opposite shore, they found a holly. Just as the first tribe had found an oak. And just as the Oak and Holly are connected, our two tribes always remember that we come from the same roots and we share the same past."

"And the man who led them across the lake was Cuillonoc. Forgive me, Tree-Father." Struath smiled and waved away Yeorna's apology. "So. What do you think?"

"I think your people move around a lot."

"About the name."

"Oh. I do not like it."

Darak's head jerked up. Yeorna gasped. Struath frowned. But Griane's face held his gaze longest. As he watched, the light in her eyes died just as surely as the sun must have when it sank into the waters of that great sea. He knew it was his fault—all their faces told him that—but he was not sure what he had done other than speak the truth.

"Is there another name you would prefer, Holly-Lord?" Struath asked.

"Nay. I just do not like that one."

Griane flinched. Hoping to make things better, he said, "It sounds like a cough."

Before he could say more, she had shoved aside the

branches at the cave's entrance and crawled out. Before the branches had stopped rustling, Darak went after her.

"I did something wrong."

Struath cleared his throat. Yeorna sighed. The fire hissed. Nothing ever seemed to bother the fire.

"Griane spent a day thinking of a name," Struath said.

"I know."

"She wanted it to be a name with meaning."

"I understand."

"A name you could be proud of."

"It sounds like a cough."

Struath cleared his throat.

"It does not feel right in my mouth."

Yeorna sighed.

"Is Griane angry because the name sounds like a cough?"

"She is not angry," Yeorna said. "She is hurt."

"But I did not touch her."

"Your words hurt her."

He had never imagined you could wound with words. He found that more frightening than anything else he had learned since becoming a man.

"Do you remember Darak's face when you described the battle in the grove?" Struath asked. "When you told him Tinnean screamed?"

He pressed his palm against the front of his tunic to ease the sudden pain in his chest. "My words made Griane feel that way?"

"Well. Not so bad as that," Struath said.

He stared into the unfeeling fire. "I do not like words."

Darak crawled back into the cave, brushing snow off. He squeezed his shoulder and squatted beside him again.

"What words should I have used?" he asked Struath.

"You could have said . . . it was a fine name. A name you liked."

"But that would be not-true."

"A lie," Struath corrected. "But only a small lie, Holly-Lord."

"Lies are different sizes?"

"Sometimes, we speak words to avoid hurting another's feelings. Those are small lies. They do not harm the teller or the hearer."

"I do not understand."

Yeorna sighed. "Suppose a girl—a girl you liked very much—made you your favorite food in the world. And it wasn't—"

"Hot apple cider."

"What?"

"Hot apple cider is my favorite."

"Oh. All right. Well, suppose the hot apple cider tasted bad."

"How could hot apple cider taste bad?"

"Forget hot apple cider," Darak said. "Say a girl asks if you like the oatcakes she made. You say, 'Oh, aye.' Even if they're hard as rocks. Or if a girl asks, 'Do you think my hair looks pretty this way?' You say, 'Oh, aye.' Even if it looks like a nest of snakes."

Yeorna cuffed Darak, but she was smiling. Even Struath's lips were twitching as he said, "What Darak means is that if you like a person, you sometimes need to hold back a little of the truth."

"But you'll end up with hard oatcakes," Darak said, dodging Yeorna's hand with a grin.

Their smiles faded as Griane crawled into the cave. Darak helped her to her feet and stood by her as she hovered near the entrance, dragging the toe of her shoe in a long arc in front of her. "I'm sorry I made such a fuss. It was silly. It's only a name."

He stood up. He always felt better standing at important moments. "It is a fine name. I like it. And I think your hair looks pretty that way."

"I . . . it's a mess." She smoothed her braid, darting an uncertain glance at Darak who suddenly seemed interested in kicking melting snow off his shoes. "Thank you."

"I am sorry I made you unhappy."

"Nay. It's your name. If you don't like it—"

"Just the last part. The Oc."

"That's the part that sounds like a cough?" Darak asked.

He thought it was impolite to mention the cough. Griane's glare confirmed that. She stuck out her tongue. Darak pulled her braid. She swatted his hand away and muttered something under her breath that made him grin. The pain in his chest eased at bit, then flared when he realized how much he would miss their strange displays when he returned to his Tree.

"Suppose you left off the Oc," Yeorna suggested.

"Names have power," Struath said. "Cuillon conveys authority and dignity. It brings to mind the founder of the Holly Tribe, but is yours alone. What do you think, Holly-Lord?"

He sounded it out and nodded. "It feels right in my mouth."

Struath nodded. Yeorna clapped. Darak grinned. When Griane smiled and hugged him, the ache in his chest went away.

Cuillon. He had a name. He only hoped it held enough power to keep the holly thorns from piercing his hands again.

Chapter 22

EACH NIGHT SINCE they had arrived at the cave, Struath had reached for another vision, but exhaustion and pain had hindered him. Tonight, he was determined to succeed. Soon, they must leave the sanctuary of the cave to seek either the Summerlands or a portal to Chaos. Only Brana could help him determine the true path.

He stared into the fire, waiting for the others to sleep. The flames beckoned him. He felt his body falling away and jerked upright when he realized his head was nodding. He called upon his years of discipline and again, felt himself drifting.

It might have been a moment later or moonset when he heard her voice.

"Wake up."

Struath knew he was curled up in his mantle, yet he was also perched on a windswept pinnacle, watching dark clouds race across the moon.

Peck, peck, peck between his eyes.

"Forgive me, Brana."

"Why should I? You never even thanked me for saving you."

Struath shuddered, remembering their last flight.

"Again, I ask your forgiveness. And offer my thanks. If you hadn't broken the Trickster's spell—"

A derisive caw cut him off. "If the Trickster had wanted the wolf to have you, you'd be dead. He's playing with you. He enjoys that. So does the wolf."

She cocked her head, no doubt expecting him to ask about the wolf again. But tonight, Struath had a more important quest."

"Brana, I need your help."

"You always need my help."

"Is the Oak in Chaos?"

"That is beyond my power of Seeing."

"Can you open a portal for us?"

"I could carry you to Chaos. Perhaps. But only the Trickster can open a portal for the others." She winked. "Unless you'd care to ask the wolf."

Always it came back to the wolf. "Why does it follow us?"

"Will you fly with me?"

"Aye, Brana. I will fly."

She rose skyward, circling above him. He raised his arms, but found himself still locked in his man's form. Brana dove. Her powerful talons seized his shoulders. Effortlessly, she ascended, the pinnacle dwindling to a tiny moonlit blot of gray in the darkness.

With a low rattling cough, she released him. He drifted downward, arms outstretched, waiting for his wings to sprout. He flapped his arms. No feathers. No wings. His fingers clawed empty air. He fell faster, tumbling helplessly through black, limitless space, just like the nightmares he'd had as a boy.

An abyss yawned beneath him. When he saw the fangs, he realized it was a gaping mouth. When he saw the yellow eyes, he recognized the wolf. But only when he heard it say, "Have you missed me, little rook?" did he finally See.

He screamed. The wolf's tongue lolled out, enveloping him in a hot, wet sheath. He struggled futilely as it drew him toward its eager maw. When fangs bit into his shoulders, a terrified cry escaped him. Then he heard the beating of wings and realized Brana had snatched him away, her defiant croak louder than the wolf's frustrated howl. They soared skyward, out of reach of those jaws, beyond vengeance, beyond terror, beyond death.

She set him down in the cave as gently as a mother laying her babe in a cradle. He woke with tears streaking his cheeks.

How could he have failed to See? All the signs were there: the wolf's malevolence, its spirit-sickness. He should have recognized that spirit the night of the Midwinter rite or later in the glade of the heart-oak. Brana was right; consciously or unconsciously, he had refused to read the signs.

Morgath had returned.

The man whom he had respected—nay, idolized. The man who had guided him along the paths of magic, opening up unimagined worlds of knowledge and power. How proud he had been that a man so wise and gifted would choose him, a skinny gawk whose only real friend was the raven who visited him in dreams.

He could still remember that morning so many springs ago when he had returned from his vision quest: the weight of Morgath's hands on his shoulders, the keen gaze that searched him, the smile that penetrated him as surely as that all-seeing eye. And the words: "Such a great gift. You will travel far."

Struath knotted his trembling hands into fists. Pride. Always, it had been his weakness. Pride had ensured his allegiance to Morgath. Pride had led him along the forbidden paths of dark magic. Even when he had used that ill-gotten knowledge to defeat his master, guilt and remorse had been leavened with an equal measure of pride.

Struath moaned softly. How could he defeat a man

who was clever enough to escape from Chaos, powerful enough to cast out the spirit of the Oak-Lord?

He reached into his pack and pulled out the sacrificial dagger. Slowly, he slid it from its sheath. The bronze gleamed dully in the firelight. His master—nay, he must not think of him as that any longer. To do so only added to his power. The Destroyer had been the first to possess such a dagger. He could still recall his wonder when he first beheld it—as if the sun's rays had been forged into metal. Recalled, too, his gasp of surprise when the Destroyer had presented him with a similar dagger at his initiation. This dagger.

"You deserve no less, little rook," the nickname a tribute to his spirit guide and to his long, dark hair. "Great men require the best tools to accomplish great deeds." Had he winked then or just smiled?

Those long fingers cupping his face. Those full lips pressing against his forehead in benediction, then moving lower, to brush his cheek, his jaw, his mouth.

Struath clamped his lips together. Even after so many years, even knowing the evil Morgath had done, his body still roused at the memories of that night. The eve of Midsummer, the air thick with the scent of wild roses. Hands and mouths exploring, bodies slick with sweat.

He had wept afterward, because the pleasure had been so intense, because he was grateful that he could give equal pleasure to his beloved mentor—and because he was so proud Morgath had chosen him for this initiation as well.

When Morgath took one of the Grain-Mother's apprentices for a lover, he had wept again. When Morgath argued that a man must sample all the pleasures of life, he had broken with him. When Morgath told him no woman could ever displace him, he had returned.

As with the flesh, so it was with spirit. When Morgath led him into the realms of dark magic, he had resisted, not only fearful of the dangers of their forbidden quest, but of yielding utterly to the strength and charisma of the older man. Always, though, he relented and returned. Until the day he murdered the wren.

After that, he went no more to that soft bed of rabbit furs, though his body still ached for the touch of those skillful fingers, that knowing mouth. Ached even more for the comfort of those arms that he had once believed would shield him from any danger, any evil. He had never dreamed that the evil lay within.

Later, he always wondered why the elders believed him. Perhaps they, too, feared Morgath's power. When he denounced the Tree-Father, he spoke no word of his own act of sacrilege. Nor did Morgath. Bound by ropes, bound even tighter by the wards erected by the priests of both the Oak and Holly tribes, Morgath offered no word, no look, not a single gesture to implicate him during the daylong council. Struath accepted the burden of silence, believing that the worst punishment he could endure was to live with his secret shame and guilt. Then the elders told him that he must perform the rite that would cast his mentor's spirit into Chaos.

That was the only time Morgath acknowledged him—the moment when he knelt next to him in the glade of the heart-oak, the dagger that his mentor had given him held aloft between his trembling fingers, staring down at the smooth white chest that he would carve open. In spite of the wards, he had felt the pull of Morgath's power, but no wards could protect him from the simple but unendurable compulsion to look into his mentor's face one last time.

Their spirits touched as they had so many times before. He touched hatred. He touched madness. Disdain for those too cowardly to seek knowledge at all costs. Determination to show no fear and a bottomless terror for the journey his spirit would undergo. It was

only when Struath touched a small flicker of love that
he severed the connection, plunging the dagger into
his mentor's chest with a great howl of despair that
echoed through the silent forest.

Struath clenched the hilt of the dagger. "You are
not my master any longer."

It had taken Morgath thirty years to escape Chaos.
Once he had sent the Destroyer back, he would de-
vote the rest of his life to discovering a way to seal
him there forever.

Chapter 23

THE OTHERS WERE STILL sleeping when Darak picked up his bow and quiver, determined to get in a day of hunting before another storm blew in. Moments after he had crawled out of the cave, he heard the rattle of branches behind him and turned to find Griane crouched by the cave's entrance, muttering imprecations as she struggled to free her mantle. He stilled her impatient fingers, untangled the mantle from the twigs that had snagged it, and pulled her to her feet.

By way of thanks, she glared at him and announced, "I'm coming with you."

"I see."

"The others don't need me, and I'm good with a sling, and we need to lay in a good supply of meat before we move on."

"All right."

"And besides, I can— What?"

"I said all right."

She narrowed her eyes. "Why are you being so nice?"

"Because if I said nay, you'd follow me." She flushed. "I've seen no sign of the wolf, but that doesn't mean it's not lurking about. So stay close and for mercy's sake, keep silent."

Apart from one cry of triumph when she brought down a squirrel, she obeyed. Even when they rested at midday, sharing a smoked fish and a few swallows of water, she remained mute. Not the brooding silence that followed his assault on the Holly-Lord, but a restful sort of quiet. He found himself enjoying her company, the widening of her eyes when he nodded toward their prey, her quick grin when he made a kill. Even more surprising was his discovery that this impulsive, sharp-tongued girl possessed a hunter's patience, a hunter's stillness, communicating with the smallest of gestures, the slightest of nods.

He spotted the deer first. Griane froze a moment later; only her quick intake of breath betrayed her excitement.

His mind formed a silent prayer to the Forest-Lord, but it was his father's voice he heard in his head.

They mostly browse for a count of twenty, but each deer has its own pattern.

The doe raised her head, scanning the trees. Seeing nothing, she tore another long shred of bark from the tree. Darak counted.

It'll look for movement. Keep still. Stay relaxed.

Again the doe looked up. Her brown eyes seemed to stare right into his. Only when she lowered her head did he allow himself to blink.

Once you've got their pattern, you move.

Four steps only, then freeze.

Never press your luck. One step too many and the deer will catch you mid-stride and be gone.

Four more steps and freeze.

Take your time. Go for the sure shot.

One step forward. Clear of that low branch. Two steps left. Beyond the screen of saplings.

Wait till you're ready to take the shot before you draw.

Mark the spot between the ribs. Bowstring back. Elbow high. Now!

She crumpled to the ground without taking a step and pure joy flooded him. For the second time in his life, he'd taken a deer with one shot through the heart. Even his father had managed the feat only once.

Griane whooped and threw her arms around his neck. He hugged her hard, glad to share this moment. Then he knelt beside the doe, stroking her neck gently as the soft brown eyes glazed over. He whispered a prayer of thanks, then made a shallow slash down the chest, careful to avoid piercing the stomach and the sac containing the intestines. He inserted his dagger under the skin and peeled back the thick hide. Steam rose from the exposed organs and he breathed it in gratefully before cutting the liver free. He sliced off a chunk and held it out to Griane.

"Nay. It's your kill."

He ate it raw, eyes closed as he savored the tender flesh.

"We'd best butcher it here," he said, "else we'll attract scavengers to the cave. I'll cache whatever we can't carry with us and come back for it later."

"Darak."

"Empty your waterskin. The blood'll make a good base for stews."

"Darak."

The soft urgency in her voice brought his head up. She was staring past him, her face pale under the dusting of freckles. Wiping his dagger on his breeches, he murmured, "What is it?"

"I don't know." Her voice shook just a little. "A man. I think."

He casually picked up his bow as he rose and pretended to examine the bowstring. All the while, his eyes scanned the underbrush. He missed him at first, so perfectly did he blend in with the shadows. Then he caught a brighter gleam of color among the sun-dappled tree trunks.

The stranger was lounging on a fallen log. Trees shadowed his face, but his legs gleamed ruddy in a shaft of sunlight. He leaned forward. A tail uncurled. He reached around, pulled his thick brush forward, and began grooming it. Without looking up, he said, "Don't gape, children. It's unbecoming."

"Merciful Maker," Griane breathed.

"Do come closer. I hate to shout."

His voice was soft as if confiding secrets, yet each word carried clearly.

"And leave the bow."

Reluctantly, Darak let it slide from his fingers. Although he firmly intended to keep his distance, he found himself walking forward with Griane at his side. They stopped just out of reach of the long arms. Griane slowly knelt; he remained standing until she seized his wrist and dragged him to his knees.

The triangular ears twitched. So did the whiskers around his sharp nose. The long red tongue lolled out as he grinned. Then he turned his attention back to his brush, examining the white tip critically before licking it into a perfect point. Darak tensed when he rose, but after swishing his brush back and forth a few times, he tucked it under him and resumed his seat on the log.

When the Trickster's mouth curved in a mocking smile, Darak realized he was clutching his bag of charms. He let his hand fall to his side, but kept a firm grip on the hilt of his dagger.

"What is your name, child?"

"Griane, my lord."

Darak muttered a curse. Names held power. You didn't offer them to strangers. Especially when the stranger was the Trickster.

"Griane." He repeated the name as if savoring it. "And do you know who I am?"

"Everyone knows of you, Lord Trickster."

"A gratifying thought. Come closer. No, not you. Just this delightful girl."

Griane hesitated, then rose and took a tentative step forward.

The Trickster clasped his white-ruffed cheeks. "Ah. That hair. Lovely."

Griane fingered her braid uncertainly. "You're the first to say so, lord."

"Well. Men can be so stupid, can't they?" The Trickster's golden gaze flicked his way before returning to Griane.

Griane shot an amused look over her shoulder. "Aye, lord."

Darak resisted the impulse to stuff her lovely braid down her throat. Judging by the Trickster's lazy smile, the god knew exactly what he was thinking.

"Have you ever met a god before, Griane?"

"Nay, lord."

"How does it make you feel?"

"I . . . well . . . a little afraid."

"That is wise. Gods can be so fickle. I think it's because we are immortal and constantly seek something new to amuse us." He shrugged. "But rest easy, my dear. I mean no harm to you or your silent companion. Today."

"I . . . thank you, Lord Trickster."

"Tell me, Griane. Do you think I am beautiful? I have been told that I am beautiful." The Trickster's mocking smile made the heat rise on Darak's face.

"You are . . . magnificent."

"Even better. More awe-inspiring. One always likes to inspire awe. Do I inspire awe in you, Griane?"

"An awful lot of awe."

The Trickster laughed. "Delightful girl. Such hair. Such wit."

"I wasn't trying to be witty, Lord Trickster."

"Which only makes you more delightful." The Trickster shot him another glance. "And you—do I inspire awe in you as well?"

"Aye."

"Ah. It speaks as well as blushes. Does it also have a name?"

"I warrant you know it."

The bushy brows rose. Griane shot him a quick glare. "Forgive him, Lord Trickster. His name is Darak—"

Darak got to his feet. "Guard your tongue, girl."

"Oh, please. It's far too nice day to quarrel. Darak is simply being cautious, my dear. Darak is a cautious fellow. Darak is also an exceedingly rude fellow, but I'll let that go. This time."

The hair on the back of his neck rose. Three times, the Trickster had repeated his name. Every child knew that was how you began a charm—or a curse. "Lord Trickster . . ."

"Call me Fellgair." His whiskers twitched. "You see? I offer a name for a name."

Darak considered reminding him that they'd offered him two names, but decided that would be pressing his luck. "Fellgair," he said. "We shall remember that name. Fellgair. It is a fine name, Fellgair."

The Trickster rolled his eyes. "Do you really think your petty charms will have any effect upon me? Next you'll be clutching your little bag again and spitting in the four directions."

Darak felt his face grow even warmer.

"Though why you should believe in the efficacy of charms when you no longer believe in the gods, I can't imagine."

The Trickster's slow smile told Darak that the god had heard his quick intake of breath. "The charms are a habit, Lord Trickster. As to believing in the gods . . . should I doubt the evidence of my own eyes?"

"Absolutely. Eyes are notoriously unreliable. Any halfway creditable shaman can cast a glamour that could make you see whatever he wished."

"Then you're not the Trickster God?" Griane sounded crestfallen.

"As a matter of fact, I am. Although Darak—dear Darak—rude Darak—the thrice-named man who accompanies you—doesn't believe in gods. Or rather, he does believe. He simply hates them. Why was that again? Oh, yes. That nasty business with the plague. Don't clench your jaw, dear boy. You'll grind down those lovely teeth."

"It was you, then. Who brought the plague."

"Did I?"

"Why?"

"Perhaps it amused me."

Rage flooded Darak. He tamped it down, struggling to keep his voice even. "It amused you to watch them die? The men who praised your cunning? The women who sang songs about your cleverness? And the helpless babes—" His voice broke and he clamped his mouth shut. Was it the Trickster's doing or his own foolishness?

"For one who cautions Griane to guard her tongue, you're perilously free with yours."

Belatedly, he realized Griane's fingers were digging into his forearm. He laid his hand over hers and saw the Trickster's eyebrows soar suggestively. He ignored the look and said, "You're right. I am too free with my tongue. I never used to be. Maybe it's just that we've come a long way and we're no closer to our goal than when we started." The Trickster leaned forward, his face intent. "And I didn't mean to say all that either. So I guess you have charmed me, after all. Or else I don't give a damn anymore."

"Well, I do consider myself charming." The Trickster flashed that tongue-lolling grin. "But I haven't cast a spell over you. Any more than you've ceased caring about the outcome of your little quest."

Griane stepped close enough to the Trickster to start Darak's heart thudding again. "Will you help us, Lord Fellgair?"

"Griane." Darak hoped she could hear the warning in his voice. He had not asked for the gift of fire, but he had accepted it—and the Trickster had promptly aided the wolf. Who knew what price he would exact now?

The Trickster tapped his lips with one elegantly lethal claw. Griane knelt. "Please." Somehow, she made the word sound more like a command than a plea. Darak stared at the stiff shoulders, the straight back. Even while he shook his head, he found himself admiring her courage.

They remained there, Griane on her knees, the Trickster on his log, staring into each other's eyes for so long that Darak feared she had been bespelled. Then the Trickster stretched out his hand. He let his palm rest against her hair, then drew his knuckles slowly down her cheek.

"What will you offer in return for my help?"

Before Darak could warn her to make no bargains, Griane leaned forward and pressed her lips against the Trickster's mouth.

Fellgair's eyes closed. He smiled, his lips still touching hers. Then he drew back to study Griane's face. "I have stolen my share of kisses from mortal women. You are the first to offer one freely."

He rose, extending a graceful hand to help Griane to her feet. Then he held out the other. After a moment's hesitation, Darak stepped forward. He caught his breath as the Trickster's peculiar scent hit him, the foxy reek at odds with the sweet fragrance of honeysuckle. With some trepidation, he took the proffered hand. The palm was spongy but rough, like a dog's pads.

To his surprise, Fellgair simply placed Griane's hand in his. The golden eyes regarded him gravely. "You will find what you are seeking in Chaos."

The words hit him like a physical blow. "Tinnean is in Chaos?"

The Trickster smiled and strolled into the trees.

"And the Oak-Lord? Is he with Tinnean?"

For one moment, the Trickster's ruddy pelt gleamed among the gray tree trunks. Then there was only everyday sunlight, and everyday shadows, and Griane's hand cold in his.

Chapter 24

FROM HIS HIDING PLACE in the thicket, Morgath watched the two figures walk upstream, the Hunter staggering a little under the weight of the doe. Saliva oozed from his jaws, the hunger pangs fiercer than the throbbing wound in his side.

Twice now, the Hunter had thwarted him. He would pay for that. The wound hindered his hunting. It had taken him five days to find their lair. Ever since, he had kept watch, but until today, he'd seen only the Hunter. A low whine escaped him at the thought that the Betrayer might have perished, although he had seen no body, nor the rock pile that marked the grave of a dead pack member.

Cairn.

He repeated the name in his mind. Words were power. Words were his connection to his true self. Lately, when he lost himself in the hunt or ripped open the belly of a hare, it seemed that he had always been a wolf, had always seen the world through these eyes, snuffed it with this nose. Unless he exerted his control, nothing would remain of the man he had been, not even his hatred. Then he would wander the First Forest, a stranger to himself.

He whined softly. He'd been alone so long, while the Hunter had his pack. Even now, the little female trotted obediently beside him, glancing up occasionally to expose her throat to him. Morgath bellied forward, hindquarters twitching in the desire to attack. The Hunter would have to drop the doe before he could use his weapons. He measured the distance. Too far to be certain. No cover to protect him. He could not risk it, no matter how much he longed for the Hunter's blood.

He whined again. The Betrayer was his primary quarry. Sometimes he forgot that was why he had come so far—to send his spirit to Chaos and feast on his flesh. He'd rip open that soft belly as easily as gutting a hare. He'd lap up the hot, salty blood. The liver, he would save for later, tender though it was. He'd have the heart first. Tear it out, just as the old man had torn his from his body. Tear it out and devour it.

He watched the Hunter struggle up the embankment. The female turned and seized his arm. When she paused to push the Hunter's hair off his face, longing filled him, more intense than the desire to hunt, to kill, to destroy.

And then he knew what he wanted. Not merely to kill the Betrayer, but to walk toward him on two legs. To speak aloud the words that would remind him of his perfidy and condemn him to Chaos. To watch the old man kneel at his feet and call him master, just as he used to.

As they disappeared into the cave, Morgath rose and stretched. Night was approaching. The time for hunting. Later, when his belly was full, he could decide which of their strong, young bodies he would make his own.

The faces of the others told Cuillon it was a bad thing for the Oak to be in the place they called Chaos. Darak's silence told him even more; he would not speak the name aloud, even when he interrupted Griane's telling to question Struath.

"Can you penetrate it with your Sight?" Darak asked.

"Nay."

"What about the portals? Can you sense them before they open?"

"Nay."

"Can you open one yourself?"

"Nay!"

The two glared at each other. Then Darak rose without a word to leave the cave. Yeorna seized Griane's arm as she started after him. "Give him time." His belly gave one of its odd little flutters as she sank back down.

"Please," he said. They all started at the sound of his voice. "Why is Chaos a bad place?"

"It is not bad," Struath said. "Not in and of itself. But it is a place of illusion, where existence is ever-changing."

"Like the seasons?"

"Imagine if autumn followed winter," Yeorna said, "and then came winter again with no spring or summer."

"Oh."

Struath stared into space, stroking the underside of his chin. Griane squirmed. The Holly-Lord resisted the urge to do the same. Struath's stories were interesting, but sometimes he preferred Darak's straightforward answers. His impatience troubled him, further proof of the changes his spirit was undergoing.

Struath placed his hands on his knees. "In the beginning, before gods or men existed, before there was sun or moon, earth or sea, there was Chaos. Out of Chaos, rose the Maker and the Unmaker. The Unmaker ruled Chaos, delighting in his realm, but the Maker longed for order. She took fire and shaped Bel, the Sun Lord, and Gheala, the Moon Lady. She created Nul, the Keeper of Lightning, and all the stars in the night sky. Her breath became the four winds and her voice became Nul's brother, Taran the Thunderer. One star, smaller than the others, fell from the sky. The Maker wept, and her tears created the waters of the world and the gods of sea and lake and river. Into the waters, the star fell and cooled and became earth. And here, the Maker placed the World Tree."

"My Tree?"

"Nay, Holly-Lord. The tree that connects the Upper World of the gods to the Middle World—"

"That's the First Forest and our world," Griane added.

" . . . to the Lower World where the Forever Isles float."

He tried to remember if he had ever felt this World Tree when his spirit had lived in the Holly. His roots had spread deep and far; he had touched many other trees. Perhaps, they had all been touching this World Tree, which had shared the energy of one among all.

"So the Maker planted the World Tree—"

"Nay, Holly-Lord. First, the Maker created the silver branches."

"The branches came first?"

"They are the dwelling place of the gods, Holly-Lord. Gods came into being before men."

"But how can the tree stand without roots?"

"The World Tree is not an ordinary tree."

"It does not make sense." Surely, if the Maker valued order as much as Struath believed, she would have planted the roots firmly in the earth.

"Some things must be taken on faith."

He absorbed this in silence. Perhaps faith was something that allowed men to believe things that made no sense.

"Shall I continue?"

"Please, Struath."

"The Lord of Chaos was jealous of the gods because they were immortal, just as he was. And so the Unmaker spilled his seed upon the emerging trunk of the Tree."

Cuillon opened his mouth to ask about this, but closed it when he saw Struath frown. To himself, he imagined a pile of sunflower seeds atop a fallen log.

"By spilling his seed on the trunk of the World Tree, the Unmaker ensured that each drop of life would contain a drop of death."

He amended the previous image to one of salmon spawning in a river. As an afterthought, he added a large tree growing out of the water. Neither image seemed right.

"Once death entered the Middle World, the Maker could not remove it. But she gave her youngest children—men—a great gift to compensate them for their short lives."

Cuillon waited patiently until he realized that this time, Struath wanted him to ask a question. "What was the gift, Struath?"

When Struath smiled, he knew he had guessed correctly. "By the time the roots of the World Tree appeared, the Maker's tears had washed away the Unmaker's seed. There in the roots, she created the Forever Isles, where men and women could await rebirth after death came for them." Struath sighed. "They are a place of great beauty."

"You have been there?"

"When I fly with my spirit guide."

"But you cannot fly into Chaos?"

Struath's lips pressed into a tight line. Fear and doubt returned to their faces. The fluttering in his belly solidified into an icicle. He had stolen the comfort the story had given them, just as he had stolen Griane's happiness when he had spoken against the name she had chosen.

"Perhaps . . ."

The hope on their faces hurt more than the fear. "I was thinking of how the rowan pulled up her roots and walked out of the First Forest."

Hope gave way to confusion. He spoke more quickly. "If the rowan could do that, when no tree had done such a thing before, then we can go to Chaos and bring back the Oak and Tinnean."

They smiled. The icicle inside his belly melted. The talk turned to ways of finding a portal, of the preparations they must make. He stared into the fire, lips pressed together to keep other questions from escaping. He was glad he had given them back the comfort he had stolen. Gladder still that they had believed the small lie.

Darak set out at first light. If Struath could not open a portal, Fellgair could. Whatever the price the Trickster demanded, he would pay it. When he heard the crunch of footsteps on pebbles, he spun around, ready to order Griane back into the cave. The words died when he saw Struath.

"The wolf is still abroad."

He nodded impatiently.

"You must not kill it, Darak."

"What?"

"This is not an ordinary animal."

"I know that, Struath. What's your point?"

"The spirit inhabiting the wolf disrupted the battle in the grove."

The bloodlust flooded him, making him gasp. He forced his clenched fists open, forced himself to breathe slowly. "You had another vision."

Struath nodded. "This spirit can move from body to body."

"Not if the body's dead."

"He will never let you get close enough for a kill."

"He?"

"He. It. Call it what you will." Struath's gaze slid away, then met his squarely. "If you try and kill it on your own, it will simply leave the body it now inhabits and take another. Yours, if it chooses. And you will be powerless to stop him."

"So how can we destroy it?"

Struath's shoulders relaxed. "I must be present at the kill to perform the rite that will consign its spirit to Chaos. Can we lure the wolf here?"

Darak resisted the urge to ask how Struath could keep this spirit in Chaos if it knew how to open a portal. "It would never come so close—not in broad daylight."

"At night, then? If you hid yourself—"

"Whatever spirit lives inside, it's still a wolf, Struath. Even with the wind in the right direction, I'd be hard-pressed to mask my scent completely. And if it's as dangerous as you say, I'd not want to risk the others."

"Of course. You're right. Above all, we must keep the Holly-Lord safe." Struath stared off, apparently lost in thought. "It wants me. If I went into the forest, faced it alone . . ."

"What's to keep it from tossing your spirit out?"

Struath smiled grimly. "I will toss its spirit out first."

"We're not talking about a wren, Struath."

The smile faded. "I am aware of the danger."

"It's too risky. If we lose you, who will wield the spirit catcher and bring back Tinnean and the Oak?" Belatedly, he realized how heartless that sounded, but he had more important things to consider than Struath's feelings. "I'll track it today."

"You keep thinking of it as you would a real wolf."

"This . . . being has inhabited the wolf's body for . . . what? A moon, maybe longer. The Holly-Lord can't communicate with the trees as well in Tinnean's body. So a spirit—out of place—might take on the characteristics of the host. Or lose some of its powers. Aye?"

The deep furrows on the shaman's forehead eased a bit. "If that were true . . . if he had lost power . . ." He shook his head. "We cannot count on that."

"We can't count on anything. But we can choose the time—and with any luck—the place to meet it. All you have to do is hold your own till I get off a shot. Can you do that?"

"I will. I must."

Darak jerked his head toward the cave. "Keep the others inside. We've food for a sennight and I'll fill the waterskins before I come back." He allowed Struath to turn toward the cave before adding, "Just tell me one thing."

As he'd expected, Struath's body tensed.

"You said the wolf wanted you."

Struath nodded cautiously.

"Will it try to kill you straight off? Or take its time?"

Struath's shoulders sagged. When he spoke, his voice was so soft, Darak had to strain to hear him over the gusting wind.

"He will want to take a long time."

Struath bent, wincing, and crawled back into the cave. The shaman had borne the miseries of this journey as well as any of them, but now both body and spirit seemed diminished by the weight of his knowledge. For clearly, Struath knew the spirit inhabiting the wolf—knew and feared it. Why was he intent on deceiving him? Especially when his silence endangered them all.

"Damn."

If he tried to force the truth from Struath, the shaman would close up tighter than a clamshell. Yeorna,

perhaps, might wheedle it out of him; she had a gift
for knowing how to talk to people. He would take her
aside tonight while Struath slept. For now, all he could
do was stalk his enemy and see what he could learn.

A day, maybe two before he'd be ready for the kill.
Until then, his conversation with Fellgair would have
to wait.

Chapter 25

IT WAS STILL DARK when Griane left the cave. Darak had been so exhausted from tracking the wolf that he never stirred. When he did, he would be furious, although strictly speaking, she had not lied. When Darak had returned last night, he had told her he didn't want her leaving the cave for any reason and asked if she understood. And she'd said "Aye, Darak" with just the right degree of resentment to sound convincing. She couldn't help it if he chose to interpret that as a promise.

After all, she had a perfectly sound reason for disobeying. Darak had his hands full with the wolf. It was up to her to contact the Trickster. Even if Darak could have gone, she was a far more suitable emissary. Fellgair liked her. He had called her "delightful" and "witty" and had praised her appearance. Her hair, anyway. And when she kissed him, he had most definitely kissed her back. The experience had proved mildly disappointing; she had assumed that kissing a god would make her senses reel and her pulse flutter and her body flush with . . . something. Mostly, she had noticed that his long whiskers tickled. Even Darak's brief, hard kiss at the gorge had been more stimulating, although it had left her lips a bit bruised.

Belatedly realizing that she was stroking her mouth with her forefinger, she frowned and broke into a trot. When she returned with the Trickster's promise to open a portal, Darak would forgive her. He would shout and threaten to wallop her, but he would understand why she'd had to go; he was willing to risk anything to get Tinnean back, too.

Although the chinks of sky had lightened to a dull gray, it was too dark among the trees to move fast. She had to guide herself with her hands, letting her feet tell her when she ventured off the narrow trail. Despite her care, she ran headlong into a low-hanging branch. She picked herself up, swiping impatiently at her forehead. Just a scrape, hardly bleeding at all. She'd just have to move more slowly. But Darak would be awake by now and he would guess her intention. She had to find the Trickster before Darak found her. Bent almost double, she hurried on.

Two ghostly forms loomed ahead of her. She straightened so quickly she slipped on the slick leaves and landed on her arse. Shaking her braid back, she looked up and recognized the twin birches where the trail veered.

Disgusted, she rose, wiping her hands on her breeches. Tinnean's breeches. The feel of the soft leather comforted her. It was easy to remember his face—it was before her every day—but sometimes, she found herself struggling to recollect his mannerisms: the sound of his laugh or the exact way he'd gnaw his fingernails. It was silly, but just touching his breeches brought him closer.

But standing here rubbing them won't bring him back.

The waterskin bumped against her hip. The stones she had packed inside it comforted her almost as much as Tinnean's breeches. She wasn't a complete curd-brain, although Darak would probably call her far worse. If she did meet up with the mysterious wolf, sling and stones would scare it off.

A pheasant burst out of the bushes. The scream escaped before she could stop it.

Curd-brain. Mutton-head. Ninny-mouth.

She bent over, one hand pressed against her side until her breathing slowed. As an afterthought, she removed a stone from the skin. She doubted she would need it. From the little she could glean from Darak's grunts and the Tree-Father's cryptic comments, the wolf—or more accurately, the spirit inhabiting the wolf—could have little interest in her. Still, there were other predators in the forest. Better to be prepared than to fumble for a stone at a critical moment.

Darak would approve that kind of foresight. She would have to be sure and tell him when she saw him—assuming he let her get a word in.

She wasn't afraid of a beating. She'd had enough of them from her Uncle Dugan, that drunken bully. Darak had smacked her bottom a time or two when she was little, if only with the flat of his hand. Still, it was a big hand and it had stung. She had called him a lot of names, but she hadn't cried. That was something to be proud of. She was less proud of the names she had called him the night he had threatened Cuillon. Darak could be domineering and he was certainly stiff-necked, but he was no wife beater.

A jay's raucous screech interrupted her thoughts. She glanced up and promptly tripped over a rock.

Clod. Oaf. Wool-gathering mutton-head.

It would serve her right if the wolf got her.

Although she had only thought the words, her hand flew to her mouth. She walked on, more slowly, hoping that an ill-wish only counted if you spoke the words aloud.

Ahead of her, a bramble bush sprawled across the trail. Just beyond it was the little clearing where she and Darak had met the Trickster. Avoiding the brambles, she waded into the deeper underbrush beside the trail, accompanied by a cacophony of snapping twigs and rustling leaves. Certainly, the Trickster would be well-warned of her arrival. Too late, she realized she had forgotten to bring an offering. Perhaps he would accept another kiss. If she were a god, she would prefer that to a dead animal.

She stumbled into the clearing, plucking stray twigs and leaves from her tunic. One hand went to her braid. Smoothing the errant wisps of hair as best she could, she faced the fallen log.

Three times, she called his name. Then, uncertain what sort of ritual was required when asking a god to appear, she faced each direction and called his name again. As an afterthought, she said, "Lord Trickster, I need you. I'll wait as long as I can, but Darak's following me, so I don't have much time and I'd be very grateful if you would get here before he does."

She had never been much good at waiting. When forced to it, she managed by keeping her mind or her hands busy. All she had for her hands was the stone, which she began tossing in the air. That left her mind too free to wander, so she pretended she was a hunter.

She turned in slow circles, scanning the branches for birds and squirrels, searching the ground for tracks of hare or pheasant. The shushing of the leaves underfoot was so loud that she gave up her circling. Head cocked, she listened to the forest. Except for two tree branches rubbing against each other with a sorrowful moan, it was utterly silent—as if all living creatures had fled.

In that eerie silence, the rustling in the underbrush was a relief. She spun around, a smile in place for the Trickster, and found herself facing the wolf.

The fear was a live thing, clawing at her throat. Her

breath came in harsh pants, puffing out in white clouds.
Her heart pounded loud enough for the whole forest
to hear.

Don't run. Wolves pursue prey that runs.

Even if she had wanted to flee, she could only stand
there, staring into unblinking yellow eyes nearly at a
level with hers. Some part of her mind recalled how
the Trickster had bespelled Darak with his eyes. She
blinked, forcing herself to look away, to note the burrs
in the creamy fur around its throat, the swirl of white
on its forehead.

Half a dozen paces separated them. The wolf could
cover that distance in one leap.

It moved and her breath leaked out in a ragged sob.
But instead of attacking, it sat down, bushy tail curling
around its forepaws.

Heat burned her cheeks. Was the demon laughing
at her? Enjoying her fear? Her hands clenched, fingers
closing around the solid reality of flesh-warmed stone.

Without taking her eyes off the wolf, her other hand
moved slowly to her waist. The wolf observed her,
unmoving. Its stillness chilled her. Her fingers moved
more quickly, tangling in the leather straps of the sling.

It's looped through your belt, Griane. Just like always.

Her fingers remembered and obeyed. Still the wolf
remained motionless, apparently content to watch her
free the sling and fit a stone into the leather pouch.

The air grew thick, crackling with energy as it did
when a thunderstorm approached. The stench of brimstone assailed her nostrils, obscuring the wolf's scent.
An odd prickling ran over her body. Even as she
swung the sling over her head, she wondered how
midges could survive in the dead of winter.

The wolf rose. She raised her foot to take a step
back, but it was like moving underwater, all her ac-
tions too slow, all her limbs too heavy. Her arm fell
to her side. The stone fell to the ground with a damp
thud. The sling slid from her nerveless fingers.

The scream roared out of her, dying in her throat when she felt warmth envelop her. She was rising, floating. The forest blurred into a dizzying smear of gray and brown and white. Far away, she heard Darak's shout, but she was flying now, faster than any bird. If she had known this giddy exhilaration awaited her, she would never have feared death.

Even before the scream faded, Darak was nocking an arrow in his bowstring. Shouting to Struath to follow, he plunged through the brambles.

The wolf's head jerked toward him. As he drew back the bowstring, he felt the earth shudder and pitch. Before he could plant his feet, a gale-force wind slammed him back against a tree. Above the roaring in his ears, he heard Struath shouting at him to get down, but he was already falling, falling out of his body, and rising at the same time. He could only stare at his outstretched fingers, wondering at the light that stained them blue. He heard the screech of rending wood and the blue shattered into shards of white so brilliant it hurt his eyes.

The gale died. The light faded. He tumbled back into himself and onto his knees next to an enormous fissure carved out of the earth.

Like a wounded animal, he crouched on all fours, trying to will his trembling hands to reach for his bow. No longer blue, he noticed, but normal flesh, the fingertips slimed with mud and damp leaves. He stared from his fingers to the rucked-up earth, recalling the time Red Dugan had gone out to plow the fields for the spring planting, still drunk on the previous night's brogac. He followed the furrow with his eyes as it zigzagged across the clearing.

Griane was gone. The wolf was gone. Smoke rose from the blackened trunk of a blasted sapling. He turned to find Struath leaning on his staff as if it were the only thing keeping him on his feet.

"What happened?" The words came out as a hoarse mumble, shaped by a tongue still thick with shock.

The very effort of raising his head made Struath reel. Darak lunged and caught him, the weight of the shaman's body dragging them both to the ground. When the convulsions began, he could only hold Struath until they finally subsided into long racking shudders.

Struath's mouth moved. Darak bent close to hear the words, but instead of speaking, Struath seized his face between icy palms. The shaman's energy invaded him, not the delicate probing he had experienced as a youth returning from his vision quest, but a brutal assault that sent twin bolts of lacerating pain through his temples. The relentless power ripped him open. His mind screamed in protest, but he was helpless to stop the invasion. Desperately, he tried to shield himself, to protect the most secret parts of his being.

As suddenly as it had attacked, the presence vanished, leaving only a dull throbbing in his head. Struath's hands fell limply to his lap. "Forgive me," he whispered. "I had to be sure. I was too weak to be gentle."

He realized then what Struath had feared: that the wolf had taken his body. He stared from the smoking sapling to the rucked-up earth and shivered.

"Griane?" Struath's bloodshot eye darted frantic glances around the clearing. He struggled to sit, arms flailing futilely until Darak seized him. Panting with the effort, he propped Struath against a birch.

"Wait."

He crawled over to his bow, retrieved the fallen arrow, and followed the fissure across the clearing. Broken branches and frenzied claw marks testified to the wolf's flight. Darak smiled grimly; at least his enemy had tasted terror as well.

He fought his way through the underbrush, shouting Griane's name. His breath caught when he saw a dark red patch on the forest floor, but it was only a clump of blood-oak leaves. Reluctantly, he returned to the clearing. He drew up short when he saw the sling.

The leather straps were damp with her perspiration. The smooth stone still preserved a trace of her warmth. He reminded himself that she was skilled with a sling, as good as most men. Skinny as she was, she was strong enough to stun a wolf at close range. Then he remembered her scream, thick and clotted as if she had been choking.

Struath's eye widened when he thrust out the sling. "That's all? No footprints? No trail?"

He shook his head.

"And the wolf?"

"Fled. That way."

"At least it did not take her."

"It tried to take her, too?"

Struath nodded. "I could smell it. The discharge of energy. You interrupted the attack. That's why it turned on you."

"That was the blue light?"

"Nay. That was me." The shaman took a deep breath. "I threw all my power. And still I could not destroy him. Only . . . shatter the energy he directed at you." Darak followed Struath's gaze to the blasted sapling. "I must pray forgiveness of the oak."

"You did that?"

A look of pain flashed across Struath's face, quickly suppressed. Darak helped him across the clearing. He caught his breath when Struath pushed up his sleeve. The skinny forearm was crisscrossed with more than a dozen old knife wounds.

"Your dagger, Darak."

Struath held the blade above his arm, murmuring a prayer. The dagger wobbled. Darak wrapped his fingers around Struath's. Together, they made a new cut.

He supported Struath while the shaman smeared his blood down the blackened trunk.

"Forgive me, oak-brother. May my blood restore you."

The words were scarcely out of Struath's mouth when he collapsed. Darak lowered him to the ground, hushing him when Struath protested. He hacked a strip from the bottom of his tunic and wound it around the shaman's arm, remembering the times Griane had performed the same service for him.

How could a girl just vanish?

Choking down the helplessness, he strode to the place where he had found the sling. Shoving back his sleeve, he sliced open his forearm and let the blood spatter onto the leaves.

"I will find you, girl. On my blood, I swear it."

He waited, allowing the determination to shift into rage. Controlled the rage, banking it to a cold fury, savoring the bitter taste of it. Only then did he make the second cut.

"And I will find you, too. Demon or man, I will find you and destroy you."

Morgath's headlong flight slowed. Panting, he collapsed beside a shallow creek.

Foolish to disobey the pack leader. His senses had been dazzled by the female's scent, by her long, straight limbs, by the possibility of possessing that scent, those legs, that sweet, human flesh.

He'd almost had her. He had touched her spirit, felt the strength of her will, her desperate struggle to cling to her body. Another moment and her spirit would have surrendered, leaving her body open to him.

And then the air had ripped apart. The female vanished, and before he could destroy the Hunter, the Betrayer had appeared to thwart him. His lips curled back. At least now he knew the extent of the Betrayer's power.

He must act soon, while the Betrayer was weak. He must find a new body, one the Hunter would not suspect. He must give up the strong jaws that could snap bone, the sharp claws that had ripped open man-flesh. But first, he had to find a place to den, deep enough and dark enough to hide him from the pack leader's ever-watchful eyes.

As if the thought had summoned him, the pack leader loomed before him in the shape of the fox-man.

The man in him longed to shape the thoughts that would make the pack leader understand. The wolf conquered. He lowered his tail, cringing. Ears folded back, he bellied forward until he crouched at the pack leader's feet.

"You have displeased me."

He tilted back his head and offered his throat.

"I told you the girl was not to be harmed. And you disobeyed."

His low whine crescendoed into a squeal. Desperately, he opened his mind to the pack leader, begging him to understand, to forgive. When the pack leader merely stared down at him, he rolled onto his side, raising his hind leg to expose his groin.

"Now I must punish you."

His bladder voided uncontrollably. He could only lie there as the pack leader raised one hand, clawed fingers spread wide. His heart thudded desperately as the fingers began to close. His whimper died on a gasp. His heart missed a beat and he convulsed, limbs flailing helplessly. His vision narrowed to a circle smaller than a vole's tunnel.

He had disobeyed. Disobedience was death. He would never know the delight of wearing human flesh again. He would never stand before the Betrayer and condemn him to an eternity in Chaos. He would never slide the killing stone between the Hunter's ribs and tear open his flesh and watch the blood pour out of his strong, young body.

The pack leader dropped his fist. "Unfortunately, killing you would spoil the game."

His heart resumed its frantic beating. He gulped air into his tortured lungs, heedless of the ache in his chest. He was alive. He still had a chance to kill.

"Use it well. I will not grant you another reprieve."

The pack leader knelt beside him. A shiver of ecstasy shook him as the claws stroked his fur, another as the muzzle brushed his ear.

"The Hunter's name is Darak. And this is how you can defeat him."

Chapter 26

IT WAS MIDMORNING before Darak got Struath
back to the cave. He kept his voice level while he
told the others what had happened. He even managed
to finish the tale without allowing Yeorna's inarticulate cries and Cuillon's stricken expression to deter
him. But the inevitable stream of questions that followed stole what little reserves of calm he still possessed. When Yeorna asked for the third time what
could have happened to Griane, he turned on her so
fiercely that she shrank away. Shamed, he stammered
out an apology and left them.

If he remained in the cave, he would only replay
the events he had witnessed. Instead, he returned to
the clearing. He examined the signs again. He eyed the
wolf's trail, but turned back without following it. He
would have his revenge, but first he had to find
Griane—and a way to Chaos.

He hesitated a long moment, then called Fellgair's
name three times. He asked the Trickster to help him.
Discarding his pride, he went down on his knees and
begged. He waited until his knees ached. Then he rose
with a muttered curse.

"Impatient, aren't you?"

Darak whirled around so fast he stumbled. The Trickster was leaning against the blasted sapling, arms folded across his white-furred chest. He strolled over to the fallen log and seated himself. "Do sit down."

He patted the log. Darak squatted just out of reach. Fellgair smiled. "If I wanted to hurt you, I could reach you anywhere."

"Aye. Well. If it's all the same to you, I'll stay where I am."

"Suit yourself." The Trickster adjusted his brush as if settling down for a cozy chat. "So. How fares the glorious quest?"

"I need your help, Trickster."

"Then answer my question."

With an effort, Darak curbed his impatience. "We cannot find a way to open a portal. Struath barely managed to save me from the wolf. And Griane . . ." The Trickster's ears pricked up at the slight catch in his voice. "Griane is gone."

"And how have you dealt with these little setbacks?"

"I answered your question."

"Oh, I see. It's a game." The Trickster clapped his hands like a delighted child. "Lovely. I'll answer your questions if you answer mine."

"Will you answer truthfully?"

Fellgair pressed a clawed hand to his breast. "Darak. You wound me."

"That's not an answer."

"Have we started playing already?"

"Not until we establish the rules."

Fellgair wrinkled his nose. "Rules are so tiresome. Oh, sit down. Or squat if you prefer."

"Truth for truth, then?"

"Truth for truth. And since you asked the last question, I get to go first. Why do you hate your father?"

It came too quickly, before he had a chance to prepare. Fellgair's slow smile told him the Trickster had seen his body tense. He wanted to say, "I never hated him." But what was the point of lying when Fellgair already knew the truth?

"I hated him for making me feel like I could never measure up to him. I hated him for never seeming afraid. I hated him for dying." The ugly words shook him. "I was a boy then. I don't hate him anymore."

"Now you simply resent him."

Damn the Trickster and his games. "Aye, I resent him. For leaving me to raise Tinnean and care for my mother and see this through on my own. And I know that's stupid. He has nothing to do with any of this and he cannot help me set things right."

"Perhaps. Perhaps not."

"What does that mean?"

"It means exactly what I said. The role he plays in this game—if any—depends upon you."

"You call this a game?"

The Trickster waggled a reproving finger. "My turn. How did you feel when Struath revealed the wolf's true identity?"

He looked down to hide his shock, but Fellgair just chuckled. "So the secretive shaman neglected to mention that Morgath had returned. Interesting."

Cold sweat broke out on his body, followed by a gut-churning blaze of fury. All the signs had been there—Struath's terror, his evident knowledge of their enemy, his doubts about his ability to defeat him. Stupid not to have figured it out—but unforgivable for Struath to have hidden this knowledge from them.

"I suppose he also neglected to mention that he was the one who drew Morgath to the grove."

In spite of his rage, he shook his head. Whatever reason Struath had for keeping the wolf's identity a secret, he refused to believe that he had deliberately opened the way for Morgath.

"Truth for truth. Your rules."

"Struath hates Morgath."

"Perhaps. Perhaps not."

"Why would he draw him to the grove?" A wasted question, but he had to know.

"Because they were lovers."

Darak could only shake his head again.

"Morgath offered his little apprentice pleasure such as he had never experienced before—or since. Pleasure and pain. Morgath enjoys both in equal measure. You're very much like him in that respect."

"I am nothing like Morgath."

"I wonder if your wife would agree."

Darak rose. "Leave my wife out of this."

"Are you threatening me?" The idea seemed to amuse the Trickster.

He choked down his anger and shook his head. "My turn. Is Griane safe?"

"For now."

Another wasted question. He should have asked where she was, how to find her. Still, relief flooded him, making his knees shake. To hide it, he squatted down again.

"My turn."

Darak braced himself, but the question was surprisingly simple.

"Why are you willing to go to Chaos to find Tinnean?"

"He's my brother."

"You'll have to do better than that."

"It's the truth. I'm his older brother. I'm supposed to look out for him. Take care of him." Darak heard the thickening in his voice and clamped his lips together. Always, around the Trickster, he revealed too much. "My turn. Will you open a portal for me?"

"No."

Then it was hopeless. They could spend years searching for a portal. Tinnean would be lost forever. The world would die. He wasn't even aware of getting to his feet until Fellgair asked, "Giving up so soon?"

The Trickster's mocking smile stiffened his resolve. "Nay. And it's my turn. How will I find Chaos?"

"You'll find it very chaotic."

"Damn it, Fellgair . . ."

"Can I help it if you ask bad questions?"

"Nay." Darak smiled through gritted teeth. "And it's my turn again." Fellgair acknowledged that small victory with a mocking bow. "How do I find Tinnean and bring him back?"

Fellgair waggled a finger at him. "Rephrase. Two questions in the guise of one."

Darak took several deep breaths. He had to think clearly. Master his impatience. Ask the right questions.

"How do I free Tinnean?"

"Much better. You will free your brother by acknowledging that your greatest strength is also your greatest weakness."

"And what is—?"

"My turn. What are you willing to sacrifice to free him?"

Anything, Darak thought. But he forced himself to consider. Would he give up his life for Tinnean? In a moment. Would he give up the Forever Isles, his spirit condemned never to be reborn? Aye. To die and sleep forever—that was not such an awful fate.

"Let me know if you'll be much longer. I'll try to squeeze in a little nap."

Could he sacrifice someone else's life to free his brother and the Oak? Could he live with that choice?

"I would sacrifice anything that was mine to offer."

Fellgair rolled his eyes. "A tad cryptic."

"No more so than that nonsense about acknowledging my greatest weakness."

"Don't you want to know what that is?"

"Nay."

"You asked before."

"I changed my mind."

"Afraid?"

"It's not your turn."

"Sit down, Darak."

"Why are you doing this?"

"It's my job. Did you ever love your wife?"

"I've had enough of this game."

"The game ends when I say so."

Although Fellgair still wore the same small smile, Darak felt sweat break out on his forehead. The Trickster was clearly waiting for him to sit. Stubbornly, he remained standing.

"What does it matter if I loved my wife or hated my father? I know—that's another question out of turn. But this is pointless." He fought for control, keeping his voice as low as the Trickster's. "This is not a game. The world is dying. How can you stand by and do nothing?"

"Giving you fire was nothing?"

"You turned around and helped Morgath."

"Of course I did. I am the Trickster. In me, chaos and order combine. I cannot support one without undermining the other."

"But order is already undermined. The Oak is lost. Restoring its spirit would . . . it would even things up."

"Order was undermined by a man. It is up to men to restore it."

Darak's shoulders sagged. "So you will not help us?"

"I didn't say that."

"But—"

"Darak." The Trickster regarded him as he might a very small, very stupid child. "Men can change their natures. Gods cannot."

"Not even to save the world?"

"It's only one world. We have many. But we do care, in our selfish, godlike way."

Darak nodded, wishing he could believe that. "Lord Trickster . . ."

"So polite. You must want something."

"If I do not return from Chaos—"

"Assuming you reach it in the first place."

"I'll reach it. I just . . . would you keep Griane safe? And the Holly-Lord?"

After all his agonizing about sacrificing his folk, here he was condemning Struath and Yeorna. Struath had betrayed them through his silence, but Yeorna. . . .

Fellgair's face became grave. "There will be no safe place if your world dies."

"There are many worlds, you said."

"And would they thank me for taking them to one, leaving all they have ever known and loved to die?"

Darak sighed. "I don't know. But they would have each other, at least. And if I knew they were safe, it would . . . ease me, is all." He shrugged. "I've no right to ask, but . . . there it is."

Fellgair regarded him with an unblinking stare. Darak forced himself to return it. "I could—perhaps—protect one. Which will it be?"

"Nay."

"Griane or the Holly-Lord."

"Do not ask this of me."

"Choose."

"I cannot choose."

"Choose one or I'll protect neither."

"Cuillon!" His voice fell to a whisper. "Protect Cuillon."

The Trickster stroked his long, black whiskers. "Griane will be wounded."

Of course, the Trickster would tell her.

"She will understand."

Wherever Griane was, she was safe. She was strong and resourceful. Cuillon couldn't even bring himself to kill a fish.

"And he wears Tinnean's body."

Darak closed his eyes. Griane might understand, but would she ever forgive him?

"And what would I receive if I promised you this boon?"

He was so tired. Tired of games, tired of trying to stay one step ahead of Morgath and the Trickster and time. Slowly, he got down on his knees. "I will beg. If that's what you want."

He raised his hands. Big, blunt, capable hands, strong enough to heave a deer onto his shoulders or bruise a woman's flesh. He winced. He had never understood why Maili had hated his touch. They had been two strangers, shut away in their own thoughts, cut off from each other. Perhaps a child would have changed that. More likely, they would simply have gone on, day after day, sharing a bed, sharing the chores, patching the chinks in the walls and the holes in their lives.

The Trickster had asked if he loved Maili. On his knees, he offered the only answer he could.

"I never loved my wife. Not as I should have. I never knew what she wanted and I never asked. Maybe I was afraid of what she'd say. I don't know, Fellgair. I used to be so sure about my life. About everything. Now all I've got are questions."

The red-furred hands were gentle as they clasped his. "My dear boy. That is the beginning of wisdom."

"I'd rather have the answers."

Fellgair smiled. "I do like you, Darak. You keep surprising me." Effortlessly, the Trickster pulled him to his feet. "You have offered three gifts in exchange for the Holly-Lord."

Had he? He couldn't remember. Trust Fellgair to keep track. "He is worth it."

"True. But some men would have negotiated the price. You offered your gifts freely."

His father had once told him that the greatest sacrifices were made willingly and thus, were most valued by the gods.

"In return for surprising me—something so few

mortals are able to do—I offer this: to survive Chaos, you must let go of your conception of reality. For going down on your knees, I offer this: to defeat Morgath, you will have to sacrifice your pride and humble yourself again. And for the story about your wife . . ." Fellgair tapped his chin with his claw. "For that, I will protect the Holly-Lord." He held out his hand. "Now we are even."

His claws were cool and very sharp. Still gripping Fellgair's hand, Darak asked, "What do you want from me? Not for Cuillon, just . . ."

"In general?"

Darak nodded.

"I want to see you weep, Darak. I want to see you break."

Fellgair's claws dug into his palm, ever so lightly, but his smile was warm, even a little sad. Somehow, that frightened him more than any of the Trickster's words. He swallowed, the fear as bitter as bile.

"I warrant you'll get your wish ere this is over."

The Trickster nodded, his smile gone. "I warrant I will."

Chapter 27

WHEN GRIANE DISAPPEARED, something inside Cuillon ripped apart, as if a bear had torn open his trunk and shredded his heartwood. Yeorna explained that this was grief. Her way of dealing with grief was to mend her robe. Struath's was to stare into the fire.

He wished Darak would return. Darak would know how to make the grief more bearable. Each time he heard a rustling at the cave's entrance, he looked up. Each time he realized it was only the wind rattling the branches, the hope drained away like water into the earth. His ages-old patience seemed to have vanished with Griane. Now, his spirit felt as frayed as Yeorna's robe.

Finally, he seized a waterskin and crawled outside. He gulped great mouthfuls of air, so clean and sweet after the smokiness of the cave. The gusting wind tore at his mantle and he shivered. Dark clouds crouched over the treetops. Darak would have to hurry or he would be caught in the storm. The branches shielding the cave rattled again. This time, it was Yeorna, her forehead creased in a rare frown.

"Darak said we must stay inside, Holly-Lord."

He held up the waterskin. "I was going to the river."

"We have water enough to last till the morrow."

A great weight seemed to settle on his shoulders. "I just wanted to do something. To help."

Yeorna patted his cheek, just as Griane used to do. The weight settled into his chest.

"I know it is hard to wait, Holly-Lord. But we must. The wolf might be nearby."

"Aye, Yeorna."

She took his hand to lead him back inside, then froze. He glanced around, fearful that the wolf had indeed appeared, but Yeorna's joyful expression belied that.

"Look." She pointed at the sunberry bush that stood at the edge of the embankment. "A wren. It's a good omen, Holly-Lord. The wren is sacred to the Holly."

He remembered the story. Remembered, too, that the wren was the bird whose spirit Struath had cast out. Seeing Yeorna's eager excitement, he kept silent, unwilling to steal her happiness the way he had stolen Griane's. The wren teetered on its perch, one wing fluttering wildly.

"Oh, poor thing. Its wing is broken."

"Can you fix it, Yeorna?" Griane could. Griane could heal anything.

Yeorna shook her head, sighing. Then her expression brightened. "But we could feed it. If we have any suetcake left."

"Let me look, Yeorna."

Her smile made him feel useful again. He watched her pick her way along the embankment. The air felt heavy as it did before a thunderstorm. Yeorna must have noticed, too; she hesitated a few paces from the wren, staring skyward.

He crawled into the cave, trying to remember the last time he had experienced a thunderstorm in winter.

He peered into Darak's hunting sack and finally dumped
the contents on the ground, sorting through fishhooks
and lures, arrowheads and coiled rope, a pouch filled
with fragments of straw and twigs, two fire bundles,
and a bag with dusty flakes of meal.

He was repacking the hunting sack when Struath
spoke his name. He looked up to find the Tree-Father
propped up on one elbow, watching him.

"I put everything back." Humans were very particular about their possessions. Struath would allow no
one to touch the curved dagger that lay next to his
sleeping place or the little pouch that contained the
round crystal that would carry the Oak's spirit out
of Chaos.

"What are you looking for?"

"Suetcake. For Yeorna."

Struath frowned. "Where is Yeorna? She didn't go
outside?"

"Do not worry. I will bring her back."

He licked his finger and dipped it into the bottom
of the pouch. A few flakes of meal clung to it. He
hoped this would be enough. Carefully holding his
finger upright, he crawled back through the branches
and rose, smiling.

Struath was still trying to puzzle out why Yeorna
needed suetcake when he heard the Holly-Lord's
shout. He forced himself to his hands and knees and
crawled under the branches, only to collide with a pair
of legs. The Holly-Lord tugged him to his feet.

"Something happened to Yeorna," he said and
pointed.

She lay sprawled beside a sunberry bush. Clutching
the Holly-Lord's arm, Struath hurried toward her.
Had she fainted? Or fallen? It would be easy enough

to lose your footing among the shifting pebbles and slick leaves.

Awkwardly, he knelt and pressed his fingertips to her wrist. Her pulse was rapid but steady. No bleeding from the ears. No visible wound anywhere. Perhaps the wound was inside, like Crel who had fallen from a ledge while driving the sheep down from Eagles Mount.

"Did you see anything?"

"Nay. I came into the cave to find some suetcake for the wren . . ." The Holly-Lord glanced around. "It must have flown away. Maybe its wing was not broken after all."

"And then . . . ?"

"When I came back out, she was lying on the ground."

Struath's searching fingers found a rock hidden in the leaves. Carefully, he lifted Yeorna's head. He could feel no lump, although her scalp felt warm. How long did it take for a lump to rise? He wished Griane were here; she would know.

Could it be some woman's ailment? Everyone knew women acted strangely at their moon-times. Of course, he had never actually seen a woman then; those days were spent in seclusion. But sometimes, he had heard laughter and whispers coming from the women's hut.

"Help me get her into the cave." He grimaced as he pulled her arm around his neck; it was forbidden for a man to touch a woman during her moon-time.

By the time they lowered her onto her wolfskins, he was shaking with exhaustion. How would he ever find the strength to face Morgath again?

"What should we do, Struath?"

He shook his head helplessly. "Keep her warm. And wait for her to wake." If she woke.

Chapter 28

WARMTH CARESSED HER, penetrating her flesh to inhabit her bones. Griane resisted the urge to open her eyes; she wanted to savor her first impressions of the Forever Isles. The golden luminescence of the light on her closed eyelids. The crisp texture of grass between her fingers. The splash of water and the soft shushing of leaves. And the breeze. Sweet Maker, the air was rich enough to eat. She breathed in the aromas of sun-warmed earth and grass, mildly astonished that her chest rose and fell exactly as it had when she was alive.

When she finally opened her eyes, a tempest of color burst upon her winter-whitened senses. The blue bolder than any sky at home, the clouds so brilliantly white they made her eyes water. Squinting, she sat up. The legends promised that your family would welcome you to the Forever Isles, but there was only a waterfall, cascading into a pool over a series of ledges so even and straight that they might have been carved into the hillside. Purple spikes of loosestrife hugged the fringe of the pool; red clover dotted the shining expanse of green grass. Purple, red, green—such commonplace words for the shimmering intensity of hues that seemed to breathe along with her.

She got to her feet. Perhaps Maili and her parents were waiting elsewhere. The legends had neglected to mention that possibility and the fact that her body would feel as solid as ever, her head still sore where the branch had scraped it. She had assumed she would be like the man in the bog, some spirit-form of herself. Instead, Tinnean's breeches clung to her and real sweat trickled down her sides.

She crouched down and scooped water into her cupped palm. Sweet, clean, and cold, she gasped as the single swallow suffused her with warmth. Then she remembered the wolf and shivered. She was almost sure she had heard Darak's voice at the end. Had he killed the wolf—or gods forbid, been killed?

With a soft moan, she sank onto the grass. Everyone was supposed to be happy in the Forever Isles. Why did she have this hard knot of grief in her chest? Frolicking on the sunlit shores, indeed. If Old Sim were here, she'd give the Memory-Keeper a piece of her mind. But he wasn't here. No one was. She was utterly alone.

She ground her fists against her burning eyes. The other spirits must be on another part of the island. Or on another island altogether. She had to stop wallowing in self-pity and find them. Together, they could figure out a way to help the others. Just because she was dead didn't mean she was going to sit around and do nothing.

Shoving a wisp of hair off her damp forehead, she cast a longing look at the pool. It would be a shame to look bedraggled when she met her family. And it was so hot . . .

She stripped and lowered herself into the pool, gasping a little at the water's chill. Seizing soapwort from the bank with one hand, she tore her braid free

with the other and blissfully scrubbed her hair for the
first time in a moon. Splashing in the water reminded
her of her first swimming lessons: Darak's pretense of
surprise when she and Tinnean dove beneath the surface to grab his ankles, his wicked grin when he
charged toward them, cutting through the shallows
like a giant boat, heedless of their shrieks of excitement and the gouts of water they hurled at him.

She had forgotten that. One of many happy memories subsumed by the bitter ones after Darak married
Maili. She had always blamed him for her sister's un-
happiness, but it took two to make a marriage work—
or fail. Shame filled her when she remembered the
words she had flung at him, the stark look on his face.
Now, she would never have the chance to take those
words back.

She dragged herself out of the pool, ashamed to be
indulging in a bath while her kinfolk were in danger.
She dried herself quickly with her mantle and pulled
on her tunic. She was reaching for Tinnean's breeches
when she heard a splash behind her and whirled
around.

Sunlight slanted through the ancient oaks shadowing the pool. A shaft of light sliced across the waterfall's spray, creating a tiny rainbow. Another danced
off the quartz chips in the boulders, making them glit-
ter like the Tree-Father's spirit catcher. On one of the
boulders, tossing pebbles into the pool, lounged the
Trickster.

"Awake at last."

"Awake? But aren't I—"

"Dead?" He shook his head, smiling. "Welcome to
the Summerlands, Griane."

She sat down abruptly on a sunlit boulder.

"Disappointed?"

"Nay. I just . . ." She shook her head. To go from
life to death to life again took a little getting used to.
"It was you, then. Who saved me from the wolf."

The Trickster rose and bowed, claws over his heart.
"I don't know what to say."

" 'Thank you, Lord Trickster' might be appropriate."

"Forgive me. Thank you, Lord Trickster."

"You're welcome, Griane." He strolled over to her
and threw himself down on the grass at her feet. His
golden eyes slanted up at her, slitted against the sunlight. As his gaze traveled up her legs, she realized
her tunic was bunched up around her waist. Blushing,
she rose and tugged it down.

"You're as lean as a vixen."

"If you're going to insult me—"

"I meant it as a compliment."

"Oh. Well. Thank you. Again."

"Again, you are welcome. Sit down, dear. Unless
you enjoy having me look up your tunic."

She sat, knees pressed firmly together. The white tip
of his brush curled over her bare toes. She considered
moving her feet, but decided that would be rude, especially after he had saved her life.

"Does Darak ever offer you compliments?"

"Aye." She tried to think of one. "He told me I
bound his wound well."

"How dull. I should have chided him when I saw
him this afternoon."

"You saw him? He's all right? The wolf didn't hurt
him? Did you tell him I was safe? I don't want him
to worry. He has enough on his mind . . ." Her voice
ran down. The Trickster was grinning and no wonder.
She was babbling like a fool.

"Let's see. Yes. Yes. No. Yes."

"And the others?"

Fellgair shrugged.

"You must take me back."

"Must I?"

"Please. They'll be worried. The Grain-Mother's
ankle needs strapping, and the Tree-Father needs warm
compresses on his shoulder, and Darak—"

"Has enough on his mind. Why not enjoy the Summerlands? There are wonders here far greater than the water." He reached up and took her hand. He was still smiling when his claw slashed open her palm.

She cried out, more in shock than pain. She tried to jerk her hand away, but he held it fast. With his free hand, he plucked a slender silvery leaf from one of the plants beside the pool and drew it across her bleeding palm. Cool relief eased the fire. Snatching her hand back, she discovered that the wound had closed, leaving only the tiniest silver scar across her palm.

"Yes, there are many wonders in the Summerlands." He turned her chin toward another clump of plants with large, glossy leaves. "A decoction of those will soothe the most troubled spirit."

"Dried or fresh?"

"Fresh is more potent."

"Steeped how long?"

"For a man spirit-sick unto death, you should steep them overnight. For a girl fretting over unrequited love . . ." Bushy eyebrows rose in a suggestive leer.

"A good dose of common sense will suffice."

He reclined on the grass, laughing. "Ah, Griane. You are as refreshing as Summerlands water. I will miss you if you leave."

"If?"

His features shifted, the delighted smile giving way to one of such feral avidity that she scrambled to her feet. "Am I a prisoner? Do you intend to hold me against my will?"

"Never." His smile belied his emphatic negation. "But humans are so changeable. Their moods shift as often as the wind."

"Mine don't. I want to return to the First Forest."

"I want. I want. You're as bad as Darak. Did I mention that I saw him today?"

"Please, Fellgair . . ."

"We had a lovely chat. About his father. His brother. His wife . . ."

Darak never spoke about Maili, not to anyone.

"You."

"Me?"

"Mmm. Darak is quite fond of you, you know."

She didn't know. He never spoke about his feelings either. Except that morning he had told her how helpless he felt.

"He asked me to protect you and Cuillon." The tip of his brush caressed her toes. "But when asked to choose between you, he chose the Holly-Lord."

She sank down on the boulder and lowered her head, grateful that her wet hair hid her face.

"I said his choice would wound you. He said you would understand."

"Aye."

"Which? The choice or the understanding?"

"Both."

He lifted her chin gently. "Are you always so honest?"

"What's the point of lying? You'd know the truth anyway." She swiveled away and began combing out her hair with her fingers.

His hands covered hers, the pads warm and rough. "Let me do that." He spread his claws. "Much more effective than fingers, don't you think?"

Numbly, she shifted on the boulder so that he could stand behind her. For a moment, his hands lay atop her head as if in blessing. Then his fingers eased their way through the snarled strands and returned to the crown of her head to start the journey again. For a long while, there was only the splash of water, and the warmth of the sun on her face, and the light touch of his claws gliding through her hair.

"All the colors of fox fur, your hair. Burnished red. Soft streaks of bronze where the sun has bleached it. And here." His claws brushed the nape of her neck. "Almost brown." Down and up, his hands moved. Down and up, in a rhythm as ceaseless and hypnotic as his gentle swaying. "When you're older, you'll have the white as well."

Her head fell back to rest against his chest. His hands drifted down her neck, smoothing her hair over her shoulders. She turned her cheek into his fur and sighed as his hand cupped the back of her head.

"Darak asked me to open a portal."

Her head jerked up, the mood broken. "What did you say?"

"I said I would not open a portal. For him."

In those slitted eyes, she found the certain knowledge that he would open one for her. But at what cost?

"Lord Trickster, if I asked you to open a portal . . . ?"

"Are you asking?"

"I . . . before I ask, I want . . . I need to know what payment you would ask in return."

"Payment?"

"Aye. What do you want?"

"What do I want?" He knelt before her, so close that she could feel the warmth of his breath on her knees. "Well. That's an altogether different question."

Bumps of cold rippled up her arms, as if the sun had gone behind a cloud and left her shivering in the shadows. Her nipples hardened and she resisted the urge to cross her arms across her breasts. She closed her eyes. Not such a high price to pay, really. What was a maidenhead compared to the world?

"All right."

"Foxes are monogamous, Griane."

Her eyes flew open.

"Often, a pair remains together for life. You didn't know that?"

She shook her head.

"Do you wish to rescind your offer?"

"I . . . I thought . . ."

"Do you wish to rescind your offer?"

"I would never leave this place? Or see my folk again?"

The Trickster rose. "You are unwilling."

"Wait. Please."

"There is nothing more to be said."

"Give me a moment. I deserve that much. You're asking me to give up everything."

"I asked no such thing, Griane. You made the offer."

"I didn't think . . ."

"No. You didn't."

Darak had said the same thing to her, countless times. Now her impulsiveness threatened them all.

"Is there nothing else that you would accept?"

"Do you wish to rescind your offer?"

"Stop saying that. Can't you just answer me? I thought you . . . liked me. Or you wouldn't have asked . . . would not have led me to believe—"

"Do not blame me for your assumptions, Griane."

"Do you want me or not?"

"Yes."

The golden eyes bore into her. A liquid glow rose up in her belly, spreading up to her taut nipples and down into her loins. The Trickster's whiskers twitched as if he could smell her heat. When he offered her a lazy smile, she knew with utter certainty and shame that he did. Of course he could make her desire him; he simply hadn't bothered when he had returned her kiss.

Why was she hesitating? If she would miss sliding down a snowy hillside or watching the Northern Dancers illuminate the winter sky, here she would never know cold. If she must forgo the tribal feasts that celebrated the turning of the year, here she would never know hunger. And if the joys of marriage and children were denied her, she would be spared the pain of burying the babes she birthed and watching

love yield to the everyday demands of cooking and
cleaning, planting and harvesting, mending torn clothes
and broken bones. She would live out her life in this
glorious cocoon with the Trickster, always amusing,
always exciting, always a little dangerous.

She would never have the chance to apologize to
Darak for her hot and hasty words. She would never
be able to explain to her folk what had happened.
They would believe she had abandoned them. But be-
cause of her, they would find Tinnean and the Oak.
That would have to suffice.

Without a word, she lay down in the warm grass.
He knelt at her feet, watching her. She realized he
was waiting for her to open her legs to him. The sacrifice had to be made willingly.

Her breath caught on a sob and she clamped her
lips together. He saw, of course. He saw everything.
She parted her legs. His claws dug very lightly into
her ankles as he slowly pushed her knees up. He was
careful not to scratch her. She should be grateful for
that.

His fur brushed her legs as he moved between them.
His palms caressed the inside of her thighs, opening
the way wider. Would a mortal lover touch her with
such gentleness?

"Are you afraid?"

Why lie when he must notice the pulse beating in her
neck and hear the quick rasp of her breath? "Aye."

Even if she returned to the world someday, even if
she offered herself to a man she loved, she would
always remember this moment, with the grass tickling
her toes, and the sun hot on her face, and the Trickster's hands, hotter than the sun upon her flesh. She
closed her eyes, willing him to do this quickly before
she lost her nerve and begged him to let her go.

She felt a tear ooze down her cheek and then the
rough slide of his tongue. He sighed. "Is anything so
delicious as the taste of human tears?"

And then there was only warm air against her body. When she opened her eyes, he was gone.

She ran, begging him to return, knowing he had sensed that fatal hesitation, promising that she was willing. She ran until her voice grew hoarse from screaming his name. She ran until her legs gave out and she slid to her knees beneath a crab apple. Her head drooped against the tree, the knotty trunk hard against her temple. And then she wept.

Something soft brushed against her wet cheek. Something white fell upon her knee. She stared at it with a dull sense of wonder, for how could there be snow in the Summerlands? Another fell and then another before she realized the snowflakes were blossoms.

She sat up. They fell faster, as if a strong wind brought them down, although only the lightest breeze blew. Still they fell, beautiful and somehow sad. Sadder still were the two dark eyes that blinked open in the crab apple's trunk.

A blossom slid past one eye, a white-petaled tear that caught on the groove of the mouth. With one shaking forefinger, she brushed it aside and watched it drift downward. Her finger hung in the air. She touched the trunk very lightly and the tree wept white blossoms.

And then she saw the others—apple, quickthorn, rowan. An entire hillside of flowering trees. A blizzard of white, cloaking the ground like new-fallen snow.

Griane closed her eyes. Grief should not be so beautiful.

Chapter 29

BATTERED BY GRIANE'S disappearance and the Trickster's revelations, Darak had little heart for another confrontation with Struath. He refused to believe that the Tree-Father had lured Morgath to the grove, that his betrayal could run that deep. But he had concealed his knowledge of Morgath's presence. No matter what explanation he might offer, Darak doubted he could trust him again.

The storm broke as he reached the cave. He was still getting to his feet when Cuillon tugged at his sleeve.

"Darak. It is Yeorna."

The Grain-Mother sat with her back against the wall of the cave, her head lowered over the turtle shell Struath held to her lips. She looked up as he approached and her eyes widened. With an inarticulate cry, she shrank back.

"Do not be frightened," Cuillon said as he crouched beside her. "It is only Darak."

She nodded, but her eyes remained fixed on him.

Before he could ask what could possibly have reduced her to this state, Struath said, "We found her outside—"

"Outside?"

"It was my fault," Cuillon said, his face miserable. "She followed me. And then we saw the wren with the broken wing. I came back to the cave for suetcake . . ." His voice trailed off.

"We think she must have fallen," Struath continued. "She was only unconscious for a short while, but ever since she awoke, she has been . . . dazed."

Darak stared at Yeorna, sickened.

"People slip, Darak." Griane's words. *"You cannot control it."*

But he could have—simply by including Yeorna in his bargain with the Trickster.

He found himself thinking of poor Pol who had been kicked in the head by the ram; ever since that day, the boy had lain in his hut, staring vacantly into space. Had he doomed Yeorna to a similar fate through his negligence?

"Darak?"

He found his horror reflected on Cuillon's face. Damning himself for allowing his emotions to show, he groped for the words that might ease him. In the end, he used Griane's.

"It was an accident, lad. At least she's awake now. That's a good sign. Sometimes, it takes days . . ." He frowned, then turned to Struath and spoke with renewed energy. "Remember that winter—years ago— when Onnig dared Jurl to slide headfirst down Eagles Mount? Jurl slammed into a boulder and was out for a full day—"

"And dazed for another two," Struath interrupted.

"But after that . . ."

"He was as miserable as ever."

Struath offered him a weary smile and Darak found himself smiling back. Then he remembered the shaman's betrayal and his smile died.

"So Yeorna will be well again?" Cuillon asked.

"I hope so, Cuillon."

"You are not telling a small lie?"

Darak shot him an impatient glance. "I don't have all the answers. If I did, Tinnean would be safe at home and you'd be—" Seeing Cuillon's stricken expression, he broke off. His shame deepened when he remembered how he'd snapped at Yeorna that morning. No wonder his presence made her flinch.

"I'm sorry, lad. I'm just . . . I'm tired, is all."

"You were gone a long time. We were worried."

"You went back to the clearing, didn't you?" Struath asked.

"Aye."

"And tracked the wolf."

"I met Fellgair."

"Does he know where Griane is?" Cuillon asked. "Did he tell you what happened? Did he—"

"He told me she was safe."

Struath sighed heavily. "Thank the gods."

"He also told me about Morgath."

Struath's hand froze in the act of making the circle of thankfulness over his heart. His expression removed Darak's last doubts as to the truth of the Trickster's words.

"Who is Morgath?" Cuillon asked.

"Tell him, Struath." He kept his voice soft so he would not frighten Yeorna. Struath's mouth worked, but no words would come. "Nay? Then I will. Morgath attacked the One Tree. He cast my brother's spirit out. And because he had no form of his own, he stole the body of a wolf and followed us from the grove so he could destroy us all." The shaman's wince sent a savage thrill of pleasure through him. "And Struath knew. All along."

Struath shook his head.

"You knew. And you hid the truth from us."

Cuillon's fingers dug into his arm. He fought the urge to fling off that restraining hand, to seize Struath by his scrawny throat and roar the accusations in his

face. Instead, the single word came out as a strangled croak.

"Why?"

Struath's face crumpled. "I failed to See." His head
came up, a trace of the old power returning to his
face. "But I did not realize it was . . ." Trembling
fingers made the sign of protection. "I did not know.
Until I had the vision." Again, the shaman's head
drooped. "I did withhold the knowledge. I endangered
everyone. You, most of all, Darak, for I allowed you
to go into the forest alone. And Griane . . ." His
breath caught. "I shall never forgive myself for
Griane."

Struath drew the bronze dagger from its sheath with
a trembling hand. "I have failed you all—as your
Tree-Father and as a man. I do not ask for your forgiveness. I do not deserve it. But I swear that I shall
not fail you again."

Yeorna's breath hissed in as Struath pushed back
the sleeve of his robe. Cuillon winced when he saw
the old scars and the bandage stained with fresh blood.
Even Darak made an involuntary gesture to stay Struath's hand, but the Tree-Father shook his head.

"This time, I make the cut unaided."

"Nay." The unexpected tone of command in Cuillon's voice took them both by surprise. "You will not
hurt yourself again."

"I must make a blood sacrifice."

"There has been enough blood."

"Then . . . what can I offer?"

Cuillon frowned. Then his face brightened. "We
shall spit. We will all swear not to fail each other and
we will all spit. Aye, Darak?"

He gave the Holly-Lord stare for stare. In the end,
he was the one who looked away, nodding curtly.

They spat into their palms. Darak clasped Cuillon's
left hand and reluctantly shifted his gaze to Struath.
The shaman was the first to extend a hand. It shook

so badly that Darak wondered if it was a trick of the flickering firelight. When he gripped the cold fingers, he knew better. He tightened his grip, willing strength into that trembling hand; only if the Tree-Father remained strong could he rescue Tinnean and the Oak. When Struath gave him a peremptory nod, he knew his unspoken message was understood.

"Now spit, Yeorna. Like this." Cuillon spat into his right palm again. Yeorna watched, her face intent. Her gaze shifted to her hands, lying limp in her lap. Frowning in concentration, she raised her left hand, darting occasional glances at Cuillon who rewarded each movement with an eager nod. Darak watched her, relief mixed with dismay. Perhaps Yeorna would recover—but how long would that take? Meanwhile, Griane was lost, Morgath roamed the forest, and Tinnean suffered in Chaos.

Cuillon beamed as Yeorna lowered her head over her upraised hand and allowed a trickle of spittle to drip into it. "Now hold your hand out to me. Can you do that?"

With the same agonizing slowness, Yeorna stretched her hand toward Cuillon. A small gasp escaped her as he clasped it and then a smile blossomed on her face.

"Good, Yeorna. Now spit into your other hand."

Yeorna's lips puckered. Her untidy hair fell forward as she lowered her head to her cupped hand. She spat with greater force. This time, her smile was triumphant.

"Very good. Now take Struath's hand."

After a moment of hesitation, she obeyed.

"Now we will swear. Struath, it is your swearing so you should say the words."

Struath glanced around the circle, his haggard face solemn. "I swear by the mercy of the blessed Maker to support each member of this fellowship with my body, my heart, and my spirit. And if I fail in my duty, may my spirit never fly to the Forever Isles, but sink forever into Chaos."

"And so do I swear," Darak said.

"And so do I swear." Cuillon turned to Yeorna. She licked her lips, eyes darting uncertainly to each of them as her mouth struggled to form the words. "If you cannot speak the words, Yeorna, you can just nod. It will still be a swearing, will it not, Struath?"

The Tree-Father nodded. Two lines formed between Yeorna's brows. Her lips parted. They all leaned toward her, as if to help her summon the power of speech.

"I . . . swear."

Cuillon threw his arms around her. The look of sheer animal terror faded as she accepted his embrace. Noting her flushed face and damp eyes, Darak touched Cuillon on the shoulder.

"Slowly, lad. Let her get her bearings."

Cuillon pulled back, but she clung to his hand, gazing into his face with an expression of such infinite pain and hopeless pleasure that Darak's breath caught. After a long moment, she raised her right hand and stared at it. Releasing her grip on Cuillon, she rubbed two fingers back and forth across the palm. When she looked up and caught him watching her, her face went blank for a moment, then relaxed into a smile.

Darak managed a shaky smile in return before he got to his feet. Catching Struath's eye, he jerked his head toward the cave's entrance. As the shaman rose stiffly, Cuillon looked up.

"We're just going to get some fresh air," Darak said.

"Now I know you are telling a small lie."

"We're not going to kill each other, damn it. It's just . . . there are things we need to talk over."

"Talk here."

Struath leaned down to whisper something. Cuillon still looked worried, but he nodded.

Darak crawled through the branches, then held them back to ease Struath's passage. The shaman struggled to his knees, impeded by his long robe. He tried to rise, but sank back down, an expression of furious shame twisting his features. Darak thrust out his hand. After the briefest hesitation, Struath took it and allowed Darak to pull him to his feet.

Although dark clouds still lowered overhead, the rain had ceased. To the west, the sky was streaked with rose and violet, the beauty a stark counterpoint to the events of the day.

"A good sign," Struath murmured.

"A fair day on the morrow, anyway."

Out of the corner of his eye, Darak caught the helpless shivering that shook Struath. He slipped off his mantle, but the shaman's baleful glance forestalled him.

"I'm fine."

"You're cold."

"I'll manage."

"Will you just take the damn mantle and stop playing the hero?" He flung it over Struath's shoulders.

An uncomfortable silence fell between them. Struath broke it by saying, "I know I have much to atone for, but if we are—"

Darak cut him off with an impatient gesture. "I took the oath and I meant it."

"But in your heart—"

"We've more important things to worry about than my heart. Or yours." Struath drew himself up, but Darak just shook his head and dragged a weary hand across his face. "We must get to Chaos. Fellgair will not help us. There's only your spirit guide."

"Brana cannot open the way for all of us."

"Not all of us. Just you and me. Nay, listen. Yeorna will need days to recover. And we cannot allow Cuillon to go to Chaos. Even with Fellgair's protection—"

"What?"

Quickly, he related his conversation with the Trickster. With the oath fresh in his mind, he revealed every-

thing, including the revelations about his father and
Maili and the bargain that had resulted in Yeorna's
injury. As difficult as it had been to share his inner-
most thoughts with the Trickster, it was harder still to
offer them up to Struath, but perhaps the shaman
could discover clues he had overlooked. What was his
pride compared to saving Tinnean and the Oak?

Struath listened without interruption, his face unreadable. At the end, Darak added, "So we can't take
Yeorna and we daren't risk Cuillon. It has to be you
and me." At Struath's helpless gesture, his voice
sharpened. "You're the shaman. Find a way."

"While you hunt the wolf." When he remained silent, Struath's face grew stern. "You have no idea
what you are facing."

"Yesterday, perhaps."

"You cannot defeat him."

"I'm still alive."

"Only because I was there."

"What do you want, Struath? Tearful expressions
of gratitude? If I had any tears to shed, I'd offer them
to Griane." Struath's head jerked back as if he had
struck him. Muttering a curse, Darak slumped against
a boulder. "This . . . wrangling . . . serves no purpose.
We both know that."

"Old habits are hard to break." The faintest smile
lit Struath's face. It died as suddenly as it had appeared. "But I mean what I say about . . . the wolf."
Darak noted that he was still unable—or unwilling—
to speak Morgath's name. "It will mean your death,
Darak. Better to go back to Fellgair. Beg him, if
you must."

"I have begged. On my knees." His mouth twisted
in a semblance of smile at Struath's shocked expression. "You told me once I'd have to humble myself
before the gods."

"Once, it would have pleased me."

"My knees can stand it, Struath. And my pride."

With sudden resolve, the shaman said, "Brana might be able to carry me alone."

"It's too dangerous."

"And hunting the wolf is not?"

"That's different."

"How?"

"I don't know!" Darak's voice rose to a shout. "It just is."

Struath's croak of laughter brought a reluctant smile to his face. "You seek Brana. Again. I'll seek Fellgair. Again. I don't know what else I can offer him, but there must be something."

Struath hesitated, then spoke in a low voice. "We need you alive, Darak."

"We need the Oak more."

"Now who's playing the hero?"

"I'm not trying to be heroic, Struath. Just practical." He shrugged. "Besides, I've already offered the Trickster anything that was in my power to give. He could have asked for my life—but he didn't."

"He wants to keep you alive."

"He wants to see me break." Darak smiled grimly. "That alone might protect me from the wolf. Letting Morgath take me would be too easy."

"Perhaps Brana will know how to win the Trickster's help."

Darak nodded, but he held little hope that Struath's spirit guide could sway Fellgair. Griane might have been able to . . . but she was gone.

Although he braced himself for the despair, it came on a wave of nausea so violent it made him gag. He spun away from Struath, choking. Only by exerting all his willpower did he keep from shaming himself. Each ragged intake of breath caught on his clenched teeth with a hiss. His ribs ached with the effort to control his panting. He concentrated on that, only that, until his breathing eased and the nausea ebbed and he could trust himself to shape Griane's name again in his mind.

It took longer before he managed to shape the other. *Tinnean.*

Once, his greatest fear was losing his brother forever. Now, he feared what he would find. Would Tinnean's spirit be shattered by madness or twisted into something unrecognizable?

A weight descended on his shoulder. "It is hard not to lose hope," Struath said, his voice very soft. "Not to look back and think 'If only I had made a different choice.' " Struath's sigh warmed the back of his neck. "All we can do is learn from our mistakes and go on. And believe that the Maker will not allow our world to die. Chaos may have the upper hand now, but in the end, balance will . . . must . . . be restored."

"Aye, Struath."

He started as Struath grabbed his shoulders and wrenched him around. "You must be strong. For Griane. For Tinnean. For all of us."

Just as he had demanded strength from Struath during the oath-taking, so did the shaman demand it of him now. Neither of them could afford the luxury of despair, any more than one could hope to achieve the goal of their quest without the other. Like it or not, they were bound together. He had always known that, of course; what surprised him was the upwelling of relief.

Perhaps his astonishment showed, for Struath's hands slid away as the shaman took a hesitant step backward. Darak captured the retreating hands and pressed them between his.

"I will be strong. I will not lose hope. And so do I swear, Tree-Father."

Chapter 30

DARAK WOKE FROM a fitful doze to find Struath slumped by the fire, his hands over his face. Cuillon sat beside him, patting the shaman's shoulder. Even before Struath lifted his head, revealing a face ravaged by exhaustion, Darak knew he had failed.

"I'm sorry, Darak. I tried."

"And you'll try again when you're stronger." Still stupid from lack of sleep, Darak groped for his bow and quiver.

"Nay."

"I may be desperate, Struath, but I'm not so foolish as to try and confront the wolf alone. But I might be able to find his lair, work out the best place to lay an ambush."

"Darak—"

"If you're still weak from your encounter, then so is he. The longer I wait, the stronger he'll grow."

"He . . . is . . . right."

They all turned to stare at Yeorna. Belatedly, Cuillon leaped up and helped her struggle to a sitting position. "Go . . . Darak."

Darak was already on his feet. "I'll be back before twilight. In the meantime, Tree-Father, you will rest."

He forced a smile as he echoed Struath's words from the previous night. "You must be strong. On the morrow, you and I will confront Morgath and destroy him."

That resolution lent new strength to his tired legs. He trotted back to the clearing and followed the trail of splintered branches deeper into the forest. Claw marks gouged the leaf-strewn earth, tufts of fur clung to low bushes. He drove himself hard, heedless of burning lungs and aching muscles. Bloodlust surged, hot and wild, but he fought it, seeking that cold, calm center that allowed him to observe the signs and choose his path. Morgath had raced mindlessly through the forest, the man's spirit helpless before the wolf's instinct for survival. He must remain the hunter, bending mind and body and spirit to the single task of tracking his enemy.

At the top of a gentle slope, he halted, panting. He waited for his breathing to ease before following the twisting skid marks to the creek below. The tracks were shallower here and obscured by leaves. He bent closer, then drew back to study the area. Frenzied claw marks churned up the ground and the faintest whiff of urine still clung to the leaves, testifying to a terror far greater than that Morgath had experienced in the clearing. Yet, he had survived the threat to belly under a nearby spikecrown bush. Darak wrapped his mantle over his arm to protect himself from the thorns and gingerly raised a low-hanging branch.

Too exhausted to dig out a burrow, Morgath had simply collapsed. Darak laid his palm against the flattened leaves, grimly pleased that his hand remained steady. Morgath had rested here, perhaps while he'd been helping Struath back to the cave; the leaves were too damp for him to have spent the night in this makeshift lair. Darak eased himself out from under the bush, smiling. This was the path Morgath had taken back to the stream. This was the place he had broken

through the thin crust of ice to drink. And then he
had moved slowly upstream, pausing frequently as if
searching for something.

But what?

Although the trail was a day old, Darak unslung his
bow. Bending low, he ducked under the drooping boughs
of a spruce. When he straightened, he saw the furry tail
peeking out from behind a tumble of boulders.

He froze, willing his galloping heartbeat to slow. He
drew an arrow from his quiver and nocked it in the
bow. The air was still, but he edged back, using the
spruce to screen him from his prey as he worked his
way downwind. One step forward. The tail remained
utterly still. Was Morgath waiting for him to get close
before he attacked? Or was he wounded? Darak had
found no trace of blood, but perhaps Struath's magic
had injured him.

Wait for Struath or go for the kill? Only Struath
could consign Morgath's spirit to Chaos. But he had
done that once before and Morgath had escaped.

One step to the right.

It had to be now. A clean kill—one shot to the
heart—before Morgath's spirit could flee to another
body.

Another step right. That small opening between
those two branches. A clear shot.

Cold sweat broke out on his body and he slowly
lowered the bow.

The wolf's haunches were splayed over the pebbled
stream bank. Small patches of snow, fallen from the
branches of a crack willow, coated the silver-tipped
shoulders. Its muzzle lay in the water, a skin of ice
around it.

Arrow drawn, he approached with caution, uncertain whether Morgath's spirit might still linger inside
the body. When he reached the bank, he realized it
was impossible. Ice encased the whiskers. The once-
fierce eyes were glazed and unseeing. He nudged the

wolf with his foot, then slung his bow and knelt beside
it, searching for a wound. Finally, he heaved the animal over, grunting with the effort.

No blood. No broken bones. No cracks in the skull.

The wolf was dead, but only because Morgath had
chosen another host.

Cursing, Darak stumbled to his feet and ran.

Turning his face to the watery sun, Struath breathed
a prayer of thanks for Yeorna's recovery. The effects
of the blow to her head seemed to be diminishing.
She could feed herself now and her speech was less
halting. She had even managed a rueful smile when
she explained how she slipped on the slick pebbles at
the top of the embankment. She was still so weak,
though. And too often, she would lapse into silence,
staring at her outstretched fingers or touching her face
and her hair as if they belonged to a stranger—almost
like the Holly-Lord when he had awakened in Tinnean's body.

Struath's breath hissed in. On trembling legs, he tottered along the embankment. The branches of the sunberry drooped under their heavy coat of snow. He got
down on his knees, rooting among the dead leaves,
heedless of the snow that tumbled onto his neck and
shoulders. His shaking fingers closed around the tiny,
frozen body. He dragged it out from beneath the
branches. His braids brushed the wren's feathers, just
as they had during his vision of the robin. He was still
struggling to rise when he heard the Holly-Lord call
his name.

They were standing together at the cave's entrance.
The Holly-Lord grinned and waved. "Look, Struath,"
he called. "Yeorna is walking."

She looked heartbreakingly frail, clinging to the
Holly-Lord, but after a moment, she shrugged off his

arm and took a small, tentative step, like a child learning to walk. She flung back her braid and took another step, more confident now.

The wren slipped from his fingers. On his knees, Struath's eyes met hers. Yeorna smiled.

The Holly-Lord raced toward him, laughing. "See how much better she is?"

"Go into the cave."

"Are you hurt? Shall I fetch Griane's magic—?"

"Go into the cave and stay there."

"But—"

"Go. Now!"

Frowning, he obeyed. Yeorna ignored the Holly-Lord's curious glance, her glittering eyes fixed on him as he struggled to rise. Moving carefully, she walked forward until only a few paces separated them.

Although he knew the truth, he heard himself asking in a weak, pathetic voice, "Yeorna?" When Yeorna pursed her lips in that familiar look of fond reproof, Struath moaned.

"It's been a long time. Hasn't it, little rook?"

Struath's heart slammed against his ribs. Belatedly, he threw up wards, weaving the thin strands of blue, green, red, and silver into a web of protection. Morgath did the same, his smile fading as the wards trembled. With a frown of concentration, he reinforced them.

Struath murmured a prayer. Morgath had stolen the wren's body and Yeorna's the same day and still had enough power to erect wards.

"Did you ever think about me?"

Struath shook his head.

"Did you care what I suffered?"

Again, Struath shook his head, unwilling to reveal all those sleepless nights.

Morgath wet his lips. "It was like living inside . . ." He hesitated, searching for the word. ". . . a nightmare. Knowing you will never wake." The sweet smile made the words even more horrifying.

"Magic is tricky in . . . that place. Because everything keeps shifting." Struath nodded dumbly, the apprentice soaking up his mentor's wisdom. "You can hear the others. Howling. And you know that soon . . . you will be howling with them."

Panting, Morgath paused to reinforce the wards. Struath must keep him talking, force him to expend more of his energy. Perhaps then the wards would fail.

"What is it like? Taking a . . . a human?"

"Delicious." Morgath stroked Yeorna's long, golden braid almost shyly. "She was my first. I'm glad she is so pretty." The tip of the braid stroked Yeorna's cheek. "Did you ever lie with her?" Morgath dismissed the idea with a quick shake of the head. "The boy . . . he would be more to your taste."

The sly glance brought heat to Struath's cheeks. Against his will, he found himself staring at Yeorna's long fingers, so like his mentor's.

"The Hunter's brother, isn't he? He has the look of him."

Thank the gods, he had not called the Holly-Lord by his title. Whatever happened, he must keep the truth from Morgath.

"I might enjoy being a woman." Releasing the braid, the fingers traced the line of Yeorna's jaw. "Their bodies have so many contrasts. Soft in some places." His hands moved lower, cupping Yeorna's breasts. "Hard in others." He thumbed Yeorna's nipples until Struath could see them jutting against the wool of her robe. "Curves." Hands cradling her belly. "And hollows." Hands cupping her sex, fingers stroking through the wool. "If she had fought, it would have been sweeter."

Struath shook as the destroying power surged inside of him. He controlled it with an effort. He must try

and shake the Destroyer's confidence, to force him to
make a mistake.

"What do you want?" he asked.

"To watch you die."

"Then kill me."

"I've waited half a lifetime. I will not be rushed."

"I understand that you'd want revenge against me.
But why destroy the whole world?"

"There are other worlds. Did you know that? The
Trickster told me. He helps me."

"You, too?"

The smile faded, then reasserted itself. "He didn't
tell you I had returned, did he?"

"He didn't have to. I've known since the beginning."

"You lie."

"Think that if it pleases you. You always loved believing you were the most powerful being in the
world."

"What other man has ever escaped . . . that place?"

"You think you did that on your own?" Struath
laughed. Although it sounded more like a frightened
wheeze, the laughter made Morgath's wards tremble.
"Has your time in the body of animals blinded you to
the truth?" Frantically, he searched for a truth to
offer, hoping Morgath would believe his pause to be
merely dramatic. He seized on Morgath's last words.
"Do you really think you 'escaped?' You poor fool,
the Lord of Chaos let you go."

Morgath was breathing hard now, but still in control. "Perhaps. He has always been generous to those
who do his work. That is why he has permitted you
to live so long."

"If you mean the wren—"

"I mean the One Tree."

Struath tried to school his features to immobility
and knew he had failed when Morgath smiled. "I felt
you that night."

It was what he had always feared, what he had refused to admit.

"The Unmaker might have opened the portal, but you drew me to the grove. So if anyone is responsible for destroying the world, it is you, little rook."

"Maker, forgive me," he whispered.

"I doubt it. But when I cast out your spirit, the Unmaker will welcome you."

"You are a monster."

"You made me that way."

"Nay."

"I sought knowledge. Truth."

"You sought power. You subverted nature."

Morgath laughed, a harsh, ugly sound utterly unlike Yeorna's. "You drove my spirit out of my body. Was that not a subversion of nature?"

"You had transgressed. You were an abomination in the sight of man and gods alike."

"And you loved me."

Struath opened his mouth, then closed it.

"When you took the wren, the power made you tremble."

"Because it was wrong."

"Because you lusted after it. Even more than you lusted after me."

Struath gathered the power, holding it close.

"You still lust after power. You love the respect you see in men's eyes. And you love the fear even more."

Struath pulled the energy from the ground, from the air, from the river below, from the feeble sunlight straining through the clouds.

"I could have sealed your fate that day. Only my silence saved you. Did you ever think of that as you drank in the respect and the fear of lesser men?"

Struath's wards trembled as the energy raged, forging him into a weapon of destruction.

Morgath's lips curled in a sneer. "You pretend to

despise me, but you envy me. Because I am strong. Because I have the will to pursue power, while you only dream of it. Because, deep inside, you know we are the same. Only I have the courage to admit it."

He had only this one chance. He could not fail.

Maker, give me strength.

Darak was racing along the riverbank when the blue light erupted. He needed both hands to scramble up the embankment, but when he neared the top, he paused long enough to unsling his bow and nock an arrow. Everything seemed to move very slowly after that, but later he realized it all happened in the space of a few heartbeats.

The spiderwebs of color glittering around Struath and Yeorna, stained blue by the spectral light. The same crackle of energy he had felt in the clearing. Cuillon, crawling out of the cave. His own shout, echoing loudly in his ears, as he urged him to get back, get back now. Yeorna whirling toward him. The stench of brimstone. Blue light spilling over Struath like a waterfall, coalescing into a single stream that hurtled toward Yeorna and shattered into brilliant white shards. A second blue stream racing toward Struath. Energy exploding all around. The bow falling from his grasp. Yeorna's body hurtling into his. Yeorna's hands clutching his arms. Yeorna's eyes, wild with fear, as they rolled toward the edge of the embankment.

A perfect black rectangle opened in the middle of the leaf-strewn slope. Something flickered in the darkness. Tiny points of white light. Stars.

He heard a familiar, high-pitched yip. "Welcome to Chaos, children."

The Trickster's foot nudged them over the edge. He heard Cuillon shouting, Yeorna screaming. Then there was only the darkness and the stars and the two of them, falling up and up and up.

PART THREE

In the beginning,
Before gods or men existed,
Before there was sun or moon, earth or sea,
In the beginning,
There was Chaos.

—The Creation of the World

Chapter 31

THEY CLUNG TO EACH OTHER like lovers.
Stars streaked past in a pale blur. It was like skidding down the icy slopes of Eagles Mount at night—
except now the ground lay above them and instead of
the shriek of wind, Darak heard only Yeorna's scream,
fading to a hoarse sob and then to silence.

And still they tumbled, the stars spinning around
them in sickening circles. Darak closed his eyes, but
that only made it worse. He opened them again to discover a milky opalescence filling the sky, now overhead,
now beneath. A false promise of dawn, of hope, in a
place that possessed neither.

Something loomed out of the light. Above, below,
above, below. A wall? A cliff? They hurtled toward it.
Yeorna screamed again. Darak could make out rocks,
creamy and jagged. Above. Below. Holding fast to
Yeorna, he hurled his body to the right, bracing himself for a bone-jarring collision. They landed as softly
as falling into a pile of fleece.

They lay panting, still clinging to each other. In the
Grain-Mother's eyes, he saw his surprise, in her smile,
the same giddiness at their unexpected deliverance.

"Are you all right?"

She nodded. He rose and extended a hand to help her to her feet.

"What happened?"

She lowered her head. "Cuillon went outside. To watch for you. Struath followed. They were gone so long, I grew frightened. So I went after them." She darted a glance at him, biting her lip. "They were by the sunberry bush. Struath was . . . he was . . ."

"For mercy's sake, Yeorna. Just tell me!"

"Cuillon was lying facedown over a boulder. I thought perhaps he was sick, but then I saw Struath reach down . . . and pull his robe up." Her voice broke. "I think I must have screamed then. Struath looked up . . . oh, gods, Darak, his face. It was terrible. And then he attacked me."

Darak kept shaking his head, but Fellgair's words rang in his head: *"They were lovers. Morgath offered him pleasure such as he had never experienced before or since."*

"Struath couldn't . . . he would never hurt Cuillon."

"There were things that happened . . . while you were hunting. I just thought . . . gods forgive me, I thought Struath was being . . . affectionate."

Struath would never force himself on the Holly-Lord. Never. Yeorna was wrong.

"I had to protect myself."

The blue light had surrounded both of them. Yeorna could erect wards, but if she possessed that destroying power, surely Struath would have enlisted her help to combat the wolf.

"You'd have done the same. Merciful gods, Darak, he's your brother."

He went very still, then abruptly turned away as if overcome with emotion. The wren. Morgath had taken the wren. And when poor Yeorna had gone to help it, he had taken her.

The sudden heaviness in the air alerted him. He whirled around and the dagger sliced open his arm.

As Morgath raised his hand for another blow, he
jabbed his fist into his belly. Morgath fell to his knees,
doubled over.

Energy crawled over Darak's skin like a thousand
ants. The ants became bees, the irritating prickles a
net of stingers that settled over him. In the wake of
the pain, numbness crept down his arms.

He seized Morgath by the hair and yanked his head
back. Against his will, his gaze was drawn away from
the slender throat, past the trembling mouth and the
flushed cheeks to the twin tears trembling on the pale
lashes and finally, to those pleading blue eyes.

Yeorna was dead. It was Morgath staring out of
those eyes now.

The dagger shuddered in his hand like a frightened
animal—or a tiny, terrified wren.

Morgath threw himself back, toppling them both.
The dagger slipped from Darak's numb fingers. Morgath twisted out of his grasp and scuttled away on
hands and knees. Darak could only crouch there,
hands trailing limply on the ground.

"Things change in Chaos, Hunter. Lucky for you.
Otherwise, you'd be dead." Morgath smiled. "Do you
have any final words before I—?"

Darak exploded out of his crouch. He heard a satisfying grunt as his head rammed into the soft belly,
another when Morgath collided with the cliff. The
numbness ebbed and strength returned to his hands.
He pinned Morgath's wrist against the wall. His free
hand gripped the slender throat.

Don't think of that. Yeorna is gone.

The air roiled, the same energy he had felt at the
bog. Behind Morgath, the cliff shimmered, the white
stone turning clear as quartz. Darak flung himself
backward, regaining his balance in time to see Morgath lunge through the stone. He thought he heard
laughter, but it faded as the cliff dissolved into a
waterfall that tumbled out of the sky.

The insistent whine died. Morgath was gone. He was alone on a star-studded plain.

The Tree-Father lay huddled against a boulder, his arm and legs twisted at strange angles. Cuillon crouched beside him, searching for his heart tattoo.

"He's gone, Holly-Lord."

Ignoring the Trickster, Cuillon stroked Struath's hand. He had disobeyed Darak and left the cave. Now Struath was dead. Darak had fallen into Chaos. Yeorna . . .

He gazed at the wren and the pressure in his chest grew heavier. Yeorna was gone, too. Morgath had taken her body. Now her spirit would never reach the Floating Islands. It would be trapped in Chaos with the Oak and Tinnean.

"Why did you open the portal?" he asked.

"Isn't that what you wanted?"

"Not like that."

"So particular. I do hope Griane is more grateful." The Trickster's breath warmed his ear. "She is in the Summerlands, Holly-Lord. I could take you to her."

Joy filled him, as fierce and pure as when he had first seen his Mountain. Then he stared down at Struath's hand. Thin blue twigs branched under the loose skin to curve around the brown mark of the acorn. "I cannot leave Struath."

"Humans do. They leave their dead to the elements. Then bury the bones in a cairn."

"Cairn?"

"A pile of stones."

Animals left their dead in the forest. Their bodies fed the carrion eaters. Their bones fed the earth. It was right. But Struath hated the cold. How could he leave him here, exposed to snow and rain, to sharp beaks and fangs?

"I will bury Struath."

"As you wish."

"You will help me."

He expected the Trickster to argue, but he simply shrugged. Together, they carved out a shallow trench in the earth and laid Struath in it. Cuillon straightened the twisted legs, folded his hands across his chest, and closed the robin's-egg eye. That way, Struath almost looked like he was sleeping.

The first raindrop fell while they were building the thing called cairn. The shower quickly became a downpour, as if the Maker wept for Struath. He was lowering a stone onto Struath's neck when he noticed the leather thong. He dug through the rocks until he uncovered the small green pouch. Tugging open the strings at the top, he removed the spirit catcher. The first time he had seen the crystal, it had sparkled as if it held the sun. Now it lay in his palm, as empty as Struath's body.

"Take it if you like, but let's be done with this." The Trickster looked disgruntled. Rain dripped off his long nose. He shook himself, sending droplets flying. "The sun is shining in the Summerlands and Griane awaits us."

"I cannot go to the Summerlands."

The Trickster sighed. "Of course you can. Just give me your hand."

"I have to go to Chaos."

The Trickster's eyes narrowed. "You cannot go to Chaos."

"Darak needs the spirit catcher."

"Darak does not know how to use the spirit catcher."

"We will find a way."

"I will not permit it."

Cuillon rose. So did the Trickster. Cuillon squinted up at him, blinking back raindrops. "I may not be as old as you, but I am still a god."

"In the very fragile body of a human."

"Do you threaten me, Trickster?"

"Not yet."

"You must open a portal."

"I cannot."

"You opened one before."

"I cannot open a portal to Chaos for you."

"Why not?"

"Because I gave Darak my word that I would keep you safe."

Cuillon swiped the rain out of his eyes. The Trickster glared at him. "Yes, you heard me. I told Darak I would protect you."

"I will tell him that you lied."

The Trickster drew back. "I never lie. I may hold back certain details, but I never lie."

"We will finish Struath's cairn. Then you will open the portal."

"Are you deaf, Holly-Lord? Or has the human body you now inhabit eroded your wisdom?" The Trickster stalked back and forth, tail lashing. "Do you want the Oak and the Holly to be trapped in Chaos?"

"When Darak and I have our brothers' spirits, you can open a portal so that we can escape."

"Can I?"

"Aye. Then you will not have broken your promise."

"But allowing you to go to Chaos in the first place is breaking the promise!" The Trickster's voice rose to a shout. He clamped his mouth shut. The fur on his neck subsided. "You have made me lose my temper." He sounded more aggrieved than angry.

"I am sorry. But I must go to Chaos. If you will not take me, I will walk through the forest until a portal opens."

"You could wander for years and never stumble upon a portal."

"Then the boy's body will die. And my spirit will be lost."

Cuillon crouched beside the cairn. Rain streaked

Struath's grizzled cheeks like tears. Raising the Tree-Father's head, he slid the pouch free and tucked the spirit catcher inside.

"I thank you for recognizing me, Struath. And for helping me. And for your stories. Even the very long ones. I hope that you are in the Floating Islands where there are many trees. But if you are not, then I will meet you in Chaos."

The Trickster muttered something under his breath. Cuillon ignored him and carefully placed the last stones atop the cairn. Sliding the spirit catcher's pouch over his head, he rose.

The rain stopped.

"It is a sign," Cuillon said.

"A sign that the storm is past."

A shaft of sunlight burst through the clouds and hit Cuillon full in the face. He smiled. An angry swish of the Trickster's tail caught him across the knees.

"I liked you better when you were a tree."

"Once we return with the Oak, I will go back to my tree. Then you can piss on me if you like."

The Trickster stared at him, then burst into yips of laughter. Cuillon was not sure why. Humans considered it a deadly insult to piss on an enemy. He thought the offer would be a fair exchange for the portal.

"I take it back," the Trickster said, wiping his eyes. "You are much more amusing as a man."

"Then you will open a portal."

The Trickster sighed and raised his hand.

"Wait!"

Cuillon snatched up Darak's bow and collected the arrows that had fallen from his quiver. He crawled into the cave and laid them next to Darak's sleeping place. He sorted through the contents of Griane's magic bag, setting aside an empty leather pouch to hold water and a roll of doeskin bandages; he would need those if the thorns returned. He thrust them back into her bag, adding three smoked fish and a few strips of venison. Finally, he drew Struath's curved dagger from its sheath. Returning to the cairn, he thrust it through the stones.

Griane would not wait in the Summerlands. Like the rowan-woman, she would grow impatient. He hoped she would understand this sign when she found it.

"Lovely," remarked the Trickster. "Are you finished?"

"Not yet."

He filled the pouch at the river and returned to the cairn, wondering if he had forgotten anything. Darak was always so careful when preparing for a hunt. Then he remembered.

"Maker, guide me to the Oak. Forest-Lord, watch over Darak."

He closed his eyes, allowing the Holly-energy to seep through him, controlling it so that only a single thorn pierced his palm. Pressing his hand to the earth, he offered his blood—Tinnean's blood. He hoped Darak would not be angry. He cut away the thorn and licked his palm clean. Looking up, he found the Trickster watching him.

"Are you sure you want to do this, Holly-Lord?"

"Nay. But I think I must."

The Trickster dragged his clawed forefinger through the air—up from the earth, across the sky, and down to the ground again, creating a shape like the entrance to Darak's hut. He grasped one corner of the invisible doorway and peeled it back, revealing a swirl of stars.

The Trickster bowed; when he straightened, his face was solemn. "May you find what you are seeking, Holly-Lord."

"Thank you, Trickster."

Cuillon closed his eyes and stepped into the void.

Chapter 32

WHEN STRUATH OPENED his eyes and saw Yeorna looking down at him, he screamed. Only when he saw the leaves of a shrub through her body did he understand.

"Forgive me, Tree-Father." A tear oozed down her translucent face; her golden hair had faded to a pale yellow.

"I am the one who should ask your forgiveness. For allowing this to happen to you."

"Nay. If only I had stayed in the cave. If only I had—"

"It is done, child. Blaming ourselves won't help the others."

"The Holly-Lord? He is safe?"

"Aye. I think so." Quickly, he told her what had happened. He struggled to piece together the final moments of the battle, but could only recall disjointed images and sounds. "I heard Darak's voice at . . . at the end."

"Then Morgath must be dead. Darak would have killed him."

"If he realized it was Morgath."

"He will. He must. I don't think I could bear this if I thought . . ."

"Hush, now." He wiped the tear from her cheek. They both started.

"I didn't think . . . I mean, our bodies are so . . ." Yeorna held up her hands, staring at them with the same disbelief and wonder Morgath had evinced in the cave.

"Perhaps it is because our spirits still remember the feel of a mortal body."

"If that is true . . ." Yeorna's forehead creased in a thoughtful frown. "Tree-Father. I believe Morgath is here."

The surge of excitement startled him. Perhaps his spirit still clung to emotions as well.

"You feel him?"

Yeorna frowned. "I don't know. It is not the same as when I felt you." Before he could voice the question, she said, "I wasn't sure it was you. Only that the energy felt . . . familiar. So I followed it. I think, perhaps, that because our spirits have touched so many times, there must be a . . . a sort of link between us."

"And you think you share something similar with Morgath?"

"Nay." Yeorna's face twisted as she turned away. Struath rose, briefly surprised by the ease with which he got to his feet. No more throbbing knees, no more aching joints. He had left those behind with his body.

"Forgive me, my dear. I only meant—"

"Nay." Her denial was softer this time, although her face was still troubled. "It is hard to bear the thought of being bound to him. What I feel . . . it might be a link between our spirits, but I think what I feel is my body."

Morgath. Alive and in Chaos.

"Can you find him?"

"I think so."

To find him. To destroy him. To achieve in death what he had not been able to accomplish in life. The intensity of his desire made him dizzy. He fell to his knees. Yeorna reached out to help him, then pulled back, her eyes wide with horror.

His outstretched hand was filled with a strange mist that swirled in mad spirals. Even as he watched, the mist burst through his upraised fingers. Frantically, he tried to contain it, only to discover that his left hand had disappeared, too. Just like Morgath when he had emerged from the portal in the grove and the man who appeared in the bog. Morgath had seized some other creature and preserved his spirit, but the man in the bog had simply melted away.

He toppled over on his elbows. Helplessly, he watched himself dissolve. Feet and hands gone. Legs dispersing in a swirl of white. Forearms eddying around him. He flailed with his stumps, screaming, as he tried to gather up the pieces of himself. He had lost his body. Chaos would not steal his spirit, too.

He was rising, flying, just as he had flown with Brana. Would he ever see her again or was she as lost to him as his body? He exerted the full force of his will to quell the terror, searching for the shaman's stillness. Slowly, he drifted downward to settle beside Yeorna. One glance showed that he was whole again, his form as tranquil and translucent as when he had first awakened.

"What did you do?" Yeorna asked. "How did you stop it?"

"I'm not sure. Perhaps human will is stronger than that of Chaos."

But it would take more than will to defeat his enemy.

Morgath ran, screaming his fury.

Half a lifetime to find a portal. Half a lifetime to escape.

He batted away the hissing moths, slashed his way through lizard-headed vines with the woman's dagger. Only when he heard himself whimpering like a child did he stop his headlong flight. He commanded himself to be calm. To ignore his trembling legs and his burning lungs and the searing pain in his side. To remember that he was Morgath. When he had been mere spirit, he had escaped the Lord of Chaos. A pockmarked hunter in ragged breeches would not defeat him now.

He would make him pay. If it cost his own life, he would make the Hunter pay. He would find the people he loved—in that miserable village, in the First Forest, in the Forever Isles. He would find them, and destroy them, and he would make the Hunter watch. He would take the girl's body, and then her spirit, and he would make the Hunter watch. He would find the Hunter's brother, and he would shred his spirit like dead leaves, and rend the fragments into powder, and blow the powder to the four winds. And he would make the Hunter watch.

He was the most powerful shaman in the world. He possessed a strong, young body. With it, he would find a portal. He would escape. He would wreak such havoc on the world that its inhabitants would look back upon their endless winter with longing. And he would make the Hunter watch it all and beg for mercy on his knees before he killed him.

Darak sat where he had collapsed. He had his dagger and his waterskin, the sling hanging from his belt and the bag of charms around his neck. With those, he would have to battle Morgath and the powers of Chaos.

The ground beneath him seemed solid enough, although it was disconcerting to see stars in the earth—if it was earth he was sitting on. Squinting, he realized the plain that stretched before him was not so featureless after all. Low scrub dotted the landscape and what might be trees or standing stones loomed in the distance. The vista was bathed in a strange half-light that was neither dawn nor dusk. The air felt heavy, perhaps from the discharge of energy that had accompanied the transformation, but at least it was warm. No need to depend on the Trickster for fire here.

His smile faded. The Trickster had lied. He had opened a portal. Darak went over the words of their conversation twice before he realized the truth. The Trickster had refused to open a portal—for him. Somehow, Griane must have convinced him to open one and the Trickster, damn him, had chosen the worst possible moment to do so. Now he was in Chaos, without Struath, without the spirit catcher, and without any idea how to find Tinnean or the Oak.

The legends said Chaos was ever-changing. That much he had seen for himself. Morgath claimed Chaos had changed his magic. If he was telling the truth, it explained why the shaman had only been able to deaden the feeling in his hands.

Chaos was a place of illusion, but real water had splashed him when the cliff transformed and real water still cascaded from the cloudless sky. Maybe if you believed in the illusion, it became real. Could willpower transform reality into illusion just as easily?

Struath might know the answers, but he didn't know whether the shaman was dead or alive. If he was alive, he'd be searching for a way to reach Chaos with the spirit catcher, but if Morgath had won, Struath's spirit was lost somewhere in this strange, shifting world.

One thing was certain: sitting here would accomplish nothing. He flexed his arm. No muscles severed, although the deep gash at the shoulder still bled freely.

He stripped off his mantle and hacked off a strip of wool. He was winding it around his arm when he noticed the flower.

He was certain it hadn't been there when he had collapsed. Had it sprung up from the drops of his blood spattered on the ground? The tiny scarlet petals looked so soft. He wanted to touch them. The flower needed to be touched. It was lonely. He was her only friend. His blood had given her life. He must protect her. Nurture her. Feed her.

He reached out his hand. The flower lunged toward him. He jerked away with a curse as the tiny petals snapped shut on empty air.

Fool. The Trickster had warned him he would only survive if he gave up his sense of reality. In his first moments here, a flower had beguiled him.

Clumsily, he finished bandaging his arm lest he leave a trail of hungry flowers to mark his path. He looked up, squinting into the distance. Had the scrubby bushes grown larger or was it his imagination? Surely, they hadn't been so close. And just as surely, there had been no path leading toward them. Now, clustered stars headed straight toward the trees—or stones—in the distance. The path began—or ended—at his feet.

Real or illusion? The path to Tinnean or the path away?

Cautiously, he tapped the star-path with his shoe. Nothing. He placed one foot upon the path. Still nothing.

In the forest, he followed the same trails as the animals. The trails led to water and to feeding grounds. They avoided natural hazards. A hunter could follow the trail or wait beside it for game. If he was skillful—and lucky—he would bring home meat. If he was careless—or unlucky—he could fall prey to another predator.

He stepped onto the star-path. "Forest-Lord, if you

can hear the prayers of a man in Chaos, guide my footsteps to Tinnean."

Scanning the scrub for danger, he set off.

Cuillon came to rest in a meadow. Yellow flowers dotted the field. The air was warm, the stillness broken only by the buzz of insects. Trees ringed the field—hazel, ash, elder, oak. Surely, Chaos could not be so bad if there were trees.

The copse trembled as if shaken by a great wind. One by one, the trees melted into columns of fog that vanished as the flowers shot skyward, green stems as thick as the trunks of birches, yellow petals bobbing above him like so many suns.

He was still trying to decide if they were real when he felt the faint thrum. He closed his eyes, desperate to pinpoint the direction of the energy, afraid that it, too, might be an illusion. Despite the prickling in his hands, he opened himself to the energy.

It felt like their grove and their Tree, their roots sinking deep into the earth and their branches reaching toward the sun. It felt more than real; it felt right. For the first time since their quest had begun, he felt whole. It was a great wonder to him that he could feel joy in a place that the others had described with such fear.

The Oak was here.

The pain surged, driving him to his knees. Thorns burst through his palms, his fingers, his nails. Green leaves sprouted. Twigs ripped open his flesh. Gasping, he abandoned his connection to the Oak so he could reassert his control over the boy's body. Long moments passed before he could move. Hands slippery with blood and sweat, he fumbled for Tinnean's dagger and awkwardly sheared the green leaves from his fingertips.

"I am Cuillon," he said and felt sensation return.

He cut two long strips from the doeskin and bandaged his hands.

"Please, Maker. Let me remain a man for just a little while longer."

Chapter 33

GRIANE SAT BESIDE THE POOL, staring out across the rolling grasslands. For just a moment, when she had first awakened, she had reveled in the early morning sunlight and the soft splash of the water. Then she remembered what had happened the previous day: her failure to fulfill her bargain with the Trickster, her desperate search for him, the gentle trees that had wept with her, and the long walk back to the pool. She had sat up half the night, staring up at the star-studded sky and praying that Fellgair would relent. Now, with the morning half gone, she knew he would not. If she wanted to leave the Summerlands, she would have to find the way herself.

She scrambled up the steep hillside. The mist from the waterfall made the rocky path treacherous, but she reached the top with only minor scrapes. Below her in every direction, the grass undulated in rippling waves. Vivid patches of yellow—broom, perhaps, or furze—gilded the hills to the south. Farther inland, she made out the dark outlines of a forest. One tree towered over the rest, trunk thrusting skyward, wide-spreading branches shadowing the smaller trees.

Her breath caught. It had to be the tree that sheltered the spirit of the Oak after the Midsummer battle. Perhaps if she could reach it and explain their quest, it might help her find a way back to her folk.

She earned more scrapes and bruises on her precipitate descent, but a few swipes from the silvery wound healer dealt with them, just as a sip of water from the pool eased the ache in her belly. She discarded the rocks from her waterskin and filled it before bundling Tinnean's breeches and shoes in her mantle. Renewed in body and spirit, she headed inland.

Despite the urgency of her mission, she still found time to admire the beauty of the Summerlands and the aura of peace that was as tangible as the sunlight on her shoulders and the air that she breathed. The song of larks and pipits accompanied her. Once, she surprised a plump partridge from the grasses; it rose on whirring wings, its annoyed chuck-chuck making her smile. Rabbits and small game abounded and she thought she caught the shadow of a deer retreating into a thicket. But, of course, there were no people. She might have been the rowan-woman on that first day after she had crossed the veil from the First Forest. At least, she thought with a touch of sadness, the rowan-woman had the alder-man to share the new world with her.

At midday, she rested at the top of a low rise. The land ahead was more thickly wooded; a small copse lay directly in her path. She was reluctant to leave the open grasslands, for here she could easily spot an enemy, but the way to the giant oak lay through the woodlands, so that was the way she must go.

She started down the rise, then hesitated, frowning at the rumble of distant thunder. A cloud shadowed the copse, but the rest of the sky was brilliantly blue. Belatedly, she realized the rumble came from the earth, but unlike the rockslides that sometimes tumbled down the slopes of Eagles Mount, the sound was as rhythmic as a drumbeat. Shading her eyes, her gaze swept the landscape, passing over the copse, then snapping back again.

She blinked once, wondering if the passing cloud created the illusion or if it was her light-headedness from lack of food. She blinked again, her mind grappling with the impossibility of what she witnessed. The trees were moving. Not just leaves fluttering in the breeze. The trees were walking.

The legends always portrayed the Summerlands as a paradise, second only to the Forever Isles in their beauty. The Memory-Keeper's tales were rich with descriptions of hot sun and long days and shadowy forests, but woefully lacking such details as walking trees. Trees that, even now, were walking up the rise toward her.

Perhaps they would welcome her—or perhaps they would view her as a dangerous intruder.

Griane turned and fled. She stumbled, sliding down the slope, but regained her footing at the bottom. Glancing over her shoulder, she discovered the trees had already crested the rise. She raced on, the continuous rumbling in the ground evidence that the trees had abandoned their rhythmic stride for a more determined pursuit. Lancing pain shot through her with each breath. She pressed her hand to her side, slowing long enough to dare another glance behind her. Her breath leaked out on a shaking sob. Ten more strides and they would be on her.

Damn Fellgair. He could have easily taken her to another part of the First Forest. Why bring her here if her presence was an abomination? And why should the trees hunt her down when all she was trying to do was leave this place?

Whirling around, she thrust out a hand and shouted, "Stop. Right now."

Incredibly, they did, planting themselves so quickly that they might have been rooted once more. Now that they were closer, she realized that they weren't simply walking trees, but some strange amalgam of tree and human. Among the mass of watchers were some that seemed more treelike than others, their skin dark and rough, their faces indistinct, as if they had dressed too quickly in the shape of men. Whether that meant they were older or younger, she couldn't guess.

They all had hands and feet, though the fingers were green and the toes looked like gnarled roots. Despite their similarities, she quickly discerned their different origins: the mottled silver of the birch's torso, the thin needles covering the fir's arms. And clearly, there were different sexes, too. Tufted red buds capped the scaly breasts of the hazel, while the oak . . . Merciful Maker, his dark-red penis was longer than her forearm. Blushing, she fastened her gaze on his broad chest, but not before she had glimpsed the heavy testicles, smooth and green as unripe acorns. Very large acorns.

When one of the tree-folk stepped forward, Griane instinctively backed away, then froze, gaping at the legend come to life. Eyes the color of Midsummer leaves regarded her. The smooth, gray face creased into a smile. Nine long fingers reached down to touch her hair. A cluster of white flowers brushed her cheek, perfuming the air with sweetness.

The rowan-woman's leaves fluttered as she gestured to the others. Soon, all their leaves were fluttering. The others approached. Surrounded by a circle of trunks, she might have believed herself to be in the forest again, were it not for the eyes of green and gold and brown that gazed down at her.

"My name is Griane."

The rowan's gray lips pursed into a knothole.

"I'm trying to get back to the First Forest." Although they continued to sway, she could not tell if they understood. When she remembered Cuillon could only communicate through touch, she seized the rowan-woman's hand, careful not to crush the delicate fingers. She poured out the tale of the Midwinter battle, the loss of the Oak, the need to find a portal to Chaos.

The rowan-woman watched her, bark grooving in a frown. The oak-man's expression remained inscrutable. After a great deal of leaf fluttering, they turned and headed back in the direction from which they had come. Defeated, Griane stared after them until the rowan-woman held out her hand.

She had to trot to keep up with the tree-folk, taking three steps for each of their strides. Only when they entered the woodlands did their pace slow. Branches rustled as they passed; shrubs leaned closer as if to inspect her. An almost palpable air of excitement riffled through the leaves. How astonishing to think that she might be as wondrous to them as they were to her.

Just as she was beginning to tire, the trees gave way to a vast open space, the mulch underfoot to bare earth. Griane peered around Rowan and confronted a wall of wood. It took her a moment to realize it was the trunk of a tree. The branches were so dense they blocked out the sunlight, the arched roots high enough for a hut to nestle beneath. This was the tree she had seen from her vantage point above the pool.

Rowan pulled her forward. Hesitantly, she stepped up to the ancient oak and repeated her tale. If the tree understood, it gave no sign that she could see. She laid her palms in one of the deep grooves scoring its bark and tried to send the oak images of the battle. The forest went silent, as if all the creatures of the Summerlands were awaiting the giant's response.

Finally, she squatted on the ground and smoothed the cool earth with her hands. With her forefinger, she drew the outline of the One Tree, sketching a holly leaf on one branch and the seven-lobed leaf of a blood-oak on the other. A rustling overhead made her look up. The oak's branches drooped lower.

She jumped up. Standing as straight as she could, she pounded her chest and pointed to the oak leaf.

Then she leaped across the drawing and became the Holly. Feverishly, she acted out their battle, then fell to her knees. How could she depict a portal when she'd never seen one? A lightning bolt, she decided. That, the tree-folk would understand. She sketched it in the earth, then drew her dagger. Pointing from her dagger to the lightning bolt, she stabbed the drawing of the One Tree.

The tree-folk swayed, their leaves fluttering wildly. She smoothed the edges of the holly leaf, shaping the lines into the form of a man. Then she dug her fingers into the earth, obliterating the oak leaf, and hurled the dirt into the air. Sweat pouring down her sides, she drew one last picture: the image of the One Tree, shattered and broken. Panting and spent, she sat back on her haunches. She had done her best. She only hoped the great tree understood.

A shudder ran up the oak's trunk. A root ripped free of the earth, dredging a crevasse that snaked across the grove, nearly toppling a birch-woman. The tree-folk's branches moaned. Roots stamped the ground. The earth shook. Griane flung out a hand to steady herself, then snatched it away when she felt the oak's bark heave.

The explosion of air made her curl into a ball, hands cradling her head. The leaves of the tree-folk twisted like tiny creatures in their death throes. Their anguish sped around the grove. Twigs and branches rained down. Birds erupted from the trees, wings slapping the air in a frantic attempt to escape the tumult. And then, with a suddenness that left her gasping, it simply stopped. The tree-folk's leaves drifted back into still-ness, the branches of the rooted ones fell silent.

The depth of their grief made hers seem small. Not knowing what else to do, Griane embraced the oak. She knelt there, her cheek resting against a ridge, her arms too short to even feel the curve of the root.

Then she crawled away and drew a new picture. A

single oak leaf. She pointed at her breast, pointed at the leaf. Crouched down and cupped her hands. Cradling the imaginary leaf in her palms, she walked back to the drawing of the shattered Tree and pretended to place the leaf at the end of one branch. She smoothed away the jagged scar in the trunk, drew new lines to reconnect the broken branch.

Rowan's sigh drifted around the circle of tree-folk. She patted Griane's cheek, then gently nudged her toward the oak. A sense of peace stole over her as she curled up under one of the huge roots. For the first time since they had started their quest, Griane slept soundly.

Chapter 34

IN THE FIRST FOREST, it must be nearing moon-set. In the unchanging light of Chaos, Darak could only judge the passage of time by his weariness. Distance, too, seemed to obey other laws here, for the trees grew no closer as he walked. Often, he lost sight of them altogether as new obstacles appeared.

Rocks sprouted pointed muzzles and rows of spikes along their backs like hedgehogs. The hedgehogs grew to the size of sheep, savaging each other with their tusks, showering blood and pebbles across the path before lumbering off, apparently uninterested in him.

Worse were the scrubby trees, whose twisted branches transformed into grotesquely deformed arms. Mouths gaped open in the trunks. Tormented eyes looked out. Groans of misery alternated with beseeching wails as their many arms reached toward him.

"Help us."

Knobby fingers circled his ankles, tugged at his breeches.

"Save us."

He ran. They pursued, screaming his name. He tore at the clutching fingers, staring in horror as they snapped off, geysering yellow slime over the stumps.

He hurled them away, but more reached for him, slipping through the rents in his breeches to touch his flesh.

"Warm," they whispered. "Alive. Real."

"You're not real."

"Touch us."

"You're an illusion!"

"Feel us."

They rubbed against him like cats, pushing him to the ground, eager fingers sliding over his flesh. Hot, fetid breath filled his nose. Crusty tongues licked his neck, his face, his lips. All those arms twining around him in a hideous embrace, all those eyes begging him for help.

Fear is the enemy. Control the fear. Control yourself.

The despairing wails became shrieks of laughter. Arms, fingers, and tongues melted into furry gray balls, sticky as spiderwebs. When he scrambled to his feet, they floated away like dandelion fluff. Had he driven them away or had they simply tired of the game?

Too late, he wondered if Tinnean's face had been among them. He told himself it was impossible, his brother could not have been transformed into one of those loathsome creatures. Yet he couldn't stop himself from reaching up to capture an errant ball of fluff. A barb darted out and he jerked his hand away.

None of the other horrors were as bad as that, not the forest of snakes that sprang up around him or the bats that swooped down to peck at his shielding arms with their curved beaks. *Fear is the enemy,* he told himself, and he endured, wondering if his ability to control his fear was his greatest strength.

After all he had witnessed, the giant buttercups looked beautiful, though a shiver ran down his spine when he realized the huge yellow heads dipped down to follow his progress. He wondered if they rejoiced when he lost the star-path, if they enjoyed the sight of him on hands and knees, scrabbling through the knee-high grass, without finding a trace of it. What he did find was a cluster of leaves, green and gleaming atop a spiky brown tussock.

He looked around for a holly, but the giant buttercups obscured everything. Perhaps one of them had been a holly before transforming into a flower. Then he examined the sprig more closely. The twig had been sheared off with a dagger. He scratched a dark spot on one leaf with his thumbnail. Blood.

He crawled forward and found more blood spots, fragments of leaves, a scrap of doeskin. It had to be some cruel trick of Chaos. He rose, spotted the trail of crushed grass, and followed it, measuring the stride.

Fellgair had promised. They had sealed the bargain with a handshake.

He shook his head, willing the signs to disappear, praying for them to be an illusion. Knowing that they were not.

Cuillon was in Chaos.

"You fool. You damn fool!" His voice rose to a shout. The heads of the buttercups reared back, then bobbed closer, as if intrigued by his outburst.

The path through the long grass was straight and clear. Cuillon had to be following the Oak's energy. All he could do was follow Cuillon. He would not allow himself to think about the meaning of the holly leaves and the blood.

He flinched when he heard the familiar whining. A buttercup tree shuddered, petals drooping. One hairy, lobed leaf shook, as if caught in a gust of wind. As the center of the leaf grew filmy, Darak could have sworn he heard the sound of chanting.

Although the edges of the leaf were still rimmed in green, the center turned transparent. He could see sky and scudding gray clouds, but he couldn't make sense of the odd latticework that framed them. Had the portal opened in the intertwined limbs of birches?

He heard the dry clatter of a rattle, smelled the scent of burning herbs. He recognized the chant now, the one they sang during burial rites. Standing on tiptoe, he peered through the portal.

A long, narrow shape swung into view. It sagged toward him, swaying a little as if suspended. It took a moment to determine that he was staring at a woven mantle, another to recognize the distinctive colors. Other tribes sang the death chant, but only his had those strands of green running through the dusky grays and browns.

Details fell into place with horrifying clarity. The shape of a body encased in the sagging mantle. The pale things around the mantle's edges—fingers. And the lattice of branches that weren't branches at all, but arms and legs, blue-white and frozen.

"Merciful Maker."

The chanting died. The mantle rocked from side to side. A face appeared over one corner. Sweet gods, it was Nionik. The chief stared back at him, eyes widening with horror. More faces appeared. Jurl. Gortin. Red Dugan. The mantle swayed violently as hands dropped away to make signs of protection. A woman screamed. The mantle tilted and a body spilled out.

Darak stared into Mother Netal's sightless blue eyes. Only when her body twitched did he rear back, clutching his bag of charms. Two white hands dug through the tangle of arms and legs in the Death Hut. Lisula stared at him, her expression as horrified as Nionik's.

"Lisula. It's Darak."

The whine intensified and Lisula winced. Gortin's face appeared over her shoulder. His mouth moved, but the portal's whine drowned out his words.

"I am in Chaos. Lisula! Gortin! Can you hear me?"

The edges of the portal were blurring. Gortin's fingers dug into Lisula's arm as he tried to pull her away. She turned her head, snapping something that made him drop his hand. Then her eyes met his again. Slowly, she extended a trembling hand.

Home was an arm's length away. He had only to grasp Lisula's hand and he would be there. As if his hand had a will of its own, he saw it reaching past Mother Netal's wrinkled face, reaching toward Lisula's wavering fingers, pale as moonlight, formless as fog.

He clenched his traitorous fingers into a fist and stepped back. The whining crescendoed, then abruptly ceased. Lisula vanished and he was staring once again into the green leaf of the buttercup tree.

His legs wobbled and he collapsed. Try as he might, he could not control his shaking, any more than he could will away the images. Nionik's face, as lined as one of the tribe's elders. Jurl's, shrunken and sagging. Red Dugan's hair, streaked with white. And what about those he hadn't seen? What of Krali and Sim? Why had he heard no children's voices? There had been some fifty men, women, and children when he had left. There had to be more than these pitiful few.

They had been standing too far away for him to see. They were back at the village, too weak to attend the rite. He'd only been gone a moon. They could not be dead.

"It's not true. It's not real."

"The world is dying," he had told Fellgair. Grand, impassioned words, but empty. His people were dying. People he had seen every day. Faces that were as much a part of his life as the air he breathed. Gone. Lost.

The very old and the very young, they would succumb first, just as they had during the plague. How many more stiff, frozen corpses lay in the Death Hut with Mother Netal? How long would the others last, weakened by hunger and hopelessness? Nionik, Jurl, Red Dugan—they were all dying. And there were more, many more—not just in his village, but throughout the world. If he did not find Tinnean and the Oak soon, they would all die.

He stood up. On shaking legs, he followed Cuillon's trail. He found a circle of dented grass where he had rested, scattered fish bones where he had eaten. And then, like the star-path, the trail disappeared.

He tore through the furry undergrowth, slapping aside the leering faces that snapped at him, mocked him, whispered that he was lost. He stumbled through gelatinous roots and man-high spiderwebs. When he spotted something gleaming on the far side of a sink-hole, he raced toward it, only to watch green wings open and carry the thing skyward with a shrill screech.

He staggered away from the sinkhole, through a thicket, and onto a starry, black beach. Waves of light arced overhead—green, white, red—shimmering like the Northern Dancers. They rippled across the sky, foaming and hissing like real waves when they broke upon the beach.

He would find the trail again. He would find Cuillon. He would find Tinnean and the Oak.

Fear is the enemy.

Fear was the pounding of his heart and the pounding of the waves. Fear was the light streaking across the sky like fiery spears flung by the Lightning God. Fear was the flashing sparks that flew up as they pelted the beach.

"I will find them!" He screamed his defiance at the sky, at the spears, at the Lord of Chaos and all the gods who watched his people die and did nothing.

Fear was a spear, plummeting toward him.

White.

Blazing.

Merciless.

Fear was an icicle, piercing his heart.

Chapter 35

GRIANE OPENED HER EYES to find the tree-folk clustered about her. She was sure she had convinced them of her need to return to the First Forest, but she had no idea how they would manage it.

You can't worry about that, Griane. Worry about what you can fix.

She tugged Rowan's hand, pointing in what she hoped was the direction of the pool. Rowan frowned, pointing in the opposite direction, but after a long, silent discussion with the others, finally nodded. Griane lingered long enough to lay her palm against the great oak and whisper a prayer of thanks. She hoped the tree understood her when she told it that the Oak's spirit would return, hoped with equal fervor that it wasn't a lie.

They reached the pool at midmorning. She filled her waterskin, then pointed at the magical plants. She tried to explain her need to Rowan, but in the end, she made a small cut on her wrist. Their leaves fluttered wildly when the blood welled up. She plucked a silvery leaf and pressed it to the wound. This caused more fluttering. She pretended to cut other sprigs from it and the one with the heart-shaped leaves. She looked around the circle of worried faces, a question in her eyes.

This time, the discussion lasted much longer. Perhaps it was forbidden to take anything away from the Summerlands. With an effort, she curbed her impatience. If the tree-folk refused permission, she would obey.

Please Maker, let them understand.

The sun had nearly reached its zenith when the tall oak-man stepped forward. He pointed to each of the plants and slowly nodded.

"Thank you." Griane flung her arms around one thick leg. The grooves around the oak-man's dark eyes tilted upward ever so slightly. Perhaps oaks were simply more reticent than other trees or perhaps he was older. There was so much to learn here, so many things she wanted to know.

You could stay. You would always have the tree-folk for friends.

Griane shook her head as if beset by deerflies, wondering if the Trickster had put the thought in her head.

She cut sprigs from each of the plants, careful to leave more than she took. She wondered what they were called, if they even had names. Heal-all, she decided for the silver-leafed one and heart-ease for the other. Imagine being the first to name a plant. Even Mother Netal had never done such a thing.

She whispered a prayer of thanks to the plants and sprinkled water from the pool around their stems. Belatedly, she realized she had no way to carry them back with her. Finally, she hacked off the bottom of her mantle, but try as she might, she could not tie the thick ends of the bundle together. The tall oak-man touched her shoulder. With signs, she showed him what she needed. He nodded gravely and entered into another silent conversation. Again, Griane waited. She could understand why the gift of the plants had taken a long time, but how could tying up her bundle possibly spark such a protracted discussion?

Finally, the oak-man unwound a long strand of ivy clinging to his chest. Griane smiled up at him. "It's perfect. Thank you."

Their pace was more leisurely now. Perhaps the tree-folk wanted her to enjoy her last impressions of the Summerlands. When she lingered beside a fat bush heavy with berries, they watched her with the same wonder they had evinced when she'd filled her water-skin. Rowan nodded when she pointed to the berries. Griane's stomach growled, but she recalled one of the Memory-Keeper's tales about a shaman who had feasted on the fruits of the Forever Isles and returned to his village the next morning to find that ten years had passed. Reluctantly, she contented herself with gathering berries. When she was back in the First Forest, she would allow herself to enjoy one.

After that, they took pains to point out other foods to her. Soon her arms were overflowing with mushrooms and berries. What a bounty to bring to her folk.

The sun was low in the sky when they reached a shore fringed with reeds and grasses. Perhaps the legends were true, then, about the Summerlands being an island. Certainly, they were right about the mist, although it was nothing like the giant fleece Old Sim described. It rose straighter than the walls of a house, the boundary between mist and water as neat and clean as if she had sketched it in the earth with a twig.

Griane gaped at the mist-wall, wondering how Rowan or any of the tree-folk could possibly breach it. The pine-man looked tall enough to walk right through it without wetting his spiky green hair, but surely, tree-folk took to water as well as Cuillon had to climbing.

She was still gazing at it when oak-men unwound the ivy that clung to their thick torsos. Willow-women lifted curving feet and sent long, slender shoots flying from their ankles. The shoots fell in perfect lines at the water's edge. The ivy twisted under and over them, binding them together. The other tree-folk shook their branches. Green leaves showered down—birch, rowan, alder, ash, hazel—arranging themselves on top of the framework of willow and vine.

A raft, Griane realized. A raft to carry her back to the First Forest.

A smaller cascade of shoots and vines and leaves landed at her feet. Hot tears came to her eyes when she realized they were offering her a basket to carry her food and healing plants. Before she could wipe them away, Rowan touched her cheek. She raised her finger to her lips and her eyes widened. Whatever she told the others made their leaves flutter. Perhaps they expected a tear to be thick and tangy like sap.

Bark-encrusted fingers caressed her hair, drooping catkins brushed her arms. All of them wanted to touch her and in turn, be touched by her. Griane patted grooved arms and leafy fingers. Whatever happened on this quest, she must live to tell the tale so future generations would know of the kindness and generosity of the tree-folk.

Rowan stepped onto the raft and held out her hand. Griane tapped the leaves with her foot and found them hard as wood. She took a careful step, bracing herself for the raft to tilt or rock as a coracle might, but it was as solid underfoot as hard-packed dirt. She was still trying to find common ground between what should be and what was when she realized they were drifting away from shore.

She clutched Rowan's arm, but the raft skimmed the surface of the water so smoothly they might have been floating in the air. She waved to the tree-folk clustered on the shore and shouted her thanks. Here and there, arms rose in salute. She caught a final glimpse of green forest and blue sky and then the world turned white.

She could not see the leaf-raft under her feet; even Rowan's features were indistinct. Sound seemed to have vanished as well. Only the feel of Rowan's fingers curled around hers held panic at bay.

As suddenly and silently as they had entered the mist-wall, they emerged. Cold seared her lungs. After the brilliant colors of the Summerlands, the First Forest looked diminished, a gray-white world of bare-limbed trees and patchy snow. Even the greens of the pines and spruces seemed faded.

She let out her breath in a grateful sigh when their raft drifted onto the bank, heaved another to feel earth beneath her feet. Rowan slipped a sprig of flowers behind her ear, a sweetly scented reminder of the Summerlands to carry with her. Griane sliced a strand of hair off with her dagger and offered it to Rowan. A thick bead of sap oozed down her face as she wound it around her wrist. Griane clung to her for a long moment, reluctant to leave the protection of those strong, encircling arms.

Long after Rowan had disappeared, Griane stood on the riverbank waving, as if the act would stave off the loneliness that enveloped her as surely as the mist engulfed the little raft. Finally, she let her aching arm fall to her side. She pulled the sprig of white rowan blossoms from behind her ear and breathed in its fragrance. Then she turned her back on the mist-wall and started upriver to find her folk.

Chapter 36

BRACING HIMSELF FOR the inevitable pain, Cuillon sent his energy in search of the Oak once more. He maintained the connection as long as he could bear it. After that, he could only lie panting, his throat raw from the screams.

If Griane were here, she would hold him. Yeorna would stroke his hair and croon one of her chants. Struath would tell a long story to distract him from the pain. And Darak would squeeze his hand and not even mind the thorns that cut his palm. All he could do was clutch Griane's magic bag to his chest and pretend he was holding her.

He forced himself to sit up, wincing as the twigs dug into his palms. His toes had burst through his shoes again, curving into long, twisted growths. How many more times could he reach for the Oak before his feet became rooted in the soil of Chaos?

He fumbled for the dagger and clumsily sheared off the newly-sprouted leaves from his fingers. His feet were more difficult, but he could not walk on them as they were. He tied his dilapidated shoes to his belt and sawed off the growths, crying out when his dagger cut the boy's flesh along with the woody protuber-

ances that grew from it. He bound the bloody stumps
with doeskin, but left the leaves that sprouted from his
wrists and ankles; they would only burst through again,
tearing new holes in Tinnean's sleeves and breeches.

He pushed himself to his feet and tottered up a
rise, following the trail of the Oak's energy. When he
reached the top, his heart tattoo quickened.

It might be any tree, rising above the thicket, but
the sweep of the branches looked so familiar that he
found himself running. A tearing pain in his side made
him slow to an awkward trot. Finally, he had to rest,
never taking his eyes off the tree, fearful that if he
looked away, it would vanish.

Please, Maker, let it be real. Please let it be the Oak.

He started off again, deliberately keeping his pace
slow. The branches that had looked so wide from a
distance seemed to dwindle along with his strength.
But of course the Oak would have changed, just as he
had. Inside, they were still the same.

His legs were shaking when he reached the low scrub.
Branches ripped new holes in Tinnean's breeches. Twigs
scraped his legs. Panting, he pushed past a squat shrub
with clusters of violet flowers and stumbled into a
clearing.

His expectant smile faded. The stubby tree was the
size of a rowan, its grooved trunk and twisted branches
studded with thorns. Only when he stepped closer did
he realize that the shriveled, brown leaves clinging to
the branches had seven lobes and that the pebbles
dotting the parched ground were misshapen acorns.

Perhaps the Oak had taken shelter in this tree, just
as he had taken refuge in the boy's body. Perhaps the
Oak was watching him right now, unable to recognize him.

"Oak? I am the Holly. I am here."

Willing himself to ignore the pain of his inevitable
transformation, he unwound the bandages on his

hands and placed his fingertips between the thorns on
the trunk.

The energy rose to meet him, pulsing like a heartbeat. Each pulse carried the memories of earth beneath them and sky above, of intertwined roots and
interlaced branches, of the first morning of creation
and the cold, dark night of their final battle. Into him
and through him, the energy flowed, filled with strange
currents he had never sensed before: the loss that
tinged the Oak's memories of Midwinter, the helplessness that ate away at its heartwood. And within
these currents, yet another. In his eagerness to reach
the Oak, he had not sensed it immediately, but now
he recognized the energy. How could he fail to when
he had touched it once before? A small pulse within
the ebb and flow of the Oak's energy, but distinct and
real and alive.

Tinnean.

*Icicles melting on tree branches. Sap rising in the
trunk.*

The boy gave him images of spring.

*New buds sprouting on twigs. Leaves unfolding on
lightning-blasted branches.*

The Oak gave him images of renewal.

Panting, he fought the pain to offer his own image:
seedlings springing up beside a fallen log.

Cuillon fell to the ground, screaming. Desperately,
he fought the transformation, calling up the essence
of the boy's humanity to keep his true self from re-
claiming him, calling upon all he knew about men:
their passion, their fierceness, even their willingness to
kill to protect their own. Black dots danced before his
eyes, mocking his efforts. His vision narrowed to focus
on a single acorn, then to a tiny nub on its cap. The
pain receded and Cuillon surrendered to the darkness.

He could feel his heart beating. He could hear the rasp of his breath and see light behind his closed eyelids and taste sour bile in his mouth. So he must be alive.

Darak opened his eyes and stared up into a golden sky, studded with puffy, pink clouds. He sat up slowly and peered inside his tunic. The sky-spear had left no mark. His fingers touched only a mat of springy hair and beneath it, firm, warm flesh. If not for the dull ache on each intake of breath, the attack might not have happened at all.

He had no idea how long he had been unconscious. Long enough for the beach to become a narrow ravine. The light stained its walls gold; the few splotches of pink made it seem as if the clouds had made the rocks blush. Ordinary-looking trees clung to ledges and ordinary-looking birds roosted in their branches. Even if the ravine was an illusion, he breathed a quick prayer of thanks; he had never expected to find beauty in Chaos.

Beautiful it might be, but dangerous, too. The walls of the ravine hemmed him in. If attacked, he would have to go forward or retreat down the steep slope. He was still trying to choose the better course when he glimpsed movement among the rocks.

Maker, let it be Morgath.

His gaze darted around the ravine, settling on two large boulders. He scrambled over loose rocks, smiling. This kind of danger he understood.

He crouched down behind a tumbled rock pile, pulled his sling from his belt, and picked through the rubble at his feet until he found a smooth stone. With the walls of the ravine at his back and the boulders guarding his flanks, he'd be well protected.

He glanced back up the ravine. Again, that tantalizing flicker of motion, as if the Watchers of the First Forest had been transported to Chaos. He caught a brief glimpse of a figure before it disappeared behind a boulder. Too far away to make out its identity.

He cradled the sling between loose fingers, waiting. His breathing slowed. The familiar calm stole over him, contrasting with the bloodlust that sang through his body.

The figure emerged again. He searched eagerly for Yeorna's golden hair and her long green robe, but it was a man who strode over the shifting pebbles with an easy, eerie grace. Not a man, he realized, but the same sort of spirit he had seen in the bog. No wonder he'd had such difficulty spotting him.

He followed the spirit-man with his eyes, wondering if he should reveal himself. He might know where the Oak was; he might have seen Cuillon. Still, the flower had looked harmless and it had tried to bite off his hand. His sling would be no defense; the rock would pass right through the creature, just as his spear had sliced through the man in the bog.

Frustration raged through him. As if the spirit-man could sense it, he stopped. His head slowly turned.

The stone fell from Darak's fingers. He tried to rise, but his legs wouldn't obey. Bracing himself against a boulder, he pushed himself upright and stumbled down the slope.

Two neat braids framed the lined face. The tunic hung on his wasted frame. The gray eyes widened as he drew near, but the fleeting expression of shock gave way to the familiar impassivity.

Darak wet his lips, forcing them to shape the words. "Hello, Father."

Chapter 37

OF ALL THE ILLUSIONS Chaos had offered, this was the most monstrous. His father stared at him, the rocks of the ravine clearly visible through his body. All Darak could do was stare back, waiting for him to change into something—a beast or a bird or one of the grotesque trees that had screamed at him for help.

His father glanced up and down the ravine. "This place is dangerous. Come." He headed down the ravine without a backward glance. Then he knew it was truly his father, as cold and distant after death as he had been in life. He wanted to shout at that rigid back that he knew the position was dangerous, that he'd been choosing the best direction. Only his concern that he would sound like a whining child kept him silent. Instead, he trotted after his father, relegated once again to the role of obedient son.

Eleven years since his father had died—and all he could offer his firstborn son was an implicit criticism for lingering in the ravine. The gods only knew why he was trapped in this damnable place; certainly, his father would never tell him. One thing was clear enough: even Chaos lacked the power to soften him.

How could his mother have loved this man? She had always been the heart of their family. When he was tired or sad—"broody," his mam called it—she always seemed to sense it. She would put down her mending and lay her hand on the back of his neck and say, "Rest a bit." And he would lay his head against her hip and she'd hum to him and stroke his hair. It always seemed that nothing could ever hurt him then, not even his father's silent disapproval.

She had a temper, though. Quick to smile, just as quick to anger, she could blister you with her tongue as surely as his father could with his belt. A reluctant smile tugged at his lips, remembering how she'd puff up like a grouse when she started in on one of her lectures. But every lecture always ended with a fierce hug and a smile that told you she loved you anyway, even if you had ruined the tunic it had taken her a moon to sew, or spilled the entire flask of elderberry wine she was saving for the harvest feast.

Griane was like that, too.

His smile faded. Where was she? By now, Fellgair must have told her of their bargain. He could imagine her reaction: the quick toss of her braid, the defiant tilt of that pointed chin. Only the trembling of her lips would betray the hurt, the awful sense of abandonment. And all for nothing. Fellgair had broken his promise and Cuillon was somewhere in Chaos, alone and wounded.

Perhaps his father could help him find Cuillon as well as Tinnean and the Oak. He might even know how a man with no magic could get them out of this place. He wanted to sit his father down and demand answers to all his questions, but some stubborn, angry, childish part of him refused to speak, lest his father suspect that he just wanted to snatch a moment's rest.

Only when the ravine dwindled to a few tumbled boulders did they stop. Darak sank down in the purple grass, too tired to keep up a pretense of strength. His father squatted a few feet away, watching him with those cool, gray eyes.

Darak unstoppered his waterskin and took a deep pull; the lukewarm water tasted delicious. He held it out to his father who shook his head. "One of the advantages of being dead. You don't get thirsty or hungry." The smallest smile creased his face. "Or tired." The smile faded as quickly as it had come. "When I first felt you—"

"You felt me?"

"Not you in particular, but a relative. Blood calls to blood here. Spirit to spirit. The closer the tie, the stronger the connection. It was only when I saw you that I realized you were alive. That's why your call was so much stronger than the other."

"The other?" Darak scrambled to his feet. "You mean Tinnean?"

"Tinnean?" The mist inside his father's body swirled, then stilled. "Tinnean is in Chaos?"

"That's why I came."

"Tell me."

In a few terse sentences, Darak told him about the battle in the grove. When he finished, his father said, "I understand now. When I felt the spirit inside the tree—"

"The Oak?"

His father hesitated. "You can judge for yourself when you see it."

"How far?"

"You need to rest."

"I didn't come to Chaos to rest."

"You're wounded."

"It's nothing."

"When was the last time you slept?"

"I don't know. It doesn't matter."

"You won't do Tinnean any good if you're exhausted. Sit down, boy."

His father stared up at him, waiting for him to obey.

"I am not a boy. I haven't been a boy since you took ill. I was ten then, doing the work of a man. That's what you taught me, wasn't it? That a man's first responsibility is to care for his family. That no man can live on the charity of his kinfolk. That no man should be useless."

His father flinched and he was savagely glad.

"I was the one who made sure my mother and brother had food to eat and skins to clothe them. I was the one who helped Tinnean set his first snare and shoot his first arrow and gut his first fish. And I was the one who came to this unholy place to find him and bring him home. So don't tell me to sit down and don't think that you can order me about as you used to. If you won't help me, I'll find Tinnean on my own."

His father's face was as unreadable as stone, but the mist swirled wildly. The outline of his body grew less distinct. Automatically, Darak reached for him. His fingers went right through his father's arm. Perhaps the gesture helped. More likely, his father calmed the agitated swirling on his own. In a few moments, his form was as opaque as ever, though he still seemed less defined, as if the effort had drained him.

Darak's anger drained away as well, replaced by shame. Instead of seeking knowledge about Chaos, he had allowed frustration to master him, lashing out like a resentful child. Abruptly, he sat down.

"Your mam always did say a good argument cleared the air."

"It takes two to argue."

Again that small smile. "She said that to me, too. More times than I can count." His father sighed. "We were always too much alike, you and I. Maybe that's why we were always butting heads."

"Aye. Maybe."

His father regarded him steadily. "Well, you're too big for me to take a belt to."

"Wouldn't do much good. Seeing as I can't feel you."

"But I can feel you. You're like . . . fire on a winter night. That's the life in you. The spirits in Chaos will be drawn to you, wanting to get close to that flame, but scared, too, because you burn with emotions and those are dangerous for us."

In life, his conversations with his father had been limited to hunting, stalking, reading the signs of the forest and the sky. Even then, he'd preferred to teach by example. Darak seized on his last words to keep the conversation alive.

"Is that why you . . . do emotions make the mist stronger?"

"Aye. Control is our greatest strength here."

"The Trickster said—"

"You have seen the Trickster God?"

Wonder made his father's face look almost boyish. In life, he'd always seemed so old, even before the wasting sickness sapped his body and streaked his dark hair gray. Maybe all boys considered their fathers old. Still, it was shock to remember that he had been only thirty-three when he died.

"Darak?"

"Aye. The Trickster. He said I would only free Tinnean by acknowledging that my greatest strength is my greatest weakness."

"Lack of control is the only weakness in Chaos. Without control, you are prey to the illusions."

"Can you control the illusions?"

"Aye. But it is . . . wearying. Better to control yourself. Some men cannot. Some choose not to. They give way to madness. Or despair. And then they vanish."

"Where do they go?"

"No one knows. Any more than we know what happens to those who find a portal."

"I saw such a man. He . . . disintegrated." His father

nodded, face intent. "But he seemed peaceful. Perhaps his spirit went to the Forever Isles."

"Or simply ceased to exist. Either way, some men seek that escape."

"You didn't."

"Aye. Well." His father shrugged and looked away. "How old is Tinnean now?"

"Nearly fourteen."

"Fourteen! I hadn't realized . . ." He shook his head. "Time loses meaning here. We remember people as they were. When I first saw you, I thought you were my brother Kelik. You've the look of him."

"Mam always said I looked like you."

The mist swirled, then stilled.

"Forgive me. I didn't mean—"

"Nay. It's just . . ." The mist swirled again. This time, it took much longer for his father to control it. When he finally spoke, his voice sounded faint. "Tell me about them." When Darak hesitated, he added, "Even if it's bad. Better to know than to keep wondering."

Wishing he had Tinnean's gift for telling stories or Griane's inexhaustible energy, Darak talked. He told of births and deaths, of good harvests and bad, trying to leaven the unhappy tales with joyful ones. He told him about his mam's passing and Maili's, but spared his father the details of their deaths and those of his troubled marriage. He said very little about himself at all, but if his father wondered at that, he said nothing.

For a long time after he had finished speaking, his father simply stared at the ground. Darak knew better than to intrude on his thoughts. And besides, what could he say? "Did you love Mam? Did you miss seeing Tinnean grow up? Did it make you proud to hear how I brought down my first stag?" They weren't the kind of men who discussed feelings. They had never discussed anything. His father told him what to do and he obeyed.

He was shocked to hear him say, "No man wants to die. Not like that, coughing up blood, too weak at the end to keep from pissing himself." He rose out of his crouch and surveyed the grass as if searching for an enemy. "You were too young."

"I tried to keep them safe. To bring up Tinnean as best I could."

His father turned toward him, frowning. "Of course you did. I only meant . . . if I had let go of my anger about dying before my time, my regrets about . . . things . . ." He swallowed hard. "I would be with your mother now."

He clenched his fists, fighting the mist that rose up inside of him, calming it with a visible effort that left his form swaying like the grass. "Perhaps that was not my fate. Perhaps I was meant to come here to help my sons."

Always, his father had seemed so sure about everything, to have the answers to every question. As a youth, he'd resented that, but as a small child, his father's strength and calm had created a cocoon of safety in the huge, frightening world. He had always believed that when he was a man, he would have the answers, too. Now, he knew better. But how could he have failed to understand that awful sense of helplessness his father must have felt at the end when he had been just as helpless to save his mother and wife?

"I've kept you talking too long."

"Nay. I'm glad . . . I'm fine."

"Still."

"I can go on. I want to reach the tree."

"It's a day's journey." His father's gaze took in his wounded arm and sweat-streaked tunic. "Maybe two."

"I'm ready."

"I know you are. But 'twould be better if you rested a bit first. Aye?"

His father was right; as tired as he felt, he'd be useless to Tinnean. He stretched out in the grass and tucked his mantle under his head, strangely relieved to have his father watching over him again.

Morgath flung himself down, panting. The woman's ankle ached. The clumsy bitch must have injured it. Crouching low in the grass had only made it worse. Another thing the Hunter would answer for. The ankle felt warm to the touch, but his whole body was sweat-drenched under this miserable robe. The Hunter would answer for that, too.

The wolf's lingering senses had helped him pick up the trail, but he had lost the Hunter's scent now and the keen vision that had allowed him to identify Reinek was fading. Soon he would only be able to rely on his human senses.

He should have finished it when they had first arrived in this cursed place, but the desire to play with the Hunter first had been too strong to resist. And he had still been flooded by sensations he had nearly forgotten: the soft brush of hair against cheek, the rough glide of wool against thighs. The giddy delight of laughter. The delicious shock of colors. And the power to shape words with lips and tongue and teeth, to give voice to them after so many days and nights of communicating with howls and whines and snarls.

His hands reached under the robe, sensitive fingertips exploring the marvelous contrasts of hard bone and yielding flesh, knobby knees and smooth thighs. His fingers traveled higher. Strange to feel only curling hair and moist softness instead of the heavy weight of testicles and penis. He lay back and closed his eyes. The woman was pretty enough. Men would desire her. When he returned to the world, he could have his pick. He wondered what it would be like to feel a man thrusting into the hidden place his fingertips were probing.

He would enjoy learning. Then he would discard her. Choose a strong, young man. He could never settle for being the passive recipient of men's lust. Besides, women's bodies were weak. If he possessed his own body, he could face the Hunter boldly instead of skulking among the rocks, an equal match to his strength—and more than his match in cunning.

His fingers stilled and his eyes flew open. Perhaps he wouldn't have to wait until he escaped Chaos. That would be his ultimate victory over the Hunter—to expel his spirit and steal his body. He stroked himself, considering. The Hunter had much to answer for. He had wounded him with arrow and dagger. Thwarted his attempt on the girl. Dragged him back into Chaos. Casting out his spirit would be sweet, but it would yield only a brief taste of the man's terror.

He wanted more.

How much sweeter and more satisfying to prolong the ordeal—to watch him tremble with fear, to listen to his screams of pain, to make him beg for the release of death. If he was patient and careful, he could keep the Hunter alive for days.

Morgath's fingers moved again, more urgently. His hips thrust against them. His back arched as the pleasure surged, and a soft cry escaped him. He settled himself more comfortably, savoring the lassitude that suffused him. A pleasant enough experience, but lacking the delicious power of penetrating a partner, male or female. And not nearly as fulfilling as watching an enemy grovel.

Chapter 38

THE FEW SNATCHED HOURS of sleep gave
Darak the strength to go on. He judged that they
covered ten miles before the next transformation oc-
curred. Between one step and the next, the grasslands
became an ice field studded with twisting, blue columns that belched smoke into the ochre sky. A few
miles later, it gave way to a barren plain, its emptiness
only relieved by rocks and stunted trees.

They spoke little, even during their brief periods of
rest. Darak wondered whether his father felt the same
reluctance to delve too deeply into the past or was
simply allowing him to conserve his energy. He
needed all of it to match his father's relentless pace.
Sweat-soaked and panting, he drove himself, so intent
on keeping up that he didn't realize his father had
stopped until he heard him call out.

Sleeve pressed against his streaming forehead, Darak
squinted in the direction of his father's pointing finger.
The thicket shimmered in the haze. Rising above the
smaller bushes, he made out the shape of a single tree.

His father nodded in answer to his questioning gaze.
Without a word, they set off again. Only when he
lifted his hand to push aside the heavy clusters of vio-

let flowers did his father speak. "The tree looks strange. But I am sure Tinnean's spirit is inside."

No words could prepare him for what he saw when he emerged into the clearing. The grotesquely twisted tree. The crumpled body that lay beneath it. And the holly leaves encasing Cuillon's hands and feet.

Darak fell to his knees beside him. Cuillon's chest rose and fell with slow, steady breaths. Alive. He was still alive. With shaking hands, he splashed water into his palm. He was rinsing the dirt from Cuillon's face when his eyelids fluttered. A smile replaced the dazed look.

"Darak."

"Easy, lad."

"They are here. I felt them."

"Don't talk. Drink this."

Cuillon obediently swallowed a few sips of water. "Struath . . . he is dead, Darak. And Yeorna."

Darak nodded, wiping water from Cuillon's chin.

"I brought the spirit catcher."

For the first time, he noticed the pouch resting on Cuillon's chest.

"That is why I followed you. I knew you would be angry, but—"

"Hush. Save your strength."

"The pain is not so bad now." Cuillon must have seen his wince for he added, "Truly. Help me sit up."

"Cuillon . . ."

"Please.

Darak eased him into his arms. Cuillon sighed. "I have made a mess of Tinnean's clothes."

"Damn the clothes."

"I have hurt his body."

Darak glanced at the blood-soaked holly leaves, then looked away.

"Would you cut them off, please? I . . . it is hard for me to use the dagger."

One by one, Darak sheared the leaves from Cuillon's wrists and forearms, trying not to think about the agony he must have endured when they burst through his skin. It took more willpower to touch Cuillon's fingers. They were an awful greenish-gray, as slender and knobby as twigs. They still bent under his ministrations, but it was the suppleness of green wood, not the resiliency of flesh.

A soft sound behind him made him look up. The mingled pain and longing on his father's face made him look away again, unwilling to witness such a naked display of emotion from the man who had always kept his feelings private. Tinnean had been a toddler when he died. Hard enough to behold the young man his son had become. To witness the changes that were now destroying his body . . . it was more than any man should have to bear.

Darak fought to keep his voice steady as he asked Cuillon, "How long has this been happening?"

"It started in the First Forest. Each time I tried to communicate with the trees, it got worse."

"Can you stop it?"

"I had to find the Oak."

"I know. I don't mean that. Can you stop it from happening again?"

"For now. But in time . . ."

Darak stared at the bloody fingers, studded with sheared-off twigs.

"I am sorry, Darak."

"It's not your fault."

"If I had been stronger . . ."

He seized Cuillon's shoulders. "It is not your fault. You hear me?"

"Aye, Darak." A small smile crossed Cuillon's face. "You are shouting."

"Aye. Well. If it'll help you hear sense."

"We have the spirit catcher."

But only Struath knew how to use it. He dared a look at his father, relieved to find him calmer. "Could you find Struath?"

"It would be sheer luck. I cannot feel him."

Reluctantly, he turned back to Cuillon. "You reached them before."

"Aye, but now . . . I think it would destroy Tinnean's body."

Darak's shoulders sagged. To have come all this way, to finally reach their goal, and still be helpless to free them.

"Let it wait, son. See to the Holly-Lord's wounds. He needs fresh bandages."

He nodded, grateful to be given a task he could accomplish.

"You are his father. I should have seen. You look so much alike." Cuillon hesitated, his smile fading. "But I thought only bad men came to Chaos."

"Aye. Well."

His father's grimace brought back Cuillon's smile. "You even talk alike." Cuillon laughed out loud. "And have the same frown."

"You're talking too much," Darak said. "Save your strength."

He peeled back the shreds of Cuillon's breeches and started sawing off the holly leaves from his calves and ankles. He looked up only once, when Cuillon said, "My human name is Cuillon."

"Mine is . . . was . . . Reinek."

"Your son's body has been a wonder to me."

The mist swirled so wildly that Darak rose out of his crouch. His father stilled him with a gesture. When he had regained his composure, he said, "My son is a wonder to me as well." His father's gaze flicked toward him before returning to Cuillon. "I am honored to see him again after so many years."

Morgath lay belly-down at the summit of the rise, squinting at the figures in the clearing. Although partially hidden by the shrubs, he could make out the figure of a third man sitting next to the Hunter. Now he had three enemies to confront.

Above the drone of insects, a familiar whining rose. He glanced over his shoulder. The tumble of rocks at the base of the rise shimmered. Through them, he saw a bare tree limb wave as if beckoning him.

Morgath crawled close enough to see a snow-covered field and beyond it, a small circle of huts. Not his tribe's, perhaps, but a village all the same. Where real people huddled together around real fires and Chaos was only a tale told by the Memory-Keeper.

It had taken him years to find a portal. In the space of—what? Two days? Three?—two had opened before him. Was Chaos gaining a hold on the world beyond? Or was it easier to detect the portals now that he possessed a living body? The first portal had only taken him to another part of Chaos. This one promised freedom.

Morgath hesitated. To leave now meant relinquishing the exquisite pleasure of punishing the Hunter. The portal whined. The tree shivered. Go to safety or stay? Flee or force a confrontation?

Morgath fell back on his haunches as the portal wavered and vanished. There would be other portals. He could have his pick. But he had only one chance to destroy the Hunter.

Once again, he bellied up the rise. He watched the Hunter help the third man to his feet. He was much shorter than the Hunter, but his form looked just as real. That meant he was alive—and a potential threat. Was he only imagining the Hunter's solicitude as he helped the small man to his feet or could the Hunter's brother have come to Chaos in search of him?

Even from this distance, it was clear that the boy limped badly. He clung to the Hunter as they made their slow way across the clearing. The Hunter settled him in the shade of a bush and squatted beside him, flexing his wounded arm.

Morgath smiled. Ignoring his protesting back, he crouched low and crept down the slope.

🍂

Darak eyed the spirit catcher resting in his palm. Despite its long contact with Cuillon's body, the crystal felt cool. Its facets twinkled with the sickly ochre light of Chaos. Such a tiny thing for the task ahead, but better prepared than he was. He shook his head, wondering if his distrust of magic could be the answer to Fellgair's riddle.

Cuillon touched his sleeve. "When I first lay in your hut, Struath came with the others."

"The others?"

"Yeorna. Gortin. And the girl like a sparrow in winter."

Darak had to smile; plump, brown-haired Lisula did look like a sparrow in winter. "Do you remember what they did?" he asked.

"The others sang and burned weeds and Struath closed his eye and rocked back and forth for a long time."

"And then?"

"Then he fell over."

Darak blew out his breath. Before Cuillon could apologize, he added, "Don't be sorry. You're no more a shaman than I am."

But Tinnean had been—was becoming one. How many times had he rushed into the hut last summer, face alight after a day spent with Struath? Too excited to sit, he'd stand over them, hands waving as he tried to describe what he had learned that day. His mam would ask questions, Maili would smile—and he would crouch by the fire, fletching an arrow or chipping a flint, until he could bear the flood of words no more and tell Tinnean to shut up about Struath and sit.

If only he had listened, tried to understand what Tinnean meant when he talked about connecting with the eternal powers of earth and air, fire and water. All he could remember now was something about breathing and stillness.

His body tensed. Breathing and stillness he understood. Those were the first lessons his father had taught him. Breathing. Stillness. Control.

He walked to the tree and knelt before it.

Merciful Maker, help me.

He rested the fingertips of his left hand against the thorny trunk.

Lord of the Forest, help me.

He raised his right hand, spirit catcher clenched in his fist.

Tinnean—if you are there—help me.

He closed his eyes.

Fear is the enemy. Control the fear. Control yourself.

He breathed.

Let go of the fear. Just breathe.

He listened to his breathing, slow and even. To the scratch of the tree's branches as they rubbed against each other in a faint breeze. To a rustling in the thicket behind him.

He whirled around, hand on his dagger, as a yellow-winged bird shot out of the underbrush.

"Never mind that, son. Let me be your eyes and ears."

He tried, but he kept losing his concentration each time a new sound reached him.

"Just breathe, Darak."

"Damn it, don't you think I'm trying?"

"Try harder."

For a moment, they glared at each other. Unexpectedly, his father grinned and Darak found himself grinning back. His father squatted down beside him. "Don't

try and pretend you're a shaman. You're not. And
you'll not teach yourself in a few moments what it
took Struath years to learn." His father leaned closer,
face intent. "But maybe if you imagined you were
hunting. That Tinnean is the quarry."

Darak nodded. Again, he raised the spirit catcher
and closed his eyes.

He was the hunter. His muscles loose, his head clear.
In. Out. Breathe.

He was the hunter. Moving through the trees. Tracking the quarry.

Silent. Cautious. Alert.

Instead of a bow, he held a crystal.

Hard. Round. Smooth.

Instead of a stag, he sought Tinnean.

Helpless. Unconscious . . .

Not that trail. Choose another. Find the one that
leads to Tinnean's spirit.

*His eagerness to learn. His wonder at the world be-
yond this world. His stubbornness to choose his own
path, no matter where it led, no matter how I warned
him . . .*

Go back. Find the place where the trail branched.
Start again.

*The child's arms, skinny as snakes. "Look, Darak.
Look at that muscle." Knobby knees peeking out from
under his tunic. "I can too run faster than you." The
sweet smile. "Listen, Darak. I can almost play the song
now." The high-pitched squeal. "I caught one, Darak!
I caught a fish!"*

He's there.

Tinnean?

Waiting.

It's Darak.

Just out of reach.

I've come to take you home.

Slow. Move too fast and the quarry will elude you.

Come out of the Oak, lad.

Close now. Almost close enough to touch.

I'll keep you safe. Just come to the crystal.

Fingertips tingling.

You want to go home, don't you?

Pain lancing through his hand.

Tinnean. Come to me. Now.

Fire racing up his arm.

Damn it, Tinnean, listen to me!

The scream exploded inside of him, Tinnean's scream tearing them both apart. Darak flung himself away from the tree. The spirit catcher fell to the ground.

"Darak? Son? Are you all right?"

He stared down at his shaking hands.

"It's not your fault."

I failed.

"You can try again."

I nearly destroyed him.

"You must not lose hope."

I've lost him.

Darak picked up the spirit catcher and thrust it into his bag of charms. He forced himself to stand. He willed his eyes to meet his father's, braced for the inevitable look of disapproval. The desperate longing nearly unmanned him.

Abruptly, his father stiffened. His gaze darted around the glade, fixed on the bushes behind Cuillon. Darak surged forward, shouting at Cuillon to move, move fast. Cuillon was still struggling to rise when the golden-haired figure emerged behind him and seized him by the hair.

Chapter 39

DARAK RIPPED THE DAGGER from his sheath and fell into a crouch. Morgath yanked Cuillon's head back, baring his neck to the dagger. Only days ago, it had been Morgath on his knees while he wielded the dagger. Morgath smiled; he remembered, too.

"We meet again, Hunter."

He could go for the shoulder or the arm, but if he missed, even by inches, he could kill Cuillon.

"Drop the dagger."

He let his shoulders sag, then came up fast. He hurled the dagger at Morgath's face and charged. Morgath flinched. The dagger flew past his ear. Darak raced forward, praying he could reach him, knowing he would not, even before Morgath brandished his dagger and screamed at him to stop.

Cuillon's eyes were glazed with shock. Blood stained his throat, but it was the slow ooze of a shallow gash, not the rhythmic spurting that indicated a fatal wound.

"Step back. Now. Or your brother dies."

Very slowly, he backed away. Morgath didn't know he had the Holly-Lord at his mercy. Maybe he wouldn't care. From the little Darak knew of him,

Morgath sought personal vengeance. But it would mean the destruction of the world if Cuillon died.

Morgath stroked Cuillon's cheek with the flat of the dagger. Back and forth, very slowly, like a lover's caress. "You've lost your hunting instincts. Else I could never have taken the boy."

Out of the corner of his eye, Darak saw his father's form tremble, then reassert itself. Let me be your eyes and ears, he had said. Had his failure at the tree distracted him?

"What were you doing when I arrived? Praying?"

"Aye."

"Painful business. But I liked seeing you on your knees."

"Let the boy go and you can see it again."

Morgath's lips twisted in a hideous parody of Yeorna's smile. "Tempting. But killing him would hurt you much more." He raised the dagger until the point hovered a finger's width from Cuillon's eye.

"Kill him and you die." Darak held up his hands. "Dagger or no, I'll break your neck before his lifeblood stops pumping."

"So. We appear to be at an impasse." Morgath's teeth gleamed in a quick, feral smile. "Unless you have a suggestion?"

Morgath was only using Cuillon as bait. The shaman wanted him. Judging from the madness in his eyes, he was willing to risk his life for the pleasure of hurting him. Darak hesitated. Attack Morgath and Cuillon would die. Offer the shaman what he really wanted and risk death himself. He would willingly exchange his life for Cuillon's, but if he died, who would free Tinnean and the Oak?

Praying he was making the right choice, Darak said, "Take me."

He heard his father's gasp, saw Cuillon's body jerk in surprise. A single drop of blood welled up on his cheek, bright and round as a holly berry.

"What's to keep you from breaking my neck as soon as I release him?" Morgath sounded bored, but his breath had quickened.

"You have my word."

Morgath snorted in derision.

"Bind me if you like. I won't resist you."

Morgath wet his lips, as if savoring the thought of a victim at once unwilling yet compliant.

"You can do what you want to me." Recalling Struath's words, he added, "Take as much time as you want."

The longer Morgath postponed the kill, the more time he would have to free himself.

"As long as the boy is in sight, I won't fight you. But once the boy is safe, you're mine."

He waited, scarcely breathing. When Morgath smiled, he knew the bargain was made.

"Your word, Morgath. That the boy goes free. That it'll be just you and me."

Morgath's smile widened. "Just you and me, Hunter."

"Let the boy go."

"You're giving me orders?"

"Please."

"Better. Better still if you made the request on your knees."

His nails dug into his palms as his fingers clenched. The Trickster had warned him that he would only defeat Morgath by humbling himself. Slowly, he fell to his knees.

"Good, Hunter. Now try begging."

"Nay." His father's voice sounded calm, but the mist swirled dangerously. "He is on his knees. That is enough."

"Hold your tongue, Reinek, or I'll make you beg as well."

"Please," Darak said. "Let my brother go. I . . . I beg you."

"Very nice. If I free your brother, will you promise to beg some more before you die?"

Darak swallowed down the bile that rose in his throat. "Aye."

"Very good. Now strip."

"What?"

"Take off your clothes," Morgath said, with the patient voice of a teacher.

Numbly, Darak obeyed. He knew doeskin couldn't repel Morgath's dagger, yet standing naked in front of his enemy made him feel horribly vulnerable. Of course, that's what Morgath wanted. He kept his hands at his sides, resisting the urge to cover himself, but he could not control his shiver of dread when Morgath inspected him.

"You haven't been eating enough. Still, the musculature is lovely. I've always enjoyed a well-made man." Morgath's gaze lingered on his genitals. The heat rose in Darak's face. Morgath's giggle only made it worse, as did the knowledge that his father was witnessing this.

Morgath jerked his head toward the tree. "Over there, Hunter."

He walked to the tree, resisting the urge to squeeze his bag of charms and give Morgath proof of his fear.

"Face me."

Morgath sheathed his dagger and ripped Cuillon's free. Keeping a firm grip on his arm, he pushed him forward.

Cuillon's eyes met his. Darak shook his head. The Holly-Lord was no fighter and he was weak from shock and pain. Morgath might wear a woman's body now, but he was still far stronger.

"Pick up your brother's belt. Tie his left wrist to that branch."

Darak followed Morgath's gaze, taking in the tiny thorns studding the branch. The dagger appeared below Cuillon's ear.

"Do it."

He nodded, willing Cuillon to obey. Only by standing on his toes did his arm reach the branch. He managed to smile at Cuillon, but couldn't hold it when the thorns pierced him.

"Does it hurt, Hunter?"

He nodded.

"Good. Tighter, boy."

Darak closed his eyes.

The pain isn't so bad. The humiliation doesn't matter. Let it go.

"You obey orders well. You must get that from your brother. Now you may bid him farewell."

Darak opened his eyes to find tears welling up in Cuillon's. He shook his head fiercely and Cuillon blinked them back.

"Forgive me, Darak."

"There's nothing to forgive."

"Enough. Back away."

For the first time, Darak looked at his father. "Go with him."

"Nay."

"Please. Keep him safe."

Their eyes locked. His father gave him a curt nod. "I will come back for you." That cold gray gaze swept over Morgath. "And for you."

Morgath laughed. "Oh, I hope so. I'll enjoy your expression when you see what's left of your firstborn son."

With a visible effort, his father controlled the mist that threatened to obliterate him. Gods, he was strong. Darak hoped he possessed a small measure of that strength. He would need it to survive what was to come.

His father's eyes bored into his. Then he turned on his heel and glided after Cuillon.

"Oh. One more thing."

Morgath seized his wrist and shoved his right arm against another branch. He bit his lip, tasting the salty warmth of blood.

"Just to see if you'll keep your word, Hunter . . ."

Darak flinched, waiting for Morgath to plunge the dagger into his chest. Instead, he carefully folded three fingers over his thumb. Their eyes met. Morgath nodded politely as if they had just been introduced. Then he sawed off his forefinger.

Cuillon screamed and lurched forward. His father's shout drowned out Darak's strangled gasp. Cuillon stopped, a handspan from the dagger's point. Morgath tossed the finger at his feet. "Something to remember him by."

Through the haze of shock and pain, Darak watched Cuillon bend down and pick up the severed finger. He cradled it in his palms, tears streaking his dirty cheeks white. His hands shook as he opened Struath's pouch and placed the finger inside, but his voice still held the Holly-Lord's enduring calm when he finally looked up at Morgath.

"I understand now why Struath sent you here. You are evil."

The dagger in Morgath's hand trembled slightly. "So I have been told. And by better men than you. But I promised to free you and I will. When your brother's body is rotting on that tree, look for me. For I will find you and make you pay for those words."

Cuillon's eyes—Tinnean's eyes—met his one last time. "I will wait for you in the grove, Darak. I know you will not fail us. And I will not fail you." He spat into his hand and laid it atop the pouch. Then he turned abruptly and limped away. With one final glance, his father followed.

Darak was still watching them when Morgath's fingers encircled his wrist again. The shaman held his arm against the branch, this time twisting it slowly.

Sweat broke out on his forehead as the thorns gouged long gashes around his forearm and punctured the flesh of his palm.

Morgath smiled and raised the dagger. He was still smiling when he drove the blade through the back of Darak's hand.

Morgath stroked his hair while he waited for the scream to die. "Now we're ready to begin."

Chapter 40

GRIANE SCRAMBLED UP the embankment to the cave, cold and exhaustion forgotten. For three days, she had followed the river north. For three nights, she had snatched fitful periods of sleep, huddled in shallow depressions among tree roots, in tiny grottos created by overhanging slabs of rock. The Summerlands sustained her. A few bites of berry or mushroom lent new strength to tired legs. A few sips of the water warmed her as well as any fire. And the fragrance of Rowan's fading blossoms reminded her of the unexpected friends she had left behind her—and those to whom she was returning.

Each night before she slept, she'd imagined their expressions. Yeorna, blinking back tears. The Tree-Father, his hand half raised to make the sign against evil, staring at her in wonderment. Cuillon's sweet smile. And Darak. He would gape at her, then frown, then hug her so hard her bones would creak. And then he'd threaten to wallop her for scaring them all so, but his grin would belie the words. They would gather around the fire and she would show them her treasures and tell them the story and, just for a little while, Darak's fears for Tinnean would ease and the shadows under his eyes would fade.

She slipped in the new-fallen snow, gasping as she righted her precious basket. The last part of the journey was always the hardest, they said, but it only made arriving that much better. Panting, she reached the top of the embankment and shouted Darak's name.

Her voice trailed off when she saw the mound of snow near the sunberry bush. Surely, it hadn't been there before. Only when she came closer did she realize that the thing protruding from it was a dagger. With trembling fingers, she grasped the hilt. It slid free with the dull screech of metal against stone. The bronze gleamed in the sunlight. Falling to her knees, she feverishly shoved away the snow. Her mittened fingers scraped against rock.

She fell back on her haunches, staring at the Tree-Father's cairn. Then she screamed Darak's name, and Cuillon's, and finally Yeorna's. Only the wind answered.

She staggered to her feet and ran, skidding on snow-slick pebbles, falling, jarring her knee so hard she gasped, rising again with a grimace to limp the final distance to the cave. No smoke. No footprints. No sounds. Frenzied, she shoved her way through the branches.

For a moment, she could only crouch in the darkness, listening to the hoarse rasp of her breath. Finally, she tore off her mittens and forced herself to crawl forward, feeling for the fire pit. Cold stone under her hands. Cold ashes sifting through her shaking fingers.

She crawled back outside. The cairn gave mute testament to the Tree-Father's death, but she saw no blood, no evidence of struggle. She ripped away the dead branches at the mouth of the cave, hacked through those on the living bushes. Midday sunlight relieved the gloom enough for her to make out Darak's bow lying beside his sleeping place, the contents of her magic bag spilled onto the ground, the furs where the Tree-Father slept hastily tossed aside.

They had fled, then, or been forced out. At least

one had survived to bury the Tree-Father. Nay, the rest must be alive, too; otherwise, she would have seen more cairns. Had the wolf attacked again? Had a portal opened, forcing them to leave suddenly? Even so, Darak would never leave his bow behind.

Griane made her way back to the cairn. The sunlight, so welcome when she awoke this morning, now mocked her. The sky should be gray, the clouds should lower over the treetops, mourning the death of the Tree-Father. She thrust the dagger back into the stones and said a prayer that his spirit might have flown to the Forever Isles.

Then she picked up her discarded basket and gazed at the endless expanse of forest. Darak would look for signs. Scout around the cave in ever-widening circles for footprints, broken branches, anything that might hint at the direction they had taken. She had several hours of light left, plenty of time to find answers. Anything was better than sitting in the cave, alone with her fear.

With Reinek at his side, Cuillon lurched across the plain. They had stopped only once, when they heard the awful scream. He thought then that he would lose Darak's father. Helplessly, he could only watch as his body dissolved. Somehow, Reinek had mastered himself and they had gone on. He did not know where they were going. He was not sure the Trickster would come for him, or if he wanted him to. If the Trickster carried him out of Chaos, Darak would be trapped here.

When the high-pitched whining began, Reinek halted, darting glances around him. Cuillon pointed to the quaking sapling. Reinek squinted at the tree as if he could not quite make it out.

"It is a portal."

"It could lead anywhere." The first words Darak's father had spoken since they had left the clearing.

The tree thinned to a pale, gray sliver. Cuillon drew closer. It might be a wintry sky or merely the reflection of sky in a still pool. The surface rippled. Something darted toward him and he stumbled backward.

The fish flopped helplessly, just like the fish he had caught that morning with Darak. Cuillon picked it up and tossed it back through the portal. Drops of water sprayed him as it dove into the pool. The ripples were still spreading out when the portal shuddered close.

"You could have eaten the fish," Reinek said.

"It did not deserve to be eaten."

"You did not deserve to be expelled from your tree. Tinnean's spirit did not deserve to be cast into Chaos. Darak—" Reinek took a deep breath and let it out slowly.

"If I had stayed in the First Forest, Darak would not be suffering."

"And if I had seen Morgath coming . . ." The mist swirled and stilled. Reinek's mouth settled into a grim line. "Looking back serves no purpose save to make men miserable. And in Chaos, to drive men mad. The only thing we can do now is get you out of here."

"I could find Struath. He would know how to use the spirit catcher." Reinek just shook his head. "Or go back to the tree and kill Morgath."

"Forgive me, Holly-Lord, but you could not even kill a fish."

"The fish did not deserve to die. Morgath does."

"It would only end in your death and Darak's."

"Then I will find the Lord of Chaos."

"Morgath is his creature. Why should he help you?"

"I am a god. Not such a great one as he is, but . . ." Reinek's expression told him this plan was as useless as the others. "I have to do something. I cannot just run away."

Reinek surprised him by smiling. "You talk like a man, Holly-Lord."

"I have been one for a long while now."

"Not so long. Not as you measure time."

"Nay. But it seems very long. It is hard to be a man."

The smile faded. "Aye, Holly-Lord. It is."

Chapter 41

HE HUNG UPON the twisted oak, staring out at the empty plain. As soon as Cuillon and his father disappeared, he had lunged at Morgath. The brief terror that crossed the shaman's face was his only reward. The belt held his wrist fast. The thorns ripped open new wounds on his back and buttocks, and the agony of the dagger, grating against the delicate bones and tendons of his right hand, took him to the edge of unconsciousness.

Morgath brought him back. Each time a new torture threatened to allow him to escape into oblivion, Morgath brought him back, sometimes with a sip of water, sometimes with a slap.

He hung upon the tree. There was no day, no night, no way to mark the passing of time save by the changes in his body. The pain ebbed and flowed according to Morgath's whim, but it was always present, as much a companion as the oak that scored his body with its thorns. He could bear the pain the oak inflicted: the spiked trunk scraping against his spine with each breath, the ache in his shoulders, the lines of fire down his arms where the thorns ripped open his flesh. For if the tree hurt him, it also helped. An odd vibration pulsed through the trunk, like a twin heartbeat. He told himself it was Tinnean, keeping vigil for him, and he endured.

Time drifted by, and he drifted with it, carried along by Morgath's tuneless humming. He hummed while he scored his chest and belly with the dagger. He hummed while he licked the wounds. Even when he sawed off two more fingers and tenderly bandaged the wounds, Morgath hummed.

The shock of the mutilation was worse than the pain, the knowledge that he would never draw a bow again harder to bear than the terror that gripped his bowels each time Morgath raised the dagger.

He tried putting words to the humming, mixing prayers and chants and fragments of old songs to give him strength. For the ability to endure this, to survive until he found a way to free Tinnean, must be the greatest strength of Fellgair's riddle. How it could also be his greatest weakness, he didn't know; he'd never been good at riddles.

But the words conjured up images: his mam crooning a lullaby to Tinnean, his father teaching him the hunter's song. Those weakened him as much as the sight of Morgath, sitting cross-legged on the ground, weaving his severed fingers into Yeorna's hair.

He closed his eyes and let himself drift back to a time when Chaos was only a name to frighten children, a time when the world made sense, when his brother's face was filled with wonder and joy. The mysteries of the unseen world evoked the wonder, but something as ordinary as the bleat of a newborn lamb could evoke the joy.

Did all children feel that joy? Had he felt it? Mostly, he remembered resentment that he was too small to do the things his father could, too small to resist his father's will. And fear, too, that he could not control the huge world around him. Then he recalled the night of his vision quest when the black she-wolf had come for him. He had felt joy then. So long ago.

He had always envied Tinnean's simple faith. Once, he had shared it. The belief that the gods would never desert his people, that spring would follow winter, that, despite all the dangers in the world, his parents would keep him safe. When had he lost that faith? Long before he'd lost Tinnean. He tried to recall the moment things had changed for him, but it seemed that his faith had just been chipped away over the years, flaking off like flint under a hammerstone.

Maybe the same thing had happened to his sense of joy. Maybe faith and joy were linked. That would explain why the simplest things could delight Tinnean: a bowl of porridge on a cold winter morning, a patch of bluebells in the spring woods. Or just running, running, running down the beach, laughing at his too-serious older brother who shouted at him to slow down.

"Wake up, Hunter."

A slap. A splash of water. And Morgath holding up the dagger again.

Pain drifted into fear. Not the burst of terror when Morgath took another finger, but a stealthy thing, creeping up on him like a predator stalking its prey. *I am the hunter,* he told it, and felt it slink back into the shadows, waiting like Morgath for him to shatter.

Heat beat down on him, hotter than the Midsummer sun. Flames flicked at him with serpents' tongues, seeking out his most vulnerable places: his shoulders, his lungs, his ribs. Drawn to the pain, feeding it and feeding on it, sometimes retreating, but never going away.

He stretched out his toes, holding himself up to

shield those weak places. *I am the hunter,* he told the
fire, and felt it retreat. Only for a few moments, only
to shift its attack to his toes, his ankles, his calves.
Finally, he let his body sag and felt the flames sear
him, reeking with delight.

He hung upon the tree, sweat rolling down his face,
stinging his cracked lips. His bag of charms pressed
against his chest, a heavy weight that made each breath
difficult. The flames grew bolder. Even when he closed
his eyes, he could see the brilliant bursts of red and
gold, shimmering like the Northern Dancers, shining
like the sky-spears.

A raven croaked, deep and hoarse. He opened his
eyes, wondering where the bird was, then realized the
croak came from him.

"I am the hunter," he said.

Morgath reached up and stroked his cheek. "Not
anymore."

Darak closed his eyes. So cool, those fingers. So
good after the fire. They traced the line of his jaw,
the curve of his lips. Drew a trail of refreshing relief
down his neck.

"Does it feel good, Darak?" Yeorna's voice, throaty
and soft. "Shall I give you more?" Yeorna's fingers
soothing the welts on his chest. Yeorna's hair brushing
against his shoulder, light as a breeze. Yeorna's breath
warm against his face, her tongue wetting his dry lips.

"I can give pleasure as well as pain."

Hair tickling his chest. Tongue licking his belly.
Cool fingers stroking his genitals.

Darak's eyes flew open. He jerked away from Morgath's questing hands and the pain leaped, fierce as
a wildcat.

On his knees, Morgath smiled up at him. "Are you
sure, Darak? Struath always loved it."

Bile rose in his throat. He gagged and fought it
down, but when Morgath leaned closer, he spat the
filth into that upturned face. A convulsion seized him,

shook him hard enough to make his teeth click against each other and shoot arrows of pain through his body. He clenched his teeth, stopping their chattering, but he couldn't control his body. He could only hang upon the tree while the arrows tore at him, and gasp when finally, the convulsions stopped and the pain subsided.

And then the flames returned, searing his shoulder. But it wasn't fire. It was Morgath, cutting away a long, bloody strip of his flesh.

There was no beginning to the pain and no end. His body was fire. His body was blood. His body was raw meat impaled upon Morgath's dagger, dangling from Morgath's fingers, disappearing between Morgath's lips.

He could not hold back the screams then. And once they began, he could not stop them. Even when his voice shattered and dwindled to a hoarse sob, the screams echoed in his head, pulsing with that other heartbeat.

"Shall I stop it, Darak?"

Morgath's voice, tender as a lover's.

"Shall I make it go away?"

Aye. Please. Anything.

"You can die, Darak. The pain would stop then."

Oh, gods, it hurts.

"Shall I help you die, Darak?"

Maker, help me. Lord of the Forest, help me. Tinnean . . .

He opened his eyes. The fire retreated, waiting in the shadows with the pain. The oak trembled, its rhythmic vibration fluttering uncertainly. Even the breeze ceased to blow, as if the wind caught its breath and waited with Morgath for his decision.

Rage roared through him, hotter than any fire, stronger than any pain, coalescing into the words that poured out of his mouth. "Damn you. Damn you, feasting on my flesh. I will not die. I will not."

Unleashed, the fire raged back, red-hot and vicious, and with it the pain, and with that, the screams, fading too slowly into silence.

Morgath called him back.

"You're strong. I like that."

He stepped close. His hands came up. Darak flinched.

"Water, Darak. Drink."

He lowered his head, lapping up the water like an animal. Only a mouthful—barely enough to wet his lips and ease his raw throat—before Morgath opened his fingers and let the water drain through them. The damp palms cupped his cheeks. The blue eyes gazed into his. The soft lips parted in a tender smile.

He felt pressure at his temples, then a dull pain between his eyes. The pain receded. He wondered if Morgath had done that.

Aye, Darak.

The voice spoke inside of him, as close and intimate as his thoughts. Fear clawed at him when he realized Morgath had invaded his spirit.

That's right. I am part of you now. I can read every thought, feel every fear, uncover all your dirty little secrets. Even the ones you try to hide from yourself.

Somewhere a man moaned.

Your moan, Darak. I feel it, just as I felt the wolf's terror when I took it. It was delicious. So are you. Even more delicious than the wolf. Or the woman. I hardly had the chance to enjoy her. You, I can savor. I will use your spirit as freely as I used your body.

The insidious presence oozed through him, a slow, deliberate invasion of mind and spirit. Each barrier he flung up, Morgath destroyed, as easily as he might brush away a cobweb. Each memory he sought to protect, Morgath pried loose and examined. Each time he retreated, Morgath followed.

Like a child with a new toy, Morgath played with him, sometimes lingering over a new discovery, sometimes surging forward to obliterate another line of defense. The shaman stripped his spirit, leaving it as raw and quivering as his abused flesh. And Morgath loved it; Darak could feel his pleasure as viscerally as he could feel his own terror and shame.

He fled deeper into himself, desperately seeking a hiding place. He only succeeded in forging a trail that Morgath could follow, a trail that led to the very core of his being. There was no place to hide, no way to shield himself.

Summoning his will, Darak attacked. He felt Morgath's momentary surprise as he retreated and his arousal when he returned.

Good. Fight me, Darak. That will make the final possession sweeter.

He concentrated on the pain, forcing his consciousness back into his wreck of a body. Again, Morgath withdrew, but in the space of a heartbeat, he was back.

Who is Tinnean?

Before he could stop them, images flooded his mind. Tinnean lurching through the village on chubby legs, frowning with the effort of keeping his balance. Tinnean racing after him when he went hunting: "Take me with you, Darak. I won't make a sound this time." Tinnean following him out of the hut, calling to his back: "Walking away won't change anything, Darak. I have found my life-path and I will not give it up."

Ahh.

Morgath's pleasure rippled through him.

So Tinnean is the brother and his spirit is trapped inside the tree with the Oak. The Trickster didn't mention that. He likes to keep secrets. Just like us. We're very much alike, you and I.

Darak reared back against the tree, forcing the thorns deeper into his body, forcing Morgath to retreat once more.

The vibration in the tree pulsed faster, whether in rhythm to his heartbeat or driven by some urgency of its own. He pushed aside the fear and the pain and the knowledge of Morgath's imminent return and focused all his awareness on that vibration, praying it was Tinnean.

Morgath's voice summoned him. Darak's spirit fled, following the beckoning heartbeat.

Chapter 42

WHEN THE AIR IN FRONT OF HIM ripped open, Cuillon stumbled and fell. He pushed himself to his feet, wondering how he could have missed the whining that always preceded the opening of a portal. Then a long nose emerged from the starry void.

The Trickster stepped into Chaos and pinched the portal closed behind him. Golden eyes surveyed him dispassionately. "You're a mess."

"Darak needs you."

"Everyone needs me. It's one of the more tiresome aspects of being a god. Hello, Reinek. Did you enjoy your little reunion with Darak?"

Reinek's mouth moved, his eyes wide as he gazed at the Trickster. After a long moment, he mastered his shock, the now-familiar frown slipping back into place. "Chaos is not conducive to enjoyment."

The Trickster's teeth gleamed in a brief smile. "I suppose not. I'm quite fond of your son, you know—in spite of his rudeness."

"Darak can be blunt."

"Who does he get that from, I wonder?"

"Will you help him?" Cuillon asked.

"I am helping him. I am fulfilling my promise to keep you safe. Although you've certainly done your best to make my task more difficult. What have you done to yourself?"

"I am changing."

"Then we'd best hurry."

"Please, Trickster . . ."

"I am not Morgath, Holly-Lord. Begging will not affect me. Although one can't help enjoying it a little." He winked and flexed his claws. "Are you ready?"

Wincing, Cuillon fell to his knees.

The Trickster frowned, but his voice was gentle. "I meant what I said, Holly-Lord. I cannot help Darak."

"Cannot or will not?"

"You've been around Darak too long. You're starting to sound like him." The Trickster raised him to his feet. "Darak made his choice. He must see it through."

"Will you help him?"

The Trickster sighed. "Trees are so single-minded. It must come from being rooted. Hear me, Holly-Lord. We all have our little tasks. Darak's is to free the Oak and Tinnean. Yours is to get back to the First Forest. Mine—for the moment—is to get you there. Will you come?"

"Do I have a choice?"

"There is always a choice, Holly-Lord."

Cuillon hesitated, clutching the pouch that lay against his chest.

"You must go," Reinek said. "I will do what I can for Darak."

The Trickster's brows rose in mock surprise. "Not coming with us, Reinek?"

"I have my own promise to fulfill, Trickster."

"What a pity. Cluran has been waiting so long."

Reinek's eyes closed briefly. "My wife would understand."

"That's what Darak said about Griane. Understanding women—such treasures. Take my hand, Holly-Lord, and hold tight. Oh, never mind. I'll hold onto you."

Cuillon shook off the Trickster's hand. He embraced Reinek, hugging him hard even though his arms went right through him, hoping Reinek could feel something even if he could not. "Tell Darak I am safe."

"I will. May the Maker guide your steps, Holly-Lord."

"May the Maker speed you to your Floating Islands, Reinek."

The Trickster rolled his eyes as he peeled back the doorway. "May the Maker save me from endless farewells."

Claws closed around his wrist. Cuillon caught one final glimpse of Reinek's stark face before the Trickster pulled the portal closed behind them.

It took a moment for his eyes to adjust to the sudden darkness, another moment to conquer the terror of floating among stars. They spread out in an intricate web of light that seemed to stretch forever. Before he had time to admire their beauty, they melted. The world blurred, as if he were viewing it through tears. The white streaks of the stars gave way to colors—gray and green and occasional blots of yellow—each spinning past, faster and faster, until he was only aware of smears of color and light and the grip of the Trickster's claws.

He clung to the Trickster as the path shuddered. Time and space slowed, stuttering to a halt. Images slid into place. Leafless trees shivering in the wind. A sunberry bush, heavy with melting snow. Struath's cairn. His journey to Chaos was ending where it had begun.

The Trickster had vanished, but he was not alone. A figure knelt by the riverbank. As he watched, it rose, shouldering a waterskin. The sun flashed on the long red braid and once again, the world blurred before Cuillon's eyes.

Griane turned toward the embankment and went very still, like a doe scenting the breeze for danger. Then she gave a great shout and clambered up the slope. Cuillon's ages-old patience deserted him. He slid down, nearly toppling them both. Her arms went around him. Her tears wet his face. He held her close, unable to do more than repeat her name.

She reached for his hand and her eyes went wide with shock. Before the questions could pour out of her, he held up one bandaged hand. "Would you help me into the cave, please? Then I will tell you everything."

Chapter 43

AT FIRST, THERE WAS only darkness and the steady pulse of the heartbeat. Then darkness gave way to the smoke-gray of a Midsummer gloaming. As the light brightened, the shadowy silhouettes around him took on form. A birch. A bramble bush. A fallen log.

When he saw the blasted sapling, Darak realized he was standing in the clearing where he had met the Trickster and confronted the wolf. He wondered if a portal had opened into the First Forest while he hung on the tree, then shook his head. Despite his nakedness, he felt no cold.

He raised his ruined hands and stared at the blood-soaked bandages. He touched the oozing strips of raw flesh on his arms. He traced the careful pattern of shallow gashes on his chest and belly, reached behind him to touch the trails of crusted blood snaking down his buttocks.

He felt no pain, only a great weariness, as if he had walked for many miles. For one terrifying instant, he thought he was dead, but his heart still raced in rhythm with that other heartbeat. He tried to pinpoint its direction, but it seemed to be coming from all around him. Whatever this place was, the heartbeat had led him here, carrying him away from Morgath. But even here, Darak could feel his presence. Morgath was following him.

His hand crept up to clutch the bag that still hung around his neck. His charms comforted him as did the knowledge that the spirit catcher nestled among them. Scanning his surroundings, he realized that this place was like and unlike the clearing in the First Forest. Several trails twisted through the trees. The one nearest the bramble bush reeked of Morgath's malevolence. Another was partially obscured by a tangle of vines and ivy. The blasted sapling stood beside the last path, but it was not the slender oak of the First Forest: between the blackened shards of bark, Darak glimpsed the blood-red heartwood of an alder.

The first man in the world had been an alder. He had walked out of one world and into a new one. Surely that was a good omen. He rested his maimed hand on the scarred trunk long enough to whisper a prayer of healing, then set off.

The trail twisted through a forest at once familiar and foreign. Here, the boulder on the little outcropping that guarded the approach to the heart-oak. A few footsteps later, the clearing in the First Forest where he had struggled and failed to make fire. It was as if both forests had somehow grown together or sprung anew from the tangle of his memories.

When the underbrush on either side of the trail gave way to waist-high stands of sedge, he quickened his pace. The bog looked as daunting as ever. He wondered if he was meant to cross. The heartbeat offered no clue.

As he waited for a sign, one of the hummocks stirred. The frost-hardened moss cracked. The hummock heaved, showering ice crystals. A hand reached up, then another.

Somehow, he knew—even before he saw the curly

dark hair or the sorrowful eyes or the pale doeskin of the tunic and skirt, as pristine as the day he had carried her to the Death Hut. He had dreamed of her, had even imagined their eventual meeting in the Forever Isles when he would finally have the chance to set things right between them. Now Maili stood before him and he had no words.

"Why did you summon me, Darak?"

"I didn't. I didn't mean to."

"What is this place?"

"I . . . I don't know. I was in Chaos and then—"

"I don't like it. I don't want to be here."

"You're not. I don't think . . . this isn't real."

"Let me go, Darak."

"But I'm . . . Maili, I'm not trying to hold you. I don't even know why I'm here."

"Don't you?"

Her form wavered and an involuntary cry escaped him. "Don't go. Not yet. It's been so long . . ."

"Aye."

She smiled and he restrained a wince. "If we could just talk . . ."

"It's too late."

"But we may never get another chance."

"Why were you so unkind to me?"

"I didn't . . . I tried to be kind. I know I made mistakes but—"

"I hated you. Did you know that?"

Numbly, he shook his head.

"I was so young and scared and you took me like an animal."

"I didn't . . ." The same useless negation, over and over. "I'd never been with a woman. I'd never even . . . I had the care of my mother and brother, and the tribe expecting me to bring back meat every time I went hunting. And helping with the planting and the harvest and the shearing."

His voice trailed off as she stared at him.

"I thought it would all just . . . work." He took a deep breath. "I'm sorry, Maili."

"You're sorry."

He flinched at the sound of her harsh laughter.

"It might have gotten better. In time."

"We were married nearly a year."

"And no matter what I did, you turned from me. I couldn't even touch your hand without you pulling away." He tried to quell the rising frustration, but the words roared out of him. "You were my wife, damn it!"

"And that gave you the right to use me as you pleased."

"That's not—"

"I never refused you."

"You never gave me a chance!" Again, his voice rose to a shout. Again, he controlled himself. "If you had, we might have gotten to know each other."

"You didn't want to know me. Any more than a stag in rut wants to know the hinds it services."

"That's not fair."

"But it's the truth."

"Nay."

"Even now, you try and hide from it."

He shook his head, beyond words.

"The truth hurts. Doesn't it, Darak?"

She laughed again, her voice rising into hoarse shrieks that shook her whole body. He stumbled backward and slammed into a tree. Stunned, he slid to his knees and doubled over, retching dryly. As he raised his head, Maili's smile faded. She shuddered and fell to her knees. Her torso swelled. Her tunic burst open. Black fur sprouted on breasts and belly. She fell forward onto hands already thickening into paws. Claws sprouted, shredding the deerskin slippers. A tail snaked out between furry haunches, grew into a bushy plume. The head reared up. Golden eyes regarded him down a narrow muzzle.

Still reeling from the confrontation with Maili, Darak could only stare at the wolf. Although he knew this was not the beast he had confronted in the First Forest, it took long moments before he recognized her. The blaze of silver on her chest. The ragged left ear. The thick tail, as expressive as a human face. Even then, he instinctively reeled back as the she-wolf bounded effortlessly across the hummocks. If Chaos could conjure Maili out of the bog, it could just as easily create the illusion of his vision mate.

Clutching the tree for support, he hauled himself to his feet as the wolf leaped to shore. Unable to move or to speak, he simply watched her and waited.

"Hello, Little Brother."

It took two tries before his voice worked. "Is it really you?"

"Of course."

"How did you find me?"

"I have always been with you, Little Brother. We are pack."

"But I've never seen you . . . not since that night."

"You never called."

All these years, he could have felt her presence, could have recaptured the joy of that night, if only he had reached for her. He closed his eyes, only to open them again when he felt a rough, warm tongue against his leg. His hand skimmed over her head in wonder; even if this was a dream, he would always carry with him the memory of her thick fur. He got down on his knees so they could be face-to-face.

"I'm . . . oh, Wolf, I am so glad you are here."

The wet nose touched his. "So am I, Little Brother."

"I thought of you. On the tree."

"I know."

"But you didn't come then." Afraid that this would sound like a reproof, he stammered an apology. Wolf stopped his words by butting him lightly with her head.

"I could not reach you there."

"Aren't we still in Chaos?"

"Your body still hangs on the tree. But your spirit came here."

"Where is . . . here?"

"Forest."

"Not the First Forest."

"Your forest. Your memories." The wolf's fur bristled. "Morgath uses them against you."

Of course, Maili would never have spoken such lies. Maili had never hated him. It was Morgath, twisting his memories, subverting the truth. He wondered if rage was the greatest strength and weakness of Fellgair's riddle, for rage had kept him from surrendering to Morgath's tortures and it boiled through him now—and quickly died. The words Morgath had conjured for Maili were the ones he had been hearing in his head ever since she had died. He would never know what Maili had thought or felt, just as he would never fully understand what had gone wrong between them. Those truths were lost to him—just as she was.

"Morgath is close."

"I know." Lingering with the illusion of Maili had cost him precious time. He longed to set an ambush for his enemy and force the final confrontation, but choosing that path would delay his search for Tinnean.

"Wolf. Do you know where the Oak is?"

She cocked her head. Perhaps she sensed the heartbeat, too. "The Oak is everywhere."

"Aye, but how do I reach it?"

"There are many paths through the forest."

Darak tried again. "I am looking for my pack. My human brother. Can you help me?"

"It is hard to hunt alone."

"For a wolf."

"For a man, too. Without the pack, you are weak."

Even as a boy, he had preferred to hunt alone. For his peers, hunting was sport. If they brought down game, they celebrated, but if not, their fathers and brothers could help feed the tribe. If he had missed their good-natured insults and the friendships they had formed, he had gained the skills that made him the best hunter in the tribe. He'd always believed he had gotten the better bargain. Now he recalled Struath's words when he had returned from his vision quest: "She hunts with the pack and will kill to defend her pups."

He had failed to grasp the full import of that message. Now he had lost his pack. Maili and his mam. Then Tinnean. And in the quest that followed, the others: Griane first, then Struath and Yeorna, and finally Cuillon and his father. But at least he had found his vision mate again.

"What should I do, Wolf?"

"We will hunt together."

The skin of his face pulled taut as if it had been years since he had smiled.

"Aye. Let us hunt the Oak."

Chapter 44

STRUATH STARED AT the twisted branches rising above the low scrub. "Could it be the Oak?"

"That . . . thing?" Yeorna shuddered.

"You're sure Morgath is there?"

"I think so." At his questioning look, she added, "The energy is weaker now."

"Perhaps Morgath is tiring."

"Perhaps. But I think I am losing my connection to my body. Nay, Tree-Father, it's all right. Somehow, it is . . . easier . . . without it."

Struath nodded. After the initial shock of finding himself in Chaos, he had felt only relief at shedding his frail human form. But his body was dead. Yeorna still had a chance to recover hers. He wasn't sure how to help her. He could still erect wards, but when he had tried to summon the destroying energy, he had nearly destroyed himself. Yeorna speculated that the energy drew on his emotions as well as his skill for its power. But how else could he defeat Morgath?

"Yeorna, if it comes to freeing the Oak or casting Morgath out of your body—"

"Nothing is more important than the Oak." Yeorna's smile was sad. "I'm not even sure I want my body back, Tree-Father. Not after Morgath's spirit has contaminated it."

"It's odd, but . . ." Struath stared back at the tree. Morgath was somewhere in that thicket. When they had started their journey through Chaos, all he had desired was the chance to face his enemy again, to wreak vengeance on the man who had destroyed him.

"What is it, Tree-Father?"

"These last days—terrifying as they have been— have brought me a sort of . . . peace. Does that make any sense?"

Yeorna nodded slowly. "For me, it has come through accepting the loss of my body forever. It seemed such a terrible thing, but now, I feel . . . freer."

"I feel like an apprentice again, relearning my first lessons. Emptying the mind. Letting go of pride and envy and jealousy."

"Achieving balance."

"Aye. For so long, Morgath cast a shadow over my life." Struath shook his head impatiently. "I let him cast the shadow. I allowed him to taint my spirit. You helped me realize that."

"Me?"

Struath smiled at Yeorna's squeak of astonishment. "You had . . . have . . . all the gifts I lacked. Your kindness, your generosity, your gift of understanding people."

"But your skills are far greater—"

"Skills can be learned." Because of Morgath, Yeorna would never achieve the greatness she deserved—and the tribe would lose a Grain-Mother of rare sensitivity. "I thank you for the lessons you've taught me. Even if you never knew you were teaching them."

Yeorna seized his hand. Although he could no longer feel her, the gesture alone comforted him.

"Are you ready, my dear?"

"Aye, Tree-Father."

Bent low, they raced through the grasslands. He saw his smile reflected on Yeorna's face—as if they were children pretending to be wind in the grass, instead of priests about to confront the greatest test of their lives. He felt the same joy he'd known when Brana first came to him, the same exhilaration he'd experienced on their first flight. He wished she could be with him now to share what might be his final moments of existence.

They crawled through the bushes. A gasp escaped him when the tree came into view, the same nightmarish thing he had seen in his vision. Instead of a robin lying on the parched ground, a golden-haired woman sat cross-legged, lost in trance. Only when they circled around did Struath realize what Morgath was staring at.

"Merciful gods," Yeorna whispered. "Is he alive?"

Before Struath could answer, he caught a sudden movement out of the corner of his eye. He rose to flee, then sank back into a crouch.

Reinek squatted down beside him, nodding politely to Yeorna. To judge from his calm demeanor, it might have been days since their last meeting instead of years. He could not imagine why Reinek was in Chaos, but if his spirit could remain unchanged after all these years, perhaps the Oak and Tinnean were safe.

There were so many questions he wished to ask, so much he could learn from Reinek, but there was no time now. He gestured helplessly at the tree. "What happened?"

"He offered himself to free the Holly-Lord."

Terror felt different in spirit-form. Not the clenching of gut or the racing of heart. Here the senses dimmed instead of intensified, as if you were smothering in a roiling mass of dirty wool. Through it, Struath heard

Reinek's voice, low and urgent. "The Holly-Lord is safe. He is back in the First Forest. Calm yourself, Struath. Breathe."

The apprentice's lessons, this time taught by a dead hunter. Darak would enjoy that irony.

"Your spirit catcher," Reinek said. "He brought it to Darak."

Struath gazed at the bloody body hanging on the tree. "He failed."

"Aye. Will you?"

Years in Chaos had not eased Reinek's bluntness. "I don't know. While Morgath is there, I dare not try."

"Can you destroy Morgath?"

When a shaman walked between the worlds, he was vulnerable, unaware of the sights and sounds of the ordinary world. Still, Struath hesitated.

"Well?"

"I don't know, Reinek. When I tried to summon the power, I nearly destroyed myself."

"We must do something," Reinek said. "Darak feels . . . far away. I fear . . . I think we are losing him."

Yeorna's whispered prayer broke off. "You don't think . . . could Morgath have taken him?"

"What?" Reinek's voice cracked.

"He has not cast Darak's spirit out," Struath said quickly. "If he had, your body would be dead. But Morgath has the power to remain in one body while possessing another."

They stared in silence at the frozen tableau in the center of the glade. Finally, Struath said, "I cannot attack Morgath while he shares such a deep connection with Darak."

"You must risk it."

"It's too dangerous."

"My son is dying." Reinek's form blurred, then reasserted itself. "There must be a way."

Struath frowned, considering. "The moment of greatest vulnerability comes at the point of disconnection."

"Speak plain, Struath."

He almost smiled. He had forgotten how alike father and son were. "Right now, Morgath's spirit is tethered to two bodies. When he leaves Darak, there will be a moment—a few heartbeats—when his spirit is sustained only by the slender connection he maintains to Yeorna's body. If I sever it, Morgath's spirit will be lost." Reinek's eyes gleamed and Struath held up a cautioning hand. "I have never done this, Reinek. Sever the connection too late and Morgath will be safe in Yeorna's body. Sever it too soon and he'll root himself in Darak's."

"What if we warded both bodies?" Yeorna asked. "That would keep Darak safe and hinder Morgath's return to mine."

"It might work. Your body would be vulnerable of course, but . . ." Struath hesitated. "Yeorna, you ward Darak. I will—"

"Nay, Tree-Father. You must ward Darak."

If he could have wept, her sad smile would have brought him to tears. They both knew she was not powerful enough to resist Morgath for long. By choosing to ward her own body, she would almost certainly lose it forever.

"As you wish, Grain-Mother."

"A bird. A beast," Reinek said. "He's taken them before."

"I cannot protect against that. But seizing another body is draining. Even if Morgath succeeds, we will have time to free Darak and—gods willing, the Oak and Tinnean."

Yeorna nodded. After a moment, Reinek did, too.

"I will make my way behind the tree. Yeorna, position yourself near Morgath. Watch him carefully. You'll see him gasp, shiver, blink. Some sign that will warn you he is breaking the trance. We must erect the wards immediately. Reinek—"

"I will stand with my son."

As one, their gazes returned to the man on the tree.

Chapter 45

DARAK'S PACE QUICKENED as he recognized the familiar landmarks: the little stream where he could always fill his waterskin, the stand of birches where he had brought down the stag, the glade of the heart-oak. He was going home. The ever-present heartbeat seemed to share his excitement, its tattoo quickening. Finally, he had found the path. Tinnean would be waiting for him at the end of it.

He raced along the trail, past the clearing where the young boar had charged him, past the little thicket where Tinnean had snared his first rabbit, past the two pines where the Holly-Lord had broken away and raced into the night. Years ago, it seemed.

He burst out of the forest, half-expecting to see his brother running across the stubbled fields as Cuillon had the afternoon he had escaped from Griane. He looked around, his eagerness ebbing as his senses registered the emptiness. No coracles on the lake. No smoke from the huts. Not even a bird roosting in the trees. The branches moved wildly, but they were as silent as the wind that shook them.

The she-wolf's low whine shattered the appalling silence. His hand tightened convulsively around his bag of charms as he discovered the sky behind him seething with clouds the mottled purple of a fresh bruise. They roiled over the treetops as if devouring the forest. White branches of lightning split the sky. Thunder growled like a giant beast and the ground shook, echoing its malevolence.

His vision mate raised her head, scenting the air. "Go, Little Brother." When he hesitated, she growled. "Go. Now."

"But what about you?"

"I will hunt Morgath."

"It's not good to hunt alone." Must he lose her so soon after finding her again?

"Sometimes the pack splits up. Some drive the prey forward while the rest wait to make the kill."

He resisted the urge to beg her to stay. Perhaps she understood, for she said, "We are pack, Little Brother. I am always with you. And you are always with me." She bared her teeth. "Good hunting."

Darak raised his hand in salute. She yipped once and bolted back into the trees, the invading darkness enveloping forest and animal.

He heard the unseen sound of rending wood and the crash of toppling trees. Fallen leaves shivered and shifted as if a host of voles burrowed under them. The burrows collapsed into jagged fissures that devoured their shroud of leaves as they snaked out of the forest. A birch shuddered. Clods of dirt erupted as its roots tore free from the earth, leaving behind a gaping black hole. It was as if the forest were disintegrating. Unless he could reach Tinnean and the Oak, he would disappear with it.

Wind lashed him as he ran. Behind him, he heard the groan of uprooted trees, the crack of shattering limbs. He dared a quick look over his shoulder and saw branches hurtling down, only to vanish before they hit the ground.

He raced toward the stream. If the maelstrom was

following him, he would not lead it to the village. The big willow tilted toward him as he skidded into the water. By the time he had scrambled across the ice-slick stones, the tree had disappeared.

Running, falling, he scrambled up the slope toward the lone oak. The ground convulsed and split open. His fingertips brushed bark as he fell. Damning his maimed hands, he clawed at the dirt, but he only sank deeper into the earth. Flailing for a foothold, he dug his fingers in again. He would not die. Not now.

The wind battered him, howling with Morgath's mocking laughter. The heartbeat pounded like a drum, no longer all around him, but beckoning from the bowels of the earth. He couldn't follow it there. He would be lost, and with him, Tinnean and the Oak.

Naked tree roots loomed above him. Dirt poured down, choking him. Blind, he reached up. His fingers closed around the oak's roots. With the last of his strength, he hauled himself up.

The roots shattered. He fell into the void, screaming Tinnean's name. Morgath's laughter echoed around him. The heartbeat beckoned him deeper. Helplessly, he plummeted into darkness blacker than any night, into cold, deep and enduring as death, and finally, into light.

The heartbeat pulsed once and his descent slowed. One moment he was drifting downward and the next he was standing in what appeared to be a cavern. The light was everywhere—in the walls encircling him, in the roof above him, in the ground beneath his feet. They sparkled like the crystal spirit catcher, so blindingly brilliant it took him a moment to make out the tree. Its trunk rose slender and straight, its pale bark smoother than any ash. Its branches brushed the walls of the cavern. The seven-lobed leaves were as blue as flowering speedwell.

The strange tree trembled as another sprouted. They were at once one tree and two, their forms melding into each other, yet clearly defined. The new tree grew proud and strong, sheltering its smaller brother with its wide-spreading branches. The Oak, he realized. The Oak as it once was. The Oak as it might be again.

The heartbeat filled the cavern, pulsing with renewed energy, with the revitalized power of a healed world, irresistible and beautiful and right. He crawled forward and stretched out his hand, yearning to be part of that world. If he could touch it, just for a moment, he would be healed as well.

You think you can escape me?

Darak leaped up, casting a wild glance around him. He was alone in the cavern, but even here, Morgath's voice pursued him.

There is no place you can go. No place so hidden that I cannot follow. I am part of you.

"Nay."

We are all part of you.

Wind buffeted him, howling with the voices of unquiet spirits.

Why did you hurt me, Darak?

Why did you hate me, son?

Why did you refuse to give me your blessing?

"Tinnean! Where are you?"

The voices mocked him.

Lost. Forever.

"You are not real."

Above the laughter, he heard Morgath's voice. *They are all real, Darak. And they are all doomed. Like you.*

The wind engulfed him, driving him backward toward the two trees. Faces loomed before him. Maili with her accusing eyes. His father, stern and disapproving. And Tinnean, so sad and hopeless. Tearing him apart with their eyes, consigning him to an eternity of Chaos with their words.

Only the heartbeat offered hope, pounding louder than ever. As if in answer, the howling crescendoed.

He staggered back, thrusting out one hand to steady himself. He had only a moment to register the supple texture of the bark before the gale struck him, as powerful as Morgath's destroying energy, as dizzying as Fellgair's vision. And then the heartbeat washed over him and into him, carrying him out of the vortex into calm.

He hung on the tree of Chaos, staring down at Morgath sitting cross-legged before him, eyes wide and unseeing. Arms leached into branches, chest seeped into trunk, toes curled into roots. He was flesh and wood, blood and sap. He was Darak and he was tree.

He floated in the tree of the cavern, unable to move, unable to breathe, yet completely aware, completely alive. He was in the earth and of the earth, rooted to it and looking down upon it at the same time.

The steady vibration rose up through him, patient as time, slow as sap rising, the energy of the world that moved with the unhurried patience of the ages. It flowed through the body on the tree, soothing the wounds, stilling the trembling muscles. It flowed through the spirit in the cavern, easing the fear, washing away doubt.

The Oak sang. Flesh and spirit recognized the song, for it had echoed in the being of every creature since the world first's dawning. The song of the World Tree, older than time, fresh as a new day.

Heat and cold, it sang, wind and ice. And with the song, he knew them. Rain, he knew, and lightning. Raven croak and wolf howl. Time he knew as well, but it was the slow unfolding of ages, not the changing of seasons, the birthing and dying of worlds, not people. Time was the gods who dwelled among his silver branches and the sunlit Forever Isles that floated in his roots. Time was the endless cycle of energy, flowing up into his trunk and out through his limbs to sink down to his roots again.

He was Darak and Tree. Mortal man and ancient

being. A single mind and the consciousness of the world.

The realization terrified him. It was too much for any man to grasp. He would shatter if he tried, his spirit lost forever. Or worse, the part of him that was Darak would simply be absorbed. He could imagine the hopeless, helpless madness of watching himself fade, observing the last spark that had once been Darak flicker and die.

Somewhere in the engulfing terror, he found a tiny point of calm. Tinnean, small but real in the immensity of the World Tree. Tinnean, assuring him without words that he could free them.

He had tried and failed with the spirit catcher. He had surrendered himself to Morgath, enduring the mutilation of his body and the invasion of his mind. He had survived the obstacles of his spirit-journey to reach this place, but even now, with the limitless knowledge that the Tree offered, he didn't understand how to free Tinnean and the Oak.

Morgath's satisfaction oozed through him. *You cannot free Tinnean. It's too late for him. And now, the Tree will destroy you as well.*

"Nay."

You think you're being noble, don't you? Nobility didn't put you on that tree. Guilt did.

"Stop."

Only when you die. Would you like that? The Tree can't free you, Darak, but I can. I could let your spirit fly to the Forever Isles.

Even as he denied it, the desire to escape, to be free surged through him.

Come to me, Darak.

The voice beckoned, sweeter than any lover's.

You want to. I can sense your desire. I can feel the blood pumping through your wreck of a body at the mere thought of it. Come to me, Darak. Leave the Tree and come to me.

The man on the tree gasped. The man in the Tree shuddered as his spirit wavered, yearning to escape, hungering even more for the kill, even if it meant destroying himself, even if it meant destroying Tinnean. He could taste the kill, sweeter than the lover's voice, sweeter than anything he had ever known or would ever know in this life or the next.

In the end, pride held him back. He refused to give Morgath the satisfaction of rising to the bait. He choked down his rage and his desire and willed the bloodlust to subside.

His father was right. Control was the greatest strength. His ability to control pain and fear. To banish weakness when it threatened to unman him. To master the dangerous world of Chaos. To withstand Morgath. To challenge anyone who opposed him.

To dominate everyone who had ever loved him.

The man on the tree breathed the words with his spirit-self. "Oh, gods . . ."

His greatest strength and his greatest weakness. For when he couldn't bend them to his will, he either walked away, as he had done so many times with Maili, or drove them away, as he had driven Tinnean away at Midwinter.

All his life, fear had been the enemy. Fear that, if he could not match his father's accomplishments, he would be less of a man. Fear that, if Tinnean left, he would be alone. Fear that, if he lost control, if he let himself go, all that he was—all that he imagined himself to be—would simply shatter, leaving nothing.

All the times he believed he was protecting his folk, he had only been protecting himself.

Let it go, Darak.

Tinnean's voice, drowned out by Morgath's laughter.

The man on the tree trembled as if his body knew the secret and was determined to expose it to the world.

Let it go.

Pain welled up from his stomach, where a remorseless fist pummeled him. Pain rushed into his chest, leaving him gasping. Pain seized his throat with greedy fingers and choked him.

Darak. Please. Let it go.

The man in the Tree shuddered with the effort of preserving his spirit. The man on the tree gasped and opened his eyes. There were two Morgaths now, one still seated on the ground, smiling in his trance, another standing behind him. Or was that Yeorna raising her arms? It must be, for there was Struath, standing beside his father. His pack. All of them watching him and waiting.

He was so afraid.

His father reached for his body. His brother reached for his spirit.

It might only have been the breeze whispering against his cheek, or it might have been his father's hand. When he felt that gentle touch, something inside of him shattered as he'd always known it would. When it did, the energy flowed through him, and with it, the song of the World Tree. And he understood, finally, that it was not trying to steal his spirit or to absorb him. The Tree simply was. The Tree lived. The Tree sang. No man could hear all the threads of the song, or encompass all of the energy, but each man could share it, and carry a small part of that power with him always.

The song of the Tree penetrated skin and bone and blood and breath, calming the terror. The energy of the Oak and Tinnean cradled his spirit, easing it back into his body. Darak's spirit surrendered to their power, even as his body surrendered to the sobs. The tears he'd never been able to weep poured down his face, fiercer than the blazing heat that scorched his chest. The sobs shook him, harder than the spasm that racked his spirit as Morgath wrenched free of him.

The twisted oak shuddered. His arms dropped to his sides. Fire raged through them as feeling returned. At his back, though, the thorns seemed to have abandoned their ceaseless rending of flesh, for he felt only warm air. Before he could make sense of it, his knees bumped against hard-packed dirt. He fell forward, screaming when his right hand exploded in agony.

"Strike now, son."

He raised his head. Strands of colored light—blue, green, red, and silver—stretched from Struath's upraised hands, weaving a web of protection around him. Yeorna loomed over Morgath, surrounding him with another web. Morgath's face twisted into a grimace. Yeorna swayed, her form melting into the strands of light, only to reassert itself at Struath's shouted command.

"Darak! Use the dagger!"

He looked around. Even when he saw the blood-stained blade protruding from his palm, he struggled to comprehend his father's words. He reached for the hilt. His fingers obeyed unwillingly, as if, like Cuillon's, they had been transformed into wood. He forced them to close around the coiled sinew. Shimmering black dots danced before his eyes, obscuring Struath's web. He bit down hard on his lip to drive them back. His father was shouting something. The urgency in his voice made Darak tug at the hilt. His fingers slipped. Blood filled his mouth, warm and salty. This is what Morgath had tasted. His blood. His flesh.

He grasped the hilt again. The scream tore his throat. When the black dots receded, he found himself on his elbows, the dagger still embedded in his hand. The greedy earth sucked up the fresh blood; like Morgath, it could not get enough of him.

Yeorna was fading, dissolving before his eyes and with her, the pretty web of colors. He crawled forward on his elbows and knees. The pouch thumped against his chest like a heartbeat. The black dots crowded his vision. He shook his head, blinking, as Yeorna disappeared. Only Morgath's face remained, growing ever smaller, a tiny white oval just beyond Struath's web of light and color.

The web shuddered. He glanced up. His father's mouth moved, but he couldn't make out the words. Struath's long braids swirled around his head as wildly as the mist claiming his form. His blue eye blazed. Darak flinched when that piercing gaze found him. He wanted to tell Struath that he had found his vision mate again, that he finally understood the wolf's message. Perhaps Struath understood for his sudden smile was as warm and proud as the day the shaman had welcomed him home from his vision quest.

A shadow crossed Struath's face. Darak squinted skyward, but all he could make out was a dark cloud descending. A gust of warm air buffeted him. Huge wings, black and iridescent, enfolded Struath. Just before they both vanished, Darak heard a raven's croak and the shaman's joyful laughter.

Morgath moaned and toppled over.

"Now, son. Strike now."

Darak flung himself forward, pinning Morgath to the ground. Nearly blinded by his failing senses, he heaved himself up. The world receded to the blue of Morgath's eyes, to the pressure building inside his temples as his enemy sought to invade him again.

Morgath's mouth opened. He slapped his hand over it. The twin pools of blue widened. Darak felt himself falling into them, just as he had fallen into Fellgair's. The shaman's scream seared his left hand. His right felt as heavy as stone as he lifted it. Morgath writhed beneath him, hips bucking in a grotesque parody of the act of love. A tear oozed from his left eye. Yeorna's eye, the same soft blue of the sky after a spring storm. It pleaded with him to yield to the pressure in his head, to let go of his ruined body and fly away like Struath. With the last of his strength, Darak brought his hand down, plunging the dagger's blade into that beautiful blue eye.

Chapter 46

CUILLON HAD LOST TRACK of the days. It seemed they had always been stumbling through the forest, but Griane assured him it was only half a moon. Her face was as thin as a fox's now, cheekbones standing out like ridges beneath huge, shadowed eyes. Sometimes, when she pressed her magic plants against his limbs, her hands trembled just a little and her determined smile slipped, but most of the time, she yipped at him as insistently as ever.

Cold no longer bothered him, but he was grateful for the feel of her body pressed against his in the night, the strength of her arms twining around him like ivy around oak. When the dreams disturbed his sleep, her whispers comforted him. When the weight of the pouch around his neck seemed too heavy to bear, the touch of her hand lightened the burden.

Other men had made sacrifices for him, some pouring water upon his roots, some offering the flesh of animals. Only when he became a man did he understand how great a sacrifice it was to give up the food that sustained them. Just as he understood now that the only sacrifice great enough to return the Oak to the world was a gift of life. Struath and Yeorna had sacrificed theirs. Surely, Darak's was not required as well.

He leaned against the trunk of a towering ash. Darak was strong, Griane told him. He would find a way out of Chaos. He would probably be waiting for them in the grove, wondering what had taken them so long. Each time she said this, he nodded, pretending he did not notice the way her voice shook when she said Darak's name.

Griane glanced back, her face creasing in a frown. "Are you all right? Do your hands hurt?"

His fingers had lost all feeling, but it would only frighten her if she knew. So he said, "I am fine, Griane."

Her eyes narrowed. She always knew when he told a small lie. He tried again. "I was thinking."

"About what?"

"Hot apple cider."

That surprised a laugh out of her. The echo of it settled in his belly, as delicious as the cider. "Hot apple cider has everything. You can feel the warmth sliding into your belly. You can chew the apple skin. And the smell . . ." Cuillon breathed deeply. "Smell is still very strong with me. I will miss that."

A spasm of pain twisted Griane's face. He tried to smile, but his mouth refused to turn up. "Do you think I have changed too much? Will the Holly still know me?"

Griane cupped his cheeks with mittened hands. "The Holly will always know you." Her face crumpled, then smoothed itself out again. "Come on. We're almost there. Then you'll see for yourself."

She adjusted her pack, shifting Darak's great bow to the other side so she could link her arm through his. They were close now. He could tell from the way the Watchers flitted anxiously among the giant trees. His joy was leavened by the knowledge that to regain his Tree, he must lose Griane and Darak. He had known that since the beginning, but he had never imagined how much they would come to mean to him and how much the prospect of losing them would hurt.

As the day waned, they quickened their pace, both of them eager to reach the grove before dark. He strained to see the Tree, but the trunks of lesser trees hid it from view. Griane's excited shout sent his heart tattoo thumping as wildly as it had when Struath had led him back to his grove so many days ago. He darted between rowan and birch and raced across the snow-dusted earth to his Tree.

He had forgotten how huge it was, how small he felt standing before it. The sweeping boughs of his Holly cast a dark shadow over the grove, shutting out what little light still filtered through the naked branches of the other trees. The scar on the Tree's trunk looked as black as the path to Chaos.

Even if he could not feel his leaves, he needed to touch them, to feel the energy of his Holly flowing through him again. Tenderly, he cupped his fingers around one leaf.

It cracked.

He stared down at the shattered pieces. The fragments drifted through his fingers. It was only one leaf. He had lost whole limbs in the battle with the Oak. He fumbled along the low-hanging branch. Twigs snapped. Leaves crumbled into dust. Something fell into his hand. He bent close, squinting in the failing light.

A berry. A small, shriveled berry, its bright red faded to the color of dried blood.

He pushed the branch aside and plunged his arms deeper. The boy's hands and feet had changed. So might his outermost branches. Inside, closer to the trunk, all would be well. A dry sob escaped him as branches broke before his questing hands. He fought his way through the sundered limbs, desperately searching for some sign of life. The Holly tore at his tunic, his breeches, his face, but he was mindless with fear now, screaming out his denial.

Griane seized him. He fought as if she were the foe. Even when she captured his flailing hands, he kept struggling until his legs gave out and his voice died and he slid to the ground. Griane held him, stroking his hair with her gentle hands. He could only sit there, as empty and dead as his Holly.

Chapter 47

PAIN CREPT INTO his consciousness with Morgath's stealthiness.

"Darak?"

He remembered the name. Once, it had belonged to him.

"Darak?"

He remembered the voice, too, but he couldn't remember who it belonged to. As the first burst of pain retreated, he became aware of other sensations: warm sun on his back, hair tickling his cheek, a small, hard lump pressing against his chest.

"Darak?"

Three times. Three times for a charm.

He opened his eyes. A tangle of hair, gold interwoven with brown. His father's shoes, the laces still in the neat bows his mam had tied before they carried his body to the Death Hut. An outflung arm, small fingers bent skyward as if beseeching Chaos for salvation. Too small to be his.

"Morgath is dead, son."

That couldn't be true. Morgath's pain fed on his flesh. Morgath's touch lingered on his body. Morgath's voice echoed inside his mind. *I am part of you now.*

"Morgath is dead. You killed him."

Then he understood. The mound beneath him was Yeorna's body. Empty now, for surely he would have sensed if Morgath's spirit lay coiled inside. They had been joined more intimately than lovers. The connection might have been broken, but the taint permeated him the way the acrid stench of charred wood hung over a forest after a lightning strike.

Yeorna was gone. And Struath. Perhaps he had carried her to the Forever Isles on those black wings. They were free. He was alive. Morgath was dead.

He should feel something—relief, vindication, triumph. All he felt was the dull ache of his wounds and that hard lump digging into his chest. Griane's chin was like that. Small and hard and demanding, even in sleep. It had felt so good, though, her body nestled against his, that pointed chin poking his shoulder. He should have told her that. Now, she was gone, too.

"Try and stay awake, son."

His father's voice brought him back, just as Morgath's always had. Except at the end. That had been Tinnean's voice. With a hoarse cry, he heaved himself up. The pain leaped, ripping him open with fiery claws, carrying him into darkness.

When he came to himself, he was lying on his back. His father's face loomed above him, creased with concern. Darak shrank away from the outstretched hands before he remembered these would not hurt him.

"Tinnean?"

He remembered the harsh croak. He had spoken with the raven's voice when he hung on the tree.

"I don't know, son." His father's voice shook just a little. "The tree is gone."

He closed his eyes. How could he have lost them? They had been part of him, shielding his spirit just as Yeorna and Struath had protected his body. In those last moments on the tree, he had felt the heat of their energy blazing through his chest.

His eyes opened. His left hand crept painfully over his belly, trailing fire in its wake, to close around the bag on his chest. The spirit catcher was still there, safe with his other charms. If he concentrated very hard he could feel the tiny facets through the soft leather. His fingers tightened around it and he restrained a wince. Was it his wounds that made it throb?

He forced his right hand to move, gagging with the pain. He turned his head, retching weakly. He retched again when he saw the bandaged stumps of his fingers and the dagger protruding from the ragged wound in his palm. Morgath had inflicted his damage with care; taking the forefinger and middle finger of each hand ensured that he would never again draw a bow or heft a spear.

Let it go.

Twice, he grasped the hilt. Twice, the pain took him. The third time, he wrenched the dagger free, his screams fading too slowly in the welcoming darkness.

His father's voice called him back, tethering him to the world and to his body and to the tiny bag on his chest. It took a long time for his fingers to reach it, even longer to loosen the drawstrings. He reached inside, sifting through the charms with his thumb to reach the crystal. Heat surged at his touch. Willing his hands to stop trembling, he rolled onto his side and upended the bag, spilling its contents onto the dirt.

The spirit catcher blazed with fire as green as Midsummer leaves. The light pulsed in a slow, steady rhythm. He cupped it between his ruined hands and felt the pulse quicken as if it recognized his touch.

His head fell onto his arm. When he heard the harsh, racking gasps, it took him a moment to realize his father was sobbing. This time, he called his father back. Only when the mist stilled and he was safe again, did Darak close his eyes.

He never knew how long he drifted, carried along by the cadences of his father's voice, sustained by its strength and its calm. Finally, he sat up, ignoring the fresh blood that seeped from his wounds.

The clearing had transformed into a grassy knoll, the plain into a meadow. The light seemed clearer now. The dew on the grass shimmered so brilliantly it made his eyes tear. Maybe everything appeared fresh and new when you were reborn. The pain was a constant reminder that his newly reborn spirit still clung to his wreck of a body. Somehow, that body must bear him to a portal and back to the First Forest.

Slicing bandages from Yeorna's mantle and binding his wounds took most of the morning. Dressing himself took even longer. He needed a full day to gouge out a shallow trench in the earth, another to gather rocks for a cairn. His body screamed in protest, but the Grain-Mother's sacrifice deserved to be honored.

Before he piled the stones over her, he crouched down and unbraided her hair. One by one, he removed the three severed fingers. Carefully, he wrapped them in a strip of wool and tucked them under his belt. He would leave no part of himself behind in Chaos.

They chanted the death-song for Yeorna and for Struath. Only a shaman could perform the rite of opening, freeing the spirit to fly to the Forever Isles. Darak prayed the Maker had guided them—and would guide his father when it was his time.

When their ritual was finished, he asked, "How do we find a portal?"

Strange that after all that had happened, he should still look to his father for answers—and be so shaken by his helpless shrug. His father's smile was as understanding as it was weary. "One will open soon enough."

"It took Morgath half a lifetime to find one."

"I think it must be harder for spirits. The Holly-

Lord spotted a portal when I heard and saw nothing. The trick is knowing if it's the right one."

Against his chest, Darak felt a blaze of heat. He patted the bag of charms. Even if he didn't know which path to choose, Tinnean and the Oak. would.

Chapter 48

THE FIRST TIME THEY heard the whining, Darak surged to his feet and staggered in the direction of the sound. The portal opened into a forest, but after a quick flare of green light, the spirit catcher dimmed. The next opened into a village where tattooed people in loincloths fled screaming.

The third was stranger still. He heard the chanting first. Then the portal opened, revealing a naked boy lying upon a shelf of black stone. Behind him stood a man in a red robe. Sweat gleamed on his bald head. As he raised his hands, Darak saw the dagger, blade pointing at the boy's chest. The man's head jerked up. Their eyes met.

A babble of voices erupted. Other figures pushed into view: men with shaven heads and smooth, bare chests, black-haired women in brown robes. And another who seemed to be both man and woman.

Darak shook his head, uncertain whether the blurring of the portal or his exhaustion had created the apparition. Half of its head was shaved, but on the left, long, black hair fell to its waist. The left side of its face was painted, the eye outlined in black, the cheek rosy, the lips swollen and red.

The crowd pointed and shouted. One man brandished a spear. Only the naked boy on the stone seemed oblivious and the strange man-woman whose lips curved in a small smile. The portal whined as the spear carrier drew his arm back. At a deep-voiced command from the man-woman, he froze. Another command, unmistakably female this time, caused the noise to subside. The man-woman reached up and removed a dangling ornament from its left earlobe. Just before the portal closed, Darak caught a blur of motion.

He crouched down to discover the sinuous form of a snake, mouth gaping open to reveal the miniature fangs and forked tongue, tail tapering to a needle-thin hook. Each tiny scale was perfectly rendered in the same metal as Struath's ceremonial dagger. The incredible delicacy of the craftsmanship exceeded anything he had ever seen. Glancing up, he found his father frowning.

"Who were they, do you think? And why would that . . . person . . . throw this to me?"

His father's frown deepened. "Did you understand what they were saying?"

"A few words, maybe. I'm not sure. There was so much noise." He hesitated, then added, "At the Gatherings. The tribes from the south. The words had that sort of cadence, that guttural quality."

"Like the ancient tongue. Struath uses it in the rites."

"They didn't look like the tribesmen I met. And it's been generations since any of the tribes offered human sacrifices." He eyed the snake with misgiving. "Should I keep it?"

His father hesitated. "The Maker only knows what magic it possesses—good or evil."

Or what payment the giver might exact in return. Hesitantly, he touched the gleaming scales with his thumb. When nothing happened, he used the heel of his right hand to shovel it into his left. Hard to believe anything so beautiful could be evil, but he had seen enough of Chaos to know that beauty could be deceptive.

With a determined nod, he flung the ornament into the grass.

They waited in vain for another portal to open. Darak allowed himself a few sips of water and a strip of venison from Cuillon's supplies; the rest he would need to sustain him on his journey to the grove. During his fitful intervals of sleep, Morgath pursued him. He jolted awake, sweat-drenched and shivering, to find his father's worried gaze upon him.

He dragged himself onto the shelf of rock where his father sat. A field of poppies had sprung up while he slept. The giant flowers nodded in the faint breeze, black eyes fixing him with a stare as unblinking as his father's.

"Son?"

"Aye?"

"Sometimes, it helps to speak of the things that trouble you."

"You never did."

He hadn't meant it as an accusation, but his father winced.

"Forgive me. I didn't—"

"Nay, you're right. Words never came easy to me." A quick smile lightened his features. "As talkative as a stump, your mam used to say of me."

"Me, too. But she'd smile after."

"Oh, aye. She had a rare smile." His father ducked his head, just as Tinnean used to. "Did I ever tell you about the day we were promised?" Again, that shy ducking of the head, this time accompanied by a sheepish smile.

"She was fourteen that summer. I was . . . what? . . . twenty, I think. Old for marrying. One morning, just after dawn, I left the hut to go hunting. And she was standing there, hands on her hips. I couldn't imagine what she wanted. I'd only spoken to her a half dozen times in all the years I'd known her. And while I'm wondering if I was supposed to say something, she gave this little nod. Like she'd made up her mind."

His father chuckled softly. "She marched up to me and said, 'I hope you're better at listening than you are at talking for I'm only saying this once. Arrows'll be good for my father. He's always admired your fletching. Rabbitskins for my mam. I'll leave the rest to you, but bring a flask of your mother's elderberry wine. They're both partial to that.'"

He chuckled again. "Gods save me, I still didn't know what she was talking about. All I could do was stare at her. Finally, she rolled her eyes and shook her head like I'm the greatest fool in the world. Which I was, now that I look back on it. And she says, 'Bride-gifts, Reinek. Gather them quick. I want to be wed by harvest time.' And then she flipped her hair over her shoulder and marched off with nary a look back."

"You must have been quick enough," Darak said.

"Oh, aye. Couldn't have done otherwise."

"Did you . . . ?" Darak hesitated. "Did you love her?"

"Oh, aye." His father grinned. "Couldn't have done otherwise."

"How did you do it? You and mam. You were so different."

"Aye. Well. We had time to work on it."

"So it got easier."

"Not really."

Darak laughed with him, gasping a little as the wounds on his belly stretched and split.

"Your mam'd put up with my silences for a time and then she'd just . . . drag it out of me. Whatever was on my mind." His father looked out over the field, his eyes soft. "I was lucky. I married the right woman."

Darak stared down at his ruined hands.

"It's done, Darak. Whatever happened with your wife. And with Tinnean." His father reached for him, then let his hand fall back to his knee. "Learn from it if you can, but don't keep chewing on it. Let it go and move on. Else you'll end up a bitter old man."

"It's . . . hard."

"I know. None better." His father sighed. "You spend your life trying to be strong for those you love. Not wanting them to see your uncertainty lest they be afraid, too. It's only when you hold your firstborn child in your arms that you realize that you're the helpless one. You'll never be able to shield him from pain or guard him close enough to keep him from harm. You can lose him so easy—to sickness, to accident. Or just to the pulling away that comes as boys grow into men."

Just as I lost Tinnean, Darak thought. Now he had a chance to set things right, as his father was trying to do.

"As for what happened back there. . . ." His father nodded in the direction of the clearing. "He maimed your body. You'll carry the scars forever. It's the wounds you can't see . . . the wounds to the spirit and the mind . . . those are harder to heal. Time helps. So does a woman—the right one, anyway. But in the end, it lies with you. You've fought so hard, son. Don't let him beat you now."

This time, Darak was the one to stretch out his hand. He laid it atop his father's, his fingers sinking through it onto hard rock. They were still sitting there when the familiar whining began.

It took him a moment to pick out the poppy whose head drooped lower than the others. By the time he had started toward it, the petals hung nearly to the ground, their brilliant red faded to a dull pink. The whining crescendoed. They were both running now, his father following his lead. Darak winced as petals brushed his flayed arms and hairy stalks slapped against his belly. Twice, he had to slow, using his ears to guide him among the forest of flowers. He nearly ran right into the portal, stopping abruptly when he saw the thick trunk of a tree through the translucent center of the flower. The spirit catcher burned his palm, blazing with green fire.

"Go, Darak. I'll be right behind you."

"Father . . ." So much left unsaid, so many things he wanted to ask.

"I know, son." The strain eased a little as he smiled. "Quick, now. Before it disappears."

Already, the portal was fading. Darak took a ragged breath and plunged into it. The shock of the cold air made him gasp. He gasped again as he careened into a tree and slid to his knees in the mulch blanketing its roots. The portal wavered. His father's form slipped through, moving with a hunter's instinctive caution. Even before the portal winked out behind him, he began to fade, legs melding with the shadows of the forest, tunic blending with the tree trunks. The wariness on his face gave way to surprise and then to wonder. He cocked his head as if listening to something Darak couldn't hear.

"I will tell Tinnean. I will tell him everything."

His father nodded, but he was drifting away, out of one world and into another. The long hair eddied and vanished. The stern mouth curled up in a smile. And then, between one breath and the next, he was simply gone.

Darak sat there, staring into the shaft of sunlight that marked the place where he had vanished. A good omen, surely. A sign that he was safe. Even now, he could be walking onto the shores of the Forever Isles, arms wide to scoop up his mam as she raced toward him.

When the sunlight struck him full in the face, he realized how much time had passed. He struggled to his knees, blinking. When he saw something gleaming on the bottom of his mantle, he thought it was a trick of the light. He bent closer. Despite the sunlight bathing him, he shivered when he saw the snake.

The hook on its tail had caught in the threads of his mantle. He must have brushed past it during that final, frantic race to the portal. Better to believe that than to imagine it had followed him back into the world.

He fumbled open the drawstrings of his bag of charms and slid the snake inside. For good or ill, he was meant to have this thing. He shivered again, certain that someday he would meet its previous owner and face a reckoning.

Staggering to his feet, he glanced up to set a course by the westering sun. His gaze was caught by the blaze of a burnished leaf, incongruous among the naked twigs of a bush. Only when he stepped closer did he realize what it was.

He had to wait for his vision to clear, for his hands to cease trembling before he dared reach for it. It took even longer to free the long strand of red hair for she had wound her talisman around the branch very tightly so neither breeze nor animal could disturb it. He murmured her name as he would a prayer before adding it to his bag of charms. Then, dragging his sleeve across his eyes, Darak headed west.

He covered a mere mile before the light faded. Spent, he burrowed into the dead leaves beneath a rowan's roots, a wounded creature seeking its nest.

The next morning, he nearly fainted as he crawled out from under the rowan. The cold numbed most of the pain, but fire raged through his right hand and crawled up his arm. He made himself stand, take one step, then another. A day or two to reach the grove, judging by the size of the trees. He could make it that far; he had to.

Too often, he found himself drifting. Without his father's voice to call him back, he wandered aimlessly among the ancient trees. He clutched the spirit catcher in his left hand, the burning in his palm warning him when he strayed too far.

He found four more circlets of her hair that day, but he was shaking too badly to free them. After a night racked by fever chills, he set out again. The trees seemed to sway, but he knew that was only the fever blurring his vision. Once, he discovered that he was talking to his father and had to lean against a tree until his mind cleared.

When he found another of Griane's talismans, he couldn't resist reaching for it. He reeled, crying out as the spirit catcher fell from his grasp. The leaves rose up to meet him. The crystal rolled away from his questing fingers, Midsummer green among the browns and duns of the forest floor. The spirit catcher winked: *You can't catch me, Darak.* Tinnean's voice. Or was it one of the shadowy Watchers circling around him?

The shadows parted as one approached, more daring than his companions and many times larger. The ground shook with each footstep. Another illusion created by the fever, for the Watchers always moved silently. The branches of the trees drooped as the giant passed. Leaves rustled as he stroked their trunks.

The giant emerged into the sunlight. Only then did Darak make out the rack of antlers, the green leaves cascading over his shoulders, the massive, furred chest. A fever-dream. It had to be. But when he closed his eyes and opened them again, the Forest-Lord still loomed above him.

Every hunter dreamed of this moment. Darak had imagined it would come after the perfect kill. The god would step out of the trees. He would smile, silently commending his skill. And then he would vanish. Now that the moment had come, Darak could only lie there, gazing up into eyes as dark as a Midwinter night.

When the Forest-Lord stepped back into the shadows, a hoarse cry escaped him. The god looked back over his shoulder. Darak struggled to his knees. He crawled toward the spirit catcher, captured it between shaking hands, and tucked it in his bag of charms.

The god was still watching him. Determined not to appear helpless, he dragged himself to his feet. His hands left bloody smears on the tree trunk. He staggered forward, weaving between the trees. No matter how many steps he took, the Forest-Lord was always just ahead of him. When he fell, the god waited. When he got to his feet again, the god rewarded him with a smile that sent a shiver of pleasure down his back. No wonder the trees sought his touch—and the Watchers. They flitted around him like dark moths, growing more substantial each time they brushed against him.

Darak stumbled, slapping a hand against a tree to steady himself. The pain didn't matter. All that mattered was reaching Hernan. He wanted to know the feel of those strong arms, the scent of those cascading leaves. He wanted to let his head droop against that chest and know that everything would be all right.

All that afternoon, he followed the Forest-Lord until the trees gave way to a clearing and a voice cried out his name. Just before the god blended with the shadows, Darak felt a large, warm paw cup the back of his neck, just as his mam used to.

Chapter 49

HE WAS ALIVE. Thin and ragged, burning up with fever, and dear gods, his poor hands. But he was alive. Griane pressed a quick kiss to his hot forehead.

"Cuillon. Quick."

After a moment, she looked up and found him staring at the Tree, oblivious to Darak's return.

"Cuillon. It's Darak. He's come back."

"It is too late."

The first words he'd spoken since discovering the Tree was dead. She should be glad—even the healing magic of the heart-ease had failed to penetrate his silence—but Darak demanded all her attention now.

As she snatched up her magic bag, Cuillon said, "It would be kinder to let him die."

Griane whirled around. She crossed to Cuillon in three quick strides, drew back her hand and slapped him as hard as she could. "Don't you say that. Don't even think it. Darak saved your life. You will not sit there and tell me we should let him die."

He touched his cheek, blinking as if awakening from a disturbing dream. The anger drained out of her. She crouched down and hugged him hard. "Oh,

Cuillon, I'm sorry. It's just . . . Darak needs us. Both of us."

"Forgive me, Griane. What should I do?"

She kissed his cheek. "Help me roll him over."

Together, they managed it. While Cuillon unwrapped the filthy bandages around Darak's hands, she rummaged in her magic bag. She had used most of the heal-all on Cuillon's wounds. She hoped the handful she had left would be enough.

Cuillon gasped. She looked up. The packet of heal-all slipped through her fingers.

Morgath had taken the forefinger and middle finger from both hands. The stumps of the missing fingers were crusted with blood and dirt. When she cut away the wool sticking to his right hand, thick yellow pus oozed from the inflamed wound on his palm. Cuillon turned his head, gagging at the sour-rotten stench. Griane just stared at the red streaks creeping up Darak's wrist.

She had once seen a man with those same angry streaks. Mother Netal had made a poultice to draw out the poison and dosed Eddin with willowbark for the fever. His arm swelled and stank. The red streaks turned black. Three men had held him down while Jurl chopped the arm off at the elbow. Eddin had died two days later.

Maggots could eat away the rotting flesh. Brogac could cleanse the wound. But she had no maggots, no brogac, only a handful of heal-all.

She shook her hair out of her eyes. "Fetch the waterskins. Cuillon! Over there." She hacked a strip of wool from her mantle, thrusting it toward Cuillon when he crawled back with the waterskins. "Wet this and clean his hands. Use the Summerlands water." Cuillon sloshed water onto the cloth, splashing them both. "Don't waste it!"

"I am sorry, Griane."

"You're doing fine. Like this. Be firm."

"But he . . . he is bleeding."

"The blood will wash the wound clean. Don't worry. Darak can't feel it."

As if to give lie to her words, he moaned.

"That's . . . he's just dreaming."

She squeezed out most of the pus and probed the wound. Small chips of bone shifted beneath her fingers.

"Wipe his face, Cuillon. With the plain water."

She sliced strips from her tunic to use as bandages and laid out her tools: dagger, bone scraper, heal-all. "Cuillon. I have to cut the poisoned flesh away. You must hold Darak's arm still. Sit on it if you have to."

"Aye, Griane." He was very pale, but his expression was determined.

She wiped her palms on her breeches and grasped the dagger. Her hand shook. Cuillon looked up. "You can do it, Griane."

Mother Netal, help me.

As if the prayer had invoked her, she heard the old healer's voice, as clearly as if her teacher stood behind her.

Cut deep, girl. Press out as much pus as you can. Scrape away the dead flesh. Let the wound bleed. Then wash it with that fancy water of yours.

Despite her fear, Griane smiled.

Do the same with what's left of his fingers. But don't use those silvery leaves just yet. Just bandage him. Not too tight. When the swelling's gone and the seepage is clear, you can seal the wounds.

Darak convulsed when she made the cut, but Cuillon held him until he slipped deeper into unconsciousness. She worked quickly, her fingers moving as surely as if they had performed this procedure a dozen times. And always, Mother Netal's voice guided her.

When Cuillon helped her strip him, she saw the full extent of Morgath's brutality. She kept her horror in check while she cleaned the wounds, applied a poultice to the raw flesh on his arms, and lightly bandaged the weeping sores on his back.

By the time they had dressed him again, the light was gone and she was sweat-drenched. She moved the bag of charms so it wouldn't chafe the wounds on his chest and felt something round and hard under her fingers. She tore open the bag and withdrew the spirit catcher. Silently, she held it out to Cuillon. He touched it with one tentative forefinger. They both gasped as it blazed with green fire.

"The Oak. Cuillon, it must be the Oak."

He nodded, but his gaze shifted to the dead Tree. When she pressed the spirit catcher on him, he shook his head and curled up next to Darak, his back to her. She tucked the spirit catcher back into Darak's bag. She and Cuillon could warm him, but perhaps Tinnean and the Oak could offer him healing beyond her powers.

Her fingers touched something soft inside the bag. A long strand of hair.

Only when she was sure Cuillon was asleep did she permit herself to weep.

Chapter 50

COLD AIR AGAINST his face. Something soft under his cheek. A girl's voice, repeating his name.

"Darak? Can you open your eyes?"

Dead leaves fluttered like moths. Patches of blue sky peeked through the branches. The sun was rising behind a fiery cloud. A white face floated in the middle of the cloud. Griane's face. Her eyes were the blue that burned at the heart of a flame and her hair stood out like the spines of a hedgehog.

"Darak, can you speak?"

She must be worried. Otherwise, she'd just order him to speak.

"Your. Hair."

Her hand flew to her head. Her tremulous smile shifted into a scowl. She blew up fast and roared down on him, fiercer than any blizzard. He closed his eyes while she told him that she'd been marking a trail and it had worked, hadn't it, and if she'd known he was only going to save one bit of hair, she might have saved herself the trouble of chopping off all the rest. When she started in on how she had pulled out so

much in the last three days that it was a miracle she
wasn't completely bald, his eyes opened again.

"Three days?"

"Since you walked into the grove. You had a high
fever. It's gone now, but you gave us both a fright,
and if you ever scare me like that again—"

"The Forest-Lord."

"What?"

"Did you see him?"

"Nay. Did . . . did you?"

He wasn't sure. Judging from the look on Griane's
face, it must have been a fever-dream, after all. Then
he remembered the touch of that warm paw.

"Spirit catcher."

Cuillon's face loomed next to Griane's. He felt his
hand being lifted. Even through the bandages, Darak
could feel the bag of charms. "They are here, Darak."
Cuillon's smile seemed more like a grimace.

"What? What's wrong?"

"Lie still," Griane said. "You'll ruin all my good
work." The scolding was familiar, but her smile was
as false as Cuillon's. Then he saw the Tree looming
behind them and understood.

He struggled to rise, but even without their restraining hands, he hadn't the strength. All he could
do was shake his head. Struath and Yeorna dead. His
body crippled. And all for nothing. He wanted to
weep, to shout, to demand an explanation from the
Maker who had allowed this to happen. But they were
watching him, their desperate eyes begging him for
hope. This brave, skinny girl and this ancient spirit,
trapped in a body that could no longer contain it. All
that remained of his pack.

*You spend your life, trying to be strong for those
you love. Not wanting them to see your uncertainty lest
they be afraid, too.*

He controlled his features, waited until he could

trust his voice. "As long as the Oak's spirit lives and the Holly's, there is hope."

"I should have stayed," Cuillon said. "Then the Holly would be alive."

"With the Oak dead, the Holly might have died, too. And taken your spirit with it. Isn't that so?"

"I . . . perhaps. I do not know."

"And you never will." Heedless of the pain, Darak laid his hand over Cuillon's. The rough gray flesh extended up his arm, disappearing into the torn sleeve of his tunic. Time was running out—for Cuillon and for Tinnean.

"We'll find a way to restore the Tree."

"How?"

"I don't know! I don't know," he repeated in a gentler voice. He fumbled for words to comfort him and again found his father's. "Let it go, Cuillon." So easy to say. So hard to do. "There is a way. There must be."

That night, he dreamed of Tinnean. His brother stood in the shadow of the dead Tree. The spirit catcher's fire blazed through the branches, clothing the naked boughs of the Oak in Midsummer green. The light made Tinnean seem taller, but his laugh was just the same.

Wiry arms wrapped around him, so much stronger than he remembered. He kept pulling away to look at Tinnean, then seizing him, pulling him close, as if he might escape again.

"You're back."

Tinnean laughed again. "Nay, Darak. It's only a dream."

"But you will come back."

"Aye."

"How? Tell me how."

Tinnean rolled his eyes. The familiar expression of impatience sent a jolt through him, just like touching the spirit catcher.

"You know."

"I don't."

"You've already seen."

"When? What did I see?"

"The Tree."

"The Tree is dead."

"Not that one."

Tinnean slipped out of his arms. Darak reached for him, desperate to keep him, but his body was leaching into the Tree, his flesh changing to creamy bark, his fingers branching into twigs that sprouted leaves as blue as speedwell.

Darak jerked awake, his cry drowning out the twitter of birdsong.

"Are you all right?" Griane asked. "What is it?"

"Nothing. A bad dream."

The dream returned the next night. Tinnean no longer laughed and the green light of the spirit catcher flickered uncertainly. He woke the third night to find his hand clenched around the bag on his chest.

His fingers twitched as if his flesh still held the dream-memory of clasping his brother's hand. That memory led to others. Walking along the shore with Tinnean, cradling the small fingers between his as if they were as fragile as the birds' eggs they had stolen from the nests in the marshes. Watching the Northern Dancers flash green and white in the night sky, Tinnean's fingers tugging his each time the colors flared. Squeezing those fingers hard to capture Tinnean's wandering attention as he instructed him how to take a sighting on the point of the Archer's arrowhead, promising that the star could always help him find his way home.

He had hoped his ordeal on the tree would satisfy
the gods. Now he knew they wanted more. If it were
only the gods, he might refuse; a man always had the
right to choose his own path. But how could he refuse
Tinnean? The dreams were clear and unrelenting.
When he'd begged his brother not to ask this of him,
Tinnean simply sighed. When he'd pleaded with him
to wait until they found another way, Tinnean said
that there was no other way. When he'd offered himself instead, Tinnean smiled and said this was his responsibility, his choice, his gift.

In the end, though, it rested with him. To deny Tinnean this terrible gift or bestow it. To keep Tinnean's
spirit safe or set it free. To hold him or let him go.

The darkness overhead was yielding to light. It must
be closer to dawn than he realized. Then the heavens
pulsated, light streaming earthward, and he knew the
Northern Dancers had returned.

A bolt of light illuminated the Tree. Another
stretched out beside it. Together, they arced together
over the grove, crackling and hissing in the music of
the Dancers. Their shapes changed with the music,
now curling up like smiles, now twisting into spirals,
then breaking away to join a third arc.

Bathed in their light, the Tree seemed to come alive
again, broken branches reaching skyward, dead leaves
glowing. The jagged scar on its trunk danced with the
luminous ribbons of light. The circled trees took up
the rhythm, limbs moaning as if in ecstasy.

The hairs on the back of his neck rose as the dance
passed over him. His temples throbbed as they had
when Morgath invaded him, and he was equally helpless to withstand this assault. Even with his eyes shut,
the light penetrated him. It found each of the places
Morgath had touched: the cheek he had caressed, the
lips he had kissed, the genitals he had fondled. It
burned his flayed arms and scarred chest and maimed
hands. And still the light danced, into his mind, into

his spirit, seeking out the hidden places where shame
and guilt crouched, where the desire to control lay,
where the desperate hope that life might return to
what it once was still clung.

With a power as relentless as Morgath's, the light
illuminated each dark corner of his spirit and scoured
it with cold fire. He pressed his lips together to keep
from crying out and waking the others. Only if he
allowed the dance to continue would he find some
measure of peace—for Tinnean and for himself. As if
the Dancers recognized his acceptance, they grew qui-
eter, their touch gentler. The merciless fire dwindled
to a pleasant glow and then to embers.

Darak opened his eyes to find the curtain of light
passing away to the south, leaving a tenuous fringe of
rose hovering over the Tree like the promise of dawn.
He watched the sky lighten from black to slate to the
soft purple of heather. Then he shook the others
awake and told them what they must do.

Chapter 51

CUILLON SIMPLY NODDED. Perhaps the Holly-
Lord had known all along what had to happen and,
like Tinnean, only awaited his signal. Griane looked
horrified and threw a dozen questions at him. When
she asked for the third time if he was sure, he held
up his hand.

"I am not sure. Of anything. But I have spent the
last three days going over and over this. If I have to
do it again, I don't think I will be able to do . . . what
I have to."

Cuillon held out Struath's pouch. His fingers brushed
against something long and hard. Even without opening the pouch, he knew it was the forefinger Morgath
had taken. He felt a strange relief, knowing that all
of him was here at the last.

Griane had to help them remove the spirit catcher.
Darak fought the urge to snatch it back when she laid
it in Cuillon's palm. The light blazed in joyful greeting.
Cuillon carefully picked it up with his thick, knobby
fingers.

"I understand now why humans burn so hot and
bright. Even if your time is short as I measure it, it is

very full." Sadness tinged his smile. "I will miss you. And hot cider." Griane's laugh was half a sob. "And laughter. And crying, too." He wiped the tear from her cheek, careful not to let the leaves scratch her. "And my name. Thank you for that, Griane. I am sorry I did not like the first one."

"Yours is better."

She hugged him hard, then released him. Cuillon turned to him expectantly. He had to say something. He would never have this chance again. He cleared his throat, groping for the words.

Cuillon smiled. "It is all right, Darak. I know."

It wasn't enough. Sometimes, the words must be spoken. "You are a better man than I ever was. Or could be."

Cuillon shook his head. "Thank you. For all you have done. And for my brother. I will always remember."

He held the Holly-Lord for the last time and whispered, "Be well." And then he added, "Take care of him for me."

Cuillon's sigh shuddered through both their bodies. The Holly-Lord was the one to step back, but Cuillon had always been stronger than any of them. He smiled, raised the spirit catcher to his lips, and swallowed it.

Taut as a bowstring, he watched Cuillon's eyes widen, then roll back in his head. Darak caught him as he fell. Griane knelt beside him, feeling for a pulse. "I think he just fainted." She looked up at him. "What do we do?"

"I don't know. Wait, I guess."

The words had barely left his mouth when Cuillon's eyes fluttered open. The hard fingertips touched his cheek almost shyly. "Darak."

"Are you all right?"

Very gently, Cuillon took his hand and laid it against his cheek, the whiskers soft as dandelion fluff. "It's me."

Darak started to shake, his body recognizing the truth before his mind could accept it.

"Tinnean?"

A quick nod, the familiar shy ducking of the head. Two skinny arms wrapped around him, even stronger than they had felt in the dream. Strong enough to hold him while he wept. Strong enough to press him close, their heartbeats thudding against each other. Strong enough to keep the joy, the wonder, the miracle from shattering him.

When he calmed, he swiped at his face with his sleeve. Then he could really look at his brother, studying him as he might a stranger. His face was the same, of course, and yet he seemed . . . older. Remembering those brief moments he had existed within the World Tree, Darak understood. He had merely touched the wonder; Tinnean had dwelled in it.

Tinnean's expression grew abstracted. "There is not much time."

Darak's guts twisted. Unable to trust his voice, he nodded.

"They are so much stronger than I am. And they are eager for the battle."

Darak knew then that Tinnean had heard Cuillon's voice and the Oak's.

Tinnean's gaze strayed to the dead giant looming over them. "We were wrong about the battle. We always believed that our prayers and our chants determined its course. But it was always their strength, their wisdom."

"Then . . . it wasn't because I stayed away from the rite?"

"Other men have missed the rite." His mouth quirked up as he glanced at Griane. "That one year, Red Dugan got so drunk he couldn't stand, never mind chant."

Relief left him weak. "I thought . . . I was afraid . . ."

Tinnean's fingers closed around his wrist. "Nay, Darak."

"I'm sorry," he blurted out, unable to look into those shining eyes. "For fighting your choice. For refusing my blessing."

"Then give it to me now. You don't have to," he added quickly. "You have already done so much. But it would mean . . . it would make me so happy."

His voice broke. Darak pulled him into his arms. There was nothing to him. A good wind would blow him over. It had been hard enough in Chaos to let go, even knowing he was freeing his brother's spirit. But now? He hugged him fiercely, wanting to keep him from this act, wanting to keep him safe, wanting to keep him. Knowing he could not.

Still, his heart clenched into a small, scared fist when Tinnean pulled away. "I must go."

He kissed Griane and whispered something to her. She nodded, tears streaking her cheeks. Then Tinnean laid his hands on his shoulders. "You must tell the tale, Darak. Of the World Tree. Of Chaos. Even of Morgath." His gaze grew stern. "Him you must speak of. Else he will dwell in you forever."

Tinnean's gaze held him until he nodded.

"This isn't good-bye. Not really. I'll always be here." Tinnean gestured around the grove, then laid his palm atop Darak's chest. "Always."

Darak covered his brother's hand with his. "Go. Quickly." He could not bear it if this were drawn out any longer. "With my blessing. And my love."

One final time, he held him.

Remember everything about this moment. How his breath comes short and hard. How his fingers dig into your back. The smell of his hair, its softness against your cheek. Remember.

Darak let him go.

Remember his eyes, as blue as blossoming speedwell.
Tinnean's left arm shook, but his smile never fal-

tered, even when the holly leaves budded on his fingers.

Remember his fingers, slender as a girl's.

The leaves burst open, shiny and green. They twined up his arm. Red twigs sprouted along his right. The sleeves of his tunic ripped as the twigs grew into branches.

Remember his arms. Remember how bony and strong they are.

Roots tore open the bandages on his feet. They spread across the ground, wriggling into the earth.

Remember his toes. Remember how skinny and pale they are.

His breeches fell in shreds to the ground. The flesh hardened as his ankles fused together.

Remember his legs. Remember the scar on his left ankle where Crel's dog bit him.

Deep runnels appeared as the bark spread up his legs. His tunic strained and split open.

Remember his belly. Every rib showing. Remember his chest. Not a hair on it.

The branches spread out from his shoulders, green holly on his left, bare oak on the right. His chest swelled, twice the size now of a man's. Green leaves slapped his jaw. Bare twigs scratched his neck. A mass of leaves and twigs sprouted from his mouth. And still, Tinnean smiled.

Oh, gods. Give me strength. His smile. Remember his smile. So sweet it fooled the bees.

Leaves and twigs twisted in his hair. Bark encased his cheeks. His nose thickened into a shapeless lump.

Maker, help me.

Blue eyes peeped out from the tangle of foliage.

"Tinnean!"

And then his brother's eyes closed, enveloped by the encroaching bark.

He did not remember falling to his knees. At some point, he was aware of Griane helping him to his feet, pulling him away. He stilled her hands and made himself look.

The Tree was tiny compared to the dead giant looming behind it. Barely twice his height. The Holly dwarfed the Oak, its green-leafed branches almost obscuring the small bare ones of its brother. The trunk rose slender and straight, the bark as pale as the tree he had seen in the cavern. As pale as Tinnean's flesh.

He closed his eyes, only to open them a moment later when Griane clutched his arm. A shudder rippled through the Tree. The battle of the Oak and the Holly was beginning. This, too, they must witness.

The air pulsated with the same rhythm he had felt in the World Tree. The energy flowed up through the earth, around the circle of watching trees, into him and through him, raising the hair on the back of his neck, just like the Northern Dancers and Morgath's dark magic. Perhaps Struath was right; he'd always claimed that magic was natural and it was only men who perverted it.

Another shudder swelled the Tree's trunk. Like his mam's belly when she was carrying Tinnean. She'd raised her tunic so he could watch his unborn brother moving inside of her. He had been thrilled and horrified, even when she told him it didn't hurt.

The boughs of the Holly shook, offering the challenge. The Oak rattled its branches, accepting. Then they attacked, lashing each other with their branches. The Holly engulfed the smaller Oak. Her voice quavering, Griane sang, the tune nearly as old as the music of the World Tree—the song to welcome spring. He couldn't sing; his mouth was dry as sand.

Maker, protect him.

The Holly's spiky leaves gouged long gashes in the Oak's branches, but the Oak fought back, battering the bigger tree. Green boughs snapped off and fell to the ground. Could Cuillon feel each bough being severed? Was it the same agony he had felt when Morgath took his fingers, one by one?

Maker, don't let him be hurt.

A great bulge ran up the trunk to the fork where the Oak and Holly branched into separate trees. The Oak swelled as the power traveled through it. New twigs burst out of the branches, became branches themselves and reached across the grove.

The Holly shivered, retreating before the Oak's newfound power. As if sensing victory, the Oak attacked, flattening the Holly's conical top, lashing the green boughs that refused to submit.

Cuillon's dying. The Oak is killing him.

The Holly dwindled, now to his height, now to Tinnean's, now to the size of a child. And still the Oak battered it. The energy raced through him, hotter and wilder than bloodlust. He found himself shaking, wanting the release that the Oak's victory would bring, terrified that it would mean Cuillon's death.

The trunk shuddered and went still. The air grew calm. The bloodlust faded, leaving him panting and spent.

The Oak stood tall and proud in the dim light of the grove. A sprig of Holly nestled near the fork of the trunk. And only a handspan from it, Darak saw two tiny flowers, the leaves heart-shaped like speedwell, the blossoms as blue as Tinnean's eyes.

Chapter 52

FOR THREE DAYS, Griane watched Darak sitting by the young tree. He allowed her to change his bandages and spread the ointment of goldenrod and Maker's mantle on his arms. He ate when she thrust food into his hands, drank when she raised the waterskin to his lips. He even answered when she spoke to him. But he never left the tree. By day, he leaned against it, one hand always touching the trunk. By night, he curled up in the shallow pit between the two roots that had once been Tinnean's feet. When the nightmares tore him from sleep, he allowed her to hold him, but clutched the roots until the shivering stopped.

Each morning when she woke, she found the dead Tree had dwindled, as if the empty shell knew that it was no longer needed. The same thing was happening to Darak. His spirit was drifting away, and if it drifted too far, she would wake one morning and find him gone as surely as the old Tree.

Prayers, pleading, magical herbs—nothing helped. When she tried telling tales of Tinnean, his pained look silenced her. At dawn of the fourth day, she crouched beside him again.

"We're low on water."

He looked up.

"And we're nearly out of food."

He blinked as if he couldn't quite recognize her.

"We still have your snares, of course, but we've nothing to bait them with save a few bits of mushrooms and berries. So I think you'd best use your sling." He peered at her, as if expecting the sling to materialize atop her head. She patted his belt. "There."

She took his arm and helped him to his feet. He swayed and nearly took them both down. Then he seemed to regain the sense of himself and planted his feet. She released him slowly.

"You'd best be off."

Darak cast a quick, stricken glance at the tree. She pretended not to see and bent down to retrieve the empty waterskins. "I'll try that way. You go west. One of us ought to find a stream." When he made no move to take the skin, she lowered it over his chest. She smiled, too brightly. "I'll meet you back here before dark."

With a quick wave, she marched off, crashing among the fallen twigs and branches like a wounded beast. Once she was out of sight, she crouched down and circled back. She was only a little less noisy, but she had never mastered Darak's gift of walking over dead leaves without making a sound.

He was still standing where she'd left him, his gaze darting between the tree and the direction she had pointed. She held her breath and prayed. He straightened his shoulders, wincing, and lurched west.

All morning she followed him. At first, he staggered through the forest, reeling against tree trunks and stumbling over unseen stones, but soon he regained some of his natural grace. Her healer's instincts screamed that he was too weak, that it had only been a sennight since the fever had abated. But she knew he had to recover some part of himself or he would never be whole again.

She feared he was wandering aimlessly until he came upon the stream. He freed the sling from his belt and picked up a stone. He cradled it in his palm, staring at the missing fingers of his right hand. Finally, he slipped the loop over his thumb and fitted the stone into the pouch.

He whirled the sling. The release cord slipped from his grasp. The stone rolled through the leaves. He got down on his knees, fumbling for it. Again, he whirled the sling. This time, the stone splashed into the stream. His head drooped. She'd already risen out of her crouch when she saw his shoulders straighten.

He piled stones at his feet. He hurled stone after stone at a boulder on the far side of the stream, adjusting the angle of his stance, the timing of his release. He slung stones overhand. He slung them underhand. He missed every shot.

He abandoned the thumb loop and knotted the sling around his wrist so he could grasp the release cord between his thumb and two remaining fingers. By midmorning, the sweat was running down his face and he was grimacing with pain at each release. It was close to midday before he hit the boulder for the first time. She bit down hard to stifle her cry and tasted blood.

He gathered more stones and kept practicing. Only when he had hit the boulder twenty times in a row did he try for a living target. The first stone soared over the branch, the next smashed into the trunk, drawing an annoyed scolding from the squirrel before it skittered higher into the branches. He moved on, taking aim at a wood pigeon with the same results.

The afternoon was waning when he froze yet again. He stood there for so long that it was all she could do not to jump up and scream at him to take the shot. He bowed his head as if in prayer, but all the while, his hands were moving: stroking the leather thongs, cradling the pouch against his belly while he eased a stone into it.

He whipped back his arm and released. She caught her breath as the stone arced overhead. Only then did she spot the black squirrel. One moment it was turning over an acorn with its nimble paws, the next it was tumbling earthward.

She breathed a prayer of thanks, then sprinted off through the trees. By the time he arrived back in the grove, she was seated on the wolfskin, pretending to examine her supply of roots and herbs. In one hand, he held the bulging waterskin, in the other, the dead squirrel.

"Oh, lovely." She smiled up at him, her stomach twisting at the thought of eating raw meat. "You did much better than I did. All I found were some dried-up berries and a few hazelnuts." She hoped he wouldn't ask to see them, since they existed only in her imagination. "Well, I'll have this skinned in no time. Maybe tomorrow, we'll go fishing. We still have your lines and hooks and—"

"Griane."

"Aye?"

"You're about as quiet as a charging boar."

She opened her mouth to deny it, but incriminating heat burned her cheeks. And then he smiled that lopsided grin of his and it was all she could do to keep from crying and flinging her arms around him and behaving like an utter fool. He flopped down beside her as if his legs could no longer support him. His lips brushed her cheek.

"Thank you."

She gave up trying and made a fool of herself.

Chapter 53

IN THE GREAT TALES, the hero defeated the evildoer, overcame certain death, and returned home in the blink of an eye with the magical elixir that saved the world from extinction. In the real world, Darak reflected, the hero—such as he was—tried to make his body obey him, keep the heroine from starving, and figure out a way to get home.

"Fellgair must be loving this." He spat out a trout bone.

Griane looked up from mending his tunic. "What?"

"Us. Sitting here day after day."

"Sitting here?" She slanted one of her chillier blue-eyed looks at him. "Up at dawn to hunt and fish and fill the waterskins and grub in the earth for roots and mushrooms." She shuddered. "I will never eat squirrel again."

"Have some trout, then." She shook her head. "You need to eat more. You're skinny as a weasel."

"Oh, and you're such a fine figure of a man, huddling there in your mantle and raggedy old breeches with so many holes you're not even decent anymore."

He blew out his breath. "I don't understand it."

"Well, you've been wearing them for—"

"Not the clothes. The priests."

"What?"

"Lisula. Gortin. Anyone. Has no one in the world noticed that the year has turned?"

She glanced around the grove. "It's not as if leaves have popped out on all the trees."

"They could go to the standing stones, couldn't they?"

Griane gnawed at the thread, severing it with a determined snap of her teeth. "The Freshening is only half a moon away. The priests will come then."

"Half a moon?" Darak lowered the fish tail. "I must have lost more days than I thought. After Tinnean changed."

He could say it now without a hitch in his voice or a hesitation before his brother's name. On their last fishing trip, he had managed to stay away from the grove two nights and return without racing through the trees, sweat-soaked and shaking, as he had that first time.

The pain of Tinnean's loss still ached, a wound that would never fully heal, no matter how many years went by, no matter how the Tree thrived. Still, it comforted him to stroke the thick, pale trunk, and sometimes—when Griane was sleeping—to talk to his brother.

He looked up and found her watching him, the mending forgotten. She always knew when he drifted. He'd catch the quick look of fear or her teeth gnawing at her upper lip. After all he'd put her through, it was a wonder she had a lip left.

She bent her head over her mending again. "Will you be glad to go home?"

He had been strangely happy this last moon. More than once, he had imagined remaining here. He could still be a hunter—of sorts—and he'd be close to Tinnean always. Griane could gather her green things and fish with him. They could keep each other warm at night. But that wouldn't be fair to her or to their folk who needed her healing skills.

As for him, any lad of ten could bait a hook or wield a sling. He might have freed the Oak, but a man couldn't live on that. What use was he with his six fingers and his hideous scars, his body aching each morning like an old man's and his spirit aching each time Morgath intruded on his memories?

"Darak?"

Damn, he'd been drifting again and scaring her.

"That's where we belong," he said. "With our tribe." Their pack, Wolf would have said.

"That doesn't answer my question."

She had the same gift of dragging words out of a man as his mam. He sighed, staring at his hands.

"You might master the bow again."

She could do that, see right into him and know what was troubling him—even with her eyes on her mending.

"You'd have to learn to draw differently, of course. I was thinking about carving a . . . a sort of brace. A piece of wood maybe, or bone, to support your left hand. And you'd need a new bow, something lighter and easier to bend."

He had carved it from a single piece of ash. Decorated it with talismans to make it strong. Brought down countless deer, two with a single shot through the heart. To discard it now . . . it would be like setting aside a part of himself.

"Or you could do something else. Be a fisherman. Or a shepherd. Or a Memory-Keeper."

"But I'm not a fisherman or a shepherd. And I'm certainly no teller of tales."

"Tinnean thought so."

"What?"

"Tell the tale, he said."

"He didn't mean me to apprentice myself to Sim." Even assuming the old man still lived.

"How do you know?"

"Merciful gods. You're serious."

"All I'm saying is that you don't have to be a hunter."

"But that's what I am. That's *who* I am."

His vehemence startled the Watchers into retreating behind the trees.

"That's who I was," he said in a softer voice. "And I want things to be as they were. I know that's stupid and I know it can never be, but . . ." He shrugged helplessly. "I can't help wanting it."

Her face crumpled. She rose hastily.

"Griane."

She waved him back, but he kept after her.

"I'm sorry I yelled."

He took her by the shoulders and made her face him.

Maili had rarely wept. When she did, her cheeks blushed pink and tears had slid down them in slow, beautiful tracks. Griane's cheeks were blotchy and streaked with tears. Her eyes brimmed with more. Her lips had nearly vanished as she clamped them together to control her sobs. She swiped at her runny nose with the back of her hand and thrust out her chin.

Fierce as a she-wolf and just as fearless. Braver than any woman he'd ever known and more resourceful than any man. Her quick temper had forced him to take a hard look at his shortcomings, while her generous spirit made him strive to be a better man. Once, he would have sworn that she'd make some poor man's life a misery with her sharp tongue by day and her sharp elbows at night. Since then, he'd learned that silence could inflict deeper wounds than words—and that he could no longer fall asleep without those bony elbows bruising his ribs and that spiky hair tickling his cheek.

Deep within him, his heart paused, then gave one heavy beat as if upon a drum. His quick intake of

breath tightened the band constricting his chest. His
skin felt raw, as if his flesh had been newly flayed,
each nerve exposed.

His hands fell to his sides. He took a step back.

"I'm an awful nag. You've said it a hundred times
and you're right."

She paused. After a moment, he realized he was
supposed to say something, but neither his mind nor
his mouth could frame the proper response. Her expectant look changed to a scowl.

"And it's your fault if I do. Nag, I mean. No matter
how hard I try, no matter what I do, nothing seems
to help."

He said something then, but it must have been
wrong. The scowl shifted to an open-mouthed look
of shock.

"It's not enough. I want you to be happy! I want
you to be whole again. Not your hands. You. In your
heart and your spirit."

"It . . . I think . . ." Marshaling his thoughts, he
managed, "Time."

"You're not coming home. Nay, I know what you've
been thinking. You're going to stay here and live like
a wild thing, and one day you'll get hurt and there'll
be no one to help you and you'll just lie there till you
die. Or worse, you'll just sit under the Tree and let
yourself waste away and the animals will eat your flesh
and gnaw your bones and what's left will be covered
with leaves and snow—"

"Griane . . ."

"—and I love you too much to let that happen so
I say stupid things like 'be a Memory-Keeper,' even
though it's not stupid, you could do it, you can do
anything you put your mind to, and if being a great
hunter is want you want—"

"You love me?"

"Well, of course I do, you great fool. Are you blind
as well as crippled?" She looked up at him, horror-

stricken. "Oh, gods forgive me. I don't know how I could have said such an awful thing."

"But . . . how?"

"I don't know how!" Anguish changed to rage so quickly that he instinctively backed away. "You think I was looking at you one day and a pink cloud appeared around you and the sun rose and set on your face and I thought, 'Oh, I love him'?"

"I only ask because . . . well . . . I think that's what happened. To me."

She went very still. A deep red suffused her cheeks and crept slowly down her throat. She stared down at the ground and said, "Oh. I see."

He sighed, relieved of the necessity to frame the words.

"That's why you could never speak her name. Forgive me. I never realized how much you loved Maili."

"Griane . . ."

"I understand now. Why you didn't want to come back. Not just because you didn't want to leave Tinnean or because you were worried about your future, but because you were afraid I'd . . . make things difficult. That you'd have to hurt me. But I'll be fine. I am fine. Nothing has to change between us. We can still be friends and I can tend your wounds, and look in on you now and then, and make you supper although you always complain about my cooking, and—"

"Griane. Stop."

Her mouth snapped shut.

"It's you. Not Maili. You."

She shook her head.

"When I said it happened to me, I meant now. A few moments ago."

A pulse beat frantically in her throat and her eyes, already huge in her narrow face, became enormous.

"There weren't any pink clouds or sunsets, but I

couldn't breathe. And my skin hurt. Oh, gods, don't cry."

She covered her mouth with both hands. It seemed to take him forever to cross the three steps separating them. At the last moment, he hesitated, afraid to touch her. She solved the problem by flinging her arms around his neck. He rested his cheek against her hair and breathed in the scent of her.

Then she reared back.

"I'll not have you because you're lonely. Or because you're grateful."

"Any more than I'd have you because you feel sorry for me. Being a helpless cripple and all."

She punched him. "I said I was sorry. For that. Not for you."

"Well."

"So." Her eyes narrowed. "If you don't stop grinning, I'll kill you."

She was still threatening him when he pulled her back into his arms. His fingers slid through her soft hair as his mouth found hers and the homecoming he longed for.

The familiar voice came from behind him. "What a relief. I thought you'd never get around to kissing her."

Fellgair leaned against Tinnean's tree, buffing his claws on the trunk.

"I might have gotten around to more if you hadn't showed up."

"Don't mind me. I'll wait."

"So will I."

"Hello, Lord Trickster," Griane said.

The golden eyes flicked toward Griane, then back to the tree. "Odd-looking thing, isn't it?"

"It's beautiful," Darak said.

"Lord Trickster—"

"I am not speaking to you." He sniffed. "Your companion has proved even ruder than you, Darak. She left the Summerlands without a word of farewell."

"I had to get back. You know that."

"And after I saved her from Morgath, too."

"I thanked you then, Lord Trickster, and I thank you now."

"Did your companion tell you about our time together, Darak?"

"Aye. Well. We talked. A bit."

"And did you tell her about Morgath?"

Darak found his unease reflected on Griane's face. Fellgair smiled broadly. "Well, you'll have a lot to discuss when you get home today."

"Today?"

"Unless you prefer to remain here?"

To face the stares and the questions. To relive the grief and the fear. To start life again with no clear idea of where he was going.

"Why now? Why not yesterday or moon ago?"

"Because I say so." Fellgair smiled. "And because you're ready now."

To see his folk, perhaps. But not to leave Tinnean. Then again, he'd never be ready for that—and the longer he stayed, the harder it would get.

"What is the price of our passage?"

"I'm feeling especially generous today. I will accept a kiss. From Griane."

Darak glanced at Griane, who nodded. She stood on tiptoe, her cheek upturned. With a quick twist of his head, the Trickster captured her mouth. His long arms swept her up, pressing her body against his. One hand traveled down her back and over her buttocks before he released her, licking his whiskers. Griane stumbled backward, only to have her hand snagged by the Trickster.

"You will have many years with your Darak. You will shout at him when he tries to bully you, slap him

when he becomes insufferable, and wrap your long
legs around him when he becomes frisky."

"You're the one who is insufferable."

"But magnificent. And you, dear boy. Shall I offer
you a prediction?"

"That depends on what I must offer in return."

The Trickster laughed. "Your hand will do. What's
left of it."

"What's left I offer freely. And with it, my thanks
for all you have taught me."

The Trickster squeezed his hand gently, although
his eyes widened in mock amazement. "The hero gains
wisdom and the girl. Happy ending, indeed."

"But not the end, I think."

"No." The Trickster's face grew solemn. "I predict
we shall meet again, Darak. Until then, guard the portal's token."

His hand tightened convulsively on Fellgair's. With
all that had happened since he had returned to the
grove, he had scarcely spared a thought for the strange
little ornament. Now his suspicions were confirmed:
somehow, his destiny was linked to the people he had
seen through the portal—and to the Trickster.

"As long as you do no harm to me or to mine, you
will always be welcome in my house."

The Trickster nodded once. Challenge made. Challenge accepted. Then he grinned. "How kind. I do
love travel. So broadening." The clawed fingers flowed
through his as if his grip had no more strength than
a child's. "Well, as much fun as this has been, it's
getting late. You'd best toddle along, children."

Darak hesitated. "I need . . . may I have a moment,
Lord Trickster?"

At Fellgair's regal wave, he slowly approached the
tree. He stroked the lowest branch of the Oak, tracing
the shallow grooves with his fingertips. The little sprig
of holly was too high to reach, but it bobbed toward

him, as if Cuillon were saying farewell. Perhaps Cuillon could see him, even from that distant Mountain of his.

Finally, he laid his palms against the trunk and whispered his brother's name. A faint tingling warmed his fingertips. He told himself that Tinnean recognized him. He told himself that he would always feel his brother's presence, even if he couldn't cross the veil separating their worlds or stand before the tree and stroke its smooth bark. He told himself that it was enough that his brother's spirit was safe. And he knew it was a lie.

Griane touched his arm. "Lisula will open the way."

It took a moment for the words to reach him. When they did, the upwelling of relief left him weak. As difficult as it would be to open his heart and mind in Lisula's presence, at least he would see Tinnean again. And while they were apart, the Oak and Cuillon would watch over him.

He squeezed Griane's hand before nodding to Fellgair. "I'm ready now."

Fellgair sketched a rectangle in the air, then grasped one invisible edge and peeled it back. At first, all he saw were trees, bathed in the same half-light as the grove. As the light grew brighter, he realized that the shafts of sunlight came from the east, although it was nearly sunset in the First Forest.

"I don't usually muck about with time, but I couldn't resist the image of you striding out of the forest with the sun shining behind you. Never underestimate the power of drama, children."

Darak bowed. "As long as the sun rises and sets, my people will tell the tale. And all will speak of the Trickster's cleverness and his generosity."

"And you say you have no gift for words. However, I must insist that you forgo any mention of generosity. I can't have people thinking I'm a slave to my affections."

With that, Fellgair shooed Griane through the portal. Darak took one last look behind him and froze.

Speedwell sprang up at the base of the tree. More shot up from the earth, a living blue pathway, straight as an arrow, leading right to him. Hairy stems clustered around his feet, heart-shaped leaves opening from them and then the flowers themselves, bright blue with round white centers.

Fellgair's smile was gentle. "It seems your brother also has a flair for the dramatic."

Remember his eyes, as blue as blossoming speedwell.
Darak bowed his head.

"He knows you, Darak. He will always know you." Fellgair sighed. "A lovely gesture. Horribly sentimental, but still lovely. Don't weep. You're forever weeping these days."

Darak scowled and dragged the sleeve of his tunic across his eyes. "I thought that was what you wanted—to see me weep and break."

"I've seen quite enough of both, thank you."

"Damn you." The curse sounded much less effective because of his laughter.

The Trickster plucked a single blossom of speedwell and handed it to him. "One should always bring back a token of the great quest."

"Will they welcome us, do you think?"

"They're already flocking out of the village."

"But how—?"

"I sent a few dreams last night. To your chief. To that ripe little Grain-Sister. Lisula, I think her name is. And one more. Let's see. Who was it?" Fellgair paused, tapping his claw against his ruff. "Ah, yes. The incredibly ancient Sim." Fellgair winked.

"You're as bad as Griane."

"High praise, indeed."

Darak stepped through the portal.

"Oh, Darak?"

"Aye?"

"When you tell the tale, do try to work in magnificent."

The Trickster's teeth gleamed. The portal closed.

They walked through a forest of budding trees. Patches of speedwell blossomed on either side of the trail, their blue contrasting sharply with the white of the snowdrops and the yellow of the primroses. Water dripped off branches from melting icicles. The air smelled of damp earth and new life.

"It's just like my dream," Griane whispered.

Astonished, he stared at her. He'd had the same dream these last three nights. A vision made real by Tinnean and Cuillon. By Struath's sacrifice and Yeorna's. By his father who had guided him through Chaos. By the Trickster and his vision mate who had taught him about himself. And by the girl walking beside him who had restored his body and his heart.

They emerged from the forest to see their kinfolk surging through the field. He raised his hand in salute and was greeted by a great shout of welcome. Griane smiled up at him. With the speedwell pressed between their clasped hands and the morning sun warm on their shoulders, they came home.

Irene Radford
Merlin's Descendants

"Entertaining blend of fantasy and history, which invites comparisons with Mary Stewart and Marion Zimmer Bradley"   —*Publishers Weekly*

GUARDIAN OF THE PROMISE
This fourth novel in the series follows the children of Donovan and Griffin, in a magic-fueled struggle to protect Elizabethan England from enemies—both mortal and demonic.   *0-7564-0108-9*

*And don't miss the first three books
in this exciting series:*
GUARDIAN OF THE BALANCE
0-88677-875-1
GUARDIAN OF THE TRUST
0-88677-995-2
GUARDIAN OF THE VISION
0-7564-0071-6

To Order Call: 1-800-788-6262

DAW 32

Irene Radford

"A mesmerizing storyteller." —*Romantic Times*

THE DRAGON NIMBUS
THE GLASS DRAGON
0-88677-634-1
THE PERFECT PRINCESS
0-88677-678-3
THE LONELIEST MAGICIAN
0-88677-709-7
THE WIZARD'S TREASURE
0-88677-913-8

THE DRAGON NIMBUS HISTORY
THE DRAGON'S TOUCHSTONE
0-88677-744-5
THE LAST BATTLEMAGE
0-88677-774-7
THE RENEGADE DRAGON
0-88677-855-7

THE STAR GODS
THE HIDDEN DRAGON
0-7564-0051-1

To Order Call: 1-800-788-6262

Mickey Zucker Reichert

To Order Call: 1-800-788-6262

Tanya Huff

The Finest in Fantasy

To Order Call: 1-800-788-6262